P9-EME-666

Almost Home

Almost Home

A NOVEL BY
CONNIE PROVOST

Memorial Editions, 2004

© Estate of Connie Provost, 2004
Printed in Canada
ISBN: 0-9736161-0-5

All rights reserved. No part of this book may be reproduced, transmitted in any form or by any means, electronic, mechanical, photocopying, recording, or otherwise without written permission from the publisher, except by a reviewer, who may quote brief passages in a review.

LIBRARY AND ARCHIVES CANADA CATALOGUING IN PUBLICATION

Provost, Connie, 1946-2004.
Almost home : a novel / Connie Provost.

ISBN 0-9736161-0-5

I. Title.

PS8631.R68A75 2004   C813'.6   C2004-905013-3

Memorial Editions
Kingston, Ontario

To my beloved husband, Jack

Almost Home

"*M*ark, welcome back! Could you come over to my office for a moment? I'd like to introduce you to one of our new teachers, Alexandra Corbett." Lisa Fletcher put down the receiver and turned to smile at Alexa. "Mark Anderson, our vice-principal, will be here in a minute. He's just back from holidays." She took off her glasses and ran a hand through her curly, dark hair.

Coming around her desk, she sat down in the armchair opposite Alexa and continued, "Mark's an excellent administrator, great with the students, tough but very fair. He also coaches basketball, and that gives him the chance to get to know the kids outside the classroom."

Alexa smiled back nervously. She smoothed her long denim skirt and looked around the principal's office. With its plants, comfortable chairs and desk overflowing with files and papers, it was organized chaos. "Tough but very fair" would also be a good description for Lisa Fletcher.

As if she were reading her thoughts, Mrs Fletcher leaned forward and gave Alexa a long, speculating look. "Riverside High isn't an easy school now, Alexa. It's changed a lot even in the five years that I've been here. We have the full range of kids. Some are very academic. They have university plans and learn in spite of us." She smiled, the sudden warmth in her eyes softening her cynical remark.

"But we also have the non readers, the kids who come wired because they live on pop and doughnuts. And the kids who fall asleep in class because they worked a night shift at the corner store. And the druggies and bullies. One of our biggest problems is absentee parenting, parents who have no time for their kids and no time to communicate with the teachers. Then they wonder why their son decides to drop out the semester before graduation." She paused and added reflectively, "Just a typical school." Her comments were interrupted by a sharp knock on the door which swung open as Mark Anderson came into the office.

Alexa watched as Lisa rose to meet him. "Mark!" They hugged each other warmly. The two appeared to be so comfortable with each other that Alexa was sure they would be a good administrative team. "You look wonderful! Summer holidays must have agreed with you and Sarah."

Mark had the wide shoulders and narrow waist of an athlete, and his skin was golden from the summer sun. He was casually dressed in golf shirt, shorts and sandals. "There's nothing like a canoe trip for making school seem very far away. We just got home on the weekend. Not quite as exotic as Greece though! We saw Jim at the grocery store yesterday, and he said that you two had a fantastic time."

"We did indeed! The islands are incredible, especially Crete. I'm trying to convince Jim that we should buy a Greek villa and go there for six months every year when we retire."

"That would last about two weeks. You couldn't survive without regular visits from your granddaughter," Mark teased.

"You're right, but I can dream, can't I?" Lisa replied. "We'll invite you and Sarah for dinner one night when we've had a chance to develop our pictures. Right now I want you to meet our newest staff member, Alexandra Corbett. She just signed her contract this morning. Alexa is replacing Murray Dean who'll be off all of semester one."

Mark held out his hand, his dark blue eyes with their long lashes studying Alexa's face. "Welcome to Riverside, Miss Corbett." His handshake was warm and firm.

"Please call me Alexa."

"And call me Mark – except when there are students around. Lisa doesn't waste any time. It's great that she could find a replacement for Murray so quickly. Believe me, I'm not trying to frighten you away, but you're in for a challenging semester. I hope she told you that Murray Dean teaches a lot of our underachievers. The kids who take English because they need the credit, not because they love Shakespeare or write poetry in their spare time."

Something in Mark's tone irritated Alexa. He was extremely attractive with his short brown hair and compact, muscular body, but she sensed that beneath his friendly manner he was shrewdly appraising her. When she answered, she managed to smile although her tone was cool. "I taught for five years in an inner city school where we saw the full gamut of students. I know I'm lucky to find this position, and I'm looking forward to the challenge."

"Good, because Murray's classes aren't easy. He manages to get the kids under control the first week. That's quite an accomplishment because they're the kind of students who reduce some teachers to tears."

Alexa was very much aware of an undercurrent of hostility which was flowing from Mark, but Lisa interjected quickly, "We're the ones who are lucky to find you, Alexa. I only learned last week that Murray had been in a car accident and wouldn't be back for at least five months. We don't find a lot of experienced English teachers in a small town like this."

"What brings you to Davenport?" Mark asked. "I just glanced at your resume. Riverside will be quite a change after five years in a city school."

The words were innocuous, but something in the tone, a hint of sarcasm or mockery, struck a nerve in Alexa. Probably the senior girls were drooling over him, but she didn't like his edge.

"I grew up here," she answered. "It will be a change to come back, but my sisters and I have been worried about my father. He's been alone since my mother died a year ago."

Mark broke in, "Sorry I've been so slow connecting the dots. You're Dan Corbett's daughter. He told me you were coming home for a while. Dan and I have been friends ever since we moved here and bought our first house. He's a good lawyer and a great fisherman!"

Alexa thought the remark was well intentioned, but it rankled. She had been on her own for twelve years, first at university, then travelling, then the years of teaching. She adored her father, but she no longer thought of herself as just Dan Corbett's youngest daughter coming back to the family home. It was disconcerting that Mark Anderson seemed willing to accept her only when he knew how she fit into the fabric of his little town. She could imagine him talking to his wife at dinner, telling her that their lawyer's daughter had temporarily joined the staff at Riverside.

Forcing herself to smile, she turned back to the principal. "I won't take up any more of your time, Mrs Fletcher. You must be very busy with last minute preparations for the semester. I'll be in the school today and tomorrow setting up my room and planning for the first classes. Carol Helmer, my department head, gave me a tour of the school this morning."

"That's great! Carol's a pro. You'll meet the rest of the staff at our meeting on Thursday morning. Mark and I will be in the office all this week, so don't hesitate to drop in with any questions. If you want to get a head start on policy around here, Mark can give you a copy of the staff handbook. There's a stack in his office for the new teachers."

Alexa dutifully followed Mark Anderson as he went back to the vice-principal's office and quickly located the handbook. When he handed her the document, a veneer of coldness seemed to cover his face. It was so deliberate that Alexa almost gasped. "Just a final word of advice, Miss Corbett." His eyes never left hers. "As you return to your hometown, I'm sure it's tempting to see the students through rose-tinted lenses. Don't do it. Murray's Pathways kids are as hard-nosed as any inner city kids I've dealt with. Begin by enforcing the school rules, not by understanding or befriending the students, or worrying about making the curriculum relevant. It's the only way to survive."

Alexa could feel her jaw clenching. After all these years, she had developed her own teaching philosophy based on tolerance, understanding and opportunities for a second chance. Nothing could be further from Mark's bureaucratic edict. Biting back a sarcastic reply, she replied, "Message received."

"And be sure to say hello to Dan for me," was Mark's parting remark as Alexa headed for the reception area. She picked up the pile of textbooks she had left in the outer office and waited until Susan Johnson, the office manager, finished her telephone conversation. "Will I survive the first day?" she asked only half joking.

"Of course you will! The first week's a zoo, but then everything falls into place. You'll enjoy most of the kids. If someone really needs AA, send them down to Mark. That's his job."

"AA?" asked Alexa.

"Attitude adjustment! It's a common teen problem."

Alexa laughed out loud for the first time that afternoon. This was a lady she knew she could turn to for sound advice. "Thanks, Susan, I'll remember that."

When Alexa got to her classroom on the second floor, she opened the windows as wide as possible to catch any passing breeze. She took a deep breath. She was still angry at Mark Anderson's dictatorial attitude, but even in the sultry heat of August, she loved the familiar classroom odour of chalk and paper, disinfectant and dust. She began to organize her desk. Finding an elastic band in one of the top drawers, she pulled her long, dark hair back into a ponytail. Now she looked like a Riverside teacher.

The afternoon passed quickly. Her anger began to fade as her excitement mounted at the start of another school year. She had fallen in love with teaching during her first internship, and the love affair had lasted. Unlike other love affairs, she thought a little bitterly.

She used a trolley to move stacks of books from the English department storeroom to her classroom and rearranged the desks into a horseshoe, smiling to herself. This was the perfect sitcom. The single teacher returns to her hometown and to her old school. She meets a handsome colleague and falls in love. Get a grip, girl, she told herself. So far, the only single man she'd met was Buzz Spencer, the head of the science department, at least twenty-five years older than Alexa and definitely not looking for romance.

Besides, the memory of David was too fresh for Alexa to even think about another relationship. No matter what the media wrote about the physical needs of a healthy thirty-something woman she was sure it would be a long time before she wanted to be close to another man. Right now her only plan was to go home, take a shower and sit on her shady patio with a glass of wine and a novel until it was time to meet Patti Barry, one of her oldest friends, for dinner.

She glanced at the clock. Four-thirty. The school alarm would be turned on in an hour. She still had enough time to set up her classroom library and begin lesson planning. She was going to be busy. Murray Dean's timetable had consisted of Pathways classes filled with kids "destined for the world of work" to borrow a phrase from her former principal, but Mrs Fletcher had decided to rearrange the timetable, and this semester, besides one Pathways group, Alexa had two Academic English classes, one junior and one senior. By the time she gathered up her books, the school was deserted except for a custodian polishing the hall floor. He nodded and called out a friendly goodnight as she passed him.

As Alexa reached her car, she looked at her watch. There was still plenty of time before meeting Patti. She decided to make a detour to her dad's house. If he were back from the office, they could have a swim before she went home to change.

When Alexa pulled into the driveway and got out of her car, she couldn't see her father's jeep. Perhaps he'd left it at the office and walked home. She rang the bell. The only response was frenetic barking from Robbie, her father's ancient Yorkshire Terrier, who still thought he was the guardian of the house. Alexa fumbled in her oversized shoulder bag, searching for her house key. She glanced around at the comfortably worn wicker furniture and the hanging baskets of fuchsias, thinking as always how much she missed her mother. How many times had she come home to find her curled up reading in one of those chairs or embroidering one of her endless tapestries? Conscious of a lump in her throat and unshed tears, Alexa turned the worn brass knob of the front door. To her surprise, it swung open easily. Then she remembered that no one in Davenport bothered to lock their doors.

Just as she stepped into the pleasant coolness of the front hall, she heard someone call out in a shrill voice, "Yoohoo, Alexandra, yoohoo!" Alexa turned around. A plump woman in a pink polyester pantsuit and high heeled pink sandals was trotting up the front walk. Verna Murphy, her father's neighbour, swayed precariously with the effort of balancing two covered dishes. Alexa ran down the front steps to help her.

"Alexandra, how lovely to see you, dear! I was just bringing over a little something for your father. There's a tuna casserole and a raspberry pie still warm from the oven." By now, Alexa was holding both dishes.

Verna continued, "Your father's working far too hard these days, and I know how lonely he's been since Arlene passed on. I try to bring him supper several times a week." She smiled at Alexa and fluttered her lashes, which were heavily caked with blue mascara.

Alex's eyes flickered over the freshly permed sausage curls and brightly rouged cheeks. It was a standing joke between Dan Corbett and his daughters that Verna Murphy was taking a proprietary interest in her newly-widowed neighbour. While her father treated Verna with the good humour he extended to everyone in his world, she brought out the worst in Alexa. Her dad was an excellent cook. She wondered why Verna insisted on perpetuating the myth that no man could boil water successfully and a constant supply of food from her kitchen was necessary to sustain him.

"It's good to have you home again," Verna was saying. "I know Dan's looking forward to having you close by." She stood on her tiptoes and brushed Alexa's cheek with her lips leaving a smudge of crimson lipstick.

Alexa resisted the urge to rub her face. "Thanks for the food. Dad's not around. He must still be at the office, but I'll put it in the fridge for him, and I know he'll enjoy it later."

Although Verna had been happy to hand the dishes over to Alexa, she now trotted close behind her up the steps. "It's no trouble at all, dear. I always say we were put on this earth to help one other. Your parents and I were great friends for so many years. Now that Arlene's no longer with us, it's only natural that Dan and I should be closer than ever. Why don't you stay and eat supper with us tonight, Alexandra? I've got plenty of food for the three of us."

Alexa paused at the front door. She had forgotten how uncomfortable she was around Verna, who always seemed to have direct communication with a higher being and his expectations for her and other mortals. The irony of the situation did not escape her. "Thanks for inviting me, Verna, but I have a dinner date later on, and I have no idea when Dad will be home."

With her head tilted to one side, Verna Murphy examined Alexa thoughtfully. "I hope your date's that very handsome man I met when you were home last summer. Your sisters are so happily married, and I know that your father would love to see you settle down as well. You're not getting any younger you know."

Inwardly Alexa was seething, and her cheeks burned, but she managed to be polite. "I really have to go now. I'll leave a note for Dad telling him that you brought over his supper."

Clearly disappointed that she was not being invited in, Verna backed slowly towards the porch steps. "Goodbye, dear. Promise me you'll eat a proper meal tonight. You're becoming much too thin. You must start taking better care of yourself. Men don't like scrawny women. I'll see you soon. You can bring that handsome boyfriend around one night for supper."

Alexa closed the front door and leaned against it. She gave a deep sigh of relief. This chance encounter reminded her of an era when one of her obsessions had been to avoid all contact with her parents' nosey neighbour. For one wild moment she was tempted to throw the contents of both casseroles into the garbage, but she thought better of it. Robbie was scratching frantically at the kitchen door. She put the dishes down on the hall table and opened the door. As Alexa scooped Robbie up for a hug, he greeted her effusively with wet kisses. Then she carried him to the back door where he headed out to the garden to inspect his kingdom.

She put the casseroles on the top shelf of her father's refrigerator and paused to inspect the contents. The shelves were almost bare: half a loaf of her father's favourite dark rye bread, some cheese, a dozen apples, half eaten bottles of jam, some wilted lettuce in the vegetable bin. Perhaps her father did appreciate Verna's contributions. It was hard to be inspired when you were cooking for one. She understood why he worked late most nights.

Alexa stood at the kitchen window for a moment and watched Robbie digging furiously in the dirt near her father's wood pile. Then she wandered into the family room which adjoined the kitchen. More than any other room in the house, it reminded her of her mother. She sank down on the flowered cushions of the loveseat and let her gaze wander around the room, taking in the familiar details, the swag curtains in heavy rose brocade, the collection of cranberry glass, the ivory afghan which her mother had so often wrapped around herself as she read. Her father had changed nothing.

Unconsciously Alexa took a deep breath. She had always been the problem daughter, the misfit among sisters who were honours students and lived for sports or band. Until her senior year in high school, her marks had been mediocre at best. She was content to scrape by, just barely staying in an Academic program because her parents insisted. She had been far more interested in her social life and then one particular boy.

Perhaps the meeting with Verna Murphy had triggered these memories. She could see her high school self standing in the shadows of her parents' verandah locked tightly in the arms of Tony Benoit, both of them giggling because they were sure that they had seen the curtains twitch in Verna's living room window.

"Let's really give her something to talk about," Tony whispered. When he pressed against her and their lips met, both of them forgot the woman lurking behind the curtains in the house next door.

For the first time in years, she thought of the unseasonably warm spring in Tony's senior year of high school, the weekend parties by the river and then one particular party. She pushed the thought away. She had paid dearly for that night and repressed its memory firmly whenever it entered her consciousness. She hadn't come home to relive her youth, but why had she come?

Escape from an unhappy relationship was only a partial answer. She clearly remembered the frantic phone call from Katie, her oldest sister, the previous New Year's. After the usual seasonal greetings and inquiries about Alexa's trip to Barbados, Katie had plunged in. "Alexa, we've got to do something about Dad. I'm worried sick. You know that he spent the holidays with us. He's just not himself. He's lost pounds and pounds and would hardly eat no matter what we cooked. Even Christy asked him, 'Grandpa, aren't you hungry?' It's pretty sad when a three-year-old notices that her grandfather's just pushing food around on his plate. I hoped we could cheer him up, but I'm beginning to think he needs professional help. It's natural to be depressed when your wife dies, and Mom and Dad were best friends, not just husband and wife, but it's been six months, and he seems to have lost interest in everything."

Alexa remembered the visits with her dad over the winter and spring. Despite Katie's penchant for exaggeration, her description had been accurate. Dan Corbett continued with his law practice and saw a few friends, but he was not the same man. She also recalled her telephone call to him in early July. "Dad, I have a surprise. I hope it's a pleasant one. I decided on the spur of the moment that I was burned out, and I'm taking a year's leave of absence. My principal has been super helpful. It's all arranged. If you think you can stand it, I want to come home. I'm sure I can find an apartment to rent and I'll do some supply work at the high school or perhaps fill in for a sick leave."

For the first time, her dad's voice was animated, "Can I stand it? It's the best news I've had in months. The question is, 'Can you stand Davenport?' You were pretty miserable here in your last year of high school."

"Don't worry about me. It's what I want right now. I've saved some money, and I may talk you into taking a winter holiday with me."

Alexa would always be grateful that her father had not asked a million questions. There was no mention of David until Alexa brought up the subject. They resumed their comfortable, bantering relationship, and Alexa soon found a apartment in an old Victorian mansion a few blocks from her dad's house. He seemed to understand intuitively that she needed a place of her own, as if having her own space and her name on the brass letterbox would help her reclaim her identity.

The sound of muted barking told Alexa that Robbie had given up his quest for a chipmunk or squirrel and was ready to come in. She opened the door, and he repeated his rapturous greeting as if he had not seen her minutes before.

Back in her car, Alexa realized that the contents of her own refrigerator were no more exciting than her father's. She thought of stopping to pick up a few things, but found she had neither the energy nor the interest. She decided to have breakfast at the local restaurant, Coffee and Company, on the way to school the next morning. It would be a chance to meet some of her neighbours.

After Alexa unlocked the door to her apartment on the second storey of the sprawling villa, she dumped a pile of books on the comfortable chintz sofa and kicked off her sandals. She needed a long shower. There was just enough time to wash and dry her hair before she met Patti.

As she stood under the hot water, Alexa shampooed her hair vigorously, feeling as if she were washing several layers of dust from both her physical self and her psyche. Suddenly she smiled. The clock *had* stopped in Davenport. In the city she never relived the past as she had in those moments alone in her dad's house. She had come here to reclaim her life, not stagnate in memories. She stepped out of the shower and into her terrycloth robe. Wrapping a towel around her wet hair, she went to the kitchen to pour herself a glass of chilled chablis. In the hall she noticed that the red light on her phone was flashing. She lifted the receiver to punch in the code to receive her messages. Almost none of her friends had the new unlisted number yet, but perhaps Patti was caught in some domestic crisis and was cancelling dinner.

Alexa caught her breath when she heard David's familiar voice. "Alexa, I know you told me not to call, but I miss you. We need to talk. Please call me. We can meet somewhere on neutral ground, or I can drive up to see you on the weekend. I can't believe..." Alexa held the phone away from her ear. When the voice finally stopped, she punched the erase button with ferocity.

She wasn't going to call. Leaving David had been hard enough after five years, but she'd finally made the decision. She couldn't go back.

What good would more talking do? In spite of her emotion, the rational part of her mind was asking how David had found her unlisted number.

She picked up the wine glass and went into the bathroom to dry her hair. As she studied her face in the mirror, her own violet eyes gazed back. She brushed back her wet hair, frowning at the white skin which never tanned even in the hottest of summers. She tried to smile at her reflection. She didn't like the woman she had become with David. It was time to find herself again, and an evening with Patti was just what she needed. This was a new chapter in her life.

CHAPTER TWO

Seated in a corner booth at The River Mill, Alexa glanced around the historic restaurant, one of Davenport's landmarks. The limestone walls and beamed ceiling provided a sharp contrast to the chrome and glass of the bistro where she had eaten with David a few weeks before. Several patrons looked vaguely familiar, but they were mostly of her parents' generation, and on a Tuesday evening the restaurant was far from crowded.

Patti was notorious for being late, so Alexa ordered a carafe of white wine and settled back to study the elegant menu. Suddenly she was engulfed in an enormous hug.

"I can't believe you're home! I've missed you so much!" Characteristically, Patti was laughing and crying at once. She threw her huge straw handbag down on the padded banquette and sat across from Alexa.

Not for the first time Alexa realized how much she too had missed Patti. With Patti she always knew that she could say and do anything and still be completely understood. Patti's blonde hair was pinned up on top of her head, but a few flyaway curls fell around her face and neck. She was perhaps more rounded than Alexa remembered, but with no makeup and in her simple white cotton shirt and capri pants, she could easily be mistaken for a college student. "How do you do it? You're the mother of two children in perpetual motion, and you look exactly the same as you did when we were in school."

Patti laughed. "Maybe that's the secret. I literally never stop. I spend the days chasing Cheyenne and Nick and the dogs. Housework gets done – or it doesn't – in the evening when Chris is home. It should keep me young for a few years yet."

"I can't wait to see the kids again. And how is Chris? Are you two still as much in love as ever?"

"Ridiculous as it sounds, yes. I can't imagine ever being with anyone else. Even my parents have come round at last when they see how happy we are and that Chris is wonderful with the kids."

Alexa nodded. Patti's parents had been far from pleased when their only daughter married her highschool boyfriend the week after she graduated from university. She sighed dramatically. "Do you have any idea how lucky you are, girl? High school sweethearts are supposed to marry and divorce, but you're the exception. It's easy to see that you're happy."

"I know I'm lucky. The hardest decision was whether I should go back to work after Nick and Cheyenne were born. The money really would have helped us with the mortgage, but the kids are young for such a short time. Even when Chris's cousin offered to babysit, I knew I wanted to be there for all the milestones. I'll have lots of years to teach when the kids are in school. I just couldn't stand the thought of taking courses every summer and marking every night when I wanted to play with the munchkins. I never thought that becoming a mother would do this to me." She leaned forward. "Tell me the truth. Do you think I'm wasting my time in mommy land without any intelligent adult conversation most days?"

"Don't be silly! Actually I'm very jealous. You've got it all. The gorgeous husband, two adorable kids, and a career that you can start again."

The waiter arrived with their wine, and they ordered their food. While Alexa chose an appetizer, Patti had time to study her friend. She was still the same Alexa with the long dark hair and smooth ivory skin, but there was something sad in her eyes and mouth even when she smiled.

"It's super that you've come home – even for a while. But I keep thinking that you'll find Davenport incredibly provincial. We're little more than a village! Every time I see the sign 'Greater Davenport – Population 15, 000' I crack up. When you were in Europe and then in Thailand, I used to read your letters out loud to Chris. We were up to our ears in baby bottles and dirty diapers, and you were backpacking through Italy and riding elephants in Chang Mai. Won't you miss all that?"

"In some ways, yes. Actually living in a foreign country changes you forever, but I felt like a permanent tourist. The Thais are such a gracious people, so warm and so proud of their culture and history, but I didn't belong! I was always the visiting foreign teacher." Half smiling, she added, "Perhaps the travel bug will bite hard again. But right now I'm happy to be back. I've been wandering long enough. I know that life in Davenport can be claustrophobic, but I'm telling myself that we're only a few hours from the city with shopping and theatre."

"What happened with you and David anyway? Both Chris and I liked him so much when we met him last summer, and you were obviously in love. Are you two really finished?"

Alexa nodded her head emphatically. "It's over." Impulsively she seized Patti's hand. "I wish I had your gift."

Patti looked at her inquiringly.

Alexa hesitated, searching for the right words. "I don't think I've got your talent for long-term relationships. When I first met David, it was absolute bliss. I didn't care that he was divorced and ten years older than me. He was my mentor. We went to poetry readings, to concerts and the theatre. I thought about him all the time, and we wanted to spend every possible moment together. Just the sound of his voice gave me the proverbial butterflies. I was completely obsessed with him."

"I could tell. When you were together, I could feel the attraction between you two. It was almost tangible."

"I didn't think we were that obvious."

"You positively glowed if David put his arm around you or even touched your hand."

Alexa smiled. "Like the love-struck heroine of some Victorian melodrama? But in a way you're right. That's the way I felt until we moved in together. Then it gradually became a nightmare. David's a control freak. According to him, I'm organizationally challenged. He has a ritual for absolutely everything – from making a salad to arranging the spices. Some women would probably kill to live with someone who's Emeril and Martha Stewart rolled into one, but after a while it became a terrific turnoff."

Patti smiled in sympathy. She and Alexa had been roommates in their university years. She remembered heaps of discarded clothing on the floor, unwashed dishes in the sink, and stacks of papers on every available surface."

Alexa hesitated. "I know I'm making this sound so petty. It's hard to explain exactly what went wrong. David became so critical and overbearing, so controlling! Once he gave me a lecture because I bought processed cheese for sandwiches. I always felt that I wasn't measuring up to his impossibly high standards. According to him, I was wasting my time teaching illiterates. He called my inner city kids 'the yard apes.'"

Now Patti looked indignant. "That's disgusting! You're probably the most dedicated teacher I've ever met. What you do with kids can make all the difference in their lives."

"I agree," Alexa acknowledged, "but somehow my work, my ideas, my music, the books I read just couldn't compare to his. He lived in an ivory tower with his graduate students, and I was down in the gutter with the great unwashed. I think he saw himself as Pygmalion, and I was tired of playing Galatea. After a while I didn't recognize myself."

Once again they were interrupted as the waiter ceremoniously served their appetizers, grilled scampi for Patti and hearts of palm for Alexa. They looked at the beautifully presented plates and began to laugh.

"This makes up for all those totally gross meals in the university cafeteria," Patti said between giggles. "Do you remember when the Vietnamese engineering students in the apartment below ours invited us down for dinner, and the mystery meat turned out to be chicken livers? You were in your vegetarian phase and thought you were eating tofu. You went back to our apartment and threw up."

"And I remember the night you tried to impress Chris with a romantic dinner," Alexa retorted. "We actually cleaned the apartment, and you roasted a chicken, but you forgot to remove the gizzard which was in a plastic bag hidden in some cavity. All we could smell for days was burned plastic. It was the middle of January, but we had to open all the windows, and the apartment was freezing."

The two finally settled down to enjoy the food. Eating was interspersed with more shared memories and laughter. For dessert they ordered a slice of Death by Chocolate and two forks. Then conversation became serious.

"How's your dad doing? I haven't talked to him since your mother's funeral."

"It's hard to say. He seems so much older now. My sisters and I have been worried about him. The house is exactly the same as when Mom was here. I keep expecting her to walk in."

Patti squeezed her hand in sympathy. "He must be happy you're back."

Alex's face brightened. "He is, and I'll try to keep out of trouble, not like the old days when I was always the one in some scrap. He never had problems with Katie or Tanya skipping school."

"I remember how much you hated algebra with old Mr Armstrong and his sarcastic comments."

"Remember his pointer? It was like a third hand banging on the desks. Next to you, the person I've missed the most is Joy. Do you ever hear from her?"

Patti looked deflated. "I've missed her too. The three of us were always together in school, but I never see her now. When I call her, she doesn't return the calls."

"We had lunch together two years ago when I was home in the summer – just after she was appointed director of Interval House," Alexa said. "She's passionate about her work with the victims of family violence, and we swapped stories about our jobs." She paused. "She and Janet had been together for about a year, and I hoped she'd join us for lunch, but she didn't."

"I haven't met Janet either. I can't decide if Joy's putting up barriers or thinks we are. The three of us were always inseparable. Why is she doing this?"

"I don't know," Alexa said slowly. "But now that I'm back in town I'm going to try to break through those barriers. Maybe she thinks everyone in Davenport is homophobic. Small towns are bizarre, especially this one. Everyone knows everyone else's business, but some things are never acknowledged. You must know my landlord, Martin MacLean. He and Matt Williams were together for years, but, according to my dad, when Matt died the town ignored Martin's grief. He said they acted as if Martin had lost a casual friend."

Patti sighed. "You're right. I love this place, but I often wonder if Cheyenne and Nick will grow up to be narrow minded bigots if they live in a town where everyone is WASP, and the rednecks sneer at homosexuals, and the intellectuals pretend they're a figment of some sociologist's imagination."

Alexa looked at her friend affectionately. "I don't think you need to worry. You and Chris are open-minded, and you can always send them to visit Aunt Alexa in the big city every summer."

"So you won't stay?" Patti asked.

"Who knows? I was lucky to get a contract this semester at the high school, but Murray Dean will probably come back in February, and I'll be out of a job. Besides," she added tongue in cheek, "I need to meet an eligible man or two to mend my broken heart. So far, there's definitely no one on the horizon."

"Then I have some news for you. Did you know that Tony Benoit's back in town?" The two women's eyes met in a long look that spoke volumes.

Alexa examined the stem of her wine glass before answering. "That really is ancient history."

"I suppose it is," Patti agreed, "but what you two had was special."

"Patti, I've never forgotten Tony. How could I? He was my first love. But I got badly burned once, and I'm not even tempted to light that fire again. Besides, we were just kids. I was sixteen, and Tony was seventeen when he left to play hockey. I made the right decision when I broke up with him."

"Of course you did. I just wanted to give you a heads-up if you see him around town."

"Why is he back?" Alexa asked curiously.

"Apparently he's not playing hockey anymore, and his marriage is over. He's going to work with his brother remodelling old houses. Ronnie's business is booming. Chris says he has more work than he can handle."

Alexa had vivid memories of Ronnie. He had never been a favourite of hers, but after a moment she said, "Good luck to them. Just don't include Tony on a list of eligible men."

"Oh, there are lots of unattached guys around." Patti was trying to be helpful. "At Riverside, there's Buzz Spencer."

"Who appears to be about sixty," Alexa interrupted.

Patti raised her eyebrows but continued as if Alexa had not spoken, "And, of course, there's Mark Anderson. Although half the women in town have the hots for him."

"Mark Anderson? The vice-principal at Riverside? He's got a wife called Sarah," Alexa again interrupted.

"No, Sarah's Mark's daughter. She's been with Mark since Jane moved in with Peter Hill, the optometrist."

"Don't tell me even Davenport is playing 'mix and match' since I've been gone."

Alexa struggled to digest this information. Perhaps his wife's leaving had produced that edge in Mark Anderson. "Mr Anderson may be hot stuff, but I certainly didn't fall for him. After David, those sardonic types do nothing for me. The other women can have him. Patti, you won't believe this, but he actually advised me not to worry about making the curriculum relevant, just enforce the school rules."

Patti's jaw dropped slightly. "With that philosophy, I can see why you weren't impressed. If he's not your thing, come over for a barbecue, and I'll have Chris invite one of his hockey buddies. Lots of them are single."

"Yes to the barbecue. No to the single friends." Alexa couldn't help smiling at Patti's single minded approach. "I've seriously sworn off men, but I'd love to spend a Saturday with you and Chris, and it's been ages since I saw Nick and Cheyenne."

"You're on! I'll let you get settled in your school routine and then you must come over. I've missed you. We've both missed you."

Alexa drove home slowly. The music of Celine Dion filled the car, and David was not there to criticize. In spite of her dismissal of Mark Anderson, there was something about him which was almost dangerously attractive, and yet in an odd way he reminded her of David. She wondered how long it would be before they would clash over yet another difference in philosophy. She took a deep breath and squared her shoulders. She was going to become the old Alexa, feisty and fearless and free to make her own decisions.

CHAPTER THREE

The rest of the week passed in a blur. Alexa was busy with lesson planning, staff and department meetings. She met the other members of the English department; Carol Helmer, the English head, already seemed like an old friend.

"The secretaries here are amazing," Carol told her. "If you're in with them and with our head custodian, Neil Chisholm, you'll survive the kids and parents. Buy Neil a bottle of good scotch at Christmas, and he'll be your friend for life."

Alexa laughed, but made a mental note of this tip. On Friday morning she brought the secretaries a box of blueberry muffins hot from the oven at Coffee and Company. Susan Johnson interrupted her frantic printing of student timetables to pop half a muffin into her mouth and roll her eyes in ecstasy. "This is delicious, but what are we celebrating?"

"An early thank you for all the help I'm probably going to need in the next few weeks and for your words of encouragement," Alexa replied.

"Relax. You're not a rookie, Alexa. Just remember our previous principal used to tell the new staff members, 'Don't smile until Christmas.'"

"I think that's a bit extreme." With a grin, she added, "But don't worry. I won't be sending many kids down to see Mr Anderson and clutter up his pristine office. I like to run my own show."

When Mark passed through the office, Susan offered him a muffin, and he stopped to chat, perching on the edge of a desk near Alexa. His eyes met hers and held, and this time he smiled warmly. "Alexa, I want you to know that this is the lady who really keeps the school running. Lots of the junior kids think she's the vice-principal!"

As Susan protested, Mark added, "It's true! We couldn't run this place without you. The only time I ever saw you flustered was my first day on the job." Both Susan and Jenny Lafrance, the attendance secretary, smiled as he began the story which was one of the staff legends.

"Susan makes herself a gourmet lunch every day," Mark explained to Alexa. "On the first day of school, I was running like mad. By the end of the lunch hour, I was ravenous, so I stormed into the staff room, grabbed a lunch from the refrigerator and wolfed it down. Somehow I didn't notice that I was eating swiss cheese and black forest ham on rye although I had packed a peanut butter sandwich. When Susan came to eat her lunch, all she could find was peanut butter and jelly on white bread."

"Is that really true?" Alexa demanded.

Susan nodded. "Absolutely. He even ate my salad and pear, leaving me his bruised apple. I never let him forget it. I keep telling him that he owes me a dinner."

"And I'm going to pay my debt," Mark joked, "just as soon as you can arrange a night out with me while your husband babysits."

Susan teased back, "Promises! Promises!"

Alexa felt a pleasant adolescent tingle in the pit of her stomach when Mark smiled at her. She found herself attracted to his easy charm and quickly reminded herself of her resolution to avoid any emotional entanglements. Mark was a fascinating enigma. With the office staff, he was warm and humorous, but their first meeting had suggested that he was at heart a cynical bureaucrat.

At the Thursday morning staff meeting, Alexa found herself watching Mark as he and Lisa welcomed everyone. This was her first chance to see Mark with the staff, and she was more impressed than she cared to admit. "Last June you voted to change the bell system," he reminded everyone. "We've implemented the changes, and this semester the students get eight minutes between classes. There's no warning bell, but that should give them enough time for their smoke breaks and bathroom treks without being late for the next class. Any longer and we have to extend the school day which interferes with the busing schedule. We've also changed the 'late' system to try to relieve some of the pressure on the office staff." Mark looked around the room, crowded with teachers, aides and secretaries. He was at his professional best, comfortable speaking before a crowd and watching the various groups, interacting with them and noting their reaction to his comments.

Alexa wondered why she felt that he was deliberately assessing her. Throughout his presentation on attendance procedures, she could feel his gaze returning to the table where she was sitting with Carol and some of the other English teachers.

"My job's still zoo patrol," he was saying. "I'll be out in the halls between classes and rounding up the stragglers after the bell rings, but I'd appreciate any help you can give. If you have a spare minute, please get out in the hall near your classroom. It's surprising how much goes down which we can easily stop with a teacher presence."

Alexa could see many teachers nodding in support. "Will the detention hall work the same as last year?" Buzz Spencer asked.

As Mark started to answer, Carol leaned over and whispered to Alexa, "Watch the woman in the white shorts. That's Julie Chisholm. She's absolutely devouring Mark."

Alexa had already noticed the tanned blonde woman who greeted Mark with an extra warm hug when she arrived at the meeting. Mark was meticulously explaining the process for detention hall referrals while Julie sat at a table at the front of the room watching him with a rapt expression as if he were speaking in tongues.

"Are they an item?" she whispered back.

"It's hard to say. I don't think so. But Julie's trying hard. They coached the junior and senior boys' basketball teams together last year," Carol mouthed behind her hand.

Mark had moved on to reporting absentees. Alexa leaned back and looked around the room. The staff was surprisingly young, and their enthusiasm was contagious. She hoped it would be a good semester even if January brought an end to her contract.

During her lunch break, Alexa tried to call Joy Saunders. She had been calling her apartment all week. Although Patti had warned her that their old friend wasn't responding to phone calls, Alexa wouldn't give up. This time she called the office of Interval House and was surprised to reach Joy at her desk.

"Joy, it's Alex! I'm the world's worst correspondent, but I've missed you. Believe it or not, I'm home. I came back to Davenport to be close to Dad for a while, and I landed a job at Riverside teaching English this semester. Can we get togther on the weekend?"

There was a long silence. When Joy spoke, her voice sounded odd.

"It's good to hear from you. I'd like to, but I can't. I'm busy this weekend."

It wasn't the words as much as the flat tone which stunned Alexa. After a long pause, she tried again. "I know it's been ages, Joy, but I really want to see you. I'm worried about Dad, and David and I broke up, and..." To her horror, Alexa felt her voice quiver. She struggled to regain her composure.

There was another long silence before Joy answered, "I'm so sorry about your mother. She and your dad meant a lot to me when you and I were at school together. I practically lived at your house for a while."

Alexa seized this opportunity, "Then come over to Dad's place on Saturday night. He's going to barbecue, and he'd love to see you again."

"I simply can't. Actually I'm packing this weekend."

"Packing? Are you moving to a new apartment?"

Joy hesitated. "My contract wasn't renewed here at Interval House. I'm moving to the city where there will be more chance to find something in my line of work."

Alexa swallowed hard. "Listen, it's a hundred degrees in the shade today. You can't go home and pack until it gets cooler. Let's meet after work for a drink. We'll go to The Blue Anchor. You can pack all day tomorrow."

"Okay, but it will have to be a fast drink. Does five o'clock work for you?"

"That's perfect. I can't wait to see you. Look for my car. It's the one with piles of textbooks in the back seat." After Alexa hung up, she realized that unconsciously she had expected her old friends would be thrilled to see her. Why had she been naive enough to believe that after so many years they could simply pick up the threads of their lives as if she had never been away?

When Alexa pulled into The Blue Anchor parking lot that afternoon, Joy was just climbing out of her car, a battered red Celica. Alexa smiled at the sight of her old friend. She remembered that in high school Joy's favourite song had been "Lost in the Sixties." In her long Egyptian cotton skirt, white peasant blouse and amber beads, the statuesque Joy still had an uncanny resemblance to a sixties icon.

Alexa pulled up beside the Celica, hopped out, and hugged Joy warmly. She stepped back to examine her old friend and said, "Time *has* stopped here. You and Patti look almost exactly the same as you did in high school. I'm the one with wrinkles and grey hairs. Do you remember Verna Murphy, my dad's horrendous neighbour? She was kind enough to remind me that I'm not getting any younger."

Joy booming laughter had not changed. She finally managed to say, "Not to worry. You're as gorgeous as ever. No wrinkles or grey hair that I can see. But you do look a wee bit more sophisticated than us country bumpkins."

The two women fell into step as they headed for The Blue Anchor patio. A very young waitress in microshorts and a cropped top took their order and quickly returned with a pitcher of beer, salsa and corn chips as Alexa lamented, "I can't believe it. I'm actually back after so many years, and you're leaving. It's totally unfair. I wanted to be near Dad for a while, and somehow I just expected that you and Patti would be around to boost me up. Just like the old days."

When she saw her friend's expression, she added quickly, "I know that's totally insane. You've both got lives of your own. Time doesn't stand still anywhere even though I want it to."

Joy said lightly, "Six months ago you would have had your wish. I thought I was here permanently. But things can change overnight."

"Can we talk about what happened?" Alexa asked. "I gave you a rundown of my life on the phone. David and I are finished. *Finito!* I want to hear about you."

As Alexa settled in to listen, Joy seemed to struggle for words. "There isn't much to say. I told you on the phone that my board of directors didn't renew my contract. Actually they suggested that I should resign 'because of our philosophical differences.' I agreed. After seven years, they gave me a decent severance package," she added bitterly. "I can take my time looking for a new position."

"But that doesn't make sense. The last time we spoke about your job things were going so well. It was a perfect fit."

"Yes, I thought it was. But it seems that some members of the board, the local pillars of society and elders in the church, didn't exactly appreciate their director being gay."

Alexa drew in her breath sharply.

Joy went on, "People talk in small towns like Davenport. I guess they do everywhere, but here we really live in the proverbial fish bowl. I never tried to hide the fact that Janet and I were living together. And there's no way that my lifestyle affected my work. I wrote proposals for them. The grants came in, and we were a going concern. Interval House is the only place for miles around where women and children in abusive situations can get away. For many people it's been a lifeline out of a personal hell." Joy's matter of fact tone did not cover her feelings.

"But, Joy," Alexa tried again. "It's not the 1950s. People are entitled to private lives. It's nobody's business that you and Janet live together."

"That's what I thought once," Joy said. "But the chair of the board suggested that my lifestyle was a concern. She even implied that with my lesbian beliefs I might not counsel our clients to return home and 'work at their marriages.'"

"That is absolutely unbelievable, " Alexa spluttered. "You have to talk to my father. This is an infringement of your civil rights. Of Janet's civil rights. I'm sure you can fight this. Please don't give up."

When Joy answered, she was obviously choosing her words with care. "Alexa, I appreciate your support. It means a lot. Even a few weeks ago, I would have agreed with you. Now it doesn't matter. Janet and I aren't together. In a strange way, I think this split with the board of directors was a godsend. I needed to stop brooding about something I can't change and get on with my life. I've never really been away from Davenport. It's more than time for me to move on."

"And Janet?" Alexa asked cautiously. "Will you tell me about her?"

"As I said, it doesn't matter now. She's met someone else. Actually a male someone."

"Oh, Joy, I'm so sorry."

Joy ignored Alexa's expression of sympathy. "There's nothing to say. At the time I was completely devastated. I actually thought she was happy. She said she had been miserable for at least a year and told me how insensitive I was." Joy's voice trailed away.

"I wish I could say something or do something to make you feel better. I understand now why you need to get away from here. But promise me that you'll stay in touch. Who knows how long I'll be here either."

"But you're working?" Joy asked.

"Yes, I have a contract at Riverside for this semester, and I'm looking forward to it."

"I know both Lisa Fletcher and Mark Anderson, the vice-principal. I worked with Mark on some cases where teenage girls had left an abusive home situation. He really seems to care about the students as individuals."

"I wasn't exactly impressed with his educational philosophy, " Alexa said dryly, "but the staff seems to love him. And I'm excited about my contract. I thought I'd have only basic English courses. The new jargon is Pathways. But Lisa changed my timetable when she saw my teaching experience. Besides a Pathways group, I've got a group of Academic grade nines and one group of university bound kids who'll keep me reading and thinking." Alexa's enthusiasm was contagious.

"You're like me. You can get lost in your work," Joy said lightly. "We're both so lucky. For most people work is just a way to pay the bills, but you and I couldn't survive without it."

"I suppose there's always the danger of becoming a workaholic. David used to say that he couldn't stand to listen to me talk with other teachers because we were completely obsessed by the trivia of our jobs."

"I think that comment says more about David than about you. At the risk of sharing my prejudices, I have to say that a lot of men expect work to be the centre of their lives but are very threatened if their female partners feel the same way." She looked at her watch. "This has been great, but I have to go. There are new tenants moving into my apartment on Sunday morning." Joy refused Alexa's offer to help with her packing and insisted on paying the tab. "Consider it your welcome home present. You can take me out when you come to visit in the city."

Alexa got into her car clutching Joy's cell number on a scrap of paper. "I'll call you soon," she promised. "We'll definitely get together."

She drove to Martin's house replaying the conversation with Joy. After she unlocked the door and dropped her books on the hall table, she saw that the red light on her telephone was flashing again. She had three messages. The first was from her father, the second David's familiar voice, "Alexa, even if it's late when you come in, please call me."

She quickly erased the message. With her mind spinning, she wondered again, how he had found her number. She would ask her father if he had passed it on. No matter how she felt she would have to call David. She couldn't stand coming home each night to another of these peremptory messages.

The third message was succinct, the voice husky with a hint of laughter. "Good evening, Alexa, it's Tony Benoit. I know it's been ages but I heard you were back in town and obviously so am I. I hope we can get together for a drink and a chance to catch up on our lives. I'll call you again."

Alexa took a deep breath. Then she erased this message as well. Her hands were trembling slightly. This really was a time warp. She hadn't seen Tony for at least fourteen years, and their parting had not been friendly. What did they have in common now?

While she tried to block out the messages from David and Tony, Alexa changed into shorts and a T-shirt. She thought of the waitress at the Blue Anchor and studied her nails critically, wondering if the Pathways kids would be impressed if she bought some black nail polish, but she found herself remembering the conversation with Joy. She had felt her friend's carefully controlled bitterness and her loneliness, yet Joy was right. What could Davenport offer a thirty-something single woman who preferred other women? Davenport, the land that time forgot. This was the perfect town for conventionally married couples like Patti and Chris. Neither Joy nor Alexa fit in.

Alexa found it hard to settle down to work. She wandered restlessly about the apartment for several minutes and flipped through her CD collection. At last she put on Kenny G. She waited until the mellow sounds of Kenny's saxophone filled the room before she picked up a copy of Michael Ondaatje's *The English Patient*. The Pathways kids would find Kenny seriously uncool, but his music never failed to soothe her. She turned on the reading light over the desk and switched on her computer. She sat down in front of the screen and began to make notes for her senior class of university bound students. When the telephone rang again, it went unanswered.

After Alexa finally felt sleepy enough to think about going to bed, she stood for a moment at the window staring out at Martin's dark garden lit only by a single patio lamp. She told herself that change is the only constant in life. She had left Davenport as a rebellious teenager. Like Joy, she understood how the town dealt with those who broke its social norms, but she had returned as a teacher who could make a difference in kids' lives. A sixth sense told her that she would soon be at odds with Mr Anderson and his attendance and detention procedures. She shrugged. She was more than ready to take him on.

She remembered Professor Harrison, her favourite instructor at the Faculty of Education, and how often he had quoted Henry Adams, "A teacher affects eternity, he can never tell where his influence stops." She thought that the kids made even the bureaucracy bearable. They were worth fighting for.

CHAPTER FOUR

*T*he next morning after a leisurely breakfast with two mugs of her favourite hazelnut coffee, Alexa listened to and deleted David's third message. She also returned her father's call from the night before.

"Hi, Dad, I'm on my way to the grocery store. What should I buy for tonight?"

"Not a thing " replied Dan Corbett. "I picked up steaks and salad fixings on my way home last night. If you like, you can make a caesar salad after you get here, and I have a year's supply of desserts in the freezer, thanks to Verna. Did you reach Joy? Is she coming over for supper?"

"No, she's got a crazy weekend, packing to move out of her apartment. I'll explain when I see you." Alexa paused, "Dad, swear to me that Verna isn't going to turn up tonight. I've already had one conversation with her in which she told me I'm much too scrawny, and her purpose on this planet is to care for you. Oh, and it's time that I found a man and settled down. I'm not getting any younger."

Dan chuckled. "Verna's gone to visit her sister for the weekend, so we're both safe for a few days. Alexa, she means well, but I know she can be a bit much at times."

"You always had a remarkable gift for understatement," Alexa said dryly.

"Why don't you invite Martin MacLean?" her father suggested. "He's doing us a huge favour by renting you that apartment at a ridiculously low rent, and I haven't had a chance to talk to him in months, not since Anne's death."

"Good idea. I saw him this morning, puttering around in the garden. I'll drop in and invite him. If it's okay, I'll come early and have a swim before we make supper. This apartment's fabulous but not airconditioned."

When she finished the call, Alexa found her car keys and wallet and went down to the patio where Martin was reading the weekend papers. Although he was casually dressed in unfashionable denim cutoffs and a well used, paint-spattered sweatshirt, Martin was an extremely attractive man whose charm lay in being totally oblivious to the effect his silver hair and dark eyes had on others.

"Good morning, Alexa." Smiling a welcome, he scooped two calico cats off the chaise lounge and motioned for Alexa to sit down.

"I can't stop now. I finally have the energy to head out to stock up on groceries," Alexa joked. "I just got off the phone from talking to Dad. You're invited to a barbecue tonight at his place. Come early if you want a swim."

Martin's face brightened. "That's very kind. Sure I won't be in the way?"

"Not at all. Dad said you haven't seen each other in ages, and he's always eager to share fishing stories with anyone who takes more interest in the sport than I do."

"Shall I bring something?"

"Dad's got it all." Then, as Martin started to protest, Alexa suggested, "If you really want to make the evening special, bring a bottle of wine. My mom always teased Dad because he's a beer drinker. Once, to surprise her, he brought home a bottle of sherry which she said wasn't fit to use even in cooking. His idea of a well-stocked liquor cabinet is several kinds of imported beer." Alexa chattered on, realizing as always that when she mentioned her mother there was a huge lump in her throat.

Martin understood. Sending her a sympathetic glance, he replied, "I can manage the wine. Thanks again, Alexa. I haven't been out for dinner in a long time, and this will be an incentive to get the gardening done early before it gets any hotter."

In the grocery store, Alexa quickly filled her cart. At the checkout, the packer, a boy of seventeen or eighteen, smiled at her shyly. He was tall and lanky and looked as if he would have been more comfortable in sweats and a baseball cap than in his regulation jacket and tie. When Alexa smiled back, he asked, "Are you the new English teacher, Miss?"

"Yes, I'm Miss Corbett."

"I heard that Mr Dean isn't going to be at school this semester."

"That's right. I'm taking some of his classes until January."

"I may see you on Tuesday then. I was supposed to have Mr Dean for English. My name's Bob Turnbull."

"Nice to meet you, Bob. I'll look forward to seeing you in class," Alexa replied. As Bob helped her load the groceries into her trolley, she asked, "So what do you think of Riverside?"

The boy ducked his head looking embarrassed. "It's a pretty good school I guess. I made the senior basketball team last year, and we won the regionals. I'm going to try out again this year. Mr Anderson is the coach. He's the vice-principal, but he's an okay guy. Keeps us working hard."

While Alexa put the bags of groceries into the trunk of her car, she reflected that if all the Riverside students were as friendly as Bob, they would be quite a change from the punkers and rappers at her last school. On the other hand, Davenport was living up to its reputation as the fish bowl capital of the world. If a student recognized a new face in the grocery store, she could imagine the town would be pulling out its collective magnifying glasses to follow any newcomer's activities. Not to worry. Her social life in Davenport would pass even Verna's scrutiny.

Later that afternoon, Alexa was mixing the dressing for the caesar salad in her dad's kitchen while he washed the romaine lettuce. Reaching for the bottle of olive oil, she lifted the heavy hair from her neck which felt sticky even in the cool of the old house. "I can feel the pool calling," she remarked.

"Go and change. Have a swim," her father encouraged her. "We can talk later. I want to hear all about Patti and Joy. I hardly ever see them, and you have the latest news."

"I'm worried about Joy" Alexa admitted. "I hope you'll have some advice for her that I can pass on."

"Legal advice or friendly, fatherly advice?" asked Dan quizzically.

"A little of both, I guess. But it can wait," she added. "If I start to tell you now, I'll never get that swim."

Diving into the pool, Alexa expertly stroked to the other end, turned neatly and swam back. Alexa and her sisters had literally lived in the pool as teenagers. Her parents' home had been the meeting place for all their friends. Once, when her father had complained half seriously, half jokingly about the phenomenal cost of snacks and drinks, Arlene Corbett had said quietly, "But we know where the girls are, Dan, and we know their friends. That's more than most of the parents can say."

After fifteen minutes of rapid swimming Alexa got out of the pool and stretched out on a flowered deckchair. Robbie, who usually lay beside her, was staring as if mesmerized at the woodpile in the far corner of the patio where he had cornered a chipmunk earlier that afternoon. Dan Corbett, shears in hand, was attacking a climbing rosebush which threatened to cover one of the patio doors.

Alexa thought sleepily that it was a perfect late summer afternoon. She closed her eyes and listened to the jazz coming from a neighbour's house across the street. She drifted off for a few moments. The stillness was abruptly shattered by a strangely familiar voice.

"Hi, neighbour!" Alexa sat up to see Mark Anderson accompanied by a small girl seven or eight years old coming through the gate into her father's garden. They were dressed in bathing suits and T-shirts.

Dan dropped his shears. "Mark and Sarah, it's good to see you!" He went over to shake hands with Mark. "I heard you were back from holidays."

"Yes, last weekend, and Sarah reminds me every day that you invited us over to swim. Unfortunately I got home so late every night from school that I told her we'd have to wait until the weekend."

Alexa jumped up. Her two-piece bathing suit which had been perfect when she tried it on in the department store suddenly seemed much too skimpy. She was tempted to pull on her father's shirt hanging on a patio chair.

Seeing Alexa, Mark stopped short. "I guess I should have called first. Perhaps this isn't a good time."

"No, no, it's great," said Dan happily, totally unaware of Alexa's feelings. "Alexa, I know you've met Mark at the school. He just bought the house behind ours, and this is Sarah, Mark's daughter."

"Hello, Mark," Alexa managed to say. She certainly had not planned to spend her Saturday afternoon with the vice-principal. She sensed that Mark was aware of her feelings, and his eyes were teasing as if he were enjoying her embarrassment.

Turning to Sarah, a wide-eyed, serious little girl, she added, "Sarah, it's nice to meet you. I'm Alexa, and I guess you know Robbie."

Hearing the sound of strange voices, the Yorkshire Terrier gave up his pursuit of the chipmunk and came over to them.

"I met him once," Sarah said solemnly. "But I don't think he liked me. Can I pat him?"

"Robbie's thirteen years old. That's pretty old for a dog, and sometimes he gets nervous if people come to him too quickly. Just put your hand out and let him sniff you." Sending out a fervent prayer that Robbie would decide to be friendly, Alexa demonstrated, putting out her hand. Sarah followed the example.

To her surprise, Robbie allowed Sarah to rub his head and then flopped down on the patio on his back, offering a rounded stomach to be scratched.

"Robbie likes you," she told Sarah. "He only does that with people he trusts." For the first time, Sarah smiled and squatted down to rub Robbie's belly.

Alexa looked over to see her father and Mark deep in conversation. "Do you want to come for a swim?"

"I'm only allowed to swim with my mom or dad," Sarah told Alexa not even glancing up at her. Her tone wasn't rude, but there was no room for argument.

Overhearing, Mark said, "It's okay, honey. You can go into the pool with Miss Corbett. I'm right here."

Sarah frowned. Forgetting Robbie, she ran over to Mark. "You promised you'd go swimming with me." She tugged on his hand. "Come on, Dad. You promised."

"Sorry, Dan, " Mark excused himself. "I did promise. Can we have a quick swim?"

"Of course, enjoy the pool. We'll have a drink when you get out," Dan answered affably.

Picking up the paperback which had fallen beside her chair, Alexa began to read, surreptitiously watching Mark and Sarah in the water. The two splashed and played as Mark rode Sarah around on his shoulders and then pretended to duck her. Sarah was clearly enjoying the game, but she shrieked nervously from time to time. After a few minutes, Mark called, "Come on in, Alexa. Sarah wants to play tag. It's more fun with three people."

Hesitating for only a moment, Alexa dived in. Although she sensed that Sarah desperately wanted her father's undivided attention, she felt a rush of unexpected happiness as the three of them romped in the water. Mark was enjoying the game as much as Sarah. He moved easily, allowing Sarah to catch him and then just eluding her touch while she screamed with laughter. At first Sarah studiously ignored Alexa, but when Mark dived under the water and pretended to snap at her toes, she clung to her with cries of, "Save me! Save me!" Mark smiled at Alexa as Sarah grew braver and swam a few strokes on her own, going back and forth between her dad and the edge of the pool.

When Dan appeared with a tray of drinks, Mark climbed out of the pool with Sarah at his heels. After swimming a few quick lengths, Alexa also pulled herself out. She stood rubbing the water out of her hair and was again aware of Mark's appreciative gaze. She reached quickly for a T-shirt and went over to talk to Sarah.

"You're good in the water, Sarah. Do you like to swim?"

Sarah answered with adult seriousness. "Not when I can't touch the bottom. When we went on our canoe trip, we had to swim in a lake, and I saw a big turtle. I was afraid that it would grab my toes when I was swimming. And I don't like the waves in my face."

Alexa smiled sympathetically, remembering her own childhood trauma about deep water. "It's really not that bad when you get used to it. Sometime I can show you how to float in the water. You just relax and pretend you're being held up by a giant rubber raft. Even if the waves cover you for a moment, you keep floating."

Sarah answered with the same unsmiling focus. "I can't do that. I only swim with my dad and when I can touch the bottom. I don't like deep water."

Alexa, who spent countless hours with her nieces and nephews, felt that she was speaking with a miniature adult who had very definite views on life. She wondered if Sarah ever played with children her own age.

As if reading her thoughts, Mark came over to them. "This has been great," he said, including Alexa and Dan, "but I have to drive Sarah over to her mother's soon."

Turning to Sarah, he asked, "Do you want to change in Mr Corbett's pool house?"

Sarah nodded. "You come with me."

"I'll take you over to the pool house," Alexa offered.

Sarah's lower lip quivered. "I want Dad to go."

"Okay," Mark said agreeably, "but I warn you that I'm not standing guard outside the door. Robbie can do that."

He was back in a few minutes. "This hasn't been the best summer for Sarah. She's been living with me except for a few visits with her mother. Sarah really misses Jane. Next summer I'm going to make sure that she has a chance to go to camp with kids her own age. Thanks, Alexa, you were great with her. Sarah loved Robbie. I keep thinking that we should get a dog, but what would we do with it while we were both at school?"

"A kitten would be easier," suggested Dan.

He shrugged helplessly. "I know, but right now a puppy is at the top of her birthday list."

Dan laughed. "The first lesson in my book of rules for fathers is 'Listen, but don't always give in.' I remember when Katie, Alexa's oldest sister, was about Sarah's age she asked for a pony. We settled for riding lessons instead, and then she switched to figure skating. Kids' interests change very quickly. It was a lot easier to buy ice skates than put up a stable."

"Perhaps Sarah would like swimming lessons," Alexa suggested. "She really seemed to enjoy the pool, but she told me she's afraid if the water is deep."

"She had a bad experience on our canoe trip," Mark explained. "One afternoon she was playing in the water by the beach. I took my eyes off her for a minute, and the next she was struggling in water over her head." He looked embarrassed as if blaming himself for a near tragedy.

Mark appeared so vulnerable that Alexa responded, "Things like that can happen quickly. She'll get over her fear of deep water as soon as she has more confidence."

Mark looked grateful. "I better round up Sarah. Her mother expects her at six."

As he stood up, Dan asked, "Mark, why don't you come back and join us for supper? It's just Alexa and me and an old friend. And I'll do the cooking!"

Mark looked directly at Alexa. His eyes were incredibly blue. "I wish I could, but I've got another commitment."

"Some other time then," Dan said easily. "I'll probably keep the pool open until the end of September. Bring Sarah over anytime for a swim."

"Thanks again. Have a good weekend and don't be nervous, Alexa. We'll get through the first day of school, I promise." He gave her a warm smile and a thumbs up.

Mark walked over to interrupt Sarah's efforts to get Robbie to play with an old tennis ball. Just then, Robbie, who had been looking extremely bored, fixed his eyes on the ball, stood on his hind legs, paws neatly folded into his chest, and began to walk about as if to a stately tune heard only by canine ears.

Sarah shrieked with delight, "Robbie's dancing, Dad! He should be in a circus. He can dance."

Mark and Dan also laughed as Alexa told her, "My oldest niece, Bailey, taught him that trick one summer, but he only dances when he's in the right mood and wants a treat."

Sarah was still talking about Robbie's amazing performance when she and Mark disappeared through the back gate.

When Alexa went to change out of her wet swimsuit, she couldn't help wondering if Mark's other commitment was Julie Chisholm. Somehow she didn't like the idea. Alexa smiled at herself. She hardly knew Mark, but after this afternoon she was forced to admit that he was very attractive. It was perfectly normal if he had found a girlfriend. Mark had a great relationship with Sarah, and she respected his efforts to be a good father. In spite of Sarah's intelligence, she would not be an easy child to live with.

When Martin arrived, he had changed into designer jeans and a casual open-necked white linen shirt. "You look great!" Alexa said warmly.

"And so do you," he replied. She was wearing a gold sweater and matching shorts. He handed her a bottle of Pinot Noir and a tray of antipasto.

"And so do these!" Alexa added, helping herself to her favourite appetizer, a marinated artichoke. Although her thoughts continued to drift to Mark and Sarah, Alexa was soon drawn into the conversation as Dan and Martin talked about recent changes in Davenport's business community. Martin was the perfect guest, harmlessly flirtatious with Alexa while he entertained them with stories about the various clients who came to his antique shop in search of treasures for their homes.

"What's the best thing about your job, Martin?" Alexa asked. She knew he had lived in Davenport for many years and was curious about what kept him there.

"The hunt," he said seriously. "Most antique dealers head for the city, but here I often get a call that someone's selling a farm, and they want me to appraise their furniture or their collectibles. I never know what I'll find. People have absolutely no idea of the value of antiques in today's market. They have a sentimental attachment to Aunt Martha's settee or bedroom suite, and it may be worth nothing, but in the kitchen there are tarnished Georgian serving spoons worth a mint which they were planning to throw out with the trash."

"I'm sure that's how many old folk are cheated," observed Dan, ever the lawyer.

"Absolutely. Last summer I went out to the country after a call from a woman who was going into a seniors' residence. Naturally she couldn't take all her treasures. None of them had any real value, but I didn't want to hurt her feelings, so I kept looking around for something I wanted to buy. We went into the kitchen, and she opened an old jam cupboard. It was filled with china. She had beautiful Staffordshire pitchers and animal figurines. They were priceless. The old lady had inherited them from a maiden aunt. She called them 'dust collectors' and stored them away. I think I could have had them for a dollar apiece." Martin shook his head in disbelief. "I offered her a fair price for the lot, and she gladly accepted, but to this day she thinks that I'm completely mad for wanting that rubbish. I even bought the jam cupboard," he added.

Alexa listened to Martin's story as she sat back and studied the two men who were part of her life again, both of them intelligent and principled. She wondered what had kept them in a small town like Davenport, or had they been happy there because they had found the right partner?

Dan refilled their wine glasses, and the three shared a companionable silence.

Martin raised his glass, "To you, Alexa. Welcome back. Both Dan and I have had wonderful years in Davenport. I hope this year's a good one for you."

"Thanks, Martin. For teachers each September is a new beginning. I know this year will be no exception."

Much later that evening while Alexa and her father cleaned the kitchen after Martin had left, she told him the latest news about Patti and Joy. Dan was sympathetic when he heard Joy's story. "Joy's your friend, and she means a lot to me too, but these cases are always tricky. Without overt evidence, it's very hard to prove that someone's been dismissed because of their sexual preference and it sounds as if Joy was ready to leave."

"Yes, I know she was," Alexa agreed. "I'm hotheaded. I was encouraging her to consider legal action when she really wants to get out of Davenport. I grew up here without really seeing the town for what it is – at least for sixteen years."

Dan gave his daughter a searching look. He understood and started to speak but thought better of it.

"It's the perfect place to live," Alexa went on, "as long as you play by the rules. Girls like boys, but they keep them at arm's length until they have an engagement ring on their finger. Girls get married and have babies. No one gets pregnant before marriage. The men play around. Women stay home with the kids."

Dan reached out to put his arm around his daughter. "Alexa, no town is perfect. There are kind people here and not so kind, but I can't forget how supportive everyone was when your mother was ill. People here do care about each other. Never forget that." He added on a lighter note, "Today even Davenport is changing. Now the women fool around, and the men stay home. Look at Mark Anderson and Jane. She simply dumped her husband and daughter and left. It's only in the last few months that she's made time for even short visits with Sarah. No wonder Mark's at his wit's end at times, and Sarah is a sad little soul."

Alexa considered this perspective. Then she hugged her father back. "Why are you always right? Thanks for being you, Dad. I know how much this town has meant to you and Mom. And it's about time that I grew up. I keep having these outbursts since I came back. I'm putting it down to stage fright. Even after all these years I still feel like an actor on opening night just before school starts."

"Let's hope you get some applause then or even better an encore for semester two. I could easily get used to having you around again."

While Alexa was stacking the plates in the dishwasher, she said casually, "By the way, Tony's Benoit's back in town." She could feel her father unconsciously stiffen as he straightened up from feeding Robbie.

"Where did you hear that?"

"Patti told me the night we had dinner together. He's going to be working with his brother, Ronnie. And then he left a message on my answering machine."

One of her father's best characteristics was that he never offered unwanted advice, but Alexa was very much aware of the unspoken question in her father's eyes.

"Don't worry," she said lightly. "I may not always be a quick study, but I learned a lot from that unhappy experience. I'm not going to excavate ancient history."

"I'm delighted to hear it," Dan said dryly. He looked at Robbie who was sitting by the door. "I think this old fellow's waiting for his evening stroll around the neighbourhood. When you're ready, we'll walk you home and maybe say good night to Martin. Rob can terrorize his cats."

As Dan had pointed out, Robbie's idea of exercise was a stroll during which each tree and shrub was thoroughly sniffed. While they walked, Alexa had plenty of time to observe her father. He moved stiffly now, favouring one leg, and in repose his face was sad and the wrinkles deeper.

Impulsively Alexa took her father's arm. "It's good to be back," she said, "even if I do miss Mom more than ever." They walked a few minutes in silence while Alexa struggled for control. She wiped away two large tears which had slid down her cheeks. Trying to find a lighter subject, she went on, "I feel caught in a time warp. Not only did I get a message from Tony, David's been calling as well. Almost no one has my unlisted number. I wish I knew how he got it."

"Alexa," Dan said patiently, "you know I wouldn't pass it on to him, but some of your friends may be more gullible. David really seemed to care about you, and people just naturally want a happy-ever-after ending."

"So did I," admitted Alexa honestly, "but it's not going to happen with David. How many times do I have to tell him?"

"Is that a rhetorical question?" Dan joked. "Because if it's not, I'd say it once more or waste a lot of time deleting telephone messages."

A few minutes later, Alexa said good night to her father and Martin. Robbie had befriended Kaspar, the older of the cats, who purred contentedly on a patio chair until Alexa picked him up for a snuggle.

"Take him up with you if you like," Martin offered. "He's good company. Doesn't say much, but he's a great listener."

It wasn't a night to be alone. Alexa carried the unprotesting Kaspar up the stairs. No flashing light on the telephone. She undressed slowly and cuddled up on the couch with Kaspar and her novel. Alexa was almost asleep when the phone rang shrilly. She hesitated, then resisting the urge to ignore it, she stretched out a hand and picked it up.

David's voice in her ear said sarcastically, "So you do come home some nights. Do you know how often I've called? Did you ever think that I might be worried about you? I tried..."

Alexa waited, feeling anger mount inside her. David had certainly been drinking, and he was in the middle of a long harangue. "... and this is ludicrous. I'm not going to let you walk out of my life and return to your childhood. Your father's a grown man. He doesn't need you hovering around. I'm going to drive up tomorrow. If we can find a decent restaurant in Davenport, I'll even take you out for lunch, and we'll talk through this like two civilized people. You owe me an explanation."

"David, I owe you nothing " She finally managed to break in. "It's over. I'm not going for lunch with you on Saturday or any other day. Go out with one of your friends. Go to the faculty club. Listen to the opera. Do whatever you like, but don't call me again." Without giving David a chance to reply, Alexa slammed down the receiver.

She took a deep breath. Oddly enough, she felt quite calm, even a little elated. Perhaps it was David's sarcasm or his carping tone. For the first time, Alexa felt that she was free of his influence. Why had she delayed in making the break? Standing up, she stretched. Kaspar yawned hugely and jumped down to follow Alexa into the bedroom. Minutes later the two were curled up together on the bed, Kaspar in the small of her back. Alexa burrowed beneath the blankets. As she relaxed and drifted towards sleep, she thought that she was ready for David's "yard apes."

At first Alexa was sure that she slept soundly, but at some point in the night she began to dream. First, she stood in front of a classroom crowded with teenagers all talking loudly and all ignoring her. When Mark Anderson appeared at the door smiling at her, the room became quiet. Then, in the disjointed way of dreams, she and Kaspar were sharing a plate of tuna. She knew that David was standing in the garden below, throwing pebbles at her windows.

Alexa woke with a start. Kaspar was now curled up on the end of the bed purring gently. Acting on an impulse, she padded to the window. The garden below was dark and silent. After a moment, Alexa crawled back into bed, but sleep eluded her. She tossed and turned for more than an hour and then gave up the pretence of sleeping. Even Kaspar had deserted her. He was sitting at the door meowing plaintively, anxious to go downstairs to familiar territory. Getting up, she opened the door for him and then decided to make herself a cup of tea. While she waited for the water to boil, she stood at the window and for the first time gave herself permission to think about David McBirney. How could such an idyllic relationship have ended so disastrously?

It was tempting to put all the blame on David. They had moved in together after a four-year romance. Neither one was a child, but, consciously or not, he had controlled every aspect of her life. Why had she allowed this to happen?

She recalled one incident shortly before she left. Typically, they were entertaining two of David's faculty friends, Andrea and Hugh Crawley. When Andrea complimented Alexa on the curried shrimp, Alexa answered honestly, "David does most of the cooking. That's his recipe."

"Cooking isn't my child bride's best subject " David drawled. "We exhausted her repertoire some time ago."

Alexa could feel her cheeks flaming although she murmured sweetly, "Very few people measure up to your standard in the kitchen. I just relax and enjoy it."

Although she tried to talk to David later about how embarrassed she felt, he refused to take her seriously. "Alexa, they knew I was only joking. You're far too sensitive, " and he bent to kiss the top of her head, pacifying her as you would a small child who was pouting over an imagined insult.

As Alexa made the tea, she wondered why she hadn't rebelled. She had avoided confrontation even when David made her angry. She was embarrassed by the way she had left. Her principal, Ray Nolan, had been supportive when she asked for a year's leave. Without telling David, she made all the arrangements. Her few pieces of furniture were put into storage in early July, and she left the same day leaving only a one-page letter behind. It had been childish and even melodramatic. No wonder David was furious. She thought cynically that he might have missed her briefly, but mostly he would have been enraged at the idea that she had made the decision without consulting him. David hated to have control taken out of his hands.

With an effort, Alexa closed the door on these reflections. As she sipped her tea, she found herself thinking about Mark. At first, she had found him cynical with a sharp edge remarkably like David's, but she remembered his vulnerability with Sarah and his delight as they played in the pool. David would never have shown Mark's emotional warmth. She wondered how many faces the man could wear. Would the real Mark Anderson ever reveal himself, or were these all facets of the same character?

The sky was streaked with early morning light, and her beautiful apartment felt claustrophobic when she decided to go out for a walk. She had once been a morning jogger. Perhaps it was time to get back into the habit.

CHAPTER FIVE

On the first day of school, Alexa was awake at dawn. She was unable to eat, and instead of the stereotypical butterflies she had a tight knot of tension constricting her stomach. When she arrived at Riverside, the staff room was frenetic. Teachers scanned class lists, making comments to those sitting near them as they recognized names. "How did Noel Parsons ever make it to grade twelve?" Buzz Spencer was asking anyone who would listen. Other teachers with coffee mugs in hand lined up to use the photocopier. Mark and Lisa were everywhere, greeting staff and students, taking telephone calls and giving instructions to the office staff. Mark called out a friendly, "Good morning," when he saw her, but there was no time to talk.

"Come up to the English office," Carol Helmer invited. "We've got about thirty minutes before we open the classrooms. Let's have a moment of sanity before the madness begins."

As they walked down the hall, Alexa checked out the groups of preppy looking students congregating near the locker bank, exchanging summer updates and giving each other high fives. A bespectacled boy called out to Carol, "I've got you for English this semester, Mrs Helmer."

"Lucky you." She flashed him a smile and added as an aside to Alexa, "That's Ron Callaghan. His brother's our student council president. Ron's about as intellectual as we get around here."

When they went upstairs together, Alexa paused momentarily on the landing. From this vantage point, she could see the school smoking area where thirty or forty kids were hanging out, lighting their cigarettes and then inhaling deeply. It was a warm September morning, but the baggy pants worn by both sexes and the hoodies were very much in evidence. One boy had concealed his face completely with the hood of his black sweatshirt giving him the sinister appearance of a medieval monk. Carol's eyes followed Alexa's gaze. "I see our Pathways kids and their buds are blackening their lungs very early in the day. Just hope it's only tobacco they're inhaling. I'm surprised Mark hasn't joined them yet. That's his beat."

As she unlocked the English office, she turned to Alexa, "I'm wearing two hats today. Kerry, our daughter, is just starting school at Riverside. So far I've resisted the urge to handpick her teachers."

"Is she here yet?"

"No way! It would be seriously uncool to show up with your mom on the first day of high school. She's waiting to take the bus with her friends, but she's been up most of the night she's so nervous. As teachers it's easy for us to forget the agony that some of the kids go through."

"Is Kerry the shy type?"

Carol laughed. "At home, Roger and I sometimes wish she'd be less assertive, but underneath – especially today – she's a bundle of raw nerves. Just a typical teenager!"

Alexa could easily identify with Kerry, but somehow talking with Carol and the other teachers left her feeling more relaxed. She promised to meet Warren Thompson, a first-year teacher, after school to see if he had survived his classes.

As Alexa had expected, her senior class of university bound students was a gift. The students eyed her speculatively taking her measure, but they were attentive, making notes while Alexa distributed the course outline and explained the procedures for their weekly writing portfolios. When the class ended with the lunch bell, only a few drifted out. Most students remained to ask questions or to talk with the new teacher and each other.

Alexa tried to suppress a smile when James Callaghan, the student council president ("Just call me Jim."), shook hands with her at the end of class, "I just wanted to introduce myself, Miss Corbett, and welcome you to Riverside. I worked in Mr. Corbett's office this summer as a junior assistant. It was a great experience. Sorry I'll have to miss your class tomorrow. I called a press conference, and Russ Pemberton from *The Chronicle* is coming to take pictures of the council. Could I have the homework for tomorrow now?"

Stacey Sawyer, a petite girl with shoulder length blonde hair, also offered her excuses, "English is my favourite subject, Miss Corbett, and I'm planning to major in it in university. I'm sorry I have to miss your class tomorrow, but this is such a busy semester. I'm the social convenor for the senior prom and I'm in the band. Mr Carroll asked if I could help when he distributes the instruments to the juniors."

Senior students were always overcommitted, agonizing over their extracurricular responsibilities and academic workload. "I'll speak with Mr Carroll. This is a heavy course," Alexa cautioned Stacey. "It's easy to get behind, and when you miss the class the assignments are much more difficult."

She sensed that the student was not pleased with the warning. "I promise it won't happen too often," Stacey said defensively, tossing back her blonde hair. "Are you available for extra help?"

"Unless I have cafeteria or hall duty, I'll be in my room at noon hour," Alexa promised, "or you can make arrangements to see me after school."

The last student to leave was Dara Babcock, a quiet girl with a spotty complexion who had sat alone directly in front of Alexa's desk speaking to no one and taking frantic notes. While she spoke, she nervously adjusted her glasses. "Miss Corbett, I wrote a lot of poetry this summer. I wondered – you know sometime when I'm handing in my writing portfolio – if I could give you a couple of poems. Would you have time to read them?"

"Of course," Alexa answered warmly. There was always an aspiring writer in a class like this, some with genuine talent. Perhaps the best part about teaching was watching the growth of these kids. "Give me your poetry whenever you like. If you want to, we can schedule some time after school to sit down together and talk about what you're writing."

Dara flushed. "I'd like that, but usually I have to go straight home and babysit my younger sisters."

"We'll find another time then, " Alexa assured her. "Perhaps you could come in at noon hour or before class."

When Dara finally left, Alexa barely had time to find the staff washroom and eat a container of yogurt before the bell rang to signal the end of the lunch hour. As she prepared to greet the afternoon class, she was thinking that Dara had never once made eye contact with her. She remembered that high school was a lonely place for those who were perceived as outsiders.

For the next few hours Alexa had no time to think about anything but the students in front of her. In the Pathways classes the kids dressed for each other. With their deliberately torn clothes, pierced body parts, and outrageous hair, they were a motley group. Their talk revolved around Saturday's bush party, and a bash planned for the following Friday night, but Alexa liked them for their candour and the bravado which was their armour as they faced the world. In an odd way, they reminded her of her younger self, tough as nails on the outside but a seething mass of contradictions within. School was something to be endured, and she had developed a bag of tricks to lure them into her world.

On the first day it was important to set up classroom rules and expectations. She was prepared for groans and muttered obscenities, but these kids needed to know the parameters before they started. Alexa broke all the rules she had learned in college by starting with a novel. She had chosen Paul Zindel's *The Pigman*, a classic story about two teenagers, John and Lorraine, who befriend an old man.

The kids responded with typical comments, "I don't do books," and "I can't read, Miss," but when Alexa explained that they would read the novel together, they gradually settled down.

While she was handing out copies of the book, Alexa played a tape of an old favourite, "Lean on Me." The class began to tune in. This was language they could understand. She started to read aloud the first chapter of *The Pigman* in which John explains why he hates school and why he was nicknamed "the bathroom bomber" the previous year. She glanced around the room. Miraculously, the kids were now completely quiet. Everyone had their books open, and they were actually following along as she read. She thought that this was one of the teachable moments which made her job the best in the world. Many of these kids had never been read to as small children, yet even as teenagers the art of the storyteller cast its spell upon them.

When she stopped to give the class a chance to discuss the book, one girl, her eyes dramatically outlined in black, spoke out, "This pisses me off! Why do we always have to talk about this stuff? Why can't we just keep reading?" Instead of answering, Alexa gave her *the look* which she had perfected at her previous school.

Another girl in a lacy black camisole worn under an open white shirt joined in. "It's the same old crap year after year. I hate English."

Alexa was making a mental note to reread the school dress code when she saw two boys in the back corner begin to chortle, and one took a playful swipe at the other's baseball cap. She took a deep breath. Her experience in the city had taught her at least one thing: Don't raise your voice. Wait for their attention, but in that waiting almost anything could and did happen.

She wanted to get the kids on side. They had laughed out loud at John's description of the school librarian, nicknamed "the cricket" because her nylon stockings rubbed together, and now they wanted to talk about their own bad teacher experiences. This could lead to disaster.

Just as Alexa was beginning to despair, Justin Murray, a good looking dark-haired boy deliberately slouching in his seat, commented, "John's a cool dude. He's got it together."

"As if a cool dude would make time for a dork like Lorraine," the Cleopatra-lookalike retorted. She stared at Justin with her black-rimmed eyes as she issued the challenge.

Without missing a beat, Justin replied, "Like he's tired of all those ditzy chicks, Amanda. They've both got crappy homes, and they need someone to talk to."

Several kids nodded their heads in agreement. They respected Justin's opinion as if he were some sort of acknowledged leader. Alexa resisted the temptation to correct his language. She had the whole semester to work on what was politically correct. For now, she was happy that the kids could relate to something they had read.

Despite laments from one student, Alison Duncan, "Where's the movie? If this is so totally cool, why didn't they make a movie?" Alexa nudged the discussion along. A few minutes before the end of the class, she handed out the first writing assignment, "The rough copy's due Friday, but you'll have time to work on it in class. You can start now, or you can choose the first book for your independent reading. Remember you can pick any book as long as I approve it. You've got time to look at the books in the classroom library, and if you find something you want to read just come up to my desk and sign it out."

For the last period in the day, the kids were remarkably quiet, but only a few went on reading, and they ignored the writing assignment. Most left their seats to browse through the books Alexa had placed on the classroom shelves. She made a point of standing near the two boys who still wanted to scuffle with each other. While the kids flipped through horror and fantasy novels, she noticed that Justin was reading the back cover of Sebastian Faulks' *Birdsong*, a novel about World War

I which she thought her senior students would enjoy.

He came up to Alexa's desk and signed out the book. Then, catching her eye, he muttered, "Miss, can I go to the washroom?"

Alexa nodded but tapped her watch, reminding him that any absence lasting more than five minutes had to be made up during a noon hour detention.

Before the class ended, about half the students found something to read in the classroom library and signed out a book. Seconds before the bell rang for dismissal, Justin entered the room and slid into his seat keeping his head down and avoiding Alexa's eyes.

The room cleared quickly. Alexa blocked Justin at the door and said quietly, "Justin, you were gone thirteen minutes. You can make up the time tomorrow at the beginning of lunch. I'll see you then. Don't forget." Her tone made it clear that the detention was not a negotiable item.

Justin shrugged nonchalantly. "Whatever. I wasn't trying to skip out, miss, but I met someone and got delayed."

"Okay, tomorrow at 11:45." Alexa made another mental note, to ask Justin why he reeked of marijuana if he were coming from the washroom.

As the students left, Alexa realized that she was hungry. There had been no time for lunch. She decided to wait for the halls to clear and then go to the English office to compare notes with Warren. After the day spent with adolescents, she was in desperate need of some adult company. She stood at the classroom window munching an apple, watching the students heading for the buses. She saw Dara Babcock walking alone, head down, and Stacey Sawyer holding hands with a tall, blonde boy.

Five minutes later, the building was strangely quiet. Alexa was locking the classroom door when a familiar voice called, "Miss Corbett, could I have a word with you?"

Whirling around, she saw Mark coming down the hall. Her first impulse was to treat this comment as a joke. "Certainly, Mr Anderson," she replied only half seriously, but as they went back into the room, she could see that Mark was not joking.

"I spent last period patrolling the smoking area. You may be surprised to hear that I found Justin Murray there chatting up a group of kids fifteen minutes before the period ended. He was supposed to be in your class."

It wasn't so much the words as Mark's tone that stung. Alexa felt as if she were being grilled like a student. Why did the man have to be so insufferable when he thought that someone was being irresponsible?

"I'm aware of that, Mr Anderson," she said in a frosty voice. "Justin asked to go to the washroom about fifteen minutes before the end of class. My rule is that students can be out of the room only five minutes. He'll make up the time tomorrow in a noon hour detention with me." She did not mention the odour which had permeated Justin's clothes. She'd handle that problem herself.

Mark was not appeased. "That's not a good way to begin the semester. There's no reason for students to leave the room so close to the end of a class. Justin Murray pushed all the rules last year. You'll have to clamp down on him now, or he'll be running the show before too long. Just remember that around here we have zero tolerance for drugs and bad behaviour."

Without another word, Mark turned and left the room. Alexa felt as if she had been slapped. She might be new to the staff, but she did not need lessons in classroom management from Mark Anderson. When she wanted help, he would be the first to know. Until then, she simply wanted him to butt out.

Still fuming, she headed for the English office. Turning a corner sharply, she almost collided with Warren Thompson. Seeing Alexa, he dropped his briefcase and dramatically pulled his dark curly hair upward as hard as he could, "What a day!"

"That bad?" Alexa asked sympathetically.

"Even worse! These kids have a five-minute attention span. I read them a short story. That was the problem. It was short! I still had forty minutes to do something with them. They don't like discussions, and they don't like to write. I'm not even s re they can read. And they hate using a dictionary. One little beast threw a piece of chalk at me when I was writing on the board. I had to write sideways with one eye glued on the crowd." He paused, "My profs never told me there'd be days like this. I need help! I'm desperate!"

Alexa sensed a ring of truth beneath Warren's performance. "I think Carol said we're both teaching a junior class. Do you want to work together? I don't have all the answers either, but at least we can pool our ideas."

Warren seized the suggestion gratefully. "That would be great! Do you have time to talk now, Alexa?"

"Sure, but I'm absolutely ravenous. Just let me get my lunch in the staffroom and then we can find a quiet spot."

Warren fell into step beside her. "You don't know how much I appreciate this. I always wanted to teach. My mom's a teacher, and I did some tutoring in high school and university. After I met my girlfriend, Marielle, I wanted to stay in the city and I thought about post-graduate studies, but I needed to pay off some of my student loans. It's going to be a long semester if this is a typical day."

"Don't give up," Alexa encouraged him. "The first day's always the worst. It's going to get better, I promise."

When she left the school several hours later, Alexa was smiling. Warren Thompson was creative and humorous, but like many teachers in their first year he had no idea what to do with a classroom of teenagers. There should be a factory recall of the students she had taught at her first school. With a few minor adjustments they'd be fine.

Warren had talked enthusiastically about Marielle. "She's a set designer. We met in university when we were both working in *Romeo and Juliet*. She was the stage manager, and I was playing Mercutio. She gets hugely upset when I talk about her moving here, and I can't blame her. She's studied in Montreal and New York. What could she do in Davenport? Design sets for the local little theatre group? She'd go out of her tree."

While she and Warren were working together planning a short story unit, Alexa forgot about Mark Anderson, but after she got into her car, she slammed her books down on the front seat. She couldn't believe it. At her dad's house on Saturday he had been buddy buddy with her. The next moment he was on a rant because he thought she let kids wander out of her class on a whim. She didn't need the Jekyll and Hyde routine. For one semester surely they could just stay out of each other's hair.

Alexa took a deep breath before turning the key in the ignition. Running down several pedestrians including Mr Anderson might be tempting, but it wouldn't help the situation. She pulled out of the parking lot and drove slowly along Front Street. About two blocks from the school, she saw Justin Murray hitchhiking on the side of the street.

Aware that she was breaking every school rule about giving rides to students, Alexa pulled over. After all, she owed Justin something for getting the class discussion back on track. Rolling down the window, she asked, "Want a ride, Justin? Did you miss your bus?"

Justin looked a little embarrassed as he opened the door and got in. Alexa waited while he fastened the seatbelt. "Thanks, Miss. I had something to do after school, a… a… meeting, and I missed my bus. I decided to hitch home."

This did not ring true. Justin Murray looked like the kind of guy who couldn't wait for the dismissal bell to split. What kind of meeting could keep him hanging around the school? She inhaled deeply. The odour of marijuana was less pungent now. Aloud, she said, "Where do you live?"

"Gilmour Street."

"That's a bit of a hike. I go right by there. I'll drop you off."

"You know this town?"

"I grew up here. I've been away for a number of years, but not much has changed." She could see his eyes scanning her hands for rings. They were bare, and she satisfied his curiosity by saying, "My dad hasn't been well, so I decided to come back for a year to be near him."

Like Mark Anderson, Justin made the connection. "I know your dad. I worked for Ronnie Benoit this summer as a go-pher. We did some work on your dad's porch. He's got a neat place. Told us we could use the pool if it got too hot."

Alexa looked at Justin out of the corner of her eye. She wouldn't have pegged him as a potential carpenter, but there was a glint of genuine enthusiasm in his eyes.

He went on, "Did you know that Ronnie's brother played professional hockey? He's back in town. Nice guy. Not at all stuck up about the money he must have stashed away. Why would someone with all that dough come back here?"

"Who knows? I went to school with Tony and Ronnie. They're local guys." Justin really had his finger on the pulse of the community. Alexa wondered idly if he did B & E in his spare time and then dismissed the thought as uncharitable. She turned off on Gilmour, and Justin pointed to a neat white frame house set back from the street in an overgrown perennial garden. Another mystery. Alexa would have guessed that Justin's parents lived in one of the low rental apartment blocks in town.

"I live with my grandmother," he said as if reading her thoughts.

As he unfastened the seatbelt, Alexa said quickly, "Justin, I didn't give you a ride so I'd have a chance to lecture you, but I've been around schools and kids most of my life, and I'm familiar with the smell of grass."

He looked startled. "I don't toke up at school, Miss." He darted a quick look at her under his long lashes. "Look, I'll serve the detention. I did go out to the smoking area at the end of the class for a quick cigarette. Some guys I was talking to were toking up. That's what you smelled on me."

Alexa looked at him steadily. She didn't believe a word of it.

"Are you going to report me to Anderson? He's hated my guts from day one, and he'd love a chance to toss me."

Alexa resisted the urge to get drawn into this argument. Mark had the reputation of being fair with the students although admittedly he had been very jaded where Justin was concerned. "If that's the case, " she snapped, "there's an easy solution. Don't give *Mr* Anderson the opportunity. I can see the smoking area from my classroom window, and most of the time there are thirty or forty kids out there. I bet you know them all. If you're having a cigarette, use your head. Stand beside someone who's using tobacco."

Justin actually looked a little sheepish, "Thanks, Miss. I promise I won't take off from your class again." He flashed her a quick smile and got out, carefully shutting the car door.

Alexa pulled back onto the street reflecting that under the charm and pseudo sincerity Justin was extremely manipulative She had no doubt that he had been smoking up, but she had let him know that she was onto his game. He had so much potential if he could get on track. There would be no report for Mr Anderson on this incident. She was more than capable of handling it her own way.

At home Alexa changed quickly and went out for a run. Already the September evenings were growing cool. She was out of practice, and at first as on the previous morning she walked, but gradually she got into her stride. By the time she rounded the pond at the golf course and headed home she was running at a comfortable pace. Her mind was calm, and she was mentally planning the next day's classes.

The telephone rang as Alexa put the key in the lock of her front door. Remembering that her father was going out of town on business and had arranged to drop off Robbie before he left, she dashed for the receiver, still panting from her run.

"Did I catch you at a bad moment?" asked Tony Benoit. "I thought the first day of school might be rough, but you sound completely done in."

Alexa couldn't help laughing. "No, I'm just out of shape. I was out running. Chasing the ghosts away."

"You too? Ever since I've come home, I've seen them. The town's full of them!"

This was the old Tony with the quirky sense of humour and a sixth sense which told him when she was down. "Alexa, I'm not trying to be pushy. I know it's been a long time, but I'd really like to have dinner with you. How about Thursday or Friday? There's a good Italian trattoria just outside town, Fasooli's. It's guaranteed to be too expensive to attract the high school kids. Unless you'd prefer Licks?"

Alexa smiled. So Licks was still the hot spot for teenagers. She hesitated, and then curiosity won. Why not? One dinner didn't mean starting a relationship. And she needed something as a reward if she survived the first week at Riverside. She found herself saying, "Friday would be perfect."

"Perfect. I'll pick you up around six thirty."

"Do you need some directions?"

There was a pause. Then Tony said, "It's a small town. I met Martin MacLean, and he told me you were renting his apartment. So, Friday at six thirty? I promise my car's more reliable than the one I had in high school."

After she hung up, Alexa wondered why she had agreed to spend an evening with Tony after all her promises not to excavate the past, and a second thought crossed her mind. In high school Tony had been trim and athletic, obsessed with hockey but playing every sport in season. What if he were now paunchy with thinning hair? She told herself that it was only a dinner, not the rest of her life. Any conversation would be better than another argument with Mark Anderson about Justin.

CHAPTER SIX

❧

*A*ll week at school Alexa avoided Mark Anderson, not an easy task since he seemed to pop up everywhere. She had cafeteria duty on Friday, and her luck ran out. She walked around, talking with groups of students, prodding them to pick up their garbage and watching for flying apples. Many of the students were drinking coke and eating poutine, their huge mounds of french fries topped with gravy and melted cheese. She wondered if there was such a thing as negative nutrition. Then she saw Mark enter the cafeteria, clipboard in hand. He headed for one particular student who quickly picked up his food and disappeared. A skipped detention was Alexa's guess.

The room gradually cleared. When only a few groups of students were left, Mark came over to her. "Hi, Alexa, how have things gone this week?"

"Fine, thanks. No major problems, and I'm really enjoying the classes. It's quite a change from my last school, but a very pleasant one," Alexa couldn't resist adding.

"I owe you an apology. I'm sorry about the other day. Justin Murray was a thorn in my side all last year. I overreacted when I spoke to you about him. I guess first day got to me, but that's no excuse." This was Mark at his most charming.

He had apologized, but she was skeptical enough to believe that it was only a matter of time before he blew up about some other infraction of school rules. She regarded him stonily before saying, "Justin served his detention with me."

"Good. By the way, I'm sure he's one of our regular users. You might want to watch him especially in the period after lunch. If you suspect he's been smoking up, give me a call."

Alexa's face betrayed nothing. She thought of Mark's "zero tolerance" policy. "I'll do that."

Mark leaned back against the wall comfortably. "Lisa and I appreciate the help you're giving Warren Thompson. The first semester is always a rough one, but he'll be a winner once he gets the kids under control."

Alexa nodded. She wondered how Mark knew about the after school hours spent with Warren. She thought of her father's comments about Jane and Sarah. "How's Sarah finding the first days of school?"

Mark's professional mask slipped a little as he groaned. "Frankly, the last week has been rough. She cries every morning before I drop her off at Margie White's house. Marg is her caregiver before school. Sarah finds it hard to adjust to new situations. The work at school's no problem for her, but she always hates a new teacher until Christmas. I made an appointment to meet her teacher, Claudette Bennett, to see if I can do anything to help."

The afternoon warning bell rang. "Dad's home this weekend. Why don't you take Sarah over for a swim? She can take Robbie for a walk. He needs the exercise, and Dad would love the company," Alexa suggested.

"I will. Thanks for listening, Alexa. I've been thinking about last Saturday and hoping that we can get together soon." With a smile he was gone, leaving Alexa more than a little confused. Did Mark make this overture to every unattached female teacher on staff? She had not reacted to his suggestion, but inwardly she was surprised by the attraction she felt for him.

Alexa had a prep period in which she had promised to meet some senior students to discuss their ideas for a yearbook. After buying a sandwich and talking with a few teachers still eating in the staffroom, she went up to her classroom.

At the end of the school day, Carol Helmer put her head around the door of Alexa's room. "It's Friday night. You need a life, woman. Are you joining us for 'the library club?'"

Alexa shook her head. Carol had told her that on Fridays some of the staff met at Bookends, a local pub, for drinks and snacks. "Next week, " she promised. "Tonight I've got a date."

"You move quickly, girl, " Carol said approvingly. "I thought you told me you were recovering from a broken romance."

"It's just a dinner with an old friend," Alexa protested. "Nothing serious."

"What's happening Sunday night?"

"Nothing I can't cancel. Probably a date with these," Alexa indicated a stack of student writing portfolios on her desk.

"Good, come for dinner. For once Roger's off duty. When you're married to a police officer, you entertain like mad whenever your husband has a weekend free, and my daughter wants to meet you. Kerry sees you in the halls and has decided that you're totally cool. Unlike her mother."

Alexa had been on the lookout for Kerry. "I'd love to," she responded.

"Come early. Bring a swimsuit, and we can soak in the hot tub. Roger will cook dinner for us. He's good, much better than I am in the kitchen."

When Alexa dropped off her attendance sheets at the office, she noticed Julie Chisholm and Mark standing at the counter together laughing and talking and completely focussed on each other. She couldn't help wondering if away from school they were a couple. Selfish monster, she jeered at herself. It couldn't be easy being Mr Mom. He needed a life too.

When Mark saw Alexa, he immediately turned to include her. "Alexa, have you met Julie Chisholm yet?"

"Not formally. Hello, Julie."

The blonde woman eyed Alexa coolly. "Hi, Alexa. You look as if you're surviving. Murray Dean always has some tough classes." She turned to smile at Mark. "Remember last year he had to take a few days off for a family funeral, and the sub quit after the first day."

"I've managed to make it through the first week."

"Alexa is a pro," Mark said. "She's getting the kids where she wants them."

Julie's cool blue eyes assessed Alexa before she spoke again. "Sorry I've got to run. I called a basketball practice. I'll see you later, Mark."

"Coming to the library club?" Mark's smile was infectious. "We all need to let down our hair on Friday, especially after the first week of school."

Alexa felt a tightening in her chest as his eyes met her. His smile made her feel desirable for the first time in weeks. "I wish I could. I've got something else on tonight."

Mark looked disappointed. "I was hoping to see you there. Well, take care and have a good weekend. You deserve it."

At home Alexa felt a momentary panic about the dinner with Tony. She stared at the clothes in her wardrobe and rejected several outfits before deciding to keep it simple. She chose a black sleeveless dress with a slim skirt and a cream linen jacket. After twisting her hair into a knot and pinning it up, she checked her reflection in the bedroom mirror. Not bad, she decided. At least it was a change from teacher clothes. She put on a pair of strappy black sandals and wondered if she still remembered how to walk in heels.

When the doorbell rang, Alexa hurried to open it. "Wow!" Tony said appreciatively before kissing her lightly on the cheek, "Alexa, you're more beautiful than ever!"

"And you're not bad yourself!" Alexa teased. Tony had changed very little. His short hair had a few blonde streaks which Alexa did not remember, but the brown eyes and taut, muscular body were familiar. Although he was casually dressed in an open-necked sports shirt and chinos, his leather jacket looked butter soft and expensive.

Tony's laugh immediately put Alexa at ease. "This is too weird. I feel as if I'm seventeen again and should be picking you up at your parents' house. By the way, do you have a curfew tonight?"

"I don't think Dad will be checking up on me. We can close the restaurant if we want to. But don't forget you're talking to a teacher at the end of the first week of school. I'll probably fall asleep after one glass of wine or imagine that I'm still on cafeteria duty and start picking up anything on the tables!"

"Let's go, Cinderella," Tony said. "Fasooli's has great food, and I'm counting on that to revive you."

When they got to the street, Tony unlocked the passenger door of a sleek black Corvette. Alexa paused, "Tony, if you wanted to convince me that we're not in high school, the car did it. It's beautiful. I remember a black Volkswagen with holes in the floor that you covered with an old carpet."

"I loved that bug," Tony replied as he got in beside her and started the powerful engine. "It was my first car and had no heater, but I'll never forget it. Most of the time the windshield wipers didn't work. Do you remember that I had to keep stopping the car to wipe off the snow?"

Alexa nodded, smiling.

"I know this car is a little over the top for Davenport, but I bought it when I signed my first pro contract. Some guys booze, and some do drugs, but my weakness is cars. I keep this one under wraps all winter, and I can't wait for spring to get it out on the road again."

"I am beginning to think that playing hockey is much more profitable than teaching," Alexa said playfully.

"True, but your career has a longer lifespan. I've got a bum knee that lets me skate with my son and do some coaching, but it meant the end to professional hockey."

When Alexa gave him a questioning look, he added, "Listen, I'm not complaining. I did something I loved for more than ten years. Then it ended. Hockey's a great game, and I think I can help kids to play it better. That means a lot. But I want to hear about you. We've got a lot of catching up to do."

At dinner Alexa told Tony about the year she had spent teaching in northern Thailand at a teacher training college, "There weren't a lot of expatriates there, but I met Jerome, a Brit from Manchester, and later we teamed up with a Dutch nurse who was at the local hospital. The three of us travelled together. We saw most of Thailand and went to Laos, Singapore and Malaysia."

"Sounds exotic," Tony commented. "It beats flying around North America and hanging out at hockey arenas. Why did you ever come back?"

"My mother was sick. I wanted to be closer to her and Dad, and it really was time to find out what teaching here was like."

Tony's expression immediately changed. "I heard about your mother. I'm sorry, Alexa. She was a great lady. I hung out at your house so much in high school that I felt as if I were part of your family and that's how she treated me."

In turn he told her about his brief, disastrous marriage and his two passions, his six-year-old son Michael and hockey. "Janice and I have joint custody, but now that Michael's in school it makes sense that he lives with Janice and her husband, Rob, during the week. I have him at least every second weekend and during the school holidays. So far it's working. Maybe at some point he'll decide to come and live with me during the week, but right now I'm not pushing it. He seems happy and knows he still has two parents who love him."

The restaurant lived up to Tony's praise. The food was delicious.

After they had ordered espresso and amaretto cheesecake for

dessert, there was a comfortable lull in the conversation. Tony leaned across the table and covered one of Alexa's hands with his. "This has been fun! Ever since I came home, I've been wondering if I did the right thing. Mom and Dad aren't getting any younger as they say, and Ronnie can use another hand in the business, but I've been gone a long time. I can't hang out at Licks anymore, and most of my old friends have married or moved away."

"I know how you're feeling. Being back is a lot like watching a rerun of my adolescence. I'm taking it one day at a time. I have a one-semester contract, but nothing after January. That may be a good thing," she added, smiling.

Tony seemed uncomfortable for the first time. "Alexa, I was really a naive kid in many ways. When you broke up with me before I left to play hockey, at first I thought you were upset that I wouldn't be around for your last year of high school. And then I thought that there must have been other reasons or someone else," he paused searching for the right words. He looked at Alexa expectantly. Involuntarily, Alexa's hand stiffened, and Tony took his away.

"A lot of things were going on," she said lightly. "The biggest was that I was just sixteen. I wanted to get out of Davenport. I wanted to go to university and see the world. I wasn't ready for any long term responsibilities or commitments." After a moment, she added, "Maybe I was jealous. You got your big break in hockey. You were leaving. I suppose I felt left behind."

"And that's why you were so upset?"

"Tony, let's talk about something else. We were kids. Who behaves rationally at sixteen?"

Tony's appeared to be focussing all of his attention on Alexa, but with a conscious effort he leaned back and took a deep breath. "Fair enough. We were both crazy kids. Have you kept in touch with anyone we used to know at Riverside?"

"With Patti and Joy. Patti's married to Chris Barry. They have two kids and a place outside of town."

"I know Chris. He often works with Ronnie on renovation projects."

Alexa nodded. "What about you? Do you see any of the guys we hung out with?"

"You won't believe this, but I often golf with Hank Patterson."

"Hank? The guy who streaked down the hall just before graduation?"

"He'll never live that down! Hank's a chartered accountant now, married with three boys. The picture of middle class respectability."

Alexa shook her head in disbelief. "What a scene that was! Do you remember Mr MacLeod, the vice-principal? I heard he tackled Hank and put him in the principal's office. Hank was suspended, but he showed up at graduation as if nothing had happened!" They were both laughing

"Streaking's a thing of the past, " Tony said. "You're at Riverside. What are the kids into now?" They talked, interrupting each other in their eagerness to share memories, until the presence of the waiter hovering discreetly with the bill made them realize that the restaurant was almost empty.

"You've held up really well for a working girl " Tony teased her as they drove back to Alexa's apartment. "I think our waiter was ready to doze off, but you kept going." When he pulled over to the curb in front of Martin's house, he reached into the back seat and handed her a huge bouquet of yellow roses.

" Tony, I'm truly overwhelmed!"

"They used to be your favourite flower," he said. "I bought them this afternoon, but then I lost my nerve and didn't give them to you when I came to pick you up in case you thought I was being a little presumptuous."

"They're beautiful. I'm touched you remembered."

He came around to open her door, and they went up the walk together. The house was quiet with just one lamp burning on Martin's patio.

"I'd like to ask you up, but it's late," Alexa began.

"Some other night."

At her door, Alexa held out her hand. Tony took it, but suddenly his arms were around her, and his lips on hers. It was a kiss both familiar and tentative. To her surprise, Alexa felt herself responding. They kissed again, more strongly this time. Then Alexa stepped back.

In response to Tony's questioning look, she murmured, "It's been fun, but it really is late."

"It is," he said softly and repeated, "Some other time. I'm away this weekend. Michael and I are going fishing. Will we see each other soon?"

"Of course," Alexa spoke lightly. "How could we avoid it in Davenport?"

A hurt look flickered across Tony's face. "I'll call you in a few days. Enjoy the rest of your weekend."

Although she was suddenly so tired that her bones ached, Alexa lay sleepless for a long time. She thought of her reaction to Tony's kiss. Perhaps they were both lonely. Tony was familiar and oddly comforting in spite of the history between them, but she had not been completely honest with him. She remembered only too well why she had broken up with him. She had closed a door on that part of her life and had no desire to open it again.

Her thoughts turned to Mark. She wondered what it would be like to have his arms around her and his mouth on hers and then banished the fantasy. He had seemed genuinely sorry that he wouldn't be seeing her at Book Ends, but at that very moment he might be with Julie. Alexa had always worked for public boards of education with no restrictions on their employees' social activities, yet she was aware that many people had crashed and burned when they mixed their careers and their sexual life. She wasn't going there. Despite this resolution, Mark's face and lips haunted her. The sky was becoming light when Alexa finally fell asleep.

CHAPTER SEVEN

*B*y the next morning Alexa resolved to remember only a pleasant evening with her old friend Tony. After her run, she attacked the mountain of marking she had brought home from school. She began with her Pathways kids' first writing assignment. She had refilled her coffee mug and was shaking her head at the abysmal spelling when she paused to reread Justin Murray's work. The students were to describe a person who was important in their lives. Justin had chosen his grandfather. The piece was not only well written but extremely perceptive.

He ended with these words, "When my grandfather died, I lost my best friend, and I knew that a piece of history had died. I'll always remember my grandpa's stories about the war. For the first time I understood that the soldiers who died in those battles were only boys, sometimes still teenagers."

Alexa paused and then wrote, "Justin, this is a wonderful tribute to your grandfather. Be sure to show it to your family." She made a note to talk with Kelly Fitzgerald, the head of guidance. Justin was a very competent writer. Why was he in a Pathways English class?

The telephone interrupted her thoughts. Please don't let it be Tony, she muttered to herself as she went to answer. She realized that their kiss had not conveyed the message that they weren't going to resume their old relationship. "Alexa, I'm so glad you're home! I was hoping you'd call me. How's Dad doing?" It was Kate, her oldest sister.

Alexa settled in for what promised to be a long conversation, "I honestly don't know. He still keeps busy with his practice, but he seems so much older, and the house is practically a mausoleum. Whenever I go there, I'm in tears expecting Mom to walk in any moment. I miss her so much, Katie. Imagine how Dad feels." She began to cry, but she managed to add, "At least he won't die of hunger. Verna Murphy has dedicated herself to warding off his imminent starvation. I think she brings him food almost every day."

Kate sounded suspiciously close to tears herself, but she gave a realistic groan. "How does Dad stand her? Is she as pushy as ever? I always thought she was preaching at me!"

"I'm surprised you remember that about Verna. I'd completely forgotten. You know I don't think she bothers Dad a bit. Maybe he likes the attention. She thinks her destiny is to be his guardian angel or else take Mom's place."

"Give me a break. I'm glad you're around to keep an eye on him." Katie launched into the latest reports on Alexa's nieces and nephews.

As Alexa listened, she was reflecting that in spite of the eight years between them she and Katie had always been close. It was Kate who had taught Alexa to swim and play tennis. Unlike their middle sister, Tanya, she had endless patience for a tag-along little girl. She was sometimes a surrogate mother, sometimes a confidante.

When Kate had finished, Alexa said, "The most bizarre thing is happening. I just escaped from a smothering relationship and two weeks ago I met an attractive man who has a cynical edge which reminds me of David. I have to keep reminding myself that I'm not getting involved with anyone."

"What's his name? Is he a teacher?" Kate was keen for more information.

"Mark Anderson. And he's the vice- principal at Riverside."

"You don't sound happy. There's nothing wrong with that. I'd say it's great."

"I wish it were. He's recently separated and bringing up his little girl, Sarah. She's a bit younger than Bailey. The staff loves him. He's a real professional, but I can't put my finger on this guy. He's dropdead gorgeous, and one minute he's all charm and the next he's a petty dictator, putting school rules before the kids."

There was a pause, and then Kate said thoughtfully, "The good thing is that you'll be working with him every day. You'll gradually find out what makes him tick. Don't rush into anything, but he's sounds interesting. You know, Alexa, it's easy to criticize, but he's got a lot to contend with too. I can't imagine managing a school and being a single parent. Is Sarah's mother never around?"

They chatted on until Kate said, "This call is going to cost a fortune, and I still haven't told you the big news. If you think Dad can stand it,

Bill and I decided we'd come home for Christmas this year. It will be chaos dragging three kids and a baby all the way from Vancouver, but I want a white Christmas again."

"Dad will be thrilled and so will I! It'll be so much fun to be together again, Katie! You remember last year David and I went to Barbados, and I tried to pretend that Christmas wasn't happening." At last they hung up with promises to talk again soon.

Alexa was restless after the phone call. She missed Kate a lot. Some of her fondest memories were of sitting cross-legged on Kate's bed watching her oldest sister get dressed for a date or try on a prom dress. Kate would braid her hair and allow her to experiment with her nail polish. She smiled as she remembered that Kate was always the one she turned to with boy problems.

Finally Alexa forced herself to return to her piles of marking, and she ploughed through stacks of papers for most of the afternoon. She had made an appointment to meet Dara Babcock at eight o'clock on Monday morning. Dara had given Alexa a folder of poetry, and Alexa kept postponing the reading. It was always difficult if the writing was sentimental drivel although she would struggle valiantly to make some positive comments.

To her surprise, Dara's poetry was fresh and original. She wrote short lyrics with crisp images that reminded Alexa of Japanese *haiku*. She read one poem entitled "First Snowfall" several times:

Snowflakes
frost the lawn
wrap the trees
with silver wire.
An old basket
fills up
with winter's harvest.

Alexa wondered where she had learned to write like that.

The telephone rang again. This time it was her father. "We have a dinner invitation," Dan began.

"Let me guess. Would it be from your friendly neighbour, Verna?"

"How did you know?" asked Dan, tongue in cheek. "She hopes that we can come on Sunday evening, and of course you're to bring 'your boyfriend.'"

"Wonderful! The good news is that you can refuse the invitation without telling a lie. My department head, Carol Helmer, invited me for dinner. I'll be dining *chez* Helmer with Carol, her husband and daughter."

"Carol Helmer? Is she married to a police officer? I know a Roger Helmer."

"The very one. Dad, I swear you know everyone in this town."

"Well, not everyone, but in my line of work I do spend a lot of time with the police. It helps when I'm caught speeding," he joked.

"Enjoy yourself, but watch out for Verna. She's really setting her sights on you," Alexa cautioned. After sharing the news from Kate, she hung up. Then she wished that she had casually asked if Mark or Sarah had visited that weekend.

On Sunday afternoon, Alexa packed her swimsuit and a bottle of wine for Carol. On her way to the car, she thought she heard Robbie barking. Only a terrier's bark could be that shrill Alexa decided as she went to investigate. Sure enough, Robbie was sitting on the sidewalk in front of Martin's house with Sarah hunkered down beside him. When Alexa got closer, she saw that Sarah's face was streaked with dirt and tears.

"Hi, Sarah, what's wrong?" Alexa knelt down beside them.

"Robbie pooped on the sidewalk, and I walked in it!" Sarah wailed.

Resisting the temptation to laugh, Alexa said seriously, "You can blame my dad. What was he thinking of, letting you walk Robbie without a poop and scoop kit?"

Sarah took a deep breath and asked, "What's that?"

"Come on up to my apartment, and I'll clean your sandals and show you."

Alexa went back inside with Sara. and Robbie at her heels. Sarah was soon distracted, as Alexa cleaned her shoes and gave her a plastic bag and paper towels for future emergencies.

Sarah wandered around Alexa's apartment and then asked, "Where did you get that sparkly elephant? It's really neat."

"I used to teach in Thailand," Alexa told her. "Do you know where that is?"

Sarah gave her a disdainful glance. "Sure. I read a book called *Anna and the King of Siam*. I saw the movie too. Siam is the old name for Thailand."

Alexa smiled. At times she agreed with her dad that Sarah was "a sad soul", but she was also a very bright little girl. She wondered if Sarah found that most adults talked down to her.

"I'm sorry that I have to go out this afternoon," Alexa told her, "but I'll walk you and Robbie back to Dad's house first."

"Okay, but don't tell him you saw me crying. Just say you met me outside your house."

Alexa nodded in agreement. She wondered if Sarah spent a lot of time trying not to upset the grownups in her life. "Has it been a good weekend?" she asked as they walked along with Robbie ambling docilely at their heels.

Sarah shrugged elaborately. "Dad and I went for a bike ride yesterday, and then we went to swim at your dad's house. Tonight I think I'll just finish my book." She added, "Julie's coming over. I don't like her. She always smells funny because she smokes cigarettes. It makes me choke if I get close to her. I don't know how Dad stands it."

Too much information, Alexa thought. She felt as if someone had just hit her squarely in the solar plexus. Where was Mark coming from? One moment he was suggesting that they get together and the next he was spending Sunday night with Julie. He probably saw himself as the Riverside heartbreaker. To change the subject, she asked, "What are you reading now?"

"*The Blue Castle*. It's way better than *Anne of Green Gables*, but the same lady wrote both books."

After Alexa made sure that Sarah and Robbie were safely back with her dad, she walked home thinking that Sarah was better read than most of her students. She was probably completely bored by school. Maybe that was one reason she was unhappy.

At Carol's house, Alexa was warmly welcomed by Roger Helmer, a big teddy bear of a man, who gave her a hug, "I don't greet all our guests this way, " he teased, "but you've been a lifesaver. Usually Kerry and I avoid Carol for the entire month of September. She's like the proverbial bear with a sore paw until she breaks in the new teachers. This year she has you, and I hear that thanks to you at least one of the first year teachers is learning the ropes."

Alexa was embarrassed. "I don't think I've done very much, but it's good to hear that I've helped Carol out a little. She's a dynamo."

"Don't talk about me, you two," Carol teased, putting her arm affectionately around Roger. Alexa looked at them. The burly police officer with the neatly trimmed hair and beard towered over his diminutive wife, and their delight in each other was obvious. Alexa couldn't help wondering if she would ever find someone who made her feel this way.

"Why don't you ladies relax in the hot tub while Chef Roger goes back to the kitchen?"

In a few minutes, Kerry appeared. She looked like a typical fourteen-year-old with her straight dark hair and long T-shirt worn over her bathing suit. "Come and join us," Alexa invited. "There's lots of room." Still wearing her shirt, Kerry hopped into the tub and settled back in the hot water with a contented sigh.

"How was your first week at Riverside?" Alexa asked.

To her surprise, Kerry was not at all shy and did not hesitate to give her impressions of the school. "I like it a lot. It's so neat to have different teachers instead of just one. This semester I have English, math, science and art. The teachers are okay, but they give way too much homework. I even have to do a presentation in art. I thought for sure that would be a Mickey Mouse course. The first day I hated English. Mr Thompson didn't seem to know what he was doing, and one kid threw chalk at him when he was writing on the board, but I think he's getting better."

Alexa and Carol exchanged smiles.

Kerry reminded Alexa of her mother. She was a bundle of energy who could not sit still for long and soon she was out of the hot tub throwing a ball for Chloe, the family Lab, to chase. "Do you know when we're going to have the first dance, Mom? I can't wait. Last year we only had dances in the afternoon."

"It's probably the last Friday in September," Carol told her. "If you listen to the morning announcements, the kids on student council will start advertising it soon." Alexa smiled, still remembering her own excitement at high school dances.

"Promise me you won't come, Mom. I'd die if you were a chaperone at the first dance."

"No promises, but if I'm there, I'll hide somewhere, maybe in a closet," Carol promised as Kerry made a face at her.

"Are we eating out on the patio?" Roger asked, appearing with plates and cutlery.

"Let's do that," Carol said. "You don't mind, Alex? We're not very formal here."

"No, it's great," Alexa replied, feeling very much at home.

They pulled shirts over their wet bathing suits and were about to sit down at the glass patio table when the doorbell rang. When Roger went to answer it, Carol made a comical face and raised her eyebrows as she whispered to Alexa, "I'm sorry. Don't blame me for this. It was strictly Roger's idea."

Roger returned followed by a stocky, redheaded man. "This is Brian Fowler who just joined our division." He made the introductions and then said, "We're glad you could make it. I was feeling outnumbered."

Brian was definitely not Alexa's type, but his round face was good humoured, and there was a sparkle in his blue eyes which suggested that he was quite aware of the setup. As he shook hands, Alexa felt a flash of sympathy for him. They were both new in town, and everyone was going to play matchmaker. When she thought that Brian was not looking, Alexa glanced at Carol and managed to stifle a chuckle. In return, Carol held up her hands as if to say, "Blame Roger if this is a disaster."

In spite of Alexa's embarrassment at Roger's very obvious ploy, she enjoyed the dinner. Both Roger and Brian had a gift for story telling. Roger told them that Brian was the officer in charge of the canine unit. "In Davenport that's one dog!"

Brian responded laughing. "And don't forget that I brought Razor with me. We're a team. He even tries to sleep with me, and like most teenagers he doesn't want to get up in the morning. He's at home sulking right now because he wasn't invited for dinner."

Kerry giggled. "You should have brought him. What kind of dog is Razor anyway?"

"A German Shepherd, just three years old and a crackerjack."

Alexa interrupted him, "Brian, you'll have to explain this to me. I'm assuming that Razor sniffs out drugs, but Davenport isn't exactly New York City. If we're the centre of the drug trade, I'm really missing something."

"You might be surprised" Roger told her. "Marijuana's a lucrative crop for some farmers north of town. They grow it in their corn fields, and we're close enough to the international border that lots of dope gets smuggled across in the hidden compartments of trucks and cars."

"We also get called away for special operations at the airport and in the detention centres and prisons, " Brian added. "But Razor's favourite work is at the schools. When he goes to sniff the lockers, he can be sure of finding a few stale sandwiches and that drives him crazy!" He winked at Kerry.

It was Carol's turn to explain as Kerry looked sceptical. "Mrs Fletcher and Mr Anderson try to bring in a team of drug dogs several times each semester. Last year for the first time we had docile dogs which not only sniffed the lockers but could go into the classrooms. As a rule, kids who bring dope to school don't stash it in their lockers. It's more likely to be in their socks or shoes, and the dogs find it every time."

"Is that safe?" Kerry was wide-eyed. "I don't want to be bitten by a dog just because some pothead brings his stash to school."

Brian reassured her. "Dogs like Razor are called docile because they're extremely well trained and good with people. Razor plays with my landlord's daughter, but he's got a great nose, and he can sniff out marijuana no matter how well it's hidden."

"I think it's kind of neat," Kerry said. "I'd like to see the dogs. When are they coming to Riverside?"

Everyone laughed as Carol explained, "That's classified information. The important part about a sweep is that it catches the school off guard. If everyone knew, there'd be no point in doing it."

"I think it's a good idea, " Alexa said thoughtfully. "Most of the kids don't appreciate dope being sold under their noses."

"You're right," Roger commented. "But in spite of that I was amazed at the fuss made by some parents and even a few trustees the first time the dogs came. Luckily, the superintendent had approved the operation, and it really had a powerful effect on the kids."

"What happens when someone gets caught?" asked Kerry curiously.

"It depends on the amount of drugs they have," Brian told her. "They may be charged with possession or with trafficking if they have a large amount. Sometimes they get off with just a warning, but we want to set an example and make sure the kids understand that using or carrying drugs at school has a serious consequence."

After Kerry left the table, Carol said to the others, "You can bet that a lot of junior students will hear about this tomorrow. It's good prevention. I don't want my daughter going to a school where the kids think they can smoke up."

Roger put his arm around her. "Don't worry, " he said. "I think Riverside's a good school. Lisa Fletcher and Mark have worked hard to make it safe. They've cleaned up the drugs and put a stop to the fights which used to go on. What do you think of the school so far, Alex?"

"I agree with you," she answered. "Where I used to teach, we needed security guards to patrol the halls, and it wasn't unusual to have knives pulled in a fight. Riverside has a definite advantage in being a small town school. Here the teachers know the kids. They don't get lost the way they do in a large city school."

"Thanks for offering some support for my oversensitive mother antennae! I know I'm overprotective at times. I drive Kerry absolutely crazy."

Brian described the training courses he had taken to become a dog handler. "We live with the dog twenty-four hours a day. I've worked with several dogs, but Razor's the absolute best. I take him over to my sister's, and my three-year-old niece rides on his back and pulls his ears, yet once I put on my uniform he knows he's working."

"I enjoyed tonight," Alexa told Carol and Roger as she got up to leave, "but unfortunately tomorrow's Monday. Roger, if you're looking for a career change, I'd hire you as a cook anytime."

At the front door, Brian said casually, "If you're free some night, Alexa, I'll introduce you to Razor."

Alexa smiled at him. "I'll look forward to it."

When she walked into her apartment, Alexa saw the flashing red light on her phone. With grim determination, she marched over to it and steeled herself for David's recriminations. Instead she heard Mark's voice, "Hi, Alexa. It's about four o'clock on Sunday afternoon. I wanted to thank you for being so kind to Sarah. She told me that she got her shoes dirty when she was walking Robbie, and you cleaned her up. She liked your apartment. I'll try to reach you later." In spite of her earlier thoughts about Mark, Alexa could feel herself smiling. This was the best thing that had happened all weekend.

She was getting ready to shower when the telephone rang. "Good evening, is it too late to call?" It was Mark again.

"Not at all. I just got in from Carol's and got your message."

"I'm not sure what happened to Sarah, but all she could talk about was meeting you. You made her feel really important by taking the time to help her. I got a report on every detail of your apartment. Thanks again. She's having a tough time right now, and this meant a lot."

"It was nothing. I saw her on the sidewalk in front of Martin's house, and one thing led to another. She's a neat kid."

"I think so too, but I don't expect the rest of the world to share my enthusiasm."

Alexa found herself telling him all about Kate and Bill's family. "I love their kids. I spent a week with them in Vancouver in the summer, and I just found out that they're all coming for Christmas. I just wish I could see them more often. They change so quickly."

"I know. Perhaps Sarah can spend some time with your older niece, Bailey, during the holidays. Sarah's a bit younger, but she'd love someone to go skiing with. I never planned to have just one child, and at times I feel like a social director arranging activities for her. It's not so bad during the school year, but celebrating holidays can be brutal. At least she has some cousins."

Alexa was surprised at how open Mark was away from school. She felt as if she had known him for a long time. He was warm and humorous and seemed willing to talk on any subject although he did not mention Julie Chisholm. "I'll see you tomorrow," Mark said at last. "Get some sleep, Alexa. After a weekend, you never know what mood the kids will be in."

Once she was in bed, Alexa switched on her reading light and rearranged the pillows, but it was hard to concentrate on her novel. She hoped that Justin Murray had stayed out of trouble since Friday, but it was Mark's voice that echoed in her mind as she drifted towards sleep. Even if he had spent the evening with Julie, it didn't seem important. The telephone call was all that mattered. She fell asleep in the midst of a fantasy of sharing a romantic dinner with him in some exotic far away setting.

CHAPTER EIGHT

On Monday morning, Dara Babock was sitting against the lockers waiting for Alexa when she arrived at her classroom. "Good morning, " Alexa greeted her as she struggled to balance the piles of student writing folders which threatened to topple out of her arms. "Here's the key, Dara. Can you unlock the door before I drop all of these?"

Dara scrambled to her feet, and Alexa saw that she had been crying. Her face was blotchy, and her eyes were red.

Inside the room, Alexa dumped the load on the desk. "What's wrong? Did you have a bad weekend?"

Dara shook her head and reached for the box of Kleenex on Alexa's desk. She blew her nose loudly and took a jagged breath, but tears were running down her cheeks. "I hate this school. I can't wait to get out of here," she choked out between sobs.

Alexa suppressed the desire to put her arms around Dara and give her a comforting hug. She didn't care about the school rules. She just wasn't sure how Dara would react to this familiarity. The girl looked absolutely distraught, but she was struggling valiantly to control her emotions. "Can we talk about it?" Alexa waited for several moments, feeling helpless as she straightened the folders on her desk, but Dara shook her head again. She looked completely forlorn.

Desperate to offer some comfort but not wanting to push too far, Alexa said, "I think a lot of students are really fed up with school by their graduating year. High school can be like a little fish bowl with the same old fish swimming round and round in their glass cage and constantly bumping into each other."

Dara bit her lip. "It's worse than that," she said finally. "It's like a prison, and I can't escape." She sat huddled in one of the front desks, hugging her knees, the picture of misery.

"Please tell me what's wrong. Maybe I can help in some way," Alexa coaxed, wishing she had the skills to draw Dara out.

Dara shook her head. "You can't do anything. No one can."

Alexa waited for a few moments, hoping that Dara would open up, but she sensed only resistance. At last, desperate to offer some solace, she took out the poems she had read on Saturday. "Thanks for showing me these. You have a real talent! When did you start to write?"

She pulled her chair over beside Dara and went on, "Our teachers' federation sponsors a writing contest every fall. I'd like to see more of your work. If you're willing, we can choose some of your poems and enter them in the contest."

As they talked, Dara gradually grew calmer, and her face brightened. "You're the first teacher I've ever talked to about writing. I was afraid people would laugh at my poems because they don't rhyme, and they're about ordinary things."

"That's why they're so special. You describe the world we all see but in a fresh way. You make us take a second look at the everyday things we took for granted."

"Is that really true?"

"Absolutely! '*To see a World in a Grain of Sand, And a heaven in a Wild Flower*' that's what poetry does."

"I like that," Dara said, repeating the quotation. "I've written a lot over the last year. If you want to see more I could bring in some of my favourites."

The first bell rang, and Alexa groaned. "Already! We're like Pavlov's dogs. We salivate at the bell. Promise you'll bring me more of your poetry tomorrow, and I'll bring you a book by one of my favourite American poets, William Carlos Williams. He's great. Some of your poems remind me of his."

Dara nodded. She gave Alexa a faint smile, but she still looked drained, and her face was pale.

"I'll see you in class," Alexa told her with a smile.

The next three hours were easy ones. Monday morning was definitely a good time to teach the Pathways kids who were lethargic from weekend parties. When Alexa had a free moment at lunch, she went to see Kelly Fitzgerald, the guidance head.

"Alexa, come in," Kelly greeted her. "I haven't had a moment to talk with you since you arrived, but I hear from the students that your classes are going well."

"I think they are. I know you're always frantically busy, but I wanted to ask you about two students, Justin Murray and Dara Babcock. Do you know them?"

"Very well," Kelly answered. "Let me guess. Justin's driving you crazy and doing nothing."

"Not at all," said Alexa. "Quite the opposite in fact. He's reading a book I put in my classroom library for the senior students, and his first writing assignment is wonderful. Why is he in a Pathways class?"

"The usual story. Justin's certainly above average. Maybe even a gifted student. But there's no support at home. Lots of alcohol problems. Maybe drugs. His parents finally kicked him out, and he lived with his grandparents where he pretty much did his own thing. His grandfather died last year, and now there's just his grandmother. I think Justin looks after her more than she looks after him. He and Mark clashed last year because he tends to break all the rules and misses a lot of school. If he's working for you, that's great."

"But he should be in a more challenging class," Alexa insisted. "I think he's even got the potential to go on to university."

"I agree," said Kelly. "Don't get me wrong. I like Justin a lot, and we talk every few weeks. If he stays in school this semester and stays out of trouble, that's a plus. I just don't think he has the work ethic he needs for a university stream."

Seeing the mutinous expression on Alexa's face, she suggested, "Why don't you talk to him? If you can get through to him, it's not too late to change his timetable."

Alexa glanced at her watch. As usual, time was running out, "I *will* talk to him," she promised. "I also wondered if you would talk with Dara." She briefly described how distraught Dara had been that morning. "She won't open up to me at all, yet I have a feeling something's horribly wrong either at school or at home. Maybe she'll talk to you. No one should be that miserable – even on a Monday morning."

"I'll do that," Kelly agreed. "I'll have time to call her down this afternoon and I'll let you know if I get anywhere."

At the end of the afternoon classes, the telephone rang. When Alexa answered, it was Susan Johnson. "Hi, Alexa, Mark wondered if he could speak with you before you leave today."

For a moment Alexa felt exactly like a student called to the office.

"Sure," she answered, "I'm coming down with my attendance. Tell him I'll be there in five minutes." She hoped that Mark wasn't going to talk about the ride she had given Justin on the first day of school. She didn't need another reprimand.

Mark was on the telephone, but he smiled and motioned for her to come in and sit down. The conversation went on and on. At one point, he held the receiver away from his ear, and Alexa could hear an angry female voice. Finally the call ended, and Mark hung up and went over to close the office door. Justin had been a model student that Monday. She hoped that Mark hadn't found out about his activities on the opening day of school.

Mark sat on the edge of his desk. "Alexa, thanks a lot for spotting the problem with Dara Babcock. Kelly brought her to me this afternoon, and we managed to get her to tell us the whole story."

"I really don't know what's going on. Dara and I had a meeting this morning, and she was very upset about something."

"Well, keep this under your hat," said Mark. "I don't want it to become staffroom gossip since a number of our senior students are involved. It seems that some of the seniors led by Stacey Sawyer and her boyfriend, Ben Copeland, have been making Dara's life a living hell. Nothing physical, just constant name calling. This type of bullying has become almost an epidemic, but usually the seniors grow up and stop playing these vicious games." Mark sounded totally disgusted.

"I can't imagine why Stacey would be involved in something like that. She's pretty and popular. Dara sticks to herself, but why should that bother anyone?"

"Who knows? Apparently it's been going on since grade school. Stacey used to make catty comments about the way Dara dressed, but now she's graduated to a smear campaign calling her 'retard' and 'bitch.' She got Ben involved, and he and some of his buddies have made obscene calls to Dara's house."

"Did Stacey admit to this?" Alexa asked.

"Total denial. Quite indignant too. She claimed that Dara's jealous of her and invented the whole story. In the end, Kelly and I found some seniors who were willing to give us statements about things they'd heard and seen."

"So what happens now?"

"It's harassment," Mark explained. "We suspended Stacey and Ben for two days and warned them that if there's any retaliation when they come back to school they can finish their diplomas somewhere else. That was Mrs Sawyer on the telephone. She's appealing the suspension, going to the trustees, for all I know calling the Minister of Education." Mark grinned. "At times I wonder why I don't just go back to teaching math. Life was so much simpler then."

"I'm still in shock," Alexa said after a moment. "Stacey can do anything she wants with her life. She's bright enough. This doesn't fit the picture. And I can't imagine that Dara was ever interested in one of Stacey's boyfriends. Why this?"

Mark shrugged. "Power over someone else maybe? Sometimes I call it 'the kick the cat syndrome.' Dara's low in the pecking order around here, and she's totally oblivious to the things that matter to Stacey. Maybe at some time she inadvertently said or did something that irritated our prom queen. Bullying is definitely the number one problem in our schools, but no one's really sure why it starts. I'm just happy you caught it. Kids shouldn't have to come here and be tormented. And I'm glad you spoke to Kelly. Just keep your eyes open when Stacey comes back. I think she'll learn a lesson, but maybe not."

Alexa stood up. "And I'm glad you got through to Dara. She was so wound up this morning, but she was determined not to tell me what was going on."

"Well, if all else fails, I can become a private detective. People seem to tell me their life stories. I wanted to give you another heads up. If you check your mailbox in the staffroom, you'll find an invitation. Lisa and Jim are inviting the staff over to their place for a get-together on Friday night. Try to come. They throw a good party, and we'll certainly need one before this week is through. It's only Monday. One down and four to go."

He paused and then went on, "Alexa, I hope we get a chance to talk on Friday night. This place is such a zoo that a civilized conversation is impossible." His eyes were warm, and Alexa felt an unexpected tingle up her spine. Why the charm if he was involved with Julie, or did he simply treat all women this way?

Alexa took a deep breath. "Friday sounds great, and thanks for the info about Stacey. I'll keep one eye on her and one eye on the rest of the class."

"Oh, I almost forgot." Mark went to his briefcase and dug around in it before bringing out an envelope. Alexa opened it to find a homemade card meticulously drawn by Sarah. A stick girl and a stick dog were standing in front of a large house. Underneath Sarah had printed, "Thank you, Alexa."

Alexa struggled to control her voice. "Tell her it's beautiful." Her eyes met Mark's. "Maybe I'll see her next weekend, and I can tell her myself."

When she got home, Martin was reading on the patio. He took one look at her face and said, "Sit down for a moment. It must have been a rough Monday."

"I've had better" admitted Alexa, bending over to scratch Kaspar's ears. "Sometimes I think that teachers are completely insensitive to what's really going on in their students' lives."

"That's probably true," Martin agreed, "but it's true about society in general. We meet people all day long, and most of us accept what we see on the surface as reality. Actually," he added with a chuckle, "I think it's better that way. I have an old friend who is a psychoanalyst, and even a dinner with her can be pretty uncomfortable. I don't always want someone dissecting my innermost feelings."

When Alexa laughed, Martin said, "That's better. Don't let the job get you down, Alexa. It looks as if you dragged home half the books at Riverside, but if you can spare the time, why don't you join me for a quick supper? I'm just making fettuccine and a tossed salad, but it'll be more pleasant if I share it with someone."

"I'd love to. It sounds better than the microwave popcorn and diet coke that I was going to have. But promise you'll come to dinner on Sunday. Dad's coming over, and I want to experiment with some Thai recipes."

"Sounds great! I'd be honoured," Martin answered with a mock bow. "Take your time, change or whatever. We'll eat in about half an hour."

It was Alexa's first opportunity to see Martin's part of the house. "It's so elegant," she exclaimed appreciatively as she wandered around his dining room. "I feel as if I'm visiting a museum."

Martin smiled. "I'm flattered, but actually it's an eclectic mess. Anne and I just picked up a few pieces we liked. Look at that." He pointed to a statue of the Hindu goddess Shiva. "Anne was so determined to have her that I carried her in my arms through three airports."

"Martin, I hope this question isn't too personal, but I've been wondering. Why did you and Anne stay in Davenport?"

"That's a good question," Martin replied thoughtfully. "We often talked about moving to a larger centre. It would have been easy for Anne to get a transfer with the bank, but odd though it seems we both liked it here. Anne was a canoeist, and she loved being able to get out on the water so easily. I built up my business, and we gradually made a circle of friends."

Alexa nodded. "I keep telling myself that the city isn't far. It's easy to go in for theatre or dinner, but it just seems that the town is so narrow-minded."

She thought of telling Martin what had happened to Joy, but he was saying, "Perhaps we would have moved eventually, but our time ran out."

Alexa understood. She hesitated a moment and then said, "Martin, you seem like the kind of person who would be happy anywhere. That's a talent I'm trying to develop."

Knowing that she still had work to do for the next day, she stood up to leave shortly before nine. As they talked on the patio before saying good night, Martin said sheepishly, "I owe you an apology. I did something quite stupid."

"I can't imagine that."

"Well I did, and it's been on my conscience. A couple of weeks ago, Tony Benoit came into the shop looking for an anniversary present for his parents. We talked about this and that. Mostly about his hockey career. When he was leaving, he turned back and said, 'By the way, Alexa Corbett and I were good friends in high school. A mutual friend told me she's back in town and teaching at the high school. I heard she was living in your apartment, and I wanted to send her some flowers as a welcome home present. Would you happen to have her telephone number?'"

Martin looked embarrassed. "Alexa, without thinking I gave him your number. Afterwards I kicked myself when I remembered that you had an unlisted number. I shouldn't have done that. I hope that Tony isn't someone you're trying to avoid."

Alexa forced herself to speak lightly. "Thanks for telling me. We *were* friends in school, and he did give me flowers. Not to worry." She added after a moment, "One of the best things about being back here is that you and Dad let me live my life, but you keep an eye out for me. I feel protected. It's a good feeling after living in a city where I didn't even know my neighbours' names."

"You made my night. Just don't let the school take over your life. I'll look forward to Sunday."

Back in her apartment, Alexa was able to get to work without interruption, but she put Sarah's card on the table where she could see it whenever she glanced up. She had some snapshots of Robbie taken that summer. She decided that she would put one in a frame for Sarah. The thought made her smile.

CHAPTER NINE

W̶hen Stacey Sawyer came back to school two days later, she acted as if nothing had happened. She stayed after the first class to speak with Alexa. "Miss Corbett, I'm sure you heard that Ben and I were suspended. I don't understand why Dara Babcock would tell such lies about us," Stacey shook back her long hair in what Alexa recognized as a characteristic gesture. "My mother's really angry, and she's appealing the suspension, but I decided to forget it and get caught up as quickly as I can." Her blue eyes were round and innocent as they searched Alexa's face.

Alexa kept her face and voice deliberately neutral. "Certainly that's the best thing to do, Stacey. You know I'm in the classroom most noon hours if you need some help with your first essay. It's due on Friday."

"Thanks, Miss Corbett, I'll see you today at noon."

Alexa was not surprised when Stacey did not appear that day or the next for extra help. She watched Stacey and Dara carefully but could sense no animosity between the two girls. Dara kept her head down as usual and spoke to almost no one. Stacey was her usual bubbly self and chatted to everyone. She volunteered her opinion and answered questions. The whole situation was bizarre. She had expected Stacey to be somewhat subdued if only for a day or two.

Justin Murray continued to turn in great work, but was usually late for class arriving several minutes after the bell had rung. Alexa assigned another noon hour detention.

"These lunch dates are becoming a habit," she told him. "You must have something more exciting to do with your time."

Justin was slouching in his seat reading *Birdsong* when she went back to speak with him. "How's the book, Justin?"

He shrugged but then said, "It's the first book I've read about World War I. I always wondered what it would be like for the guys fighting in the trenches. The movie would be even better."

"Maybe it will be a film some day. The author has written a lot of other books, and one of them, *Charlotte Gray*, has been made into a movie. I haven't seen it yet, but it got good reviews."

"What's that one about?" Justin asked.

"Charlotte Gray is a woman who goes behind enemy lines in World War II and spies for Britain. I'm just starting to read it now, but I'll lend it to you when I finish."

"Neat," said Justin.

Alexa plunged in. "You know, Justin, you write really well, and you're reading novels my senior class reads. Isn't this an easy class for you?"

Justin shrugged. "Miss, your class is okay, but school isn't my thing. I can't see doing two or three extra years at college after this. I need money, and I want to get a job. I liked working with Ronnie Benoit this summer. Maybe I'll take a carpenter's course after high school. If I make it that far!"

Alexa glanced at her watch. "Get some lunch, Justin. A carpenter has a good trade, but at least think about what I said. You're a bright guy, and at some point you might want to think about college or university."

In an instant, Justin's fists clenched and his eyes narrowed. "You just don't get it, miss. In my family people don't 'think about college or university.' I need to help out my grandma. All she's got is her pension." He left the room without a backward glance, closing the door noisily behind him. Alexa felt a flash of anger, but in a moment of clarity she reflected grimly that she had no right to impose her values on Justin. She understood why his short term goal was earning money, not getting an education.

When Tony called that night, Alexa thanked him again for the roses.

"I'm glad you liked them. I'm sorry I didn't have a chance to call before, but I stayed with Michael for a few days while Janice and Rob went to his uncle's funeral. I just got home this afternoon. Dad's off duck hunting this weekend, and I promised Mom and my sister that I'd go up to the cottage with them. It's beautiful at Beaver Lake in September. I wondered if you'd be able to come with us."

"I remember your family cottage. It sounds idyllic, but this weekend I'm all booked up. Lisa and Jim Fletcher are having a staff party, and then I've got a date with Dad."

"Too bad," Tony said lightly, "Mom will be disappointed. She's probably been cooking up a storm ever since I said I'd invite you."

"Say hello to your mom for me. I'm sure I'll see her soon." They chatted for a few more minutes before they hung up. Alexa had always felt uncomfortable around Tony's mother who thought her sons could do no wrong and regarded any girlfriend with deep suspicion. A weekend with the Benoit family would have been high school revisited. She didn't need that trip down memory lane.

By Friday, Alexa had mixed feelings about the Fletchers' party. She wanted to meet the rest of the staff. Most of them she knew only as friendly faces in the halls. Warren Thompson was bringing Marielle. Alexa had heard so much about her that she felt as if they were already friends; however, she pictured herself as the only single in a crowd of couples. She wondered how she would feel if Mark and Julie arrived together.

"Will I be the only teacher flying solo at this party?" she asked Carol.

"No way! Roger's working nights. I'll be there alone as usual. I have to chauffeur Kerry to swimming, so I'll be late. Both of us are counting the days until she can get her driver's licence! Don't worry, girl. Half the staff will come alone, or their other half will drop in for a few minutes. It'll be a blast. We all need a chance to hang out away from the kids."

Lisa and Jim Fletcher lived in a beautiful old farm house on the River Road outside of town. When Alexa parked at the end of their long driveway, the horizon was dark with threatening rain clouds. She could hear music coming from a huge tent set up on the lawn, and as she walked across the grass, Jim and Lisa came to greet her.

"It's good to meet you at last," Jim said. "You were a life saver when Lisa got the news about Murray. She was frantic for a couple of days until you appeared on the scene."

"It was great timing for me too. I just got home, and Dad showed me the ad. As soon as I dropped off my resume, Mrs Fletcher called and asked me to come to the school for an interview. At first it was strange to be back at Riverside, but I'm enjoying it."

Jim poured her a glass of wine, and soon she was engulfed by teachers introducing themselves and their partners and exchanging shop talk. Before long Warren was pulling her aside. "Alexa, meet the love of my life!" He had his arm around the shoulders of a diminutive dark-haired girl with an engaging smile. "Marielle, this is Alexa, the teacher who saved my sanity!"

Marielle kissed Alexa on both cheeks. "I am so happy to meet you. Warren, he tells me that you help him so much with the bad classes."

Alexa was enchanted. "Warren, let's escape from this mob for a moment and walk down to the river. I want to talk to you and Marielle, and conversation is impossible here."

Wine glasses in hand, they were trying to move through the crowd when Buzz Spencer descended upon them and seized Alexa's elbow. "We need to talk," he bellowed, "never have a chance at school."

Alexa turned back to Warren and Marielle. "See you later," she mouthed, and with a wave they disappeared.

To Alexa's surprise, the dour Mr Spencer was warm and affable. Alexa thought cynically that alcohol had its uses. Like a bulldozer, he ploughed through the crowd and dragged Alexa off to the veranda where they found a quiet spot. "I knew your mother," Buzz began. "We worked together on an environmental committee to save the wetlands. Arlene was a wonderful woman. Totally organized and kept us all on track when we got up on our soap boxes to rant."

As usual, Alexa found it impossible to talk about her mother without emotion. "I find it so strange to come home and know that she's gone. Of course I was here for several weeks at the end, but somehow when I moved back here, it hit me all over again. And each time I go over to Dad's house I want to break down."

Buzz got out a large linen handkerchief and blew his nose loudly. "People are wrong when they say you get over losing someone you love. You never really do, but with time you learn to handle the pain a little better. My fiancee died almost thirty years ago in a car crash. I don't often talk about this to anyone, but I remember that day as if it were yesterday. And I also remember how happy we were together."

Alexa impulsively took Buzz's hand, "Thanks for sharing that," she said. "I don't talk about Mom a lot either, even with Dad. It's good to be with someone who knew her."

Buzz bowed his head. "Talk to me whenever you want, Alexa. Just remember Arlene was a happy woman. She was so proud of Dan and your sisters and you."

"I know, " Alexa replied, "but I wish I'd spent more time with her after I went to university. She had chronic leukemia for years, but never seemed terribly sick. Just tired sometimes. Now that she's gone I wish we could have had more time together."

"Don't," Buzz said. "You had to make your own way. She was glad you did. The first time I met her she told me that her youngest daughter was teaching in Thailand. She wanted you to be independent. Don't have regrets."

Alexa blinked back tears. "Buzz, thanks again. You don't know how much this conversation has helped me."

Jim Fletcher appeared with a tray of food. "Alexa, don't let this man monopolize you. Everyone's eating. Come on, you two."

When Alexa joined the line at the barbecue pit, she found herself next to Julie Chisholm. In spite of her jealousy, Alexa had to admit that the tall blonde woman was stunning. Julie smiled. "Alexa, I hardly ever see you around the school. We're looking for a volleyball coach. Any interest?"

"Sorry, Julie, I have to say no. I've promised to be the staff advisor for the yearbook, and that will keep me busy this semester."

Julie examined her with cool composure. "Oh, yes, I forgot that Mark told me you're replacing Murray only until January. Well, good luck. I haven't heard anything negative from the kids yet." She pointedly turned away from Alexa and began to talk with David Turner, one of the other physical education teachers.

When they walked away, Alexa felt as if she had been dismissed. Looking around, she saw Carol and Warren waving at her to join their table. The rest of the evening passed quickly. In spite of Julie's snub, she felt lighthearted. Once she looked up to see Mark standing nearby with Julie possessively holding his arm. She shrugged and went back to her conversation with Marielle. When she was in university, Alexa had studied French, and she welcomed the opportunity to use the language again.

As the evening went on, some of the teachers danced on the patio. In the laughter and conversation, Alexa thought only briefly that she had talked with almost everyone except Mark. After Warren and Marielle stood up to leave, Alexa glanced at her watch to see that it was nearly midnight. At that moment there was a heavy clap of thunder, and torrential rain began to pour down.

Jim Fletcher was heading for the house with a tray of glasses, and picking up another tray Alexa followed him. By the time she reached the veranda, her shirt was soaked and her hair dripping. Jim found some towels, and they dried off before starting to work together in the warmth of the big kitchen putting away the food and stacking the dishwasher. Alexa had almost finished rinsing plates when Lisa and Mark came in.

"This is wonderful," Lisa said. "It's great to get up the morning after a party and not spend the day cleaning. Thanks for helping, Alexa."

"And the rain held off until the end," Mark added. "This was a fantastic party, guys. I've never seen the staff so relaxed. Alexa, I didn't even have a chance to talk to you. Whenever I looked for you, you were always deep in a conversation."

"I talked to a lot of people I only have a chance to say hello to at school." She turned to Lisa and Jim. "Thanks so much for the evening. I feel that I'm part of the Riverside staff after tonight."

"I told you before we were lucky to find you," Lisa answered. "You've been a wonderful addition to the English department." She took the towel from Alexa's shoulder, "Come on. It's time to stop. You've done enough work for tonight."

Alexa glanced out the patio doors. "It's still pouring, but I'm going to make a run for my car."

"Then I'll lend you a jacket and an umbrella. You're parked at the end of the driveway and you'll be drenched by the time you get there." Lisa answered.

"I'll say good night too," Mark said, putting on his jacket. "Good night, Alexa, and drive carefully. The roads will be slick with all this rain."

After thanking Lisa and Jim again, Alexa dashed down the driveway. She got into her car, shrugging out of the wet jacket and started the engine, giving the windshield a few minutes to clear. She was just backing out of the drive when she felt a peculiar bumping sensation. Some sixth sense told her to stop. Using the umbrella as a shield, she got out to investigate. "Oh, no!" she muttered. The rear tire on the left side of the car was flat, and the rain was continuing relentlessly.

Getting back into the car, she quickly ticked off her options. She had a spare tire, but the thought of changing it in the rain and mud was not appealing. She checked her watch again. Twelve-thirty. Her dad would still be up. Feeling like a high school student, she reached for her cell phone, but before she could call, she saw Mark standing beside her window, water pouring off his hair and jacket.

Alexa rolled down the window an inch. "Where did you come from?" she asked. Without replying, he ran around the car and got in.

"Cripes, what a storm!" he said. "It's raining so hard that I thought I'd follow your car. On a wet night, the River Road can be treacherous with all its curves. When I didn't see you drive past, I came back."

"And tonight I get a flat tire!" Alexa groaned. "I feel like a high school kid. I didn't want to bother Lisa and Jim, so I'm going to call Dad."

"That's what dads are for! But don't drag him out tonight in this weather. It's late. I'll be glad to drop you off at your apartment. It's on my way home, and you can call a garage in the morning to change the tire."

"Thanks. I'd appreciate that, but it's too bad that you had to get soaked again."

"No problem," Mark said easily. "Just lock your car. It'll be safe here. Come on. Let's run for it."

Mark had left his engine running, and the car was warm. Alexa could feel her damp clothes and hair steaming. She was both relaxed and wide awake. "You're a hard person to talk to," Mark teased. "Each time I saw you, you were surrounded by people."

"It was a good party. Did you meet Warren's Marielle? She's a sweetheart, but between my rusty French and her English our conversation was a challenge."

"I was watching Warren. He lights up like a Christmas tree when she's around," Mark commented. "I wonder how long we can keep him at Riverside. I think Marielle would find Davenport pretty confining. I've been wondering how we can keep you around too," he added.

They lapsed into comfortable silence. Alexa wondered if it was strictly professional interest that had sparked Mark's last comment. She wished she knew at what point in the evening Julie had left.

After a moment she said, "I never heard how you ended up at Riverside. You didn't grow up around here?"

"My sister Joanne and I spent a lot of summers here with an aunt and uncle who had a big place in the country. It was great for two city kids. Jo liked it so much she married a local dairy farmer. They live about twenty miles from Davenport. I taught in the city for a few years, but when there was an opening for a math teacher at Riverside, I jumped at the chance."

When Mark pulled up in front of Alexa's apartment, she found herself asking, "Would you like some coffee, or are you going home to relieve the babysitter?"

"Coffee would be wonderful. I'm childless this weekend. Joanne picked up Sarah after school, and she's keeping her until Sunday."

As they were going up the stairs to her apartment, Alexa paused and looked back at Mark. "This place is Martin MacLean's pride and joy. I was so lucky to be able to rent it. It's a minor miracle after the concrete boxes we call apartments in the city."

When Alexa unlocked the door and turned on the hall lamp, Mark whistled appreciatively. "I'd heard that Martin and Anne completely renovated this house, and it's magnificent." He inspected the hall. "Look at these doors. They're solid hemlock. You'd never find that in a new house."

Alexa smiled at his enthusiasm. "You're like my dad. Every time he comes over here he finds something new to admire."

Mark followed Alexa into the kitchen exclaiming at the sight of the cherry cabinets. Then he looked at Alexa. "You're soaking. Why don't you go and change into something dry?" He spotted Alexa's espresso machine on the counter. "I'll make the coffee if you show me where you keep the beans."

In the bathroom, Alexa quickly stripped off her wet clothes and put on a soft denim shirt and drawstring trousers. She rubbed her wet hair with a towel and tied it up in a loose knot. By the time, she got back to the kitchen with a dry towel for Mark, the aroma of the freshly ground beans filled the room, and the espresso was beginning to drip.

Mark turned around and held out his hand for the towel. As he gazed at Alexa, barefoot and with water still shining in her hair, there was an expression of longing in his eyes. Alexa went to him and impulsively put the towel around his neck. In a heart beat, they were in each other's arms. Mark buried his face in Alexa's wet hair and sighed.

For a moment, they held each other tightly. When Alexa drew back, she felt Mark's lips. They were warm and firm and tasted of the Merlot he had been drinking. It was a heady taste, like a promise. They kissed again.

This time it was Mark who drew back. "Ever since that first day in Lisa's office I've wanted to do that. You looked so beautiful and so nervous, but I wasn't planning this when I came up for coffee." He took another step back. "Do you want me to leave?"

Alexa was puzzled. Their kisses had been wonderful. Why did Mark seem so aloof now? "Of course not," she said. "The coffee's ready. I'll get some cups."

Avoiding Mark's gaze, she busied herself getting out espresso cups and saucers, putting sugar and a plate of almond biscotti on the oak table. She found that her hands were trembling, and the preparations calmed her.

By the time she poured the coffee, and they sat down opposite each other, Mark seemed relaxed. He reached for a biscuit hungrily, "I can't believe I'm eating again after all the food tonight, but this is delicious."

They sipped the strong coffee, and Mark smiled at her, "Feeling warmer now?"

She nodded.

"I want to apologize again for acting like a tyrant the first week of school. You were new to the staff, and I forgot that you're an experienced teacher. You're doing a great job with our most difficult kids."

"Thanks. I love being back at Riverside, " Alexa said. "Each of my teaching jobs has been so different, but this one is the most comfortable. I feel as if I belong."

"Where did you first teach?"

"When I was an intern studying for my education degree, I did three teaching stints. The first was in a small composite school in Ingleside where I had the chance to teach kids ranging from grade seven to twelve. I loved all my placements, but at the end of the year I just wasn't ready to settle down. I had saved some money from tutoring and summer jobs, so a girl friend and I decided to backpack through Europe. It was a great year, and the following summer I got a job in northern Thailand at a teacher training college. What a learning experience that was!"

As she talked, Alexa remembered a similar conversation with Tony, but this was different. Mark was a teacher, and she talked easily about the problems she had faced working so far from home. "It was so different from the theory we had learned in university. I expected a language lab and a VCR. Instead I was teaching English with chalk and a blackboard. We had almost no books. Even paper was scarce. I had brought a tape recorder and loads of cassettes and CDs, but most of the time there were problems with electricity or the batteries would be dead, so I taught songs to all my classes, and the students who had notebooks wrote down the words. What they really loved was active learning. I taught them all the games I knew and learned how to smuggle English into the phys-ed lesson. That was a blast."

She looked at Mark, who was watching her intently. "As the year went on, I was really homesick. I got a lot of e-mails from my family and friends which kept me sane, but I was more than ready to come home at the end of a one-year contract. The big surprise was that returning was such an adjustment. I went from a college where everyone respected teachers and learning to an inner city school where the kids booed the principal at the first assembly. It was reverse culture shock. I almost didn't make it through the year."

Alexa suddenly realized that she had been talking for a long time. She started to ask Mark a question when he leaned across the table and took her hand in his. "Alexa, this has been fun, but we've had a long day." He hesitated. "I've been wondering if you have any plans for tomorrow."

She looked at him questioningly.

"It's supposed to be a great day, and I thought I'd drive to the beach."

"To Picton?"

Mark nodded. "I couldn't believe that place when I first discovered it. We not only live on the shores of one of the largest lakes in the world. We also have a sand dune beach practically at our doorstep. Talk about lucking out."

"I know. Picton's magic. It's been a special place for me ever since I was a little kid. I'd love to go."

"Could you be ready around ten? I'm always up early so I'll organize a picnic lunch. Just bring your swim suit and a towel."

"You're on. It's the best offer I've had all night."

At the door Mark put his arms around her. "Sleep well," he said, bending to kiss her.

Alexa closed her eyes. Involuntarily her lips parted. Mark drew back, leaving her wanting more. "I'll see you in the morning," he said softly.

CHAPTER TEN

*A*lexa awoke to a sunny September morning with mist hanging over the grass by the golf course. It was a summer morning with just a hint of the chill of autumn yet to come. Standing by the kitchen window waiting for the coffee to drip, she thought about Friday night. She asked herself what she was doing. Just days ago she had decided not to mix her social life and her career. She smiled ruefully as a voice in her head said, "You're going to the beach. That's all. For once listen to Carol. Get a life. Relax and enjoy the day."

Alexa sat down with a bowl of blueberries and cereal and a large mug of coffee. She reached for a pen and paper and began to plan the menu for Sunday night. She remembered telling Patti that in the year she lived with David she did almost no cooking. After David's needling criticism, she was looking forward to preparing a dinner for her dad and Martin, who would be appreciative guests. She got up and went over to her collection of cookbooks, looking for her mother's recipe for key lime pie. She was quite sure that this wasn't one of Verna's specialties. Then she jotted down a list of items she could pick up on Sunday at the Davenport Deli. An hour later with the pie in the refrigerator, Alexa had showered and was marking a set of papers. When she heard the doorbell ring, she was overwhelmed by the surge of excitement she felt.

"You're actually out of bed," Mark teased her. "I'm ten minutes early. I thought you'd still be asleep, and I'd have to wait while you showered and dressed." He was carrying a large brown paper bag, but managed to hug her by way of greeting. "I brought coffee and bagels to revive you."

"What service," she teased back. "Something must be upsetting my sleep patterns. I'm usually not a morning person, but today I was up at dawn and astonished myself by being domestic."

Mark laughed. "I guess that means you've had breakfast. I haven't. Do you want to share a bagel with me?"

"Sure," Alexa replied, as Mark sat down at the table and opened the bag. "It's a good thing I've started running again. I don't want to look like a blimp by the end of the semester."

Mark was already spreading cream cheese on a whole wheat bagel. "I'm feeling virtuous this morning," he said grinning, "because I went for a run too. On a school day it's so crazy getting Sarah to her sitter's that there's no time. If I'm really lucky, I get a few minutes to use the weight room at school at the end of the day, or sometimes Sarah and I go back at night. She loves to go to Riverside and explore or she reads or does her homework while I use the treadmill."

"By the way, I was very impressed when I was talking to Sarah last Sunday. I'm sure she's read more books already than many of our students."

"That's probably true. Both Jane and I read to her from the time she was a baby, and as soon as she could talk she had a lot of her favourites memorized. She's got a list of books she wants for her birthday, starting with Jane Austen because she watched *Sense and Sensibility*."

"I didn't read Jane Austen until her novels were assigned in university. I'd say you have a precocious child."

"I know, and it's not always easy. I thought about your suggestion for swimming lessons, and I registered Sarah on Thursday night for the fall session. She's also going to Brownies on Tuesday. That should give her some social life outside of school, and I only have to play chauffeur two nights a week. Speaking of driving ..." He pulled a card from his wallet and handed it to Alexa. "Before I forget, this is my mechanic's number. I called him this morning, and he's going to send one of the guys from the shop to change the tire on your car. You can pick it up after we come back from Picton."

Alexa frowned slightly. She had been wondering which garage she should call, but Mark seemed to think he was in charge. His attitude reminded her of David. She hesitated a moment before taking the card and saying automatically, "Thanks, Mark. I appreciate this."

Mark had made short work of the bagels. "Let's go, kid," he said with a smile. "There may be a line up for the ferry, and I want us to have as much time at the beach as possible."

The September morning was warm and hazy as they drove along the highway which followed the shoreline of the great lake outside town. When they reached the ferry, Alexa felt a childlike excitement. "What is it about this place? Whenever I come here, it feels like an escape from reality."

They drove onto the boat and then got out of the car to stand on the deck leaning over the railing. While the ferry chugged across the Bay of Quinte to Prince Edward County, seagulls swooped overhead uttering their harsh cry. They looked down, watching the dark blue water of the lake churn to milky foam in the wake of the engines.

After the ferry docked, it was a ten-minute drive to the beach. All summer it had been crowded with families, children running through the shallow water and building sandcastles, teenagers throwing frisbees, and lovers walking hand in hand, but on this September morning it was almost deserted except for a family setting up a beach umbrella and unpacking a cooler for a picnic. Two small boys played at the very edge of the water, the younger burying his brother by covering him with pailfuls of white, powdery sand.

Alexa and Mark smiled at each other in delight. "The sun's hot now. Let's change and go for a swim before it gets too cool," Mark suggested.

When he came back, Alexa was already lying on the sand on a large blue beach towel. She was wearing a two-piece yellow bathing suit which covered her full breasts but displayed her slim waist and flat stomach. "This is my idea of heaven," she said.

"And mine! We can imagine we're in the Bahamas or anywhere at least a thousand miles from Riverside. Let's walk to the end of the beach," he said pointing to a clump of trees silhouetted against the horizon, "and then we can go for a swim."

"Good idea."

He reached for her bottle of suntan lotion. "Here, I'll oil your shoulders so you don't burn." Alexa lay motionless on her stomach, as he knelt beside her and began to massage her shoulders, using a gentle, circular motion which sent a quiver down her spine.

"You are good," she purred. "Did you study massage therapy along with mathematics at university?"

Mark stood up. "Thank you, ma'am, just a natural talent," he said with a fake southern accent. "All the ladies tell me that."

"I bet they do. Shall I return the favour?" she asked, retying the straps of her halter top and reaching for the bottle of sunscreen.

"Just my nose," Mark replied seriously. Standing on tiptoe, Alexa dabbed the lotion on his nose and on his forehead for good measure. Standing close like this, it felt as if there were an electric current running between them. Mark looked down at her. "Much more of this, and I won't be able to control myself, ma'am. We'll be arrested for indecent exposure or creating a public spectacle." He was half joking, half serious.

Alexa looked around. The only other people on the beach were totally involved in their own activities. "It might almost be worth it," she said reflectively, but when Mark reached for her, she said, "On second thought, I think we should walk and burn off our excess energy that way."

As they walked along, Alexa reflected that there was something incredibly innocent in playing on a beach. Sometimes they ventured into the water to splash each other and kick up spray. Sometimes they walked at the very edge of the water where the sand formed smooth ridges between their toes. At first they talked about the party and school, but then Alexa turned to him. "I told you part of my story last night. I'd like to hear yours."

Mark looked at her. He knew many attractive women and had met Alexa only a short time before, but with her he felt that he wanted to form an emotional bond. He tried to analyse the reasons for this. She was a highly competent professional, but underneath the polished exterior he sensed a longing and vulnerability which spoke directly to him. Sometimes when she was unaware that he was studying her he had seen a look of sadness in her eyes.

Mark remembered that her mother had died the summer before. Dan and Arlene Corbett had lived in Davenport for years, and most of the town had attended the funeral. He vaguely remembered seeing Alexa then. His memory was that of a beautiful young woman in a simple black dress standing near her father at the reception after the funeral. Had she been with someone? He couldn't remember. He remembered only her face. He had been intensely aware of Alexa ever since he had first seen her in Lisa's office, and these feelings made him vulnerable. How could someone who was almost a stranger have this effect on him? Since his wife had left, he had taken great care not to become involved with anyone. Sarah was a huge responsibility, and he couldn't cope with another desertion. Yet Alexa's violet eyes led him to believe that beneath the laughter and wit there was quite another woman. Like Alexa, he was quick to joke about himself, but he had always found it difficult to put his feelings into words.

Finally he plunged in. "Alexa, I suppose everyone's story is unique, but mine seems pretty ordinary. I've been coaching almost as long as I've been playing sports, and it seemed natural to go into education. I met Jane in my second year at university. She was one of my roommate's high school friends. We hung out with the same crowd. I guess we just gradually drifted together. It was the first serious relationship for both of us, and we married right after graduation. Jane has a degree in fine arts, so she was ecstatic when she was hired as an assistant curator in a small art gallery. I was teaching senior math, and life was good. When Sarah was born, a woman who lived in our apartment building acted as a caregiver, and Jane went back to work right away."

Alexa was listening intently. She sensed that for the first time she was seeing the real Mark, not the efficient administrator known for his quick decision-making and his patient firmness with students.

Mark continued, "As Sarah got older, we kept talking about leaving the city. It was impossible even on our combined salaries to buy a house unless we went to the distant suburbs and commuted for hours every day. The city is fantastic for twenty-something singles, but we didn't want our daughter to grow up calling an apartment home and playing on concrete. Sarah was five when I saw a math position advertised at Riverside. I had almost completed my administrative qualifications, and Lisa told me that the vice-principal in Davenport planned to retire in a year's time. It seemed a perfect solution to our problems. We could afford a house here, and I was in seventh heaven."

He paused and then continued, "I think if I had been less caught up in my career and being a good dad to Sarah, I would have known that the move would be a disaster for Jane. She said she wanted a change, but the truth is that she had always worked in the art world, and there are no opportunities in a small town. After we moved and bought our house, she was busy doing the decorating thing for a while, but then the nesting was completed, and she took a good look at the town."

Mark interrupted himself to ask, "Is this boring?"

Alexa shook her head emphatically. "Not at all."

By now they had reached the far end of the beach, and they sat down side by side on a driftwood log watching the breakers far out in the bay.

Mark went on, "I'll try to make a very long story short. Jane was really disillusioned with Davenport. Sarah and I were both in school all day, and she had time on her hands. She decided to take some photography courses which were being offered at night through the trade school here. I was happy because she was involved in something and stopped complaining. Looking back, I can see that our marriage was falling apart. We lived in the same house, but there was no real sharing or emotional bond except that we both loved Sarah."

With a rueful smile, he added, "I was the proverbial dumb male. She met Peter, the guy she's with now, through her courses. When she told me she was leaving, I was in shock. We didn't have a great relationship, and I knew she wasn't really happy, but we had Sarah, and I hadn't played around. I kept thinking that every marriage has its rocky patches, and things would improve." He shook his head as if still wondering at his own naivety. His face had the vulnerable expression which never failed to move Alexa.

In the silence that followed, she impulsively reached for his hand. "Mark, I'm sorry things turned out that way. Sarah's wonderful, but it can't be easy being a single dad and Mr Vice-Principal."

He held her hand tightly. "I'm beginning to learn that, " he said ironically. "Thanks for listening. It's hard to talk about this. The whole male pride thing gets in the way." He gave her a mock tough guy smile.

As they started to walk back along the sand, Mark put his arm around her. "I didn't plan to bleed all over you this morning. It was going to be a great beach escape, but since we seem to be having true confessions I have a feeling that I'm not the only one walking around with a few personal scars." He looked at her inquiringly.

After a moment, Alexa said, "Mark, maybe we're both naive or at least not very perceptive. In the city, I was involved with a man called David, someone I thought I cared about. We'd been together for almost four years when I went home to be with my mother the summer before she passed away." Alexa could feel tears coming to her eyes, and she blinked rapidly behind her sunglasses as she looked out at the sparkling water. In sympathy, Mark pulled her closer.

"It was a heartbreaking summer. When I went back to the city in September, we decided to live together, and the relationship just fell apart. It's easy for me to blame David who's very controlling, but I was so numb that I avoided confrontations until I couldn't stand the stress any longer and just wanted out. I was able to get a leave from my job and I decided to come back here for a while to be near Dad. My sisters and I are worried about him. After he spent Christmas in Vancouver with my oldest sister, Kate, and her family, she said that he wasn't eating or sleeping." She smiled at Mark. "I think he's doing better now that he's got me around to worry about."

"You're right. Your dad is very discreet, but as soon as we became neighbours, and he told me that his youngest daughter was coming home for a few months I could tell how much it meant to him."

Alexa felt it was time to change the mood. She began to pin her hair up as she said, "Let's go for that swim now." They waded through the shallow water and then swam out beyond the first breakers.

Both were strong swimmers, and for a while they swam parallel to the beach until Mark called to her, "Let's catch a wave." Treading water, they waited for a large wave and used its momentum to body surf back to shallow water. Exhilarated but frozen, Alexa ran for a towel. For the first time the September breeze felt cold.

"That was great!" Mark enthused. "If there's another Saturday like this, we have to bring Sarah here. She'd love it."

Alexa smiled at the word "we."

Mark went to the car for the picnic hamper, and they carried it into the shelter of the dunes where they used an outdoor grill to start a fire. Mark roasted hotdogs and toasted buns while Alexa spread out the rest of the food on a beach mat. Unable to resist the temptation, she bit into a peach and laughed as the juice ran down her chin. "You thought of everything," she said appreciatively when Mark poured chilled white wine into two goblets.

He held one up. "To us," and they raised the glasses to their lips, "and to years of September picnics."

"To us," Alexa murmured.

They were ravenous, but tried to eat slowly, savouring the feast and refilling their glasses. After they were filled with food and wine, they lay side by side on their towels, fingers entwined. They talked of their childhoods and families, of their own high school days and their first teaching experiences. Alexa felt warm and safe. "Mark," she began, "I have to ask you a question. Is there something between you and Julie Chisholm?"

Mark rolled over on his stomach and took both of Alexa's hands in his. "It would be easy to lie about this," he said, "but I can't. I told you that when Jane left I was totally shocked. I joked about it, but a big part of it was male pride, and I felt disillusioned because I thought that we'd made a commitment to each other and to Sarah. I was ready to try again, but she didn't want any part of it. I walked around for days like a zombie, feeling that my whole world had fallen into pieces. Then, as the weeks passed, I began to realize that in some ways things were actually better. Our marriage hadn't been the greatest, and at least Sarah didn't have to live with parents who argued or sulked. She missed Jane, but kids are resilient, and she seemed to settle into the new routine."

Mark paused as he saw the expression on Alexa's face. "I'm not blaming Jane totally. I was certainly part of the problem. I wasn't very sensitive to her needs. Unless we'd moved back to the city, I don't think she would have been happy."

"Julie and I have been friends since I came to Riverside. We coached boys' basketball together, and we both love the game. I'm not proud of this, but last spring we were on a real high when the senior boys won the regional championship. We went out to dinner with the team and their parents to celebrate. Somehow we ended up back at her house and in bed together. Julie's a great person, but I'm not in love with her. I know it's a cliché, but it was just sex."

Mark looked directly at Alexa. "I feel like a real jerk about what happened. It may sound arrogant, but after that Julie seemed to think we had an understanding or something. Finally I told her the truth. That I liked her and hoped we would remain friends, but I didn't want to continue the relationship she thought we were beginning. I didn't see her all summer. Then last weekend she came over on Sunday night, and we put together a coaching sche 'ule for this year." For the first time he laughed. "Sarah doesn't like her, and I think the feeling is mutual, so I wasn't fighting her off at the kitchen table or anything like that."

Alexa unconsciously let out her breath.

Mark leaned over and kissed her. For Alexa his mouth worked the same magic as it had the night before, but it was a gentle kiss with only a hint of passion. Then Mark spoke seriously. "Alexa, I don't sleep with every woman on staff if that's what's bothering you. And I don't go around saying 'I love you' to a woman because I spent the night with her. I've never talked as openly with anyone as I have with you today.

We've both been through a lot of changes in our lives. Let's take the time to get to know each other."

"Maybe I just wonder how any man could resist Julie. She's gorgeous."

"At the risk of making you suspicious, I agree. Julie's a very attractive woman, but that's all. Now it's my turn. I couldn't help noticing last night that you had a huge bouquet of yellow roses in your living room. I assume you have an admirer, unless Martin or Dan believes in extravagant gestures."

"Touché" Alexa said. "An old friend from high school brought me those last weekend when we had dinner together. Now it's my turn to say that he's attractive and rich," she added mischievously, "but that chapter of my life is over."

"Good," said Mark smiling, "I was hoping that you'd be willing to spend some time with a poor teacher."

After their day together, Alexa felt very close to Mark. She wanted to get to know every part of him, but she said lightly, "I'll check my social calendar. I think we can arrange that." In spite of the shirt which she wore over her bathing suit, Alexa was shivering.

Mark reached for her, his breath warm against her face, his lips searching. They kissed deeply, and Alexa relaxed against him. Just as quickly he pulled back. "It's getting cool now. Let's go into Picton and explore before we have to catch the ferry back to reality."

In the old village he parked the car, and they strolled past the century-old houses with their elaborate gardens and wraparound verandas. They went into Noah's Ark where Alexa bought a wonderful set of exotic animals for Nicholas and Cheyenne. Mark exclaimed over the intricate olive wood carvings.

After they stopped at The Brown Bear and ordered cappuccinos, Mark excused himself to make a call on his cell phone to his sister. He returned smiling. "Why do I worry? Sarah's in her element on the farm. Jo and Ray will bring her home tomorrow. Alexa, let's go to the farmers' market and pick up some things for dinner. Then come back to my place. I'd love to cook for you tonight."

Alexa hesitated for a moment. "Do you have other plans?" Mark asked.

"No, I was just thinking of all the marking I should do this weekend, and tomorrow I've invited Dad and Martin for a Thai dinner."

"If that's the only problem, I have a solution. We'll stop by Lisa's house, and you can pick up your car. You can get some marking at your apartment. I'll build a fire in the fireplace, and let you get some work done while I cook."

"You're too good to be true."

"I'm glad you think so, but remember I spent years in the classroom. It's not always easy cramming marking into every weekend and trying to have a life too."

At the outdoor market they shopped for cider, fresh fruit and vegetables, crusty homemade bread and sausage. As they stood on the deck of the ferry with Mark's arm around her shoulders, Alexa said softly, "Thanks for a perfect day."

"I want it to be the first of many, and it's not over yet. Sarah says I cook better than her mother. I'll try to live up to my reputation as Mr Mom."

At Mark's house, Alexa sat in front of the blazing fire, trying to concentrate on a stack of essays. Mark had refused all offers of help in the kitchen. "Don't interrupt the Galloping Gourmet," he teased. "A masterpiece requires concentration."

When the pungent odour of garlic and spices became too enticing to ignore, Alexa went into the kitchen. Wrapped in a chef's apron, Mark was stirring a bubbling pot of spaghetti sauce and chopping apples and pecans for a salad.

"It smells wonderful," Alexa said. "How long before we eat?"

Mark handed her a mug of hot cider. "Back to work, Miss Corbett. Dinner won't be ready for a while, but lunch was hours away. Have a bread stick if you're hungry." Then he whispered in her ear, "What's really attracting you, the cook or the food?"

"The food, of course," Alexa said demurely, retreating to the living room where she tried to concentrate on a particularly dismal piece of student writing. Away from Mark's magnetic presence, she was aware of a small voice in the depths of her subconscious. *You've had a fab day, but you hardly know this man, and his teaching philosophy couldn't be more different from yours. Will you even see him again when your contract ends? You just escaped from one dead-end relationship. Surely you learned something from that?* Resolutely, Alexa silenced the voice. It was a day out of time and a magical one.

When they finally sat down to eat, she decided to concentrate on the food. She sampled the dishes and smiled at Mark. "You are a good cook. The salad's wonderful and the sauce is to die for." As Mark poured her a glass of red wine, she protested, "No more. I usually drink a glass of wine a month. This could become a habit."

"It's supposed to be good for the heart, and guaranteed to help you relax after all that marking." Over dinner they talked about their first cooking experiments. Mark laughed when Alexa described the meals which she and Patti used to make in university. "I know what you mean about trying to impress a date when you can't cook. Once my roommate, Paul Davidson, tried to roast the contents of a can of Spam for his girl friend. He had no idea what he was doing. He thought Spam was some type of exotic spiced ham – and I suppose it is."

"Patti wasn't the only bad cook. I remember trying to make a lemon meringue pie. The filling looked like some type of yellow glue. Patti said it reminded her of wallpaper paste. We ended up putting it into parfait glasses and trying to hide it with whipped cream! I wonder why we didn't just throw it out and run down to the bake shop."

"Speaking of desserts, " Mark said, "I don't even pretend to bake, but Sarah loves chocolate éclairs, and we have some in the freezer. Would you like one?"

Alexa absolutely refused, but watched with admiration as Mark polished off two with coffee. "How do you do it and never gain a pound?"

"It must be all that running around at school, and then there's basketball. I work as hard as the boys when we're on the court."

As they carried the plates into the kitchen, Alexa tried to turn the conversation to school. "Justin Murray's really impressed me this semester. He can actually write, and we have intelligent conversations about the books he's reading. I know you don't believe in second chances, but perhaps you should revise your opinion of him."

For just a moment, Mark looked annoyed, but he refused to take the bait. "I don't know what you mean by second chances. We gave him more chances than I can count last year, and he persisted in doing his own thing." Seeing the look on Alexa's face, he hesitated and then went on. "I know his home situation isn't the greatest, but that excuse only takes you so far. At some point he's got to become responsible for his own actions." He made a deliberate effort to be fair. "He does seem to be trying harder this year. Maybe it's your influence."

While Alexa wondered if he was trying to flatter her, Mark put his arms around her. "Why are we talking about Justin right now? There's a full moon tonight. Let's go out and moon gaze." Unable to resist, Alexa let him lead her outside and soon they were stretched out side by side in two deck chairs on Mark's small patio. A huge harvest moon hung in the sky, flooding the lawn and garden with its light. Alexa felt happier than she had in months. They lay quietly for a long while, and then Mark reached for her hand. "The next few weeks will be really busy at school, and the weekends won't be much better. There's basketball, and I have to spend time with Sarah until she gets settled in school."

Alexa swallowed hard. "Mark, I understand completely. You don't have to explain. I know there's really no time for us to be together. You don't have to say anything more."

If Alexa had known Mark better, she would have seen his face change. He had what his sister, Joanne, called "a stubborn streak a mile wide." Now his chin jutted out slightly, and a frown line appeared. Without letting go of her hand, he sat up and swung around so that he was sitting on the edge of his deck chair looking at Alexa. " I know I've got two strikes against me." Before she could interrupt, he went on, "First of all, I'm a parent trying to fly solo."

This time, she did interrupt. "I told you I like Sarah. Not because she's your daughter, but because she's a neat kid. She's terribly serious and funny all at the same time."

"I know. Sarah's my daughter, and I love her. But you saw her that Saturday at your dad's. She's become my velcro child since Jane left. She's at my heels every minute, and she throws daggers at any woman I talk to. It's easy for me to say, 'Don't take it personally,' but most women would find it difficult after a while."

"Am I 'most women?'" Alexa asked.

Mark shook his head. "No, you're not, and this isn't coming out the way I want it to. I know Sarah likes you. She keeps talking about your apartment. She was very impressed that you had worked in Thailand. Alexa, I love her, but I'm trying to warn you that she can be demanding. Our family doctor is setting up some sessions for Sarah with a counsellor. I don't want her to be traumatized by her mother leaving, and it's hard for me to know when she's really hurting and when she's just trying to manipulate me." He smiled. "I should have studied psychology in university, not math and computers."

"It sounds as if she's a typical kid. Okay, I've been warned about Sarah. You said you had two strikes against you. What's the second?"

Mark took a deep breath. "This isn't easy to put into words, but I just have a feeling that you're not too comfortable with the idea that I'm vice-principal at Riverside, and you're on staff. I know I came on too strong the first day of school, but I'd even ask for a transfer to another school if that would make you want to spend time with me."

Alexa answered honestly, "Mark, I guess the vice-principal thing is a bit of a hangup for me. Today's been idyllic, yet I can't help thinking that on Monday we're back to 'Mr Anderson' and 'Miss Corbett.'" She hesitated, searching for the right words. "But the truth is that I would probably still be hung up if you were the local bank manager. I had a bad experience in high school when I felt the eyes of the town gossips were on me. It turned me off small towns and getting too friendly with anyone here. Probably that's one reason why I chose to teach in the city."

There was a very long silence. Mark wondered again why he felt so drawn to Alexa in such a short time. He thought of Julie. It was easy to have a casual relationship with an attractive woman and share a bed with her, but that was not what he wanted. "I wish I could remake the world for you," he said softly. "People will always gossip, but we've got nothing to hide. We're both dedicated professionals. That doesn't mean we can't have a life outside school." He brought the palm of Alexa's hand to his lips and kissed it softly.

"You're beautiful, and this has been a wonderful day. I told you that I don't talk easily about my feelings, but with you it's been different. I'd love to have you stay with me tonight, but I'm not going to ask you. I want us to get to know each other first. We have a lot of time. Let's not rush things." He stopped again, "I'm hoping that you do want to see me outside of school."

When Alexa nodded, not trusting herself to speak, he bent over her. They kissed for a long time, his mouth first soft, then firmer, his tongue making her body turn to liquid fire. At last he pulled her up. "Let's go inside. It's cold out here."

They sat in front of the dying fire with Alexa's head on Mark's shoulder. Mark said softly, "This is perfect." He brushed back her long hair and traced the outline of her cheek and mouth. Slipping his arm around her waist he drew her to him, and they kissed hungrily while he murmured endearments.

At last Alexa drew back. "Thanks for today. You really spoiled me. I could get used to it so quickly."

"That's the idea. There *are* some good things in small towns."

"I hate to break the spell, but I can feel reality calling. It's getting late, and I've got guests for dinner tomorrow night. Will you and Sarah come too?"

Mark thought for a moment. "I hate to say no. I'd love to spend the evening with you, and Dan and Martin, but Sarah's going to be tired when she gets home. I think she needs an early night if she's going to cope with school on Monday. Alexa, I know you've got things to do on Sunday, and I need to go into the school and deal with some attendance problems before I meet Sarah and Jo. I'll call you on Sunday night, and you can fill me in on the dinner party."

"That sounds like a plan," Alexa agreed. "I told you that next Saturday I'm going to visit my friends, Patti and Chris, and their kids. The munchkins are both younger than Sarah, and she might enjoy them. Would you like to come? Chris is an easy going guy. You two will have something in common."

Mark pulled her close. "I'd love to, and thanks for including Sarah. She needs to be around other kids."

Mark insisted on walking Alexa home. "We could cut through Dad's garden," she joked. When she unlocked the apartment door, he reached for her and drew her into his arms, drinking in the essential woman-scent of her. Her lips were a teasing combination of softness and hidden passion. With an effort, he released her. "I'll call you Sunday night," he promised.

Mark walked home slowly along the street, dark except for the occasional streetlight. He had felt an instant physical response to Alexa. It would have been so easy to spend the night together, but then what? A sixth sense told him that he would have possessed her body but not the essential woman. She was worth waiting for. He promised himself that on Sunday he would look at the second semester timetables. Even if Murray Dean came back, there must be some classes available to keep Alexa at Riverside. He'd talk to Lisa about it on Monday.

CHAPTER ELEVEN

❧

*T*he next morning Alexa dressed casually. She was going out to the deli so she could get an early start on dinner. When the doorbell rang, she smiled, wondering if Mark had decided to bring breakfast again. She opened the door to find David McBirney standing outside. Alexa's hand went to her mouth. For just an instance the old attraction surfaced. He looked exactly the same, the silver hair carefully brushed back and the cool grey eyes assessing her, taking in her sweat pants, the oversize T-shirt and running shoes.

"Going to the gym?" he asked.

"David, what are you doing here?"

"I could ask you the same thing," he replied.

A wave of emotions swept through Alexa. First, there was anger and annoyance that he felt he could drop in like this, but she also felt a knot of apprehension in the pit of her stomach. David was quite capable of making a scene. She had no time for his theatrics.

"I live here," she said calmly.

"Alone?"

Alexa stared at him, not giving him the satisfaction of a reply.

He took silence for consent. "Your feminist friends would be proud of you for upholding the sisterhood."

Again there was silence.

"Aren't you going to invite me in?"

"I'm not dressed for guests."

"I don't think I qualify as a guest."

Alexa thought quickly. David never made scenes in public. She checked to make sure she had her keys and wallet with her. Then shutting the door behind her, she said, "I'm going out. Do you want to join me for breakfast before you leave?"

A wave of anger crossed David's face. He shrugged. "Where are you going?"

"There's a coffee shop a block away. I'm going there before I meet some friends."

The two walked along without speaking. Then David broke the silence, "I think I deserve an explanation. You simply left. Why didn't you talk to me if you were so unhappy?"

"I left because it was the right thing to do."

"Come on, Alexa, I want the truth. Was there someone else?"

"The truth is that I'd simply had enough – of everything, of a relationship which wasn't going anywhere."

A tiny muscle twitched in David's cheek. "And where did you want it to go?"

Alexa was tight lipped. When they reached Coffee and Company, she went in first, calling out a greeting to Costa Apostolova, the owner.

"Hi, Alexa, " he called back from behind the counter. "We don't usually see you on Sunday. I see you brought a friend. Sit anywhere you like. The menus are on the table. Coffee now?"

"Two coffees would be great."

Alexa chose a booth in the far corner. She sensed that David was gritting his teeth and trying to keep his temper under control. When Costa brought coffee, she ordered a bran muffin and blackberry jam.

"Nothing thanks, I've eaten " David muttered.

"Sure? The muffins are all fresh." Costa waited, pen in hand.

David shook his head.

When they were alone again, he looked at Alexa. "I thought you were happy. You had a career which you said you enjoyed. You had friends. We had a beautiful apartment and, I thought, a very satisfying life."

"David, it wasn't working for me. I wasn't happy."

David was obviously trying to control himself. His jaw was clenched. "Alexa, I know you were upset after your mother died and you were worried about your father, but that was a year ago."

"I wanted something different. I needed a change."

"Was it the biological clock ticking away? Did you come back here," he looked around the tiny restaurant with something of a sneer, "hoping to meet a man and have a baby? Is that what this is about?"

Now it was Alexa who was angry although she chose not to reveal it. "No, that's *not* 'what this is about'. I don't expect you to understand. The only thing we ever promised each other is that we would not get involved with anyone else while we were living together. I kept my promise."

She looked up as Costa brought her muffin. "Thanks, Costa, this looks wonderful."

"More coffee?" he asked. They both shook their heads.

Alexa deliberately cut the muffin in two and began to spread one half with blackberry jam. She wasn't hungry, but she wasn't going to let David see that he had ruined her appetite.

He resumed the conversation, pursuing her last remark. "And should I understand that you are involved with someone else now that you've left?"

She shook her head suddenly tired of the whole scene. "I'm sorry you had to drive all the way up here for nothing."

"You're keen to get rid of me, aren't you?"

"I told you I have things to do. I'm meeting some friends. It was good of you to come, but there's nothing more to say."

"I have a great deal more to say. For a start, I've missed you, and I was worried about you. You didn't even leave a forwarding address. I pictured all kinds of things which might have happened if you were depressed or upset."

Alexa wasn't going to give David the satisfaction of asking how he got her address and telephone number. It would have been easy for him to use some pretext and charm one of the secretaries at her previous school. "Well, as you can see, nothing did happen to me. I'm well and happy."

David tried a new approach. "Alexa, I can't believe you're happy here. You love shopping, going out for dinner and seeing films. What do you do in Davenport? Rent videos? It doesn't even have a cinema."

"Actually I haven't had a lot of time for films. I have a contract at the local school and that's keeping me very busy."

"You always told me that Davenport was a fish bowl. How can you live here?"

"Very easily." By now Alexa had finished her muffin. She folded her napkin neatly in two. "David, I don't expect you to understand. Our relationship is over. Thanks for your concern, but I have to leave now."

They both got up. David's hands were balled fists deep in his pockets. "It's not over, Alexa, no matter what you think now." He threw some money on the table and walked to the door. Without looking back at her, he was gone.

Alexa exhaled sharply. If she had been alone, she would have dissolved in tears, but with a supreme effort, she went over to the counter where Costa was making a pot of fresh coffee. His eyes were sympathetic. There was one other couple in the tiny restaurant, and he spoke softly, "Are you okay, Alexa?"

She nodded, trying to smile, but not trusting herself to speak. She walked slowly back to her apartment. There was no sign of David's car. Drawing another deep breath, she unlocked her car and scanned her grocery list. It swam before her eyes as tears ran down her cheeks. She leaned back in the seat and allowed herself to cry. At last, she blew her nose, wiped her eyes and checked her appearance in the mirror before turning the key in the ignition. She felt as if she were suffocating. David always had to have the last word, but no matter what he said it was over. She had handled the scene without running away, and she wasn't going to let it ruin her weekend. It was time to go to the deli and then begin to cook.

Alexa was busy chopping vegetables for the chicken curry and pad thai when the telephone rang. She fought a momentary panic, but it was her dad. "Hi, sweetheart, I tried to call you yesterday, but you were out, and I didn't leave a message. How was your staff party?"

"The best!" Alexa replied. "Are we still on for tonight? I invited Martin as well. This apartment's wonderful, and I had dinner with him one night last week when I was feeling down."

"Martin's a good guy," her father agreed. He hesitated for a moment. "Alexa, I wondered if I could bring a guest."

"Of course, I'll have lots of food. Anyone at all, as long as it's not Verna, " she added quickly.

"It's Heather Robinson. I don't think you ever met her, but Heather and I went through law school together, and we've kept in touch over the years. She's staying here at the Travellers Inn tonight getting ready to interview a key witness in a case she's involved with. I thought she'd appreciate a change of scene from the four walls of a hotel room."

"Sure, bring her along and come over whenever you like. I told Martin we'd eat about six thirty."

While she cooked, Alexa forced herself to concentrate on the preparations. She smiled thinking that her father had actually sounded shy and a little embarrassed when he spoke about Heather. She wondered if they were more than friends. Her parents had been so perfect together that she couldn't imagine her father spending the rest of his life alone. She wanted him to be happy.

When her father and Heather arrived, Alexa immediately felt comfortable. Heather was a humorous silver-haired lady with a youthful face and figure dressed casually in a denim jacket and pants with a bright scarf tucked into the open neck of her shirt. She immediately took off her jacket, found an apron and began to help Alexa by stirfrying vegetables, leaving Dan to open the wine they had brought.

"Alexa, this is wonderful! It was so kind of you to invite me too," Heather said. "I wasn't looking forward to the standard roast beef and mashed potatoes in the hotel dining room, so I jumped at the chance to get out when Dan called. I can bone up on the case tonight," she added.

Alexa studied Heather and her father as they laughed together over a picture of Dan and his three daughters on Alexa's desk. "I can remember when you looked even younger than that," she teased. She looked at Alexa. "Did you know that your dad was considered the flashiest dresser in our class? I remember that he wore a pink tuxedo jacket to our graduating ball, and your mother wore a pale pink gown. They were a smashing pair."

Alexa learned that Heather had two daughters: Jan, who was also a lawyer, and Shawna, who was teaching in Malaysia. The previous Christmas Heather and Shawna had spent the holidays together by meeting in Thailand.

"Shawna loves to scuba dive," Heather told her. "We were going to spend a few days at Pattaya Beach, and I thought I'd surprise her by taking a scuba diving course before I left. I'm sure the instructor thought I was mad. I was the only grandmother in a class of teenagers or twenty-something young people. At least I learned enough to get over my fear of deep water. In Thailand I mostly snorkled and hunted for shells, and the water was beautiful, so blue and clear. It was the first Christmas since my husband's death, and I kept wishing Jamie had been with us. He would have loved the trip."

Both Dan and Martin were lavish in their praise of the food. "This is delicious," Martin said, helping himself to another serving of noodles. "And you're absolutely radiant. I'm glad that you recovered from your blue Monday."

After dinner the men volunteered to do kitchen duty while Alexa and Heather talked over tea. "Davenport's a pretty town," Heather said wistfully. "It's such a change from the city. Your father invited me over to his house this afternoon, and we swam and sat by the pool for a while. I met his neighbour, Verna Murphy."

Alexa decided to be charitable. "Yes, she's taken good care of Dad in the last year. He must have a freezer full of dinners she's brought over."

Heather smiled. "I think she was checking me out. She'd make a good Crown Attorney. With more time, she'd have learned my whole life story." The two women's eyes met in mutual understanding.

"There's not a lot to do in small towns," Alexa said, almost apologetically. "Verna worked as a teller in the bank, but she's been retired for several years now and seems to spend most of her time working in her garden and cooking for Dad. She brings out the worst in me, but he's more tolerant. He makes her feel important by appreciating everything she brings over."

"That's typical of Dan." Heather hesitated. "Alexa, your father and I are just good friends. He's still grieving over Arlene, and I can't seem to accept the fact that Jamie's gone."

"I'm glad he has you to talk with. My sisters and I have been worried about him."

Before going to bed, Alexa reorganized her briefcase for Monday, checking to see that she had put in the marked assignments. She was propped up on her pillows reading when Mark called. "It's been quite a day," she began, resisting the impulse to tell him about David's unexpected appearance.

"I found today so long. I kept thinking about what you were doing and wishing Sarah and I were coming for dinner."

"I was hoping to see her this weekend." Then Alexa described Heather. "I liked her a lot. She's friendly and down to earth. Dad was in such a good mood. It would be great if eventually they become more than friends."

"You're turning into a matchmaker! Your father strikes me as someone who will make his own decisions although it wouldn't hurt if you and your sisters added the seal of approval to his friend."

"Tanya would probably be shocked if she knew that Dad had even looked at another woman. She's the conservative one, but Katie and I would be turning cartwheels just to see him be more like his old self."

"Give him time."

"How's Sarah after her visit to the farm?"

"So far so good. This is the first Sunday night she's gone to sleep without crying about school. She had a wonderful weekend being spoiled by Jo and Ray and her cousins."

"I'm glad! Tell her about next weekend with Patti's kids. She'll have something she can look forward to."

"She'll want to know if they have any animals."

"All kinds. The last time I was there they had two dogs and more cats than I could count, as well as rabbits, and I think there was a goat."

"That's Sarah's idea of heaven."

As they said good night, Mark said softly, "Get some sleep, Alexa. Monday is always a busy day."

Alexa tried to fall asleep, but her thoughts were full of the day's events. Why had David come? She didn't feel that he was dangerous, but he had certainly been angry. He loved control and he had lost it.

When at last she slept, her dreams were a jumble of images. She and David sat in a restaurant while Mark watched them from a doorway. She slept lightly and was wide awake as soon as the announcer's voice on her clock radio shattered the stillness of the bedroom.

When she arrived at school, she checked her mailbox in the staff room and headed up to the classroom. As soon as she came through the doors at the top of the stairs, she could see Dara standing by the lockers with Ben Copeland a few feet away. When he heard the sound of footsteps, Ben turned around quickly and strode down the hall and out of sight. Dara remained, ashen-faced, clutching something in her hand. Alexa hurried towards her. After a quick glance at Dara's face, she dropped her briefcase and unlocked the classroom door. "Come into my room, Dara," she invited. Without speaking, head down, Dara followed her and collapsed into a desk, drawing her knees up and hiding her face. Her shoulders were shaking, and Alexa could hear the sobs wrenching her body. "Please talk to me, " she begged, "or should I call Mrs Fitzgerald?"

To Alexa's relief, Dara finally looked up, reaching for a wad of

Kleenex from the box on Alexa's desk. After a few moments, she took a long shuddering breath. "Last week something really horrible happened," she said between sobs. "I stayed after school one night to work in the library on our major history essay, and when I got back to the senior locker bank there was something lying on the floor. I picked it up." For the first time her cheeks had some colour as she continued, "It was a totally gross photo of Stacey Sawyer. She was lying on a bed without any clothes." She gulped, her eyes meeting Alexa's for the first time.

"Oh, Dara, what did you do?"

"The next day I brought an envelope from home and I put the picture in the envelope and gave it to Stacey. I just said, 'I found this on the hall floor.'"

Alexa understood how hard this must have been for Dara. "Did Stacey say anything?"

"No, she just gave me a dirty look and put it in her locker."

While Alexa was wondering what support she could offer, Dara's eyes filled up again. "I didn't say anything else to her. I just wanted to forget it, and I didn't want her to be mad at me, but this morning Ben was at his locker when I got to school. I started to get out my books and just ignored him, but he came over and sort of smiled. He said, "I heard you liked the picture I took of Stacey. Here's another one. Why don't you come over to my place some time? I've got lots of others.'" Dara was crying hard again.

Alexa could not restrain herself. "What a smartass," she said before she could stop herself. "You don't have to put up with this, Dara. Let me speak to Mr Anderson."

Dara shook her head vehemently. "No, I don't want him or anyone else to know. Promise me you won't say anything to him. I can't survive here if I rat people out. But I don't want any more of this filth." She flung what she had been holding to the floor. Alexa bent to pick it up. It was another photo of Stacey. This time she was lying on her stomach across a bed. She wore only a black thong, and she was pouting seductively at the camera.

Alexa hesitated for only a second. "You're right. It is filth, and you don't need to deal with this. If you don't want to talk to Mr Anderson, I'm going to make you an appointment with Mrs Fitzgerald. Maybe she can see you today. We have English right after lunch, and you can certainly miss that class. I won't tell her what it's about, but you must promise me that you'll talk to her."

Dara nodded, struggling for control once more.

"Why don't you stay here until the first bell goes? I'll go down to guidance now and see if Mrs Fitzgerald's around." Alexa almost ran downstairs. Already the reception area of the guidance offices was full of students waiting for appointments and reading the notices on the bulletin board. Kelly, still wearing her coat, was talking to a tall serious looking boy. After a few minutes, she beckoned Alexa into the tiny cubicle which was her office.

"I won't keep you," said Alexa. "This place is a madhouse. I just wanted to tell you that I'm seriously concerned about Dara. I saw her as soon as I got here this morning being harassed by Ben Copeland. She doesn't want to speak to Mark, but she said she'd talk with you. Do you have time this morning or right after lunch?"

"I wish I did, but I'm already late for a guidance heads' meeting at the board office. I can see her tomorrow," she added quickly seeing the stricken expression on Alexa's face. "The seniors are beginning to panic about university deadlines, and I'm booked solid, but I'll squeeze her in somehow."

Alexa tried to pull herself together. "That should be fine. I can see you're frantic. Dara talked to me a little, but I'd like you to speak with her as well."

"Not to worry. I'll do my best, and if I don't get anywhere, I'll persuade Dara to confess to Father Mark " Kelly quipped. "By the way, I've been meaning to tell you that you've been looking fantastic. I'm glad the stress of the job isn't doing a number on you."

Alexa left the office wondering if she should go to Mark, but she hated to betray Dara's confidence. She convinced herself that things would be okay for just one day. When Dara arrived for English, she told her that Mrs Fitzgerald would see her as soon as possible on Tuesday. Dara looked exhausted, and Alexa found herself adding, "Why don't you go down to the library this period? We're just reviewing for our novel test, and I'll give you the handouts." At least Dara could avoid Stacey for one period.

After school Alexa procrastinated about starting a mountain of marking by going down to the staffroom for coffee. On the way she stopped at the office to hand in her attendance sheets. Mark was behind the counter talking to two students, but he gestured for her to go into his office. After a moment he arrived and closed the door. "Don't look at my desk, " he begged. "I'm swimming in paper. Not my strong suit." He paused to look at her longingly. "And I'm going a little crazy." He pointed to his large office window. On the other side of the glass, Susan Johnson was calmly dealing with the latest student crisis. "I wonder what Susan would say if she looked up and saw me kissing you. Would she run screaming to your rescue or suggest that I buy a window blind?"

Alexa tried not to laugh. "It's not fun, is it? When I saw you in the cafeteria at noon you looked as if you were going toe to toe with Shawn Bethune, one of my Pathways kids."

Mark groaned. "I think Shawn's turning into another Justin Murray. And the worst part is that I don't even have time to talk to you now. I'm due at Sarah's school for a teacher interview in fifteen minutes. I called Jane and asked her to come too."

His face brightened. "This morning Lisa reminded me that tomorrow night we have a school council meeting. Usually we're ready to go out for a stiff drink when we get out of there, but it means I'll have a babysitter for Sarah. Could I drop in for a late night visit?"

Alexa replied with mock seriousness, "Certainly, Mr Anderson. No matter how late it is I'd love to be briefed on the educational issues which concerned our school council and I might even offer you a cup of strong tea."

"All I'll want is a little sympathy." Mark picked up his briefcase and looked at his desk. "The paper will have to wait until tomorrow."

In the staffroom Buzz Spencer and Phil Maloney, the history head, were having coffee at one of the tables. "Alexa!" Buzz greeted her. "Come and join us. How was Monday?"

"Good, I think the kids were still comatose from the weekend, and things were surprisingly quiet."

"I noticed that too, " Phil commented. "My main problem is getting my North American history students to open their mouths. I feel like an entertainer. They want me to turn on the VCR every period and plug in a documentary. It doesn't exactly lead to stimulating discussions."

"This year's seniors are not the sharpest knives in the drawer," Buzz agreed, "but today I turned them loose with their first dissection, and they all managed to stay awake. That's progress. If I use chalk and talk, their eyes glaze over."

Alexa laughed. "Jim Callaghan cornered me at lunch today, and I agreed to chaperone the school dance on Friday night. You two gentlemen can tell me what I let myself in for."

"You'll be in good company," Phil said. "Our student council president made the rounds, and I think most of the heads and the administration will be out in full force. It's a long night, but not too hard. Lisa insists that the student council hire two off-duty police officers who work the door and pick up anyone under the influence of drugs or alcohol. The teachers circulate and watch for trouble spots. It's pretty tame. Last year a group of kids tried to come in the cafeteria windows without paying. Just the typical run of the mill nonsense."

"I always sign up for the first video dance," Buzz added. "Most of the kids are completely mesmerized by the big screens. I can't stand the music, so I pick up some earplugs and use them when it's my turn to supervise in the gym."

Phil nodded. "You're right. This is the best dance to supervise. I remember two years ago the student council brought in a punk group. The kids got so hyped up that Mark and I spent the whole evening separating groups who were trying to mosh. At one point I had two kids lifted right off the ground, trying to keep them from bashing their heads together. I'm too old for that, not to mention that some kid could decide that I was assaulting him and try to charge me. Now we have video dances, and if the kids get too crazy, the music is turned off, or the DJ switches to a slow number. That clears the floor in a hurry."

"You two are the greatest. I've filed all this information away, so I won't feel like a rookie. It sounds do-able. At my last school things got so out of control with gang fights and kids from other schools crashing our events that we virtually banned dances. There's not a lot to do in Davenport on Friday nights, at least until the hockey season starts, so this keeps the kids off the streets and in a safe place."

That evening Alexa decided to call Joy. Several weeks had passed since they met at the Blue Anchor, and she had been wondering if her friend had found work. Joy picked up her cell on the second ring. "Alexa, I planned to call you this week! I've got so much to tell you."

Alexa could tell from Joy's voice that things were going well. The two spoke quickly, their sentences overlapping as they caught up on the news. "I just signed a six-month contract," Joy said, "but it could become a permanent position. It's with a not-for-profit housing corporation that does most of its work with single moms and their families. They were looking for someone to work as a counsellor and co-ordinate programs in health and wellness. It's exactly what I wanted and builds on the kind of work I did at Interval House. They just offered me the contract this afternoon, and I'm still six feet off the ground. And how is Riverside? Are you surviving September?"

"What a wonderful chance for you! And I'm more than surviving." Quickly Alexa described her classes and some of the staff. She added, "I've decided you were right about Mark Anderson. He's a good vice-principal and totally involved with the school."

"I know. When I worked with him, he seemed really sensitive to the issues some of the girls were facing."

Alexa reflected that this was high praise coming from Joy. She found herself telling her about the scene with David on Sunday. "I got through it, but when I finally got back to my car I just let it all out and cried."

Joy sounded sympathetic. "I'd say that's a normal reaction. It sounds as if you handled it very well. Just don't be surprised if he contacts you again. I'm always amazed that otherwise intelligent males can't seem to comprehend the word 'no.' If you think David's harassing you, be sure to talk to your father. He's in a great position to advise you."

"Joy, I've really missed you. Once you get settled, let's get together one weekend. I need to get into the city. Each time I buy a weekend paper and see the theatre that's on I'm desperate to get away. Maybe I can pry Patti loose from her munchkins, and she'll come too."

"That would be fabulous. It's been a long time since the three mouseketeers were together. I'm apartment hunting tomorrow," Joy told her, "but I'll call you as soon as that's over. Have you seen *Mamma Mia*?"

"No, that would be perfect. I need a 'feel good' girls' only evening." They hung up after Joy promised to contact Alexa before the weekend.

When Mark called that night, he was apologetic. "Alexa, I don't like this at all. I wish we had more time to spend together. This afternoon I felt that I was just shoving you aside. Today was such a rat race."

"Don't worry. I understood completely. How was the interview with Sarah's teacher?"

"Quite good, actually. Jane didn't show up, but I got a lot of information. Mrs.Bennett thinks Sarah is doing better this week. She knows that Sarah's bored silly by the language arts program and finishes all her work quickly. We decided that when her assignments are done she can go to the library to work on some independent projects. Mrs Bennett also suggested that the kindergarten teacher would love an extra pair of hands. Sarah can help with reading circle or recess."

"That's perfect! She'll enjoy the younger kids, and it would be a good motivator to do something she likes when she finishes her work."

"Thanks for taking an interest. It's more than her mother's doing right now. Sarah's basically a good kid, but she stresses easily," he broke off. "I'm already thinking about tomorrow night. Courtney Adams, one of our senior students, is coming over to babysit. Sarah thinks she's pretty neat, so we can have a few minutes together after the meeting."

"Now it's my turn to say 'take it easy.' See how late it is when the school council finishes its meeting. If you want to go straight home, that's okay. We'll have Saturday together."

"Not a chance. Seeing you will be the only thing that keeps me sane!"

On Tuesday night Alexa drove home wondering what she could have for dinner that would be quick and easy to prepare. When she signalled to turn onto Bridge Street, she automatically looked in the rear view mirror. Directly behind her was David's familiar black Audi. She blinked in disbelief. It was definitely David at the wheel.

As the familiar knot of tension formed in her stomach, Alexa slowed down. She felt a surge of anger. If David wanted to talk to her again, she'd be happy to oblige, but it was going to be in a very public place. She drove along Bridge Street almost at a crawl and turned into Martin's driveway. David's car was nowhere in sight. She was sure he had been right behind her. What was going on, and why was he stalking her?

Taking her briefcase out of the car, she walked over to chat with Martin who was deadheading some roses. Minutes passed, but there was still no sign of David. By now Alexa's stomach was churning. She said goodbye to Martin and went up to her apartment. While she changed into jeans and a pullover, she expected the doorbell to ring at any moment. Unable to stand the tension any longer, Alexa knew she had to leave. Picking up her keys, she shut the door and almost flew down the stairs. Before she knew it, she was knocking at her dad's back door.

"Alexa, this is a surprise! I was coming over to see you tonight. Have you eaten yet? We have a good selection in the freezer," he added with a smile.

Alexa hugged her father and picked up Robbie who was barking hysterically. She felt about sixteen again as she blurted out, "I have to talk to you, Dad!" She told him the whole story of David's unannounced Sunday morning visit and their conversation. "And on my way home I saw his car behind me on Dundas Street. He was wearing dark glasses, but I know it was him. I must have freaked out because when I turned onto Bridge and looked again the car was gone. Is he stalking me or something? I can't take much more of this."

Dan Corbett let her talk. When she had unwound, he said, "Alexa, I'm speaking strictly as your dad, not as a lawyer. This morning David called and made an appointment to see me at the office at three o'clock. If we had discussed legal issues, I couldn't have this conversation with you because of confidentiality, but it was strictly personal."

Alexa nodded. "What did he want?"

"At first I couldn't tell. The conversation didn't seem to be going anywhere. He asked about you and wanted to know if I thought you were well. Finally he asked why you had come back to Davenport. Naturally I said that he should discuss that with you."

"This is too weird. Why can't he just admit our relationship is over and bow out gracefully?"

"I don't know, but try to see it from his point of view," Dan said, as he had so often to his daughter when she was distressed. "David's had a charmed life. He's brilliant and he's used to getting what he wants and receiving accolades from his students. In his own way he does care about you, and from his point of view things were going well between you. He didn't expect you to leave."

"Dad, do you like David?" Alexa demanded.

Dan chose his words with care. "David can be charming when he wants to be, but your mother and I worried that you were so much under his spell. I imagine he can also be controlling."

Alexa nodded. "I was miserable the last year with him, but I was tired of arguments and having my feelings brushed aside, so mostly I went along with his ideas. That's not at all like me."

"I think you made the right decision in leaving, but David's hearing something else. Apparently when you talked to him on Sunday you said something about 'a relationship that wasn't going anywhere'. I think David interpreted this to mean that you want a permanent relationship. I suppose marriage."

"I could never marry David. I don't love him."

"I know, but don't be surprised if he approaches you again."

They sat in silence for a moment. Alexa shook her head in disbelief. "Too too intense. I told him on Sunday that I don't want to see him again."

Dan smiled for the first time. "David's far from stupid. He'll get the message eventually. He did say that you've changed."

"I have!" Alexa got up. "Dad, I'm hungry. Maybe we should raid your freezer. What do you feel like eating?"

When Mark arrived after the school council meeting, Alexa was drinking a fruit smoothie and making up a test for her senior students. She was surprised to see that it was after eleven. "You look whipped," she said.

In response he opened his arms. When she came into them, he hugged her tightly.

"What a night! I felt as if we were being nibbled to death by mosquitoes. It's hard to believe that the most pressing issues in education are the number of kids in the smoking area and the cost of the band trip. Lisa always gives a thorough principal's report. She explained the stats for next year. With the projected enrolment for September we'll need another computer lab and more gym space. It fell on deaf ears. They really don't care about facilities or staffing issues, as long as their little Johnny or Jeannie is being served now. Sorry," he added sheepishly, "I'm always on a rant after these nights."

Alexa laughed. "Don't forget I'm in the education business too. I can empathize. If you didn't care, you'd be a rotten vice-principal."

"True, but I take the job far too seriously. It comes home with me. I wish I could learn to leave it at the office. Along with the paper work," he added with a grin.

Alexa couldn't resist. She leaned over and kissed him softly. "Does that help?"

Mark responded so enthusiastically that she broke away laughing. "Do you want a drink? Coffee? Beer? A smoothie?"

Mark checked his watch. "Look at the time. I feel like Cinderella. There's school tomorrow, and Courtney needs to get home, but I'd love a smoothie. I've been drinking bad coffee all night."

When Alexa stood up to go into the kitchen, he followed her making himself comfortable at the table. Alexa was reaching into a cupboard for a glass when she heard him say, "I forgot to give you the latest newsflash. Your favourite student skipped both his afternoon classes, biology and math. I think he's missed at least six math classes already this semester. Then he was stupid enough to hang out at school. I caught up with him last class in the smoking area and told him he would have an in-house detention all day tomorrow. I'll keep him under lock and key in the office. The teachers can send down work for him."

Alexa felt a sudden and irrational flood of anger. She was furious at Justin, but also with Mark who seemed to be gloating about Justin's latest transgression. She whirled around to face him. "I presume we're talking about Justin Murray."

"The very one."

"I'm sure Justin was pleased by your news. It's just the ticket to make him want to come to school, and I'm sure you were delighted to be vindicated in your opinion of him." She had a lot more to say but forced herself to stop, although she glared at Mark.

He stood up from the table and made a movement towards her but stopped. He held up his hands in the classic gesture of surrender. "Alexa, I'm sorry. We disagree on the subject of Justin, and I shouldn't have mentioned him at all. It's just that it's been a very long day, and the kid gets under my skin. Even I can understand skipping class on a beautiful fall afternoon, but why would he hang out at school in the smoking area where he knew I'd find him? Sometimes I think he wants to get kicked out."

Alexa exhaled noisily, struggling to regain her composure. "Maybe he does." She remembered Justin's comments about needing money. "School isn't where he's at right now. Why don't you let Kelly speak with him tomorrow or the next day? Maybe he should try the alternative learning centre where he could work and take a home study course."

"Maybe that's the answer. I know I'm not getting through to him." He looked at his watch and gave her a half smile. "Let me give you one piece of good news. My family doctor called to say that Sarah has an appointment with a child psychiatrist who's supposed to be excellent, Dr Laura Ahmid. Before the council meeting, I called Jane to tell her about my interview with Sarah's teacher, and she offered to take Sarah on Friday night to sleep over. I'm supervising the school dance which doesn't end until eleven thirty, but after that I'm yours. If you still want me," he added.

"And I'm one of the dance chaperones. We can have a romantic evening checking the kids for alcohol and drugs."

"It's a deal," he said. "But after the dance, look out. We're off duty and the night's ours."

After Mark had left, Alexa paced the floor. She knew Mark thought he was being fair in his treatment of Justin, and the kid couldn't keep breaking school rules when they didn't suit him, but the bigger picture was that she and Mark had very different beliefs about students. How could their relationship survive if they continued to butt heads over philosophical differences?

CHAPTER TWELVE

*T*he week went by quickly. As usual Dara avoided speaking to anyone in English class, but she wrote an excellent novel test and seemed pleased with the comments Alexa had written on her paper. Alexa checked with Kelly on Tuesday after school. She had seen Dara, but there was nothing new she could report.

"Just keep watching her," Kelly said. "I think she's coping with the Stacey-Ben thing. I told her that if the harassment continues, I'll have to go to Mark, and she understood. I encouraged her to give you some of her poems for the writing contest, and she brightened up."

"What's the situation like at home?" Alexa asked.

"Nothing special. Both parents work, and Dara babysits her younger sisters after school. I've met her mother at parents' night. I'm going to help Dara apply for some university bursaries. She would certainly qualify, and she's got the ability to go on. She may just be in a senior slump, wondering what she's going to do next."

"Thanks for the update. I can't help worrying about her. She's such a loner."

On Friday in the period before lunch, Alexa read the final chapter of The Pigman with her Pathways English class. It was a disturbing chapter, and for once all the kids wanted to talk about what happened.

Shawn Bethune managed to dominate the discussion for a moment by saying loudly, "I told my dad about this book."

He was interrupted by guffaws and derisive comments.

"Sure, Shawn!"

"Since when did you and your old man talk about books?"

Even Alexa suppressed a smile. Although Shawn was bright, he did not seem like the type for literary discussions, but he ignored the dissenters. "My dad says that something like that happened here."

"You mean the party? We have those every weekend."

"No," Shawn said, trying to control his temper. "My dad said that about ten years ago there was this old guy who lived downtown over the pizza place. He used to let some of the older kids hang out in his apartment. One day he just disappeared, and when the owner of the building went looking for him, they found his body. Somebody had beaten him up, and he was dead."

Alexa could feel the blood draining from her face, but luckily no one noticed. They were too intent on the bombshell which Shawn had dropped.

"Like some kids killed him?" someone asked.

"Yeah. My dad said that the weird part about it was that everybody knew kids hung out at his place, and people said he had dope, but in the end a kid in Grade Nine was charged with his murder. Not the older guys."

The class was buzzing.

"I never heard about that."

"Did he go to jail?"

"As if some little kid would off him. Sounds like the cops just wanted to wrap up the case."

At last Alexa managed to intervene. "Shawn, what's the connection with the book? Lorraine and John didn't kill Mr Pignati."

"Yeah, he died of a broken heart after the kids trashed his house," Amanda said eyeing Justin. "Do you still think John has his head together?" she taunted.

Justin shrugged elaborately. "Kids make mistakes, and then they have to live with the consequences, right, miss?" He looked at Alexa.

"It was a pretty big mistake," someone muttered.

Alexa took a deep breath. She moved to the classroom windows which overlooked the soccer field at the back of the school. Just then she saw a police van pull up. She recognized the driver, Brian Fowler. He got out followed by two other officers, and from the back of the van the men released three dogs. Alexa assumed that one of the German Shepherds was Razor. She took another deep breath, forcing herself to be calm. She hadn't expected a canine search so early in the semester.

"We've heard some interesting ideas," she said to the class. "Read the last chapter again over the weekend. We'll continue the discussion on Monday. Next Wednesday is our test on the novel, so today I've got a review sheet for you. You can work in pairs, but I want it handed in before the end of the period."

She hoped that would keep them occupied. The students moved their desks together and after the usual buzz of conversation settled down to work as the PA clicked on.

Someone muttered, "I wonder what Anderson is going to preach about now?"

Then they heard Lisa Fletcher's voice. "Please excuse this interruption. I'd like all teaching staff to close their classroom doors and keep students in the rooms for the rest of the period. We have three dogs conducting a search of the school. We need to keep the halls clear."

There were a few muttered protests. "Of course, they'd pick a Friday, the night of the first dance," one student, Kevin Gibson, said in disgust.

But when Justin needled him, "What's the matter, Gibson? Planning to buy?" he subsided.

Alexa gave both boys an icy "No more nonsense" look, and they reluctantly picked up their pens. The school was quiet. Alexa thought that they must be searching the first floor lockers.

After a few minutes, the class became absorbed in their work. A muted bark and the sound of footsteps suggested that the officers had moved to the second floor. Alexa was helping a pair of students with one of the questions when they heard a sharp knock on the door. Everyone jumped.

Alexa opened the door to see Mrs Fletcher with one of the officers and a black Labrador Retriever. "Miss Corbett," Lisa Fletcher said, "we'd like you to bring the students out into the hall. They can leave their books and jackets in the class. The search will take just a few moments."

"The students don't need to worry," the officer added. "Casey's a docile dog and well trained." As if to support the comment, the dog sat placidly beside his handler, tongue lolling. The officer reached down to fondle his head.

Alexa turned back to the students. She noticed for the first time that Justin Murray looked ashen. "Just leave your jackets and books in the classroom. They're going to search the room, and we'll go out in the hall until they finish."

The officer took the dog to the other side of the hall as the students filed past. For once they were very subdued, and no one made a comment. Mrs Fletcher, the officer, and the dog went into the room.

To break the tension Alexa joked, "Let's hope no one brought their lunch to class. We don't want Casey to be distracted."

There were a few moments of silence. Suddenly they could hear frenetic yapping from the room.

Mrs Fletcher appeared in the doorway. "Miss Corbett, could you come here for a moment please?"

Inside the room Alexa saw the officer holding up a black jacket while the frenzied dog leaped about barking hysterically. "Do you know who owns this?" the officer asked.

Alexa started to move towards the desk.

"Don't come any closer," the officer cautioned. "Casey gets very excited when he's working."

Alexa stopped in her tracks. "Justin Murray, I think. I was just going to check the name on the notebook on the desk."

The officer flipped over the notebook, revealing Justin's name.

Lisa said quietly, "The students can come back to class now. We'll ask Justin to come to the office with us." When the students filed back into the room, the officer with the jacket drew Justin aside. He left with the principal and the police officer.

Throughout the rest of the period, there was barely a pretence of working. The low buzz of conversation filled the room. As the bell rang to signal the lunch hour, Alexa collected the review sheets, but for once the students did not rush from the room.

"What's going to happen to Justin?"

"Did the cops arrest him?"

"Fletcher's going to have him expelled, right?"

"Don't we have any rights? How can the cops just walk in here? Is this a dictatorship or what?"

"I'm going to get my mother to call the board office. She'll give them hell."

"They're like the gestapo!"

Alexa tried to answer calmly, "We don't know what's going to happen. Maybe nothing. We don't know what – if anything – the officer found."

After most of the students left, Cindy Burgess stayed behind. "Miss, there is lots of dope around. Especially before a weekend. If I was principal, I'd bring the dogs in every Friday. Lots of the kids feel the same way. I smoke, but I don't do drugs, and I don't like all that pot in the smoking area. It gives us a bad name!"

When she was finally alone, Alexa shut the classroom door, sat down at her desk and put her face in her hands, first Shawn's story and now this. It was impossible to escape from your past in Davenport. In high school, Alexa had not been a regular drug user, but she had partied with kids who were. She knew the story of Lennie Warren very well. Some of her classmates had used his apartment as a regular hangout, a warm place to smoke up away from their parents and out of sight of the police. Alexa remembered with a shudder that in the September of her third year in high school, she had gone with some friends to Lennie's apartment. She had found it depressing with its filthy furniture and fetid air and pathetic that an old man was so desperate for company that he hung out with high school kids. She had never been tempted to go back.

When the story of Lennie's murder broke the following March, the town was abuzz. Tony's brother, Ronnie, had been a regular part of that scene, but Tony told the police that he and Ronnie had been watching a hockey game that night. When Alexa had asked him if Ronnie was involved, he became furious and refused to talk about it.

She couldn't recall why a younger student had been charged with the attack although the kids speculated that he was a juvenile and, therefore, it was convenient to pin the blame on him. She remembered that the following September when Tony left to play Junior A hockey Ronnie also went away. She heard that his parents had sent him to a private school, a military academy, but by that time she had no contact with the Benoits.

Perhaps at this very moment Justin was being charged. She had wanted to believe him when he told her that he didn't use at school. Why would he be stupid enough to bring dope to class?

Alexa had never seen the school so tense. Even in the staffroom where she retreated to grab some lunch, the teachers were on edge, and rumours were flying. One story alleged that the dogs had searched four classrooms and found four drug stashes. Alexa did not add to or contradict the rumours. In truth, no one knew what had happened.

When Carol Helmer appeared, Alexa appealed to her. "Carol, when will we find out what's going on?"

Carol shrugged. "I feel sorry for Lisa and Mark. They'll be deluged with phone calls from angry parents and queries from the local newspaper. Everybody wants a drug free school, but nobody wants their son or daughter charged. All the parents think the board's Safe School Policy is great – until it affects them personally. Going by what happened last year, at some point Lisa will get on the PA and make an announcement to the school. At least the dance tonight should be fairly quiet " she added.

"Great! Because it's going to be a long afternoon."

"Did you get hit up by Jim Callaghan too?"

When Alexa nodded, she said, "A group of us who are chaperoning are going out to eat first. Come with us to Book Ends. We stick to coffee before a dance, but the food's good."

As Alexa had predicted, the afternoon dragged along. The students were always restless on Friday, but this was heightened by the morning's events. Just before the dismissal bell, Lisa Fletcher made an announcement. "As a result of the canine search today, two students have been charged by the police. The students will not be returning to Riverside this semester. I want to remind all of you of the board's Safe School Policy which specifically forbids carrying illicit drugs of any kind on school property. You all know that tonight is our first school dance. Have a good time and stay safe."

Alexa had not seen Mark all day. She hoped he would have time to join the teachers at Book Ends. He and Lisa arrived just after everyone had ordered, and both of them looked drained. After they had flagged down a waitress and added their orders to the others, Buzz asked, "So what really happened today after the dogs came in? Can you give us the scoop?"

Lisa shook her head. "I'm sorry, I can't. Just what I said to the kids this afternoon. We had enough time to take the dogs into four different classrooms. Unfortunately they found bags of marijuana in two classes. The amounts are large enough that both students have been charged with trafficking." She rubbed her forehead. "After that I seemed to spend most of the afternoon talking to the superintendent or the local paper."

"We were lucky to get the dogs so early in the school year," Mark added. "Hopefully the kids learned something from this." Alexa thought that he looked exhausted.

"At least tonight will be quiet," Phil Mahoney predicted. "The kids know we'll have officers supervising, and most of them were shaken up today. I had a junior class just before lunch, and they were petrified thinking that the dogs were coming into our room."

Mark held up two crossed fingers in the sign for good luck. "Let's hope. I'm not in the mood to break up fights tonight."

By the time the dance began at seven thirty, the two off-duty police officers were at the doors with Lisa and Mark circulating nearby. Alexa had drawn cafeteria supervision for the first hour, and, remembering Buzz and Phil's words of advice, she kept one eye on the windows while she talked to a parent chaperone and some students who were operating the canteen.

In an hour Carol came to relieve her. Drawing Alexa aside, she said, "You won't believe what happened. Two junior students arrived with huge tankards of peach cooler in their backpacks. Mark said you could hear them clinking as soon as the girls walked in. The stuff has at least ten per cent alcohol content, and the kids are only fourteen. Mark and the police officers are talking to them now, trying to find out how they got the booze. Lisa and Buzz are at the front door. Can you go into the gym? Phil's the only chaperone there."

"No problem," Alexa replied. "And we thought it would be a quiet night."

In the gym the kids were gyrating to the music or standing in groups watching the videos. Alexa noticed that most of the crowd was made up of juniors. The senior students were out looking for more sophisticated entertainment.

After a few minutes, Mark appeared at the opposite side of the gym. Alexa watched while he gradually worked his way through the crowd towards her. When he was next to her, he had to speak directly into her ear to be heard over the cacophony of the music, "I don't know about you, but I may not last until eleven thirty. This place is hopping!" Alexa nodded in agreement, but there was no way they could talk.

When the dance ended, the chaperones uttered a collective sigh although the second half of the evening had been easy. Alexa's greatest crisis was talking to Alison Duncan, a girl from her Pathways class who was sobbing hysterically because her boyfriend was dancing with someone else. The students were mellow, and Jim Callaghan thanked all the teachers profusely for their help.

In the staffroom, Mark whispered to Alexa, "We're out of here. I'll see you in ten minutes at your apartment. I've got a bottle of white wine in the trunk of my car – unless of course you'd prefer a glass of peach cooler."

Just then Carol and Phil came in. "Come on, you two. We're going to Jenny's," Carol invited. "We all need a beer after tonight, and Lisa's coming with us."

Mark looked at Alexa. At times she was totally unfathomable. He didn't know if she was looking forward to being with him or if she'd prefer to go out with the staff. Her face revealed nothing. "Alexa, do you want to go?" he asked.

All evening Alexa had been thinking of nothing but Mark, but she said, "Sure, it's nice of Jenny to invite us." She wondered why Jenny Lafrance, the attendance secretary, had invited the chaperones to her house. When the others burst out laughing, she looked puzzled.

"Alexa, Jenny's is the pub at the Travellers Inn," Carol explained. "We often go there after a dance because it's quiet and seriously uncool. We don't have to worry about meeting our students."

Alexa could feel her cheeks burning and she felt a flash of unreasonable irritation as Mark put his arm loosely around her shoulders. But the irritation disappeared as quickly as it came. This was not David with his barbed sarcasm. Mark was gently teasing. "Kiddo, you need to get out more." He turned to Carol. "We'll have to show her the town's hot spots."

Alexa managed to smile when Carol said, "Let's do that. We can find ten minutes in our hectic schedules to give you the grand tour, Alexa."

On their way to the parking lot, Mark murmured in her ear, "Alexa, let's have one drink and leave. I just want to be with you."

She smiled into his eyes. "Good idea. After today I need some down time, and not with half the staff chaperoning us."

At Jenny's, Alexa found herself seated near the open fireplace between Lisa and Phil. "Thanks for chaperoning tonight, Alexa. The kids on student council appreciate it," Lisa said.

"It's a real window on the kids' lives. I'm always amazed at how they pair off. By the way, I wanted to congratulate you on the staff newsletter you publish each week. It's the best one I've seen and a good way for us newbies to keep up with what's happening around the school."

"That was Mark's idea. He called it The Devil's Advocate because our sports teams are The Devils. He's going to make a good principal some day."

"And what's the Iron Man Award?"

Phil who was sitting on her other side overheard the question. "Mark started that when he came. When a teacher's away for part of a day, other teachers get on-calls to cover the classes. We call them 'blueys' because Susan prints them on blue paper. It's probably the assigned duty everyone hates the most. Mark tracks the on-calls, and the teacher who accumulates the most in a semester receives the Iron Man Award at a staff meeting along with a gift certificate. That sweetens the poison."

Alexa smiled. "Someone's been kind to me so far. I've only had two blueys, but at least I know I'm in the running for a major award."

She and Mark left in separate cars, and as she drove home Alexa thought about the conversation. Mark was a good vice-principal because he was a team player who did his best to motivate the staff. She must remember to tell him that the next time he was feeling less than euphoric about his job.

Mark was at the apartment before her. He presented her with the wine and three long-stemmed yellow roses. Then he dramatically staggered to the couch and flung himself on it, holding out his arms for her to join him. "They don't print money in large enough denominations to compensate for a day like this."

Although Alexa desperately wanted to talk about Justin Murray, she waited while Mark found glasses and poured their wine. Before she could ask a question, he said, "I'm so wound up. This is one time when I should forget the whole school scene, but I can't. It's great to be with you. You know what's happening at Riverside, and I can count on you not to pass on anything I say."

"That goes without saying. If it helps, let's talk. It won't go any further."

"Did you hear about our junior girls with the cooler?"

"Yes, Carol told me."

"We questioned them separately, and they were scared to death. They don't make a habit of this. They had brought the stuff to the dance because they were going to a sleepover with some of their friends tonight, and one has a birthday. Both of them told us that Ben Copeland bought them the alcohol. We called their parents who were not too pleased, as you can imagine. The girls are lucky. They're only getting a suspension. The police won't charge them. We asked the parents to speak to them, and if the stories are confirmed we'll have to deal with Ben on Monday. Do you remember who he is?"

"Of course. He's Stacey Sawyer's boyfriend, who was suspended for harassing Dara."

"That's right. Supplying alcohol to minors is a serious offence especially when you're eighteen. This may be the end of Ben's career at Riverside, and the police will certainly lay some charges."

"It's so stupid. These kids just don't think of the consequences before they act." She could not wait any longer. "Mark, what's going to happen to Justin?"

"The police found ten small bags of marijuana in his jacket. They charged him with trafficking. The only break for Justin is that he's just sixteen, and this is his first offence. He'll probably end up on probation with community service."

"But was it really his? Someone could have planted it on him," Alexa said a little desperately.

"Justin admitted it was his."

"We all did stupid things in high school."

"I won't argue about that, but we can't condone selling drugs."

"What about school? Is he finished at Riverside?"

"He's finished for now. Kelly talked to him. He can register for courses through the board's alternative school. Remember you suggested that the day I caught him in the smoking area after he skipped all afternoon? Justin's far from stupid. He'll probably look for a job and take some home study courses. Next September we'll let him come back if he has a clean record and has completed at least one course."

"What a waste! He's bright. He could have done anything he wanted."

Mark put his arm around her. "I know I look like the enforcer after our first conversation about Justin, but we cut him a lot of slack last year. It may be hard for you to accept, but the truth is that Justin knew what he was doing. He's selling, and I expect he's been doing that for a while. As you told me, right now going to school is low on his list of priorities. If it makes you feel any better, yours was the only class in which he was producing any work."

Alexa interrupted, "It doesn't make me feel better. I feel that the whole system failed him."

"Maybe it did if by 'system' you mean society as a whole. From what Kelly tells me, his parents just washed their hands of him, but we're offering a traditional education, and right now he's not buying. It doesn't mean that the doors are closed forever. Justin's making some bad choices, and now he has to face the consequences." He took Alexa's hand and brought it to his lips. "Don't blame yourself. You helped to keep him in school longer than anyone else."

Alexa played with the stem of her wine glass. She didn't feel like drinking. "We just don't see this in the same way. I hate to lose a bright kid."

"And I hate to lose the little time we have together. Alexa, one reason you're so special is that you care so passionately about the kids, but right now let's talk about anything besides school."

Alexa sighed. Like Mark, it was hard for her to shift gears. She got up and turned on her CD player. The haunting music of Enya filled the room as she came over to sit beside Mark. "Tomorrow's going to be a good day. What time is Sarah coming home?"

"Jane will probably bring her around noon. I'll call in the morning and check."

They sat in silence for a few minutes totally at peace with Mark's arms around her, and her head nestled on his chest. Softly he began to kiss her face and neck. "I've been dreaming about this all week," he whispered.

Alexa could feel a dangerous excitement filling her as they caressed. She was certain that Mark was aware of her responsiveness. He kissed her deeply cupping her face in his hands and drinking in the warm fragrance of her skin.

Mark had been telling the truth when he said that thoughts of Alexa had haunted his dreams and his waking hours. He had imagined how well their bodies would fit together, and even her lightest touch brought him to a heightened responsiveness. It would be easy to spend the night here sharing her bed and exploring each other's bodies, but he hesitated. He sensed a hidden core in her that he could not discover simply by sleeping with her, and he wanted all of her, not just her physical essence.

He could also sense how distraught she was about Justin. She was trying to hide it, but he knew she was close to seeing him as the enemy.

In truth, he and Kelly had spent countless hours with Justin the previous year, trying to convince him that he was not exempt from school rules because he had been through a rough patch at home. Like Kelly, he had thought that Justin was a talented kid, but his patience had worn thin when he deliberately flouted the school's expectations and missed an ever-increasing number of classes.

To Alexa's surprise, he drew back and kissed the top of her head. "It's late. Could I come over in the morning and bring you breakfast?"

She hid her surprise by yawning and stretching. "I'm sure it's my turn to cook. Come over in the morning, and I'll make us some blueberry pancakes."

"Is ten o'clock too early?"

"No, that's fine."

After he left, Alexa was too tired to replay the events of a very long day, but she fell asleep with her senses filled with Mark and wondering why he had not acted on the attraction between them.

On Saturday morning there was still no sign of Mark by quarter past ten. Knowing that he was always early, Alexa had made coffee and mixed the pancake batter shortly after nine. She was beginning to think that something had happened to him or Sarah when the doorbell rang.

"I'm late and I apologize," Mark said smiling. "This place smells wonderful, and so do you." He kissed her lightly.

When they sat down to eat, Alexa studied him carefully, "Mark, you look like a cat which has just ingested a large yellow bird! What's happening?"

"My face always gives me away. I'm a lousy poker player. This morning I was just going out the door when my buddy, Paul Davidson, called. Did I tell you about him?"

"Wasn't he the fellow who roasted Spam for his girlfriend?"

"Yes, *chef extraordinaire*, that's Paul. We shared an apartment when we were finishing our degrees in math, but I went on in education, and Paul did a post graduate degree in computer studies. He's done really well for himself with a major computer company. Last year they sent him as a manager to Bermuda."

"Does he have an opening for a secretary in February?" Alexa joked. "I'm not a bad typist. What an opportunity that would be!"

"Paul's going home at Christmas for his sister's wedding in Calgary.

He asked me if I wanted to use his place over the holidays. How would you like to spend a few days in Hamilton?"

Alexa gulped. "It sounds fabulous," she hedged, "but Kate, my oldest sister, is coming here for Christmas with her husband and kids. Our family hasn't been together in ages."

Mark got up and picked up the calendar on Alexa's desk. "Once in a while our board of education does something humane. Christmas falls on a Friday this year, and we get out of school a week before. We could fly down on Friday night and come back on Monday or Tuesday. Bermuda's not far, and you'd still have time to get ready for Christmas. What do you think?" He beamed like a small boy .

Alexa studied the pattern on her coffee mug. As if he understood, Mark said, "I shouldn't have sprung this on you, but I was like a kid with a new toy when Paul made the offer. At least think about it. We don't have to decide now." He reached for her hand. "I'm not trying to pressure you. Paul has an apartment on the top floor of an old colonial house. He has two bedrooms, but if you didn't feel comfortable with that his landlord runs a bed and breakfast in the rest of the house. We could book a room for you there."

Alexa shook her head. "That's not a problem. The apartment sounds fabulous." After a moment she asked, "Would Sarah come with us?"

"I guess I'm not that far in my planning. She wants to go to Disneyland in March break. I know Jo and Ray would take her for a few days at Christmas." He grinned. "One thing's for sure. Jo's going to receive an amazing Christmas present from me. I couldn't have survived without her. She's the original earth mother when it comes to kids." He looked intently at Alexa. "We've got lots of time before Christmas to talk about this. Bermuda's not the most popular destination at that time of year. The sun worshippers are heading for Mexico and Barbados. I'm sure we could pick up flights even at the last minute."

"It's a great invitation. Paul sounds like a wonderful friend."

"He is. I keep hoping that his next assignment will be Hawaii or Puerto Rico. What a great way to see the world that would be."

When Mark left to meet Sarah, Alexa's thoughts were in a turmoil. Part of her mind urged, *Say 'yes'! It will be a fantastic holiday before the whirl of Christmas begins. You know you want to be with him. What better opportunity?* But another voice chided, *You've been there and done that and thrown away the T-shirt. Why are you ignoring the danger signs and getting involved with a man whom you may never see again after January?* Alexa sighed. She had only to remember Mark's mouth on hers and his honesty as he spoke about his feelings after Jane left to know that Mark was no David. She wanted to be a part of his life. Someday soon she would tell him everything, including the last year with David and David's persistence in pursuing the relationship. She knew that Mark would listen without judging.

A moment later the telephone rang. It was her father. His voice sounded happy and relaxed. "Hi, Alexa. Heather's going to be here again on Sunday night. Will you come for dinner? I've invited Martin too. Heather enjoyed talking to him."

"I'd love to if you really want me."

"Of course I do, or I wouldn't have called."

"Dad, it's my turn to ask if I can bring a guest. Mark Anderson and I have been spending some time together. Would you mind if I invite him?"

Dan sounded surprised but very pleased. "Not at all. Is Mark the reason you've been looking so happy lately?"

"He certainly helps." She added impulsively, "Dad, I can't believe how different I feel with Mark than with David."

"That's a good thing," Dan said dryly. "You've had a couple of bad experiences, and I was afraid you were swearing off all men. Some of us are pretty good guys!" They talked for a few more minutes. Just before hanging up he said, "Be sure to bring Sarah tomorrow. Heather and I are cooking and we'll keep her busy."

About an hour later Mark returned with Sarah whose eyes were red from crying. "I don't want to go," she told Alexa. "I feel sick because I didn't sleep all night." Alexa and Mark exchanged glances over the top of her head.

Alexa knelt down beside her. "Sarah, we promised to visit my friend Patti. She has two children who have done nothing but talk about meeting you. They live in the country with lots of animals, but they don't have other kids close by to play with. If you're sick, you don't have to come, or if you get there and you want to go home, your dad can take you. Patti will drive me home later."

Sarah continued to look unhappy and went over to sit down on Alexa's couch, wrapping her arms around herself and snuffling. Trying to distract her, Alexa went on, "I'm bringing some presents for Patti's children, Nick and Cheyenne. I got them a set of carved animals and some books. Do you want to see them?"

Sarah shook her head obstinately. Finally Mark said, "Sarah, I'll take you home. Alexa can go to see her friends, and you can meet them some other time."

Sarah considered this. "I'll go," she announced at last, "but only if I can sit in front with you, Dad. I feel like I'm going to throw up when I ride in the back seat."

Mark started to protest, but Alexa interrupted, "That's fine. I can sit in the back. I don't get motion sickness."

When they were on the highway, Sarah seemed to recover completely. She asked Mark unending questions about the animals she was going to see and pretended that Alexa sitting behind them with the gift bags for Nick and Cheyenne did not exist.

As they got out of the car at Patti's, Mark pulled Alexa close and whispered, "Thanks for putting up with us. Sarah's first meeting with Dr Ahmid is on Monday. I hope that this doctor is as good as I've heard."

In spite of the bad beginning, Alexa had a great afternoon. It had been more than a year since she had seen Patti and Chris's children, but Nicholas immediately brought her the framed photograph she had sent from Chang Mai of Alexa mounted on an elephant.

"That's you," he said. "Were you scared?"

"A little," Alexa told him. "I had a small blanket to sit on, but I was high off the ground, and the elephant was swaying from side to side when he walked."

"But you didn't fall?" he asked gravely.

"No, I didn't," she assured him. "The elephants in Asia are well trained. Usually they work in the forests moving big logs with their trunks, and they always have a trainer with them."

"Like the circus," he said.

At three, Nick was already a book lover, and he wanted Alexa to sit with him on the porch swing and read the new books she had brought When Patti tried to intervene, Alexa insisted it would be fun. Nick sat mesmerized through *Where's Spot?*, but it was a book on shapes which Alexa had bought for Cheyenne which he really loved. When it was time to identify the shape, he would roar with glee, "Square!" or

"Triangle!" or "Rectangle!" and urge her to read the page again.

Chris laughed. "Listen to him," he said to Mark. "Have you ever seen a senior calculus class so seriously into math? You can tell Patti's a good teacher."

Mark smiled. "At some point, kids' enthusiasm seems to take a nose dive. Maybe I should have taught kindergarten."

Cheyenne was a two-year-old dynamo who identified all the animals in the set Alexa had brought, but she couldn't sit still for long. After a moment, she dropped the giraffe she had been playing with. "Wabbits!" she said to Patti. When no one paid any attention, she repeated loudly, "I feed the wabbits."

For the first time, Sarah looked intrigued. "Usually in the afternoon, we go to the barn to feed the rabbits," Patti explained. "Do you want to come with us?" When Sarah nodded, Cheyenne took her hand, and soon Sarah was in charge, shepherding her around the barn and garden and visiting the animals including a lamb which had been added to the menagerie since Alexa's last visit. She fell in love with Stuart, a huge brown rabbit, and carried him in her arms to show Mark. She bent over him, her cheek against the silky fur, totally absorbed in stroking his long ears.

After Sarah and Cheyenne left to play with some kittens which were sunning themselves by the garage, Patti said to Mark, "Stuart's housetrained. We've got a lot of rabbits, but Stuart was given to us by a family who lived in an apartment. He uses a litter box like a cat. Why don't you take him home? Our kids won't miss him, and he'd be good company for Sarah."

"You'll like Stuart. He's a friendly fellow," Chris added. "When we first got him, he insisted on sleeping at the foot of our bed. I woke up one night and thought I was feeling Patti's hair against my face, but when I reached out, and the hair moved, I knew I'd made a mistake."

Mark laughed. "I slept with my dog when I was a kid, but I don't know anything about rabbits." He thought for only a moment. "Okay, if you can give me the 'Bunnies for Dummies' course before we leave, I'll take him home with us. Sarah will be in seventh heaven, and she'll be your friend for life."

Late that afternoon Chris and Mark fired up the barbecue while Alexa helped Patti set out salads and rolls. Cheyenne was already sleepy and did not resist being fed her supper early and having a bath. "Let me do it," Alexa begged. "I'm an old pro after Katie's children, and it's so much fun to play in the water."

"Usually it is," Patti agreed. "Cheyenne's been a water baby since she was born, but Nick used to get red in the face and scream bloody murder. At times I couldn't stand it any longer, and Chris took over."

When they were ready to sit down at the wooden picnic table, Sarah insisted that she wanted to sit between Mark and Patti. Chris smoothed over a difficult situation by saying, "Aren't I lucky! I get to sit with Alexa and Nick."

Alexa tried to smile, but her face felt stiff and unnatural. She wondered how much more of this she could stand. The Wicked Girl Friend was not a role she wanted. In spite of Mark's encouraging smile, Alexa wished that Sarah had stayed home, preferably with a babysitter whose idea of a treat was a nice bowl of oatmeal, but the next moment she forgot her frustration when Nick looked up at her adoringly and said, "Mommy made cupcakes, but you have to eat your veggies first."

After they had cleared the table, Patti and Alexa managed to have some time alone together while Patti made coffee and got out the treat, a plate of chocolate cupcakes. "You and Mark are perfect together!" Patti enthused. "I know Sarah's going through a rough patch, but she'll be fine. Trust me! She needs Stuart to fuss over."

"Don't get too excited," Alexa warned her. "I like Mark, but we're just getting to know each other. He's not the sarcastic guy I told you about at the River Mill. Remember? We've both been through bad relationships, and Sarah is a problem. When I first met her, I never thought she would dislike me so much."

"Relax, girl. Sarah doesn't dislike you. She's just testing the waters. Since her mom left, all she's got is Mark. It's natural for her to be possessive when she sees her dad with a beautiful lady. And Mark is gorgeous," she added mischievously.

Alexa hugged her friend. "You see life through rose coloured glasses, but I love being around you. Especially now that I'm old and jaded."

"Don't worry," Patti said airily. "I've got a good feeling about this." Alexa resisted the urge to remind Patti that she had approved of David as well.

When they went back to the porch, Sarah ran to Alexa with Stuart in her arms. "Alexa, my dad says I can keep him! I can take him home!" She was beaming at Alexa as if they were best friends.

Alexa smiled back, and this time it was a natural smile. "That's great, Sarah. Stuart's beautiful. You can make him a bed where he can sleep when you're at school."

"And I'll feed him, and I'll brush him, and I'll walk him every day. Just like Robbie."

By the time Nick was in bed, Sarah was asleep on the living room couch with Stuart beside her. Mark covered her with a blanket, and the two couples sat outside on the porch drinking coffee and talking lazily. Patti had a barrage of questions for Alexa and Mark about Riverside. After listening for a while, Chris remarked, "Teachers never stop talking shop. When I get together with other carpenters, we talk about sports. Why is that?"

"I'm sure you get tired of hearing about school, but we can't leave teaching alone," Alexa explained. "For me, it's a sort of love-hate thing. I can't imagine doing anything else, maybe because I'm still a kid at heart, but at times it's so frustrating that we unload whenever we can."

Mark added, "Being with Alexa is great because we both feel the same way about work, but we'll have to watch it, or we'll turn into a boring middle-aged couple obsessed with our jobs!"

"Hey, I didn't mean that you guys were boring," Chris interjected, "but I've gone to enough teacher parties to know what the conversation will be about."

Patti leaned over to give him a kiss. "Poor you!" Turning to Mark and Alexa, she said, "I've been telling Chris that next year I'd like to go back to work at least part-time. Ever since Alexa came back I've realized how much I miss it – and the adult conversation that's sadly lacking around our munchkins."

As they drove home, Alexa turned around to watch Sarah curled up in the back seat with Stuart in her arms. She turned to Mark. "If you're lonely tonight, you can always cuddle up with Stuart. I think he's part of the family now."

"Stuart's no substitute for you."

"I should hope not," Alexa glanced over at Mark and saw him smiling. "By the way, I almost forget to tell you that Dad called this afternoon with a dinner invitation for Sunday. Heather's visiting this weekend. If you and Sarah would like to come, you're included."

"Let's see how Sarah's feeling tomorrow. If she's in one of her grumpy moods, I'll try to find a babysitter for a few hours. I don't want her to ruin your dad's dinner party. Can I call you in the morning and let you know?"

"Of course. Dad's laid back about these things, and he specifically invited Sarah to come. He's a marvellous grandfather, and he misses Katie's kids even more than I do. She reached for his hand. "Let's hope Stuart or Dr Admid is a miracle worker. If I get much more ice from Sarah, even the 'yard apes' at my last school will look good."

"'Yard apes?'" Mark asked. He didn't ask for an explanation. Something in Alexa's tone told him she was completely serious about Sarah.

CHAPTER THIRTEEN

" So far, so good," Mark said when he called late on Sunday morning. "Sarah's in fine form today. She insisted on going to Sunday school because she's really impressed with her teacher, Lori Green, one of our students, and since she came home she's been completely focussed on Stuart. She made him a bed, fed him, and encouraged him to do aerobics. I didn't know rabbits required that kind of attention."

He sounded so serious that Alexa laughed. "It sounds like a lot more fun than grading tests. I know Lori. She's on co-op this semester. Usually she's at Maple Grove Elementary School, but at the beginning of the semester she was doing some work for the English department and came into my Pathways class to help out a few times. The kids loved her. She's totally cool."

"I'll bring Sarah to your dad's for dinner tonight, and I'll spirit her away if she's not happy. I don't want to ruin the party."

"That's good. Even if Sarah isn't speaking to me, Heather and Dad will enjoy spoiling her."

That afternoon as Alexa was changing into wool pants and her favourite Fair Isle sweater the telephone rang. "Hi, Alexa, we haven't seen each other for a while." It was Tony, his voice warm and familiar. "I wondered if you'd be free sometime this week for dinner. There's a bed and breakfast place outside of town called The Victorian Rose that's just opened a dining room. From what I hear, the food is fabulous. And I thought I could invite Ronnie and his wife, Jenna, to come with us. They don't seem to get out much."

Alexa hesitated for only a moment. "Thanks for the invitation and thinking of me, Tony, but I'm going to say 'no'. I'm seeing someone else right now." She hoped Tony would understand and accept her refusal.

"I'm sorry to hear that. I enjoyed the evening with you at Fasooli's." Tony waited for Alexa to offer more information. Finally he said, "Well, good luck this semester. I'm sure we'll see each other around town, and if you change your mind give me a call." He sounded hurt and a little bitter.

Alexa replayed the conversation in her mind several times as she brushed her hair and pinned it up. She knew she would not have enjoyed a dinner *en famille* with Ronnie, but second guessing herself was one of her worst characteristics. She had been hurt and always hated to hurt someone else. She told herself that it was better this way. Tony wouldn't be alone for long. He had recovered quite nicely before.

By the time Alexa got to her dad's house, everyone was gathered in the kitchen. Sarah had been helping Heather to set the table, but she was more interested in her new friend. She immediately dropped the place mats and came over to Alexa. "Look, Alex! Look what I've got for Stuart! Mr Corbett gave me one of Robbie's collars and a leash." Turning to Mark she added, "Can I take Stuart out for a walk now?"

"Okay, Sarah, but promise you'll be careful and not go too far. We don't know if Stuart's going to enjoy that kind of exercise." When she had gone, Mark smiled at the others and put his arm around Alexa. "Patti was the answer to a prayer when she gave us Stuart. I haven't seen Sarah this happy in weeks. She's spent the whole day with that rabbit, and the change in her is amazing!"

Dan smiled. "I can see that. They're inseparable. Stuart's a good pet for her, and a lot easier than the dog she wanted." He grinned at Alexa. "It's great to see everyone looking happy. Dinner won't be ready for a few minutes. Why don't we take some drinks out to the deck and enjoy the last of the afternoon sun while it's still warm?"

Heather and Alexa were the first to sit down at the patio table and were soon deep in conversation when they heard the garden gate creak open. They looked up to see Verna Murphy holding Sarah firmly by one arm. She marched her up to Mark. "Mr Anderson, I want you to know that I just rescued your little girl. She ran right into the street after her rabbit. They were almost hit by a car!"

Sarah burst into tears and breaking free ran to bury her head against Mark's chest.

"What happened, Sarah? Are you all right?" he asked gently, taking Stuart from her, but Sarah was crying too hard to answer.

"I was outside watering the flowers," Verna went on, "when I saw her come though the gate to the sidewalk. She was having trouble holding the leash and she dropped it. The next thing I knew the rabbit was hopping across the street, and she was chasing him right into the road. It's a miracle the driver was going very slowly and stopped before he hit her."

Mark lifted Sarah onto his lap and dried her tears. He smiled up at Verna. "Thank you so much. We're very lucky you were watching out for her."

"I'm Verna Murphy, Dan's neighbour. I don't think we've met, but I've seen you outside working in your yard, and I met your wife at the church."

Shifting Sarah to the chair beside him, Mark stood up and held out his hand. "Sarah's mother and I aren't together now. I'm Mark Anderson. Thanks for reacting so quickly. Stuart's our new pet, and Sarah's just getting used to him."

"Come and join us for a drink, Verna, " Dan invited. "You know everyone. You met Heather when she was here last weekend. What can I get for you?"

The little woman looked slowly around the group. She nodded at Martin and eyed Alexa curiously for a moment. When Heather smiled at her, she did not smile back. "Yes, I met Mrs Robinson. Nothing for me, thanks. It's almost supper time. I must be going."

In spite of Verna's protests, Dan insisted on walking with her. "Come on, Martin. You'll have a chance to see Verna's flower beds. They're gorgeous."

When they disappeared out the gate, Martin could be heard asking, "How do you keep your roses blooming for so long? Do you have a trade secret?"

After they were gone, Sarah stopped snuffling and said loudly, "I don't like that lady. She jerked my arm hard and she yelled at me."

"What happened?" Mark and Alexa spoke almost together.

By now Sarah seemed to have recovered, and she shrugged off the question as if the answer were obvious. "Stuart didn't want to go for a walk. I think he wanted his supper. He tried to hop over to the grass, and when I picked him up to get him to walk on the sidewalk I dropped his leash. Then he hopped onto the street. I didn't see the car until it was right in front of us. But the man stopped and got out. He was nice. He helped me catch Stuart."

Mark hugged Sarah tightly. "You have to be careful, sweetpea. I couldn't stand to lose you or Stuart. You frightened Miss Murphy. She thought the car was going to hit you, and she was trying to help. We'll send her a thank you card tomorrow. You can sign your name and Stuart's."

Alexa found herself echoing her father's words. "Miss Murphy really does mean well, Sarah. I'm sure she was terrified when she saw Stuart take off like that." She looked at Heather. "I know Dad. He'll smooth her ruffled feathers if anyone can."

Heather rose and held out her hand. "Come on, Sarah. It's time for dinner and time for you to feed Stuart. Let's go and see if we can find him a carrot or two and some lettuce leaves."

Unprotesting, Sarah took her hand, and as they went into the house Alexa heard her asking, "Do you have any carrot tops, Heather? That's Stuart's favourite treat."

Mark put his arms around Alexa and pulled her close, resting his cheek against her hair. "Alone at last. I've missed you so much today. Do you think you can put up with Sarah's mood swings?"

"I've been wondering that myself. Look at her just now. She's all sweetness and light with Heather. If I had asked her to help me make Stuart's dinner, she would have given me the cold shoulder. Perhaps you could book me an appointment with Dr Ahmid. I'm beginning to think I need it much more than Sarah does." Alexa was not entirely joking.

The next morning it seemed to Alexa that she had just fallen asleep when the telephone rang. She reached out blindly for the receiver to hear Mark's voice. "Good morning, my love, did I wake you up?"

She struggled to sit up but fell back wearily against her pillows. "What time is it?"

"Almost six thirty. I'm sorry to call so early, but I wanted to catch you before I left for school. I'm afraid I've got some bad news."

By now Alexa was wide awake. "Mark, what's wrong? Has something happened to Sarah?"

"Sarah's fine. Lisa just called me. Dara Babcock made a suicide attempt last night."

Alexa inhaled sharply, and Mark went on quickly. "She's in the hospital, but the doctor thinks she'll be okay. Lisa had a call from Roger Helmer, Carol's husband, who's the investigating officer."

"What happened? How did she do it?" Alexa was close to panic.

"I don't have a lot of details right now. Apparently Dara was babysitting her sisters, and when her parents got home they found her. She'd taken a lot of aspirin and some of her mother's sleeping pills. Luckily her mom and dad didn't waste any time. They took her to emergency right away, and they pumped out her stomach."

Alexa was now standing beside the bed, her free hand clenched in a fist. "I feel so guilty. I knew something was wrong. If only I'd tried harder to make her talk to me." Inwardly she was cursing herself, wondering if her failure to report the incident with the pornographic picture and Ben Copeland's subsequent harassment was the catalyst which had pushed Dara over the edge.

"Look, Alexa, you're not superwoman, and as far as I know you're not clairvoyant. We can't always predict the future. You were there for her, but Dara wasn't ready to talk. Don't beat yourself up over this. Are you listening?"

"Yes, I'm listening, but what can I do?"

"Nothing right now. We're going to speak to all of Dara's teachers before classes start. The official word is that she's in the hospital with a virus, and we expect her to be back at school within a few days. Dara seems to be a loner, so I don't know if the other kids will get the real story or not. If you hear any rumours among the seniors, just try to keep things as low key as possible."

"I will, and Mark, thanks for letting me know before I got to school."

"I was worried about how you'd react. I'll fill you in on the details after school or tonight. We're going to keep this quiet if we can. Dara has enough problems. She doesn't need the story buzzing through the whole school."

"Thanks again, Mark. I appreciate the call. How was Sarah when you got her home last night?"

Mark's voice relaxed. "Kids! She never mentioned Verna again. She went to sleep like a baby with Stuart on the blanket beside her as if nothing had happened. Alexa, promise me you'll take it easy today. We'll talk again tonight."

While Alexa was showering, she began to cry. Mark was right. She could do nothing but try to quell the rumour mill, but she cried because her overtures to Dara had been ineffectual, and she cried for all the Justins and the Daras, kids who had so much potential but might never realize it because of their circumstances, and she cried for the petty cruelty and inhumanity which was part of any school and of society as a whole. Later, as she dried her hair and sipped a mug of coffee, she struggled to pull herself together. At this rate, she'd be useless at school. She couldn't change human nature, but she could make things a little better for the kids in her classes.

Early in the day Alexa was surprised that none of the kids seemed to be aware of the reason for Dara's absence. It was a quiet Monday, and the juniors were speculating about the school dance and the fate of the girls who had tried to smuggle in the drinks, but she had a quick reality check when she met her senior class just before lunch. Jim Callaghan immediately cornered her and asked, "Miss Corbett, is it true what the kids are saying about Dara? I heard she tried to commit suicide last night. Should we send her flowers from the student council?"

Alexa hoped that for once her face did not betray her emotions. "Where did you hear that rumour, Jim?"

"One of the girls on her bus has been telling everyone that Dara took an overdose." He looked apologetic. "I'm not trying to add to the furor. I just thought since she's a senior we should do something to show we care, like send flowers or something."

"It's a nice thought, but I understand that she's in the hospital for a couple of days because of some type of virus."

"Oh, well maybe I should talk to Mrs Fitzgerald in guidance before we do anything. Sometimes the kids start stories that are completely wild."

Jim's forehead was wrinkled with a concerted effort to be politically correct.

The Pathways kids arrived for their afternoon class with the usual pushing and shoving and exchanging ᴄ ᶜinsults. Shawn Bethune wasted no time, "Hey, Miss, what's this about some girl, Darlene, who tried to off herself last night? She's in one of your classes, right?"

Alexa took a deep breath. "I don't teach anyone called Darlene. One of the senior girls is in the hospital with a virus."

"A virus?" Shawn looked sceptical. "Come on, Miss, give us the goods."

Pat Fortier intervened. "Lay off, Shawn. You don't even know the kid's name."

Samantha McGill interrupted before Shawn could open his mouth.

She was not one of Alexa's fans, and now she gave her a look of pure hate. "And we're the dummies. You couldn't talk to us about anything important."

While Alexa was framing her reply, Pat leaped to her defence. "Shut up, Samantha. All you do is bitch about school and make out with your boyfriend. If you're so smart, find another class. Miss Corbett wants to get started."

Samantha flounced to her seat, mouthing an obscenity under her breath. She stared balefully in Pat's direction as Alexa said, "Pat's right. We have to get started." She began to distribute a worksheet drilling writing errors she had found in their last journal entries. "You've got ten minutes to complete this, and then we're going to watch the video of 'The Monkey's Paw', the short story we read on Friday." The students slowly settled down with occasional groans and muttered imprecations.

When Alexa brought her attendance sheets to the office after school, Susan told her that Mark and Lisa were in a meeting. She made tea in the staffroom and went in search of Warren. His tie was loose, and his shirt sleeves rolled up as he sat surrounded by stacks of student assignments. "Hi, Alexa," he greeted her. "You teach Dara Babcock, don't you? Are the rumours the kids are spreading true?"

Alexa filled him in, and he shook his head in sympathy. "You never know, do you? I often wonder what kind of hell some of our kids live in." He reached for a mug of coffee and indicated the untidy desk. "This is my hell. The kids are screaming to get their work back, so this is going to be an all-nighter."

"The constant marking is the worst thing about teaching English," Alexa agreed. "Did you have a good weekend at least?"

"It was great! Why do weekends last only two days? Marielle's just started a new job as an assistant to a set designer who's working on a production of *The Scarlet Pimpernel*. He took us out for dinner at *Le Papillon*, and then we went on to a theatre party." He grinned. "It was quite a contrast to life in Davenport."

Alexa nodded. "I can believe that. I miss the city too. Olympia Pizza doesn't cut it when I want cannelloni, yet I can't believe how this place is growing on me. How are the classes going?"

Warren smiled as if he understood why Alexa was feeling warmer towards Davenport. "Much better, thanks to you. Can we work on the unit test? I thought I'd get to it on the weekend, but I ran out of time."

"Sure, I've got my rough draft here in my briefcase."

When Alexa finally got home, she found that she was restless. She thought about dinner but decided to go out for groceries first. She was pulling on a sweatshirt when the doorbell rang. It was Mark and Sarah.

Mark was smiling. "Hi, the cook just quit! Sarah had an appointment after school, and we decided we should go out to eat. Sarah wants chicken fingers. Would you care to join us?"

For once Sarah looked happy. "I wanted Stuart to come too " she broke in, "but he ate at home. Now he's sleeping on my bed."

They drove to Sarah's favourite fast food restaurant, and she chattered away throughout the meal about a play they were doing at school. "I'm going to be the fairy godmother, and I have to learn a lot of lines, and I have to find a costume."

"When's the show?" Alexa asked.

"At Christmas. Can you help me make a tall, pointy hat with sparkles?"

"Sure, I'd love to. When you know exactly what kind of costume you want, we could go over to my dad's house. Up in his attic there's an old trunk we can raid filled with costumes that my sisters and I used to wear. I think there's a blue skirt with silver stars. That might be just the thing for the fairy godmother to wear."

Sarah was curious. "How many sisters do you have?"

"Two, Kate and Tanya."

"Are they old like you or young?"

Alexa smiled. "They're even older than I am. In fact, Katie, my oldest sister, has a little girl, Bailey, who's about your age."

"Maybe she wants the costumes," Sarah suggested.

"She lives in Vancouver, so she doesn't come here too often, but she's coming for Christmas. You can meet her then."

"I'd like a sister," Sarah said thoughtfully.

Mark asked playfully, "What's wrong with a brother? Is this discrimination?" but Sarah was concentrating on dipping her chicken fingers into a container of honey sauce and had lost interest in any discussion of siblings.

After she finished eating, she ran off to the children's play area giving Mark and Alexa a private moment to talk. "Sarah's a different kid since Stuart joined us," Mark said. "I think you got your wish for a miracle worker. I wasn't part of Sarah's meeting with the doctor today, but she wants to talk to both of us next week."

"I can't believe the change in her. We had a real conversation tonight."

"Sarah doesn't dislike you," Mark protested, echoing Patti's words, "but for a while I think she disliked the whole world." He paused, "So what rumours are flying around the school?"

"Unfortunately the word's out. The junior kids were talking about Friday's dance, but apparently a girl on Dara's bus told everyone she knew that Dara had taken an overdose, and Jim Callaghan approached me about sending flowers. Even the Pathways kids had heard the rumours. Just a typical Monday at Riverside. How is Dara?"

Mark looked upset. "I can't believe I was naive enough to think we could keep this thing under wraps. She'll be okay physically in a day or two. Roger Helmer had a meeting with us after school. He said the hospital might keep her for a couple of days just for observation. I told you before that Dara's been tormented by Stacey off and on for a long time, but this fall things came to a head."

Alexa nodded.

"It seems that Stacey's boyfriend, Ben Copeland, has been taking nude photographs of Stacey in suggestive poses."

Unconsciously Alexa covered her cheeks with her hands as if to block out this image. Mark said, "I know. I reacted the same way. Maybe Ben hoped he could sell them to an Internet site or to some sleazy magazine. But being the jerk he is he couldn't resist bringing them to school to show off to his buddies. He must have dropped one by mistake, and Dara picked it up in the hall. I can't imagine what she thought, but she put it into an envelope and gave it back to Stacey."

Alexa felt like a hypocrite. This was the perfect moment to tell Mark that she knew about this incident, but instead she said, "That's unbelievable. Stacey always looks like Miss Preppy, all that shiny blonde hair and innocent blue eyes."

"I agree. And anybody else would have left it alone, but Stacey told Ben, and he and some of his friends started tormenting Dara. The latest is that they've been calling her 'butch' and 'dyke' and suggesting that she might like to go to bed with Stacey, and Ben would take pictures."

Alexa gulped. Once again she felt totally responsible for Dara's suicide attempt. Why was she such a coward? Why couldn't she talk to Mark about this? After a moment she said, "I understand now why

Dara's been so miserable. She was probably too embarrassed to talk to anyone about this."

"And I imagine she was afraid that no one would believe her. Tonight Roger is contacting both sets of parents. Judging from Mrs Sawyer's reaction to Stacey's suspension, he may not get much support there, but after the incident at the dance we've got enough on Ben to keep him out of school for the rest of the semester, and if the Copelands cooperate he could be facing some additional charges, not just procuring alcohol for minors."

"Do you think Dara will come back to school after all this?"

"I hope so. Kelly went to the hospital to see her today, and Dara asked for some homework. Kelly's also had the chance to talk to her parents. She told Roger that she's going to arrange some counselling for Dara and probably for the family as well. They don't seem like bad people, just busy and preoccupied. The mom has two part-time jobs and more or less leaves Dara in charge of the younger kids."

"If she stays in the hospital, I'll visit her tomorrow after school, or if she's at home I'll drop by with some flowers or a book."

"You're exhausted. I know you care about Dara, but she needs professional help, and Kelly will make sure she gets it. It's critical that she takes care of herself and gets away from the pressure of school and the other kids." Mark sounded vehement.

Alexa had never seen Mark react so strongly. The potential suicide had obviously affected him deeply. "You're right. I wear my heart on my sleeve and that's no help at all."

"On Saturday night you and Patti were talking about visiting Joy for a weekend. Why don't you plan that for next Saturday?"

"What will you and Chris do?"

"We'll manage. Chris asked me to play golf with him sometime, and I can help him close his pool for the season. We'll take good care of the kids."

"I don't doubt that for a moment." Alexa leaned across the table to squeeze Mark's hand. She remembered how concerned she had been when she first came home that the town gossips like Verna would watch her every move. Now it didn't seem to matter. People could think whatever they liked. They would anyway. "I'll call Joy tonight to see if she's up for a visit."

The next afternoon when Alexa pushed open the door of the

hospital room, she thought that Dara was asleep. There was no one else in the double room, and she was a small mound under the tightly pulled sheets of the hospital bed, but when Alexa closed the door and approached the bed, she opened her eyes.

"How are you feeling?" Alexa asked.

"I'm okay, Miss Corbett" Dara answered groggily. "I've got a sore stomach. That's all."

"Maybe this will make you feel a little better." Alexa was carrying a wicker gift basket which she set down on the bedside table. Dara actually smiled as she sat up and reached for the small brown bear surrounded by pale yellow roses and daisies. "That's from the teachers," Alexa told her, "and this book is from me. You're going to love Margaret Atwood if you haven't discovered her poetry yet."

Dara flushed. "Thanks a lot, but I don't deserve any of this, Miss Corbett. I feel like such an idiot. I don't know how I can go back to school and face everyone. I know all the kids will be talking about me."

Alexa couldn't deny this, and she took Dara's hand impulsively. "Whatever rumours are circulating you know how long they last. Some junior kids at the dance smuggled in alcohol and got suspended. It's the buzz in the halls for a day, and then the next story breaks. That's a high school for you. I talked to Mr Anderson before I came here today. He or Mrs Fletcher will call your parents tonight. I don't know very much about all this, but Mr Anderson asked me to tell you not to worry about a thing. He said that the police finished their investigation, and Stacey and Ben aren't coming back to school this semester."

Dara released a huge sigh. "That makes me feel better, but I'm still not sure I want to go back. For one thing I'm going to be so far behind."

"You've only been gone for two days, and all the teachers will help you catch up. I know high school hasn't been great for you. Most of us look back on our years in school, and we have some bad memories, but you've had a really rough time. But you think positively. You're an exceptional writer. Don't waste a gift like that. I majored in English and French at university, but I don't have your talent for writing poetry. Mrs Fitzgerald will help you with your university applications. She says you've got an excellent chance of getting a scholarship or bursary, and I'll be right here tormenting you until you enter the poetry contest I told you about. That will look good on your resume," she teased.

Dara smiled wearily. "All right," she said. "I'm not sure what I'm going to do about school, but I promise I'll enter the contest."

"That's great! I'm going now. You look as if you could use some more sleep. I'm going to leave my telephone number. You can call me anytime if you want to talk, and I'll see you soon. I hope in class."

Alexa walked slowly down the hospital corridor. Dara was far from stupid. She doubted that she had been deceived by Alexa brushing aside the suggestion of rumours. She wondered if she had any friends her own age that she could talk to. She had talent, but other than Kelly Fitzgerald, Mark and Alexa, there didn't seem to be a lot of supporters in her corner.

When Alexa got home, she ate a bowl of soup, but she felt sleepy and listless. She promised herself that she was going to start using the weight room after school. Perhaps a new exercise program would give her a burst of energy. While she was channel surfing, watching snatches of the programs her Pathways kids always talked about, the telephone rang. She picked it up, thinking that Mark must be back from driving Sarah to her Brownie meeting.

"Alexa, I feel I owe you an apology." For once David's voice did not sound arrogant or sarcastic, yet she felt herself becoming tense. Her shoulders and neck felt as if she had been lifting heavy weights. "I shouldn't have appeared at your door unannounced and expected a warm welcome. I'm sorry about that."

Alexa searched for the right words. "It was a bit of a shock, and then I saw your car behind mine last Monday. I didn't expect you'd be back in Davenport so soon."

"I know. I made an appointment to speak with your father at his office. I didn't plan to drop in on you again."

At least David was being honest. Alexa could picture him stroking back his hair as he offered this explanation, but she was not appeased. "David, I don't understand why you thought it was necessary to talk to Dad. I was as direct as I could be when we had coffee together on Sunday."

" I've really been worried about you, and I'm still looking for an explanation of why you left like that. Was it something I did or said which upset you?"

Alexa bit back the urge to tell David that the world did not revolve around him. Instead she replied, "David, I'm just repeating myself. People change. I realized that I no longer wanted the big city rat race and the type of life we had."

"That's hard for me to believe. You always said that you hated small towns where the only spectator sport is watching the neighbours. You seemed happy with our physical relationship. Was that the problem?"

This time Alexa was blunt. "No, David, that wasn't the problem. You're a good lover, wonderful in fact, but that was all."

"All?" David seemed totally bewildered. "It seemed to be enough. We were wonderful *together*, Alexa. We still could be. I want you to come back when you finish your contract there." He hesitated. "I told you that I miss you. We could be married. I can't imagine life without you."

Alexa was at a total loss for words. Finally she said, "David, I'm very flattered, but we've become two very different people. After my mother died, I thought a lot about my parents and the kind of marriage they had. You thrive on the excitement of your university career and the pace of the city. That's not what I need now."

"What do you need?"

"A slower pace for one thing. And a relationship that's based on shared values and mutual respect."

"That's what I thought we had. Listen, Alexa, we need to talk about this in person, not over the telephone. And you left some of the books I gave you here. Could we get together for dinner or a drink on Saturday? If you don't feel like driving into the city, I'll come to Davenport."

For the first time since Alexa had known David, he sounded tentative, almost humble, but Alexa felt detached. *It was an affair,* she told herself, *a convenient living arrangement which suited him. He loved to mentor, and she was a good student, listening to his ideas and allowing him to massage his ego. She shared his bed and perhaps his intellectual life, but there was no strong emotional bond. They never once used the word "love." David would always be a world unto himself.*

Aloud she said, "Thanks for the invitation, David, but it's impossible. And please just keep the books."

David continued to protest, but at last they said goodbye politely although Alexa could feel the waves of resentment which David emitted even through a telephone receiver. Rejection was a new and bitter experience for him, yet somehow Alexa felt that for the first time he had actually heard her message and she hoped that in time he would accept it. He had little choice.

Almost immediately Mark called to see if plans were going ahead for the weekend with Joy. After she gave him the details, he said, "I'm so glad you're getting away. Alexa, get some sleep this week. For once the students can wait a few days to get their work back. The world won't stop turning."

"No, of course it won't. I'm becoming obsessive, but I've decided to start a weight training program tomorrow, and I'll be recharged. The kids won't recognize me as the human dynamo."

"Alexa, you're perfect as you are. Don't change," Mark said softly.

CHAPTER FOURTEEN

*A*s Alexa had hoped, Saturday was the ideal antidote for the stress of the week. It had been years since the three friends were together just having fun. In the morning they went to Costa Brava where Alexa tried on swimsuits, and Patti and Joy modelled exotic lingerie which left them all hysterical with laughter. Ignoring the haughty sales assistant, Patti finally selected a sheer black nightgown although she gasped at the price tag. "There's almost no material," she protested.

"It's worth it. You're paying for the effect it will have on Chris!" Alexa told her. She was holding two swimsuits, a black bikini and a crimson maillot. Unable to decide between them, she bought both.

After lunch and sangria at the Blue Cactus, they took a taxi to Serenity Spa where Alexa had "the transformation", a manicure, pedicure and facial, and Joy and Patti decided to be completely decadent with a seaweed wrap and a massage. Later at Joy's apartment they dropped their shopping bags and changed quickly before leaving for dinner and *Mamma Mia*.

Over drinks and munchies, they talked into the late hours of Saturday night, sharing the details of their present lives and their memories of high school. Patti and Alexa howled with laughter while Joy recalled a Christmas dance which she and Alexa attended as a couple. Joy had rented a tuxedo and Alexa borrowed a strapless black dress from Katie. Both had worn red roses. "I can still see Mr MacLeod's face when we got up to dance," Alexa chortled. "Why did we decide to do that? I suppose Tony was away playing hockey, and I didn't want to sit home alone. In those days, girls didn't go stag to the Christmas formal."

"And I was languishing over Eric Johnson who didn't know I was alive," Joy added.

"Mr MacLeod? Who was he?" Patti asked, wiping tears of laughter from her eyes.

"Don't you remember? He was the vice-principal," Alexa replied. "I'll never forget him because he caught me the only time I forged a note from my mother."

"When did that happen?" Joy asked.

"In my senior year, Mom wrote me a note because I had a dentist appointment. I was supposed to be excused at 1:45, and I changed the time to 11: 45. I thought I was being very clever using the same colour ink as my mother, but somehow he knew and called home. That was one of the times when my parents gave me the 'we're very disappointed' lecture."

"Where were you planning to go?" Patti wanted to know.

"Tony and I thought we could get away with cutting part of the morning and having a long lunch hour at his house while his mother was at work. We thought we had a foolproof scheme, but it didn't work," Alexa said ruefully.

Patti sighed. "It's amazing how your perspective changes when you have kids. What we did was so innocent. I shudder when I think what Nick and Cheyenne may be doing when they're teens."

"The good old days weren't always innocent," Alexa said thoughtfully. "Since I've come back, I've been haunted by the ghosts of our high school days. Do you remember the murder of Lennie Warner?"

"Vaguely, " Patti replied. "There was something bizarre there. I remember that some of the kids in our year used to hang out at his apartment and smoke up or whatever, and then when he died, a young kid none of us knew was charged."

"I went there once."

Both Patti and Joy looked at her in surprise. "To Lennie's apartment? You weren't part of that crowd," Joy said.

"It was before I started to date Tony. One of the girls in our French class, Marnie Walker, invited me, and I went with her. I tried to pretend I was having a great time, but I hated it. The kids were all smoking pot and drinking beer, and Lennie was trying to be cool and part of the scene. Ronnie Benoit was there that night, and when he and Marnie disappeared into a bedroom I left."

"You never told us that before," Joy said.

"I know. There were lots of things I didn't tell you two both before and after Tony. I guess I was just trying to fit in somewhere and tired of following in the footsteps of two perfect sisters."

"I didn't know you felt that way," Patti told her, leaning over to hug her. "Of the three of us, you were the one with self-confidence. You always seemed so sure of yourself. Like you knew exactly what you wanted."

"It was mostly an act. I said I wanted to be my own person, but I followed whatever crowd I was in."

"Don't be so hard on yourself. You were just a kid. You've got to allow yourself to be human. That's what I learned from the whole miserable scene of breaking up with Janet and leaving Interval House. We're only human. Most of the time we just do the best we can. We can't save the world. We can't even save another person."

Now it was Alexa and Patti's turn to look at Joy. "Where do we get these Messiah complexes?" she asked. "It's definitely a woman thing."

"Thanks, Joy. I needed to hear that right now " and Alexa began to tell them about Justin and Dara.

On Sunday morning at brunch, they vowed to plan a getaway weekend every year. Joy summed it up. "We need to let our hair down once in a while and get a little crazy, and I've missed you guys so much." Alexa and Patti drove home with Beatle tapes playing loudly and feeling as if they were eighteen again.

Mark's sister, Joanne, had invited Alexa, Mark and Sarah to a family party that night. Alexa was looking forward to meeting Dorothy and Jim Henderson, the aunt and uncle Mark and Jo had stayed with as children. She had no time to be nervous about meeting Mark's family, and she was still on a high from her weekend away. In the car she chattered on, telling Sarah about Mamma Mia. "I promise to take you if we can get some tickets. You'll love it. At the end, everyone was up dancing to the music like a big party. I bought you the CD, so you can listen to the songs before we go."

Sarah was thrilled at the prospect of a trip to the city. "When can we go?" she demanded. "How about next weekend? My friend, Angie, went with her mom to see *The Lion King*. Can we see that too?"

"Let's wait a few weeks. Then we can do some early Christmas shopping while we're there. We'll only have time to go to one play, but you can pick the one you want to see."

Mark smiled at their enthusiasm, yet he seemed preoccupied. While Sarah talked away about her Saturday with Nick and Cheyenne, Mark was unusually quiet although he reached for Alexa's hand and give it a squeeze when Sarah said, "Cheyenne's such a baby. I have to watch her all the time, or she gets into trouble."

Alexa thoroughly enjoyed Joanne's dinner party. Almost immediately she felt included in the family circle as she studied Joanne, so much like Mark with her brown hair and disconcertingly blue eyes. She was casually dressed in a red turtleneck sweater and long black denim skirt. Like Mark, she was friendly and outgoing, greeting Alexa with a quick hug, "I feel as if we already know each other. Mark talks about you constantly."

Everyone was talking at once as they sat around the living room and helped themselves from a large fruit tray on the glass coffee table. Over the mêlée of voices Alexa could hear Sarah asking, "Aunt Jo, where did you get these baby melons? They're awesome. We always buy the great big ones."

"We grew them in the garden specially for you," Joanne replied. "I'm glad you like them, sweetpea, because it's very hard to peel such tiny fruit!" She and Alexa smiled at each other while Sarah speared a melon ball and popped it into her mouth.

Alexa talked for a long time to Mark's Aunt Dorothy, still vibrant at eighty. She and Jim had just celebrated their fifty-fifth wedding anniversary. "What an accomplishment that is!" Alexa said in admiration.

"It doesn't seem like fifty-five years, and the best part is that we still laugh together. He's the only man I know who listens to the opera on Saturday afternoon while he watches the baseball game on television."

"And you're the only woman I know who'll let me eat fruitcake sandwiched between shortbread cookies for Christmas breakfast," Jim interjected.

"Well, you've never complained about my onion and peanut butter sandwiches!"

"Onion and peanut butter?" Alexa asked.

"I use Spanish onions and slice them very thin. Try it sometime. It's delicious."

Alexa looked across the room to smile at Mark who was talking to his brother-in-law. That morning she and Patti had sung along with one of their favourite Beatle songs, "When I'm Sixty-Four."

For the first time she wondered if she and Mark could possibly grow old together, sharing the challenges and joys of life, building a strong relationship like this one over the years. She was already so comfortable with Mark. Perhaps "comfortable" wasn't a romantic word, but this was what she wanted, caring and openness and sharing everything they were and would be.

At the dinner table she watched Ray carving the roast of beef while Jo organized the dishes of vegetables. Both of them looked happy and relaxed. Alexa wanted to be part of this. Later, when they said good night with a sleepy Sarah leaning again Mark, Alexa said impulsively, "Thanks so much for inviting me. I had a wonderful evening. I'll call you soon with a return invitation."

After Sarah went to bed so tired that for once she did not insist on her usual routine of books and stories, she and Mark sat side by side in front of the fire. Alexa stretched luxuriously. "What a fabulous weekend. First I get to spend some quality time with Joy and Patti. Then I meet your family. I can't imagine anything better. Your aunt and uncle should write a book about the secrets of aging well. They're very special."

"I loved visiting them when I was a kid. They always had so much fun with each other and just naturally included Jo and me. We were like their favourite grandchildren." There was a moment of silence, and Alexa's heart beat faster as Mark kissed her. She kissed him back and put her arms around him, wishing they could slip off their clothes and make love in the warmth of the flames. She closed her eyes and leaned against him, playing with this fantasy until she heard Mark say, "Alexa, I want to show you something that was in my mailbox when I got home from school on Friday night." He went over to the bookcase and picked up an envelope addressed to "Mr Mark Anderson" in spidery handwriting. Inside was a folded piece of paper and a message which appeared to be typed using a machine with a very worn ribbon. Alexa noticed that the "o's" were almost illegible:

Mr Anderson, you appear to be a fine young man. I feel it is my duty to tell you that you are making a mistake in seeing Alexandra Corbett. She is not the kind of young woman you should be associating with, and she is sure to be a bad influence on your Child. She had an Abortion, and any woman who kills a child is breaking God's law. I do not think you are the kind of man who can accept immoral behaviour. I am sorry to send you this letter without signing my name, but I think it is best that I remain anonymous.

I have only your interests at heart and trust that you will do your Christian duty.

Alexa was completely stunned by what she read. She held the paper in her hands for a long time, staring blindly at the page. She blinked away unshed tears. Finally her face crumpled. Tears rolled down her cheeks although she did not make a sound.

Mark put his arms around her. "I'm sorry," he murmured against her hair. "I shouldn't have given this to you. But we've grown so close, and I didn't want any secrets between us. Please don't cry." He kissed a tear which had rolled down one cheek.

Alexa struggled to get her emotions under control and at last she spoke almost tonelessly, "Who could have written this filth? Who could hate me that much?"

Mark looked helpless. He kissed her again. "Please try not to be so upset. At first I was just going to rip it up, but so many strange things have been happening that I thought I should keep it." She pulled away from his embrace and stood up.

He watched her as she walked over to the window and stared out at the quiet street. He could hear her sobbing and quickly got up, going over to put his arms around her from behind, nuzzling the side of her neck. They stood like that for a moment, and then Alexa broke free. She turned around to face him. "I suppose you think I owe you an explanation."

Mark was clearly upset. "Alexa, you don't owe me anything." He was unconsciously echoing the words she had used to David. "Can't we just forget it? It's sick. Some crazy wrote that letter. I know it's not true."

"What's not true?"

"What the letter said."

"And what if it were? Would your feelings change? Would you then sit as judge and jury? Would everything be different between us?"

"That's not fair," Mark interjected sharply. "I'd never judge you, and one crank letter from a fanatic doesn't change anything between us."

Without another word, Alexa went to get her jacket.

Mark was shocked not so much by her words but by her expression.

"Please wait. You can't leave like this. Let's talk about it. At least let me walk you home."

"No. Sarah's upstairs asleep. I need to be by myself and have some time to think about this." Ignoring the stricken expression on Mark's face, Alexa slipped on her jacket and went out, closing the front door quietly behind her.

She began to walk quickly. At first her thoughts were a jumble of emotions, but gradually she allowed the quiet of the night to surround her. She deliberately chose the longest way back to her apartment, and after a few minutes felt a little calmer. She refused to think about the letter or Mark. Instead she concentrated on the peaceful street and the pools of light sent out by each house she passed. Usually Alexa liked to speculate about the life inside each home. Often the living room curtains were open, offering clues about the family they contained. In one room she could see floor-to-ceiling bookcases. A man and woman sat reading in armchairs beside the fireplace. In another a solitary woman slouched on a couch in front of a television set.

At last Alexa allowed her thoughts to turn back to the hateful anonymous letter. What drove a human being to send that kind of message? Revenge? A quest for power? Or was it really the misguided belief that your duty was to inform and protect a child from an adult sinner? Alexa shuddered. She had a sudden understanding of the depths of loneliness and frustration which led someone to keep a secret for years and then, empowered by hidden knowledge, write a letter and furtively watch its effects. She pictured an empty life with no fulfilment except to observe from the sidelines. She shivered. As a child she had lived near such a person, someone who watched and noted events. She thrust the thought away.

That night Alexa lay sleepless for hours. She resisted the idea of calling Mark. It would be so easy to pick up the phone and be comforted by his voice, but somehow she could not make the call. She wondered if he were very angry. She knew she had behaved badly, but the letter had come as a complete shock. Twelve years was a long time, time enough to start a career, to marry and have children. Events which had happened more than a decade before had seemed to be neatly wrapped and then carefully entombed in a locked compartment. Now time seemed transparent, a series of compartments through which she was condemned to drift. Nothing was finished. She felt destined to relive the past endlessly. Why would Mark want to be part of that?

The next day at school it was easier for Alexa to think of other things. Kelly Fitzgerald found her in the cafeteria at lunch hour. "I've got good news," she said. "I thought you'd want to know that I talked to Justin Murray and his grandmother today. He's working for Ronnie Benoit again and he's decided to enrol at the alternative school. I faxed them his transcript, and he's going to start with an English course. He also mentioned that he still has one of your books."

"When you're talking to him again, tell him to keep it," Alexa replied with a smile. "When does he have to appear in court?"

Kelly shrugged. "Probably not for a month or two at least. There's always a backlog of cases. Lisa will be called as a witness, but it's a first offence. I expect the judge will be lenient if Justin's enrolled in a school part-time and working."

"Do you think he can stay clean?" Alexa asked

"I wish I knew. I don't think Justin has a serious drug problem. I know he drinks regularly, and he needs money. In a strange way, this may be a good thing for him. Neither Ronnie nor Tony will put up with any nonsense at work, and if Justin wants to learn a trade, he'll pick up the basics of carpentry from them. I'm going to stay in touch with him. There's always the possibility of setting up an apprenticeship. Who knows? There may be a happy ending after all."

Alexa nodded. "School certainly isn't the only way to learn. I had my Pathways class just before lunch. Those kids are counting the days until they can get out on a co-operative learning experience. Talk to them about snowmobiles or cars, and they come alive. Put them in a classroom and they're caged animals!"

Kelly looked around the room, frowning at a boy who was winding up to throw a container of yogurt. "It looks like feeding time at the zoo," she said with unusual cynicism. "Remember even the zoo keepers need some nourishment. Be sure you eat something before you go back to class."

She was about to leave when Alexa put her hand on her arm, "Any news from Dara?"

"She's coming in tomorrow, but I don't think she'll be back."

"You can't let her quit school. She has to come back!" Alexa knew she was becoming far too emotional about this.

"It's not really that bad. Dara was carrying an extra subject this semester because Lisa doesn't want the seniors to have a double spare. She only needs English and history, and she can continue with those through the alternative school. I don't think she's ready to face the other kids right now."

"She promised me that she'd enter the teachers' writing competition," Alexa said despondently.

"She can still do that. I'll remind her."

Alexa was feeling down when the final bell rang. Her classes didn't seem the same without Justin and Dara, but as she was straightening the room, gathering up books and papers, Warren knocked on the door smiling broadly. "I can't wait any longer," he said. "Let's go to the English office and find Carol. I've got something to tell both of you."

Carol was marking tests at her cluttered desk. "You're like a dog with two tails," she greeted Warren. "Please don't tell me you got married this weekend! Alexa and I want an invitation to the wedding."

Warren was literally grinning from ear to ear and looked about sixteen years old. "Don't worry. You'll both be there. No, I have other stupendous news." He paused for effect. "On Saturday morning I had an interview with St Michael's Academy. They offered me a contract for next semester teaching English and drama!" Giving them no time to react, he went on, "I hate to leave Riverside so soon, but now Marielle and I can be together and when I'm living in the city it'll be easier to take some post-graduate courses."

Alexa hastily suppressed a twinge of jealousy as Warren described this dream job, but she threw her arms round him. "I'm so happy for you! St Mike's is a good prep school with small classes. You'll be on cloud nine. I just couldn't see Marielle living happily ever after in Davenport."

Carol added, "It's great news, but Riverside is going to miss you. Kerry's been talking nonstop about your classes for the last few weeks. She's decided you're way cool. Promise your kids won't hear the news until January, or they'll be getting up a petition to keep you here!"

"Don't worry. They'll be the last to know, but there's another part to all this!" Warren looked at Alexa. "You'll have a contract for semester two. Even if Murray Dean comes back in February, the school will need another English teacher."

"Bingo! I thought of that right away," Carol said, beaming at Alexa.

"You two are way ahead of me. Let's not count on it. Maybe when the English position's advertised, Lisa will hire someone else."

"And maybe she won't, " Carol answered. "I'm not trying to give you a swollen head, but everyone here knows you're doing a great job. Except for your university kids, you don't have the best classes, but you're getting through to them, and that's not easy."

"You're the first ones to hear about this. I'll talk to Mrs Fletcher and Mark later this week. I wouldn't have made it this far without you two, and you've still got a few months to bring me along so I'll be a real pro by the time I hit St Mike's."

Both of them vowed to keep the news a secret. "But swear you'll stay in touch and meet us whenever we brush the hayseeds out of our hair and come to the city," Carol joked.

"That goes without saying. I may even be able to get you some theatre tickets," Warren promised.

"Warren, you're a babe!" Carol laughed as Warren blushed.

Alexa left the English office still thinking about Warren's news and wondering what it would mean for her. She forced herself to go to the weight room and use the treadmill and the rowing machine. The room was deserted. Students and staff had finished their workouts and drifted out, but she could hear the thwack of the ball as the senior girls' volleyball team practised in the gym across the hall. She was half-heartedly doing arm curls with hand weights when Sarah appeared at the doorway. "Sarah, what are you doing here?" Alexa exclaimed.

"I went to see my doctor tonight after school. Now Dad's in the office talking to somebody. Then we're going to order a big pizza, half with pepperoni and half with veggies, but no mushrooms. Do you want some?"

Alexa carefully laid down the weights. "Just give me time to shower and change. I've wanted a pizza all day."

Sarah smiled at her. "Maybe Dad can order two pizzas."

CHAPTER FIFTEEN

ℰꙮ

When Alexa closed the door, Mark wanted to rush after her. It took all the self-control he had to let her walk away. Silently he cursed his decision to show her the letter. It was ugly and vindictive, but he had never imagined that Alexa would react this way.

He went to check on Sarah who was sleeping soundly. He was tempted to call Alexa as soon as he thought she was home, but she had said she wanted to be alone. Although he resisted the impulse and tried to plan his schedule for Monday, his thoughts were elsewhere. Surely she hadn't been serious when she accused him of sitting in judgement. He didn't care about her past, but he felt a knot of tension in his stomach as he wondered if she would try to cut herself off from him completely.

At last he went to bed, but unable to sleep, he thought about Alexa. With her cloud of dark hair and her eyes a strange shade of blue so dark as to be almost violet, she was beautiful, but he told himself it was not difficult to find attractive women. He responded to Alexa not just because of her physical appearance, but the special way she tugged at his deepest emotions. Alexa met life with her arms wide open. Whether she was talking to Sarah, teaching a class, or walking on the beach, she was fully present in the moment. He had never met anyone quite like her before. Mark knew that he had been able to share his feelings with her as with no one else, yet he was very much aware that Alexa had wrapped herself in a protective coating, and there were many parts of her life which she had not revealed. He wondered if she would ever fully open up to him.

As usual he was busy on Monday dealing with a series of incidents involving attendance, discipline, and personal issues brought to him by staff and students. Lisa was at the monthly principals' meeting, and when the superintendent called to tell him that Mrs Sawyer was appealing Stacey's suspension, Mark took meticulous notes but felt only impatience that Lisa had to defend every action the school took.

After school there was no time to look for Alexa since Sarah had an appointment with Dr Ahmid. Mark wasn't in the habit of noticing decorating details, but as he sat in the doctor's reception area he felt himself relax in the cocoon of the wingback chair. The room was furnished in pale blues and greens, and the low table beside his chair had a lamp instead of institutional fluorescent lights glaring down from the ceiling. Green plants in ceramic pots filled the corners. He picked up a sports magazine and idly flipped through it, unable to concentrate.

In a few minutes, the office door opened, and Dr Admid appeared. "Mr Anderson, Sarah and I thought you might like to join us now." She stood back to let him precede her through the door, a tiny woman dressed in a long skirt and silk blouse. The office was like a small family room. Sarah was sitting cross-legged on the floor, playing with a family of bears all dressed in colourful winter sweaters and scarves. Dr Admid sat down on a couch near Sarah and motioned for Mark to join her. There was nothing clinical about the room. A writing pad with a page of notes lay on the coffee table. Again Mark felt himself relaxing. The tension in his neck and shoulders was gone.

"Hi, Dad," Sarah said. She seemed more interested in dressing the bears than talking to anyone.

"Sarah and I are just getting to know each other," Dr Ahmid began in her quiet voice. "She was telling me how she feels when she goes to visit her mother. Sarah, do you want to tell your dad about that?"

There was a long silence. Sarah tied a yellow scarf around the mother bear's neck and looked at it critically. At last she said, "I don't like to go there. I want Mom to come back to our house."

Mark unconsciously sighed. "Sarah, can you tell me why you don't like to visit her?"

Sarah shrugged and untied the scarf. She picked up a red one instead. "I don't like that guy who lives with her. He's always hanging around, and sometimes he kisses her in front of me. It's gross."

Mark could feel himself stiffen. "His name's Peter. I'm sorry you don't like him. Maybe your mother could come for a sleepover at our house. She could spend a night with you there."

"You mean like it was before, and you'd be there too?" Sarah asked.

"No, I'd go to stay with Aunt Jo and Uncle Ray or maybe with Aunt Dorothy and Uncle Jim," Mark answered.

"Why can't you stay with us?"

"Sarah, we talked about this before. Your mother wasn't happy when she lived with me. We both love you very much, but now we live in separate houses." Mark glanced at Dr Ahmid. She was listening carefully to their conversation.

"Why can't we just be together again?"

"I know you want that to happen, but your mother likes Peter, and she's happier now that she's living with him."

Sarah didn't answer. At last she said, "When I go to visit Mom, does Alexa come to stay at our house?"

Mark was startled. "I told you that Alexa is a friend of mine from school. I like her a lot, but right now we're just friends. When you're away, Alexa and I do some things together like go to the beach or supervise a dance at school, but she doesn't sleep at our house."

Again there was no comment from Sarah who was now undressing all the bears. Mark was getting no help from Dr Ahmid, but he tried again, "Do you like Alex?"

"She's okay. She's nicer than Julie. And she doesn't stink of cigarettes, and her friend Patti gave me Stuart."

Mark went on, "No matter what happens, you and I are always going to be together. We're a family."

Sarah considered this. "Are Mom and Peter a family?"

Mark swallowed hard. "Yes, they are."

"But they don't want me around."

Mark struggled to find the right words. "I don't think that's true. Your mother loves you a lot, but she's had a lot of changes in her life too. Sometimes grownups have problems, but that doesn't mean they stop loving their kids, and Peter's just getting to know you."

After a moment Dr Ahmid said, "Sarah, would you take the bears into the reception area where Tasha's working? I want to speak with your dad for just a moment."

After Sarah had left carrying the bear family, Dr Ahmid gave Mark her full attention. "Mr Anderson, like most children whose parents separate, Sarah is struggling with the changes and what they mean to her. She's very bright, and often with a bright child we talk a lot and try to use words to help them deal with their pain. Sarah can verbalize how she feels, but it's going to take some time for her emotions to catch up with what she says. Let her have that time."

Mark nodded. "I know. Sometimes I feel that I'm living with another adult, and then I realize she's a kid who's hurt and just wants to go back to the time when Jane and I were together."

Dr Ahmid stood up. "If you'd like me to see Sarah again, Tasha has my appointment book."

"Thank you. I think it's helping her. She's very comfortable with you." The two shook hands.

Dr Ahmid smiled, suddenly looking very young. "Then I'll see her again in two weeks."

Mark took Sarah back to the school with him. At noon hour there had been a fight in the boys' locker room, and one of the parents was coming in to protest the suspension which followed. When they walked in the front door, Mark said, "Sarah, I'll be busy with a parent for a few minutes. Then we'll order pizza for supper from Olympia. You can look at the takeout menu in the office and pick what you want."

"Can I go down to the gym?"

"Yes, but if there's still a practice going on, you'll have to sit on one of the benches and stay off the court."

Mark watched as Sarah walked down the hall in the direction of the gym area. At this hour she considered the school her personal playground, and all the staff knew her. He waved at Neil Chisholm, the head custodian, and went to check his phone messages.

The meeting went on much longer than Mark had planned. When the parent finally left, Sarah was sitting at Susan's desk, happily swinging her feet and using coloured markers to draw a picture of the pizza she wanted.

"Hi, Dad, I saw Alexa. She wants pizza too."

Mark felt as if he had just received a standing ovation as his team won the basketball championship. He resisted the urge to let out a blood curdling yell of happiness. Instead he managed to contain himself and went over to Sarah to give her a bear hug. "You're amazing! Did I ever tell you that before?"

"Oh, Dad!" Sarah wriggled self-consciously, trying to free herself. "You can't do that at school. Some of the big kids might see us."

"No big kids here," Mark said, pretending to look around.

"There are some big girls in the gym playing volleyball, " Sarah answered. "That's where I saw Alexa."

"She was playing volleyball?" Mark pretended to be serious.

"No, she was working out in the weight room, so I asked her if she wanted pizza, and she said she'd wanted some all day."

"Thanks for inviting her, Sarah." Mark couldn't control his smile. "We can order as soon as we get home. I'll ask Alexa to meet us there."

"Dad, I'm starving. Let's order now, and we can eat at the table in your office. It'll be like a picnic."

Mark started to protest, "Alexa has been here all day. Maybe she'd like to get out of the school." Just then Alexa came into the office. She had changed back into the black pantsuit she had worn in the classroom that day, and her hair was still damp from the shower and curled softly around her face. "I vote with Sarah," she said. "I haven't eaten anything since noon hour, and I'm hungry too."

Mark raised his hands, smiling, "Okay, okay, I know when I'm outnumbered," and he reached for the telephone.

Alexa seemed to be ignoring the scene on Sunday night. She and Sarah wasted no time in polishing off the pizzas as they talked, and when Mark excused himself to deal with a student who had come into the office to call home after the practice, he came back to learn that Sarah was going for a bike ride with Alexa on Friday after school.

"Are you sure you want to bother, Alex?"

"Of course, it's not a bother. My old bike's still at Dad's. I'll check the tires this week. It'll be fun. Maybe later we can use Martin's barbecue and cook our supper."

After they had cleaned up and were putting on their jackets, he said quietly, "When do we have a chance to talk?"

"On Friday, " she promised. "There's a lot I want to tell you."

"With Sarah around?"

"Sarah goes to bed early. There'll be time then," she replied, and with that he had to be content.

On Friday between classes, Kelly appeared in Alexa's classroom with a folder. "The promised poems from Dara," she explained. "She didn't come in until this morning. Apparently she hasn't been feeling well, and she apologized several times for cancelling out on Tuesday."

Alexa took the file eagerly. "I'll take care of these. Do you think I should call her, or would that just add to her stress?"

"Go ahead. I think she'd like to hear from you. Part of the problem is that she feels like a quitter for dropping out this semester, but she's already got her materials for the home study courses, and she'll be busy with those. Maybe she'll be ready to come back for semester two. We made an appointment to go over her university applications next week, so at least she's not giving up on that."

"I can submit her poems, and please let her know that I'm more than willing to tutor if she has a problem in English, and I'm sure Phil would help her with history."

"Good. The more we stay in touch the more likely it is that she'll consider coming back. She could finish her year through distance education, but she's desperate for some human contact."

"I'll give her that," Alexa promised.

When Sarah arrived at Alexa's door after school, she looked listless and pale. She was carrying Zeke, her battered stuffed monkey. "Are you feeling sick, Sarah? You look a little tired."

Sarah shrugged irritably. "My throat feels funny, sort of scratchy. I don't think I can go for a bike ride with you. Dad drove me over. Can I lie down on your couch and watch television?"

Alexa tried to touch Sarah's forehead to see if she felt feverish, but Sarah froze and then pushed her hand away. "Don't you touch me!" she shouted. "I hate you doing that. You're not my mother. My dad and I are happy, just the two of us. I don't see why you always have to come around."

Alexa inhaled deeply. She felt as if someone had punched her hard in the stomach. "And I hate the way you're acting," she snapped. "You're bright and funny, and your dad loves you very much, but you make him unhappy with your sulking and bad moods. Don't do that to him. He's such a good guy. It's not fair."

"I don't care! I don't want you hanging out with my dad, and if I have to see you, I'm going to run away. Then he'll be sorry he didn't pay more attention to me."

Alexa resisted asking Sarah where she would go. To her mother and Peter's house? Or was she planning to move in with her best friend, Angie?

For a moment, the two glared at each other. Sarah's eyes were filled with anger and with a cool contempt which Alexa found totally disconcerting. She was prepared for tears or more shouting, but without saying another word Sarah lay down on the couch and used the remote control to flip through the channels, stopping to watch a game show and quickly becoming absorbed in the inane actions, ignoring Alexa completely.

After a moment, Alexa poured a glass of apple juice and set it down on the table beside the couch. From the kitchen window she could see Mark and Martin talking on the patio below. "I'm going down to the patio. If you feel better, come and join us," she invited. "Martin has something neat he wants to show you." She forced herself to sound calm as if she had never shouted at Sarah.

Sarah clutched her monkey and did not even look away from the television screen. Alexa wondered if she were really sick or thinking, *No way, lady. I won't give you the time of day. Not after the way you yelled at me.*

She closed the door quietly behind her and went downstairs. When Mark patted the lounge chair beside him, she sat down and asked, "What's wrong with Sarah?"

"She says she's sick, and her throat's sore. I tried to give her some baby aspirin, but she didn't want to take them. Actually I think a big part of the problem is that she was supposed to go shopping with her mother tomorrow for a new winter jacket and boots, but Jane called after school and said she was busy on Saturday, and they'd have to postpone it for a week." He looked exasperated. "I wish she understood what that does to Sarah."

"That's hard on her. And I know you've got a basketball tournament on this weekend."

"If Sarah's feeling better, I'll take her. If not, I'll call Courtney to see if she can babysit again."

"If you're stuck for a sitter, I can help out. I don't know if Sarah would like that, but I don't have anything special planned for tomorrow except the usual marking. If Sarah's feeling better by the afternoon, we can make some chocolate chip cookies and take them over to Patti's munchkins. They'd be happy to see Sarah again, and she could bring Stuart for a visit."

"Thanks, but you've got a life too. You don't need Sarah in one of her sulky moods." He looked tired and tense.

"Really, I don't mind."

Martin had opened a bottle of wine while they were talking. Now he brought them both a glass and said, "Let me put some souvlaki on the barbecue. Maybe Sarah will brighten up if she has something to eat." He turned to Mark. "I told Alexa that I have a set of Matryoshka dolls we bought in the Soviet Union which I was going to give Sarah. I'll bring them up to her before dinner, and if she doesn't want to eat, they may keep her amused."

Alexa went upstairs to check on Sarah, who was asleep. It was tempting to condemn her mother. How could she let Sarah down repeatedly? Sarah was quicksilver, her moods varying from moment to moment, but she was also funny and perceptive. Jane was missing so much.

In spite of Martin's efforts, Alexa could see that Mark was tense and preoccupied. While she talked to Martin, he frowned, looking as if he were wrestling with some problem more weighty than a babysitter for Sarah. She wondered if he were thinking of what she might confess when they were alone. She felt a prickle of apprehension but tried to concentrate on Martin who enjoyed the opportunity of sharing his beautiful home with guests. When he surprised them by producing a tray of baklava for dessert, Alexa tried to tease him. "Martin, the magician, what hat did you pull these from? Or is there a Greek bakery in Davenport I haven't discovered?"

"One of my clients knows I have a sweet tooth, and she often brings me a treat when she comes from the city. These were in my freezer next to an almond cake. I can also produce a bottle of ouzo, but I thought we'd pass on the Greek coffee." He explained to Mark, "Greek coffee's a lot like Turkish coffee. It's incredibly strong and served in tiny demitasse cups. We could never drink more than a few sips because the bottom half is full of coffee grinds."

Alexa smiled at this description. "That's my assessment exactly. I've even tried to drink the coffee while sucking on the traditional sugar cubes, but it wasn't much better. In Athens I discovered that if I ordered 'American coffee', the waiter brought a packet of Nescafé and a cup of hot water. It wasn't great, but better than the alternative."

"I can't compete with you world travellers," Mark commented good-naturedly, trying to be part of the conversation. "The farthest I've been is Mexico." He looked at his watch. "If you two come back to my place, I promise to make us some genuine American coffee. I want to put Sarah to bed early. And, Martin, thanks so much for thinking of giving Sarah the dolls, but why don't you wait until she's feeling better and can appreciate them?"

Martin diplomatically declined the invitation for coffee saying that he had to return some telephone calls. Tucked into her own bed, Sarah woke up long enough to drink some juice before falling asleep again. When Mark came back downstairs, Alexa was sipping her coffee. "This is good. Almost as good as the coffee in France, " she teased.

"Don't go there, " he begged. "I love Sarah, but at times I think I should have wandered the world for a while before becoming a father."

"She's worth it. You'll have lots of time to travel later."

"Do you want more coffee while I call Courtney to see if she's free to stay with Sarah on Saturday?"

While Alexa poured a second cup for each of them, he made the call and came back saying, "Neighbours can be wonderful at times. Courtney's away this weekend, so I talked to her mom who's sending her niece over to babysit on Saturday."

"That's good. Now you can go to the tournament and concentrate on coaching." She put down her cup. They smiled tentatively at each other. "Can we talk about last Sunday and the letter?"

"Of course, if you're sure you want to, but you don't have to explain anything to me. The world's full of crazies. Let's leave it at that."

Alexa shook her head. "No, I'm tired of secrets. I want to tell you about my senior year in high school."

Mark started to protest, but she held up one hand, "Please just listen." She took a deep breath. "You know, Mark, this happened so long ago I almost feel as if I'm telling you someone else's story." She closed her eyes and then began. "In July before my senior year in high school, I found out that I was pregnant. I was sixteen, and I had dated only one boy. His name was Tony Benoit. He had just signed a contract to play Junior A hockey, and he was going to leave town in August."

Mark had moved to the couch beside her, and he held one of her hands in both of his.

"My mom and dad were wonderful. They were horribly upset, and my mom cried a lot, but they didn't condemn me or Tony, and I knew they would be there for me no matter what I decided to do. We talked and talked about all my options. I knew I didn't want to get married, and I wasn't ready for any long term commitments. I wanted to go to university, and it would be years before I could support a child on my own. Mom and Dad offered to help if I kept the baby, but I didn't think that was fair. They had raised their own family. They didn't need to raise a grandchild. Dad asked me if I wanted to end the pregnancy, but I felt that what was inside me was alive. I couldn't even consider that."

When she paused again, Mark took both her hands in his. "You don't have to tell me any of this."

Alexa freed her hands and brought them up to her cheeks. She took several deep breaths and went on as if he had never spoken. "Finally we decided that I would go out to North Vancouver. My mother's younger sister, Aunt Krista, is a teacher there. She arranged for me to take courses through an alternative school. In those days there was nothing like that in Davenport. We decided that after the baby was born my dad would arrange a private adoption, and I would finish the semester there. I flew to Vancouver in August without even saying goodbye to my friends. It was a nightmare. I still dream about it sometimes. When I got there, I was incredibly homesick. I had never been away from my family before and I just kept crying. I couldn't seem to stop. Aunt Krista and I spent most of our time on the telephone talking to Mom."

Mark put his arm around Alexa's shoulders, and she looked at him, her eyes glistening with unshed tears. "In the last week of August just before school started, I lost the baby. My aunt and uncle took me to emergency right away, but the doctor couldn't get the bleeding to stop. The cramps and the hemorrhaging were terrible. I was just a kid, and I was so frightened. And I felt guilty, as if I had somehow caused the miscarriage by being so upset."

Mark put his arms tightly around her and pulled her close. "Alexa, I'm sorry. I'm so sorry you had to go through that. You were so young and so alone."

Alexa tried to smile at him. "The bizarre thing was that when it was all over I came home and finished my senior year here. No one knew what had happened except my family. I know Patti and Joy suspected that something was wrong, but I never told them about the pregnancy. Most of the kids just thought I went away for a holiday because I was upset after I broke up with Tony, and he left to play hockey." She smiled for the first time. "I hadn't been a very serious student, but that year I hit the books, and for the first time my marks were high enough for university."

"You never told Tony that you were pregnant?"

"I know it sounds strange, but he never knew. Twelve years ago it just seemed that it was the girl's problem, and anyway I couldn't face his family. They were so proud of him. I was afraid his mother would think I was trying to trap her son at the start of his brilliant and lucrative hockey career."

Mark held her tightly. "I hate to see you so upset, but I'm happy that I know about this. One of the reasons I love you is that you care so much about people. I see it with the kids at school, and I see it with Sarah. You light up when you talk to her. Let's try to forget the letter. It's ugly, and it's not part of our lives."

Alexa shook her head. "I know I was upset last Sunday, and I behaved badly, but I knew even then that this was going to haunt me. I'll keep asking myself who sent the letter and why."

"Is that so important?"

"It is to me. You'd think I'd have learned by now that you can't keep a secret, especially in a small town like this one, but I thought no one knew about this except my parents and my sisters. Obviously I was wrong. Someone knew and then made some assumptions."

"Alexa, I want to build a life with you. Everything isn't going to be easy. We're not kids anymore, and we each have a past. I want to get to know all of you." He watched her face carefully, trying to read her emotions.

Alexa blinked as a large tear slid down her cheek. "I feel so lucky to have met you."

Mark leaned over to kiss the tear away. "No way, I'm the lucky one. Please stop crying. I can't tell whether you're happy or sad."

"I'm happy. I want us to be together, and it was such a relief to tell you about Tony." She tried to smile. "And there's more. You still don't know everything about David, and even before Tony I wasn't a model student like my sisters. I'm embarrassed by some of the things I did in high school."

"And you don't know everything about me. When I knew Jane was leaving, I said and did some pretty rotten things."

Alexa was quiet for a moment. She wanted to talk about Sarah and her threat to run away, but there had been enough drama for one evening. At last she said, "You're right. We've been excavating the past. No more tonight."

Mark sensed that Alexa was still deeply troubled. "Would you feel better if we showed the letter to your dad?"

"I thought about it, but I don't think so. Perhaps if you get another one. But Dad's been through so much with losing Mom, and now for the first time I see that he's beginning to be happy again. He doesn't need this to worry about. He's been gold for me, always there when I needed him. It's time for me to stand on my own feet and not go running to him with every problem."

Mark kissed her gently. "Correction, it's time for us to share our problems." They kissed with more intensity. As Alexa relaxed against him, Mark let his lips slide down the soft skin of her neck and whispered, "I wish you would stay tonight. Can I tempt you with a queen-sized bed? I even changed the sheets this morning."

Alexa laughed for the first time. "Believe me, I am tempted, but Sarah doesn't need to wake up in the morning to find a strange lady in your bed."

"You're hardly a stranger!"

"I know. But she's got enough changes to deal with right now. And I know at times she resents me being around."

"Although I don't like it, you're right – for now. And try not to worry about Sarah. I think she's coming round."

Alexa recalled the shouting at her apartment and felt more than a little sceptical. For a long time, they held each other tightly. Alexa could feel the tension draining from her body as Mark caressed her. Finally she broke away. "I should go home. You'll have a very early start tomorrow morning with the boys."

At the front door Mark took her face gently in his hands as they kissed. "I love you," he said again. "And I hate saying good night like this. Sarah's sound asleep. I'll walk you home and jog back."

"I'm a big girl," she teased. "The streets in Davenport are deserted at this time of night. I don't think there's much danger of being kidnapped."

"You never know," Mark said pretending to be serious. "Today one of the kids in the cafeteria showed me a story he was reading from *The National Enquirer* about extraterrestrial kidnappings. I don't want to take a chance on losing you."

"Don't worry. I don't get lost easily. I'll jog home and call you as soon as I'm safe inside my door."

Mark drew her close and pressed against her, cradling her body with his. "No matter what happens we're going to keep each other safe." He kissed her to seal the promise.

CHAPTER SIXTEEN

On Saturday afternoon Alexa called Joy, and they decided to meet for an early supper at an inn half way between Davenport and the city. Alexa felt happy as she drove along Highway 401. The trees were turning yellow and orange and crimson, a deep purple red that she had never seen anywhere else in the world. In this part of the country the soil was thin, and limestone outcrops bordered the highway. In the distance she could see rolling farmland, the occasional farmhouse with its peaked roof and the glint of the setting sun shining on the lake.

She was surprised to find herself thinking of Davenport. The town with its spreading trees, stately old homes and surprisingly monumental churches had been a trap from which she longed to escape, but coming back more than a decade later she recognized its charm and understood why her parents had been so happy there.

Alexa slowed the car as she turned off the highway into the small Victorian town where she would meet Joy. She was early, but she recognized Joy's car parked outside a second hand bookstore, The Old Authors' Farm. Joy was immersed in a conversation with the bookseller and holding a copy of The Prophet's Camel Bell. "Alexa, look at this! It's the only one of Margaret Lawrenc 's books I don't own. It's out of print now, and I'd almost given up looking for it."

Alexa smiled. It was so typical that they would meet in a bookstore that neither one of them was even surprised. She gave Joy a hug and asked the bespectacled man at the counter, "Do I have time to look around, or are you just closing?"

"Take your time," he answered. The counter beside him was piled high with stacks of books and yellowed magazines. "I've got the kettle on, and a client's bringing in some boxes of books from his uncle's estate, so I'm going to be here for a while yet."

Joy's eyes lit up, and Alexa said, "My landlord, Martin MacLean, says he always gets an adrenalin rush when he goes out to evaluate an estate. We're the same, Joy, except with us it's books, not furniture or dishes."

"I just couldn't drive past this place. Who knows what treasures we'll find?"

It was dark by the time Alexa and Joy walked across the street to the inn with their arms full of books. "I'm sure I'll end up as one of those eccentric old women you read about in the papers. When they die, their house is completely filled with books. Every room, even the bathroom, is lined from floor to ceiling. There's only a narrow path through each room. I'm already halfway there, and I realized it when I moved," Joy said, half joking and half serious.

"I'm the same. Books are the one thing I can't resist. Make that two things, books and food. Did I tell you that I've taken up weight lifting?" Seeing Joy's incredulous look, Alexa quickly added, "Well I'm not exactly pressing a hundred pounds yet, but I've got a routine in the school weight room. I decided if I didn't do something this semester, I wouldn't be able to get into my clothes by Christmas. Some nights all I do is sit in front of the computer or mark student assignments."

"What happened to Mark? I was hoping he'd bring some variety into your life."

"He does, but he's busy too. This weekend he's got a basketball tournament." Over dinner she talked about Mark and Sarah and found that she was telling Joy about the anonymous letter and the reason why it upset her so much.

Joy was a good listener, attentive and empathetic. She reached across the table for Alexa's hand. "Alexa, I never knew any of this. What insensitive creatures teenage girls can be! That summer I was a live-in nanny at the lake for Judge Stinson's two horrendous daughters. They were spoiled brats, and I was having an identity crisis of my own. I remember Patti calling me to say that you'd gone away to Vancouver to stay with your aunt, but you were back when school started, and I didn't think any more about it. I was just too wrapped up in myself and my issues."

Alexa knew Joy was completely nonjudgmental and talking to her was therapeutic. At last she said, "Thanks for listening. I'm really at a crossroads. Mark's very special. I feel I can trust him and I actually think about what it would be like to have a life with him, not just now but ten or twenty years from now. He has the most amazing aunt and uncle who've been together for more than fifty years, and they still seem to have fun together. They're best friends, as well as partners. But in spite of all this good stuff, I look at Davenport and wonder if I'd be happy in a small town again, especially there."

"Everyone wants that special person who's going to be there for the long haul. It sounds as if Mark might be the one. And neither of you is chained to Davenport. I seem to remember that you told me Mark taught math before he was an administrator. There are lots of teaching jobs around now."

Alexa toyed with her coffee cup, turning it round and round in its white saucer. "That's true. But it would be better for Sarah not to have any more changes. She doesn't see a lot of her mother, but she'd see her even less if she were living in the city. And Sarah's a whole other problem. She blows hot and cold when I'm around. Mark warned me about that, but it's still hard to take She's such a bright kid, and often I wonder what she's really thinking, and I suppose I'm dragging a lot of baggage from being with David and generally being suspicious of happy-ever-after endings." She paused, "That's a lot of 'and's'. What about you, Joy? You look really together. Are you happy?"

"Who's ever completely happy? I love my new contract and being in the city with the chance to go out whenever I want, but I think about Steve the way you do about David. He always told me I was hypercritical and obsessed with my work. He said it controlled our lives."

"I know Steve is a musician, but was that his only work?"

Joy laughed. "Believe it or not, he has a degree in psychology and for a while he was a case worker for a social service agency, but it wasn't for him. He said he didn't want his heart broken every day. And his heart was really in composing music. There's not much money in that, and he thought I was condescending about it." Joy paused, "Maybe I was."

"And maybe not. Our ex-lovers are great at laying a guilt trip on us."

"As you said, I've got some baggage to sort through, but at least I'm meeting people. I've joined a woman's health club, yoga and swimming and the whole nine yards. I couldn't get that in Davenport."

"I have a real love-hate thing going on with our hometown," Alexa confessed. "I can see the charm which totally escaped me as a teenager, but I keep thinking what I'm giving up by living there. I loved going out to a film on impulse or getting a craving for Thai food at midnight and picking up the phone for takeout from Bangkok Village, and the concerts..." Her voice trailed off.

"Life's a series of tradeoffs. Give the thing with Mark some time. I think he's a keeper. And he's right about the crazies among us. Someone who writes an anonymous letter to dredge up your distant past isn't worth thinking about."

"Joy, you're a keeper too. Good friends aren't easy to find. That's something I missed in the city. I knew a lot of people, but it was so surface. With you and Patti it's real. I thought a lot about what you said last weekend, about losing the Messiah complex and being human and accepting yourself. It's true. I'm my own worst enemy."

Alexa drove home after dinner feeling totally relaxed. When she was with Joy or Patti, she was truly accepted. She identified closely with Joy, and they faced the same issues: the search for meaningful work, the need to be loved and to be part of something bigger than a social unit of one.

She thought of her father and what a lot he had taught her over the years, not by lecturing, but by the way he dealt with people, accepting them for what they were, finding each one interesting as a unique individual. And then there was Mark. She had always hated the expression "soul mates." She and Mark were separate entities, but she identified with his struggle to be the best father he could be to Sarah and to bring out the best in the kids and teachers he worked with at school. She was beginning to feel that no matter where they lived Mark might be part of what she was searching for.

Sarah's sore throat developed into a heavy cold, and Mark spent Sunday trying to entertain her. "We read most of the afternoon," he told Alexa on the telephone that night. "She brought back some books from Jo's house when we had dinner there, and she wanted me to read Jane Eyre, but I talked her out of that, so we settled on a book of fairy tales. I thought they would be easy going, but it was total gore. Lost children and old crones with pots of boiling water. I wonder why people think that violence began with television?"

Alexa laughed. "Joy and I found an awesome bookstore on Saturday. I bought Sarah all of L.M. Montgomery's Emily books. They should be pretty safe." She went on, "Sarah may be ready for Jane Eyre, but you're probably not. I remember I read it in my first year of high school and thought it was the most romantic book in the whole world. When I read it again at university, I realized how much I had missed."

Mark listened as Alexa told him about her evening with Joy. "You two are wonderful. I don't think men talk about their lives in the same way women do. Chris and I mostly talk about golf or hockey. We never mention feelings or personal relationships. What's wrong with us?"

"Nothing. It's the differences between men and women which make life so interesting. I'm sure that you were reading fairy tales and worrying about your basketball team."

"You're right," Mark acknowledged. "St. Pat's are the ones to watch this year. The boys are going to have to work their butts off if they want to make it to regional competition again. We have one or two hotshots, but they're still not playing together as a team." He broke off. "And I missed you. I've already booked a sitter for next Saturday. We're going to have a night out with no children or rabbits or basketball. Just the two of us in a romantic restaurant. Where should we go? Do you want to try Fasooli's or The Victorian Rose?"

"The Victorian Rose sounds perfect. I haven't been there, but Dad and Heather loved it, and I trust their judgement. Thanks, Mark. I'll think about it when I'm on cafeteria duty."

By now the week had a rhythm. Over a Monday morning coffee with Warren, Alexa asked, "Are you still procrastinating about talking to Mrs Fletcher?"

Warren looked sheepish. "It's going to happen this week for sure. I actually wrote it on my calendar. I tried on Friday, but she was busy. I know she's a good principal, but for such a small lady she actually scares me." He grinned. "I wasn't the best student in high school, and when I go into her office it brings back memories – none of them good. I start to feel guilty when I walk in the door even though I don't think I've done anything wrong."

"That's why she's such a good administrator. She's got that presence. Too bad they can't package it and sell it to education majors – at least the ones who want to teach teenagers."

At lunch time when the intercom summoned Alexa to the office, she understood how Warren felt. She was glad that she was wearing her bronze suede jacket and matching skirt. Mrs Fletcher had an extensive wardrobe of suits and matching accessories, and Alexa usually felt underdressed by comparison. Even Susan looked harried and only nodded in Alexa's direction instead of giving her the usual cheerful greeting and tidbit of news.

When she was called into the office, Alexa looked carefully at both Lisa Fletcher and Mark. Their faces were grave and composed in a way she had not seen before. "Thanks for coming so quickly, Alexa. We'll try not to cut into your noon hour too much so you have time to eat," Lisa began. "We've received some terrible news. One of our senior girls, Lori Green, was killed in a head-on crash coming to school this morning."

Alexa could feel the blood draining from her face. "What happened?"

"You probably didn't know her." Lisa went on. "Lori was on full-time co-op this semester at Maple Grove Elementary School. Usually she took the bus, but this morning the Grade Three class was going to visit a farm, and she drove herself so she could be there early to help the teacher. They were going to leave just after nine o'clock."

"I knew her. She helped out in the English department at the beginning of the semester." Alexa looked over at Mark. She tried to emulate his composure but failed utterly as tears rolled down her face. "She helped me with the Pathways class," she said between sobs. She was struggling to comprehend this senseless tragedy. How could this have happened to Lori who had been so sweet, so good with even the roughest kids? She remembered that she had been Sarah's Sunday school teacher. Mark was staring straight ahead.

"The police think that Lori was killed instantly. Her car was going around that bad curve just north of town on Highway 41 when it was struck head-on by a vehicle coming from the opposite direction but on the wrong side of the road," Lisa continued.

Alexa shook her head in disbelief. She wondered how such a senseless accident could happen on a Monday morning on a rural road. Mark and Lisa exchanged glances, "Alexa," Mark said gently, "We wanted you to know that the other car was driven by Justin Murray."

When she could trust herself to speak, Alexa asked, "How badly hurt is he?"

"He died before the ambulance could get him to the hospital," Mark said quietly. He did not mention the conversation with the police in which Brian Fowler had told them that they had found beer bottles in Justin's car and suspected that he had been drinking most of the night and was on his way home after a party.

Mark watched Alexa carefully, wondering how she would react to this shock. Her face was ashen, and she swayed as if she might collapse. He noticed that she was wearing a favourite piece of jewellery, an old-fashioned gold locket decorated with a small circle of pearls set around an amethyst which she had told him belonged to her grandmother. She fingered this now as if to draw strength or comfort from it. Instinctively he went over and put his arms around her. "Go home this afternoon. I'll find someone to cover your classes."

With an effort she pulled herself together. "I can't do that. I have the Pathways kids, and they all knew Justin and Lori. I've got to stay."

"Alexa," Lisa added, "sometimes we have to look after ourselves before we can help someone else. The board's emergency response team will be here all afternoon. David Siegel, the head psychologist, and his counsellors will be available for the kids. Probably everyone will hear the news over the noon hour, and the students will need to talk about it with their friends. They'll provide strong support for each other to get through the grieving, and we'll let them know that there are also counsellors available. We're waiting for some information about funeral arrangements."

Alexa nodded. "Don't worry about me. I'll be okay. I can't leave the kids. They may just want to talk to each other, but at least I'm someone they know. They don't know Dr Siegel."

At that moment there was a knock on the door, and Kelly Fitzgerald came into the office. Her eyes were red and puffy. As she and Alexa hugged each other, she whispered, "We'll get the kids through this." Turning to Mark and Lisa, she said, "Alexa has the Pathways kids last period today. I know most of them, so I'll be with her. Sometimes it helps to have two adults in the room."

Alexa gave her a grateful look. "I know it will help me."

The rest of the day was a blurred jumble of impressions. Most of the students knew Justin as well as Lori and her younger sister, Karen, who was a junior at Riverside. Groups of students gathered in the halls or the cafeteria sobbing and hugging each other. Kelly and some of the student council had set up a table in the main hall near the office with yearbooks open to pictures of the two students. Students wrote their thoughts and words of farewell on banners and in a memory book placed beside the yearbooks. Someone put a pink rose beside the memory book and, as the afternoon went on, other flowers and bouquets appeared. Some had notes or brief messages tucked inside.

Mark paused to read a few. Tears welled up in his eyes as he read one brief poignant note, "Why did you do it, Justin?"

Last period almost all the Pathways kids were in Alexa's room. She thought they would choose to cut class and be with their friends, and she was moved by their presence. Following Kelly's cue, they pulled the desks into a tight circle and talked. As always, the kids were brutally frank. There were tears, but there was also anger.

"He had it all, man."

"Like, if he was so smart, why did he have to drink and drive?"

"Yeah, he killed Lori."

"Don't say that, man. Like, do you think he had a friggin' gun or something?"

"When he got loaded and got into that car, it was like waving a gun."

"He was on the wrong side of the road. She never had a chance."

"Like, do you think he planned it or something? It was an accident. That's all. Just a friggin' accident. Accidents just happen."

"Yeah, right, tell that to Karen and her mom and dad."

Alexa and Kelly simply listened, blinked back their own tears, passed out Kleenex and broke all the rules by hugging students when they broke down.

Mark came into the staffroom after school and sat with the teachers. The next few days there would be collective mourning. The Greens planned to hold a one-day wake, and the funeral would be on Thursday afternoon.

"What arrangements are there for Justin?" Buzz asked.

"We're waiting to find out. The police are still trying to contact his parents."

Turning to Alexa, Mark said, "Lisa's waiting for the superintendent to get back to her, but we want to cancel classes on the day of Lori's funeral so everyone can attend. I'm not sure what we'll do for Justin, but we think you and Kelly should represent the staff at his funeral. You two probably knew him best." Alexa nodded, knowing that she would cry again if she tried to speak. The day had been mentally and physically exhausting, and she was at a breaking point.

The whole school attended Lori's funeral, and Mark took Sarah. She was confused by the closed casket. "Where's Lori?" she asked. "I want to say goodbye to her. She was my best teacher." She cried quietly, as Mark tried again to explain the inexplicable.

Although there was no wake for Justin, the church was crowded for the Friday funeral. Alexa and Kelly introduced themselves to his parents and grandmother, but the three were almost comatose, their glassy eyes making Alexa wonder to what extent they were medicated. Alexa found a seat at the end of a pew filled with her students. Just as the service was starting, Mark squeezed in beside her. "I couldn't let you do this alone," he whispered.

Bob Latimer, the young minister who took the service, spoke directly to the teenagers in the church. His message was one of hope, and he reminded them that the school would plant two trees in memory of Lori and Justin and a small plaque would be fastened to each. He spoke of the cycle of life, and when he read the memorial poem, "Do Not Stand at My Grave and Weep", there were audible sobs throughout the church. Alexa was emotionally exhausted, torn between grief and anger. It was all so senseless, the loss of life before either Lori or Justin had a chance to reach their potential.

After the service when the students hugged each other and cried, Alexa felt that all her tears had been shed, but she watched Mark with admiration. He seemed to know instinctively what to do and say to bring the kids some comfort. A group of boys was hotly debating where the school should plant Justin's tree. Shawn Bethune interrupted the debate. "In the smoking area. Like, that was Justin's favourite place. Man, you could always find him there," and then he stopped abruptly as if realizing that the vice-principal was listening.

Another boy vehemently disagreed. "Not in the smoking area, man. How long's that tree gonna live if you put it there?"

"Why's that, Pat?" Mark asked. "Are you worried about the smoke or the kids trampling it as they rush out between classes for their fix?"

"I guess smoking's pretty stupid, sir." Pat Fortier looked embarrassed. "I'm gonna quit this year before I start playing hockey. I made a promise to myself, and I'm really gonna do it."

"Good man! I'm going to check with you before Christmas. Free lunch on pizza Friday if you can stick with it."

Pat gave him a thumbs up. "It's a deal."

They stood for a long time outside the church as if unwilling to go back to their normal routine, as if by lingering they could keep Justin with them. When they finally walked back to their cars, Mark spoke quietly to Alexa, "Are you going to be okay?"

She nodded. "I don't have any tears left. I'm numb, and it's not a bad feeling."

"Will you come over tonight, or do you need to get some sleep?"

"I have a few things to do, and then I'll call you. I don't want to be alone."

At school Alexa went up to her classroom to gather some marking and materials for the weekend. She sat down at her desk. What she had told Mark was true. For the moment, there were no more tears. She looked around the room. So much had happened here since the beginning of September.

She looked at the circle of desks and could almost see Justin slouching in his seat with his handsome face and incredible smile, but his carelessness had cost Lori her life. She felt torn, loving him and hating him simultaneously. If only she could turn back the clock to that first day when she had given him a ride home. Could she have said or done something which would have altered the path he was fated to take? For just a moment, she longed to put her head on the desk and cry, but then she remembered Joy's words, "We can't save the world. We can't even save another person." And she remembered Mark saying, "Right now he's making some bad decisions." How prophetic those words seemed now. She could not be the judge and jury who tried Justin Murray. She would continue to care passionately and try her best to light a spark in her students, but she couldn't remake their worlds.

Her eyes went to the front seat where Dara had sat frantically taking notes, enclosed in her own bubble of loneliness and despair. There was still hope for Dara. Quickly Alexa picked up her briefcase, locked the classroom door behind her and went to the empty English office. She dialled Dara's number and waited. When Dara herself answered, she said, "Hi, Dara, it's Alexa Corbett."

"Oh, Miss Corbett, " Dara's voice sounded muffled as if she were very far away.

"I've been thinking about you, and I've missed you in class. How are you?"

"I'm okay I guess. I saw you at Lori's funeral, but the church was so crowded, and you were sitting near the front. I didn't have a chance to talk to you."

"You knew Lori?" As soon as she said this, Alexa thought that it was a small town, and Dara probably knew most of the kids in her age group.

"Yes, we taught Sunday school together. I didn't really know Justin, but I knew who he was. He went to the same grade school I did. He always said hello to me."

"He used to be in one of my classes." Alexa exhaled sharply, "I'm having a hard time with all of this." Then she caught herself. Surely this was not the kind of thing teachers said to students.

To her surprise, Dara answered, "I am too. You know it's funny. I hated school, but it's really weird working alone at home. It's just me and the books."

Impulsively Alexa said, "I know you have to babysit a lot, but if you're free tomorrow, maybe we could meet and we'll have lunch somewhere. It would be good to talk to you."

"My dad's home tomorrow. I don't have to babysit."

"Let me pick you up – around twelve-thirty?"

"You're not too busy?"

"No, I'd love to see you."

Dara gave Alexa directions to her house, and Alexa hung up feeling that at last she had something to look forward to.

When she arrived at Mark's house, she felt almost human again. Although she was tired, she wanted to see Sarah and be with her and Mark. They walked over to her father's house and borrowed Robbie for a walk. The nights were getting cold, and they were bundled up in sweaters and jackets, but went twice around the park before they headed back. Her dad made them hot chocolate, and Sarah began to talk excitedly about their theatre trip to the city. She had finally chosen The Lion King, and they had tickets for early December. "Dad and I are going Christmas shopping when we're there," Sarah told Dan. "We're going to buy presents for my grandparents and for Alexa and Robbie. I can't tell you what they are, but I'll give you a clue. Alexa and Robbie are going to look like twins."

Mark laughed at Alexa's puzzled expression. "Sarah, it's supposed to be a surprise. If you give out any more hints, she'll guess."

Sarah giggled with delight when Alexa said, "No, I won't. I have no idea unless you're planning to get both of us new collars. Robbie's looks as if it's been used as a teething ring."

Alexa kissed her father good night, and they went back to Mark's house. When Sarah went upstairs to get ready for bed, she sat down on the padded cushions in the wide window seat of the living room. This room was beginning to feel like home. She leaned back, watching the flickering flames in the fireplace and allowed the exhaustion of the past week to dissipate.

After Mark sat down beside her, she said, "I wanted to tell you that you were wonderful today. I was watching you, and you seemed to know just what to do and say to help the kids."

Mark reached for her hand. "When I was in Grade Seven, my older brother, Timothy, committed suicide. I don't think my parents ever got over it. Both Jo and I feel that we lost part of our childhood trying to help them cope."

"How terrible! You never told me that before."

"Some day we'll talk about it, but not tonight. We've had enough tragedy for one week."

"There's so much about you I don't know."

"I feel the same way about you, but we've got a lifetime to get to know each other."

Just then Sarah called from upstairs, "Okay, Dad, I'm ready for my story now."

Mark leaned over to kiss Alexa. "Come up with me."

Alexa shook her head. Ever since the scene with Sarah at her apartment, she had been treading cautiously afraid of provoking another outburst.

"Then don't go away. I'll be back."

"Don't worry. I'm not going anywhere."

When Mark returned, Alexa was leafing through a magazine. "Is she asleep?" she asked casually.

"Not yet."

"Did she say anything about my being here?"

Mark raised an eyebrow. "Well, to be honest, she asked if you were staying here tonight." In answer to Alexa's unspoken question, he went on. "She's acting like a Victorian chaperone."

"Just staking out her territory." Alexa replied cynically.

It was becoming easy for Alexa to believe that Mark was a permanent part of her life. On Sunday afternoon, they took Sarah and her friend, Angie, to pick apples at Joanne and Ray's farm. The two girls worked energetically to fill one basket and then, losing interest, ran off to explore the barns. Alexa and Mark worked away for another hour and then walked across the fields to a small pond at the back of the property. In spite of the sunny skies, the wind was cold, and Alexa thrust her hands into her jean jacket pockets. "It feels as if winter will be here sooner than I'd like. Was it only yesterday we were complaining about the heat at school?"

"How was your lunch with Dara?"

"I'm concerned about her. She knew both Lori and Justin, and their deaths have had a huge impact on her. She says she's writing some poetry and coping, but I'm not so sure."

"Is she seeing a counsellor?"

"Yes, every two weeks, and that seems to be going well, but I'm worried that it's not enough. She needs some friends she can call and talk to. She hated school, but the odd thing is that she misses the classes. She doesn't think much of the correspondence material she's working with. I made her promise that she'd call me next week, and we'll set up a tutorial session in the morning before school or in the late afternoon."

"Maybe that will be enough to lure her back in semester two."

"I hope so. Dara could add so much to a class. Whatever happens, I don't want to lose her." Alexa looked fiercely protective.

Mark put his arm around her. "Alexa, I've been thinking, and that's always dangerous. In a school the size of Riverside, there's going to be some staff changes for second semester." Alexa smiled to herself. Mark had obviously not heard Warren's news. He went on, "Lisa will find a contract for you if she can. She knows you're doing a great job with the kids. But I'm not married to Davenport. Perhaps we should talk about looking for jobs somewhere else."

Instantly Alexa was wary. She stopped walking and turned to face him. "What made you think of that right now? Did you get another letter?"

Mark shook his head. "Relax! Nothing like that. It's just that you were so upset when you read the letter that I thought this might be a solution. You said that Davenport's like a glass cage with someone watching your every move. That's what small towns are like, especially when you have a very public job like teaching. It's just the way it is. It's never going to change."

"Let's think about it. It's good to know that the cage door is open, and we can fly away, but it's also good for Sarah to be close enough to her mother to see her sometimes. When I first came back, I felt that I was renewing my neurotic affiliations. Now I'm beginning to change my point of view."

"I like that. 'Renewing my neurotic affiliations.' Who said that anyway?"

"I did, but to be honest I think Leonard Cohen said it before me."

"That's what I love about you English types. I never know if you're being clever or quoting someone. Math nerds can't do that."

"And I'm impressed. I didn't think math nerds would know anything about Mr Cohen."

"Most of us are literate even though we teach math," Mark protested.

When they reached the pond, they sat down in a sheltered spot beside a huge granite boulder. Mark pulled two Ida Red apples out of his pocket, and they munched away. Then Mark moved closer and put his arm around her again. "In spite of the wind, it's a perfect October afternoon."

Alexa pretended to misunderstand. "It must be the apples. They're fantastic at this time of year."

Mark pulled her close, warming her face with his breath and kissing first her closed eyes, then the side of her face and finally her lips. Her mouth opened to his kiss. "You taste like apples," she murmured as she luxuriated in the sweetness of his breath.

"I wonder why?" Mark slipped his hands under her jacket, holding her tightly. Alexa felt a surge of warmth as his hands encircled her breasts. "This is heaven, but it's not enough. I love you, and I want to be able to spend an entire night with you. I'm tired of saying good night after we've spent an evening together."

Alexa pressed against him, no longer teasing. "I love you too, " she said for the first time. "I think we should go to Bermuda at Christmas."

Mark was so surprised that he pulled back to look at her face. "Do you really mean that?" he demanded.

She nodded, laughing. "Yes, to both. I love you, and I've been thinking about your suggestion. Bermuda would be my idea of heaven."

Mark gave such a delighted whoop that the ducks which had been placidly paddling near the reeds at the edge of the pond flapped their wings in alarm as they readied themselves for flight. "I don't believe it! You actually said you love me and you said 'yes' to Bermuda. I'm going to call Paul tonight and then I'm going to book some flights before you change your mind." He crushed her to him, and Alexa felt a warmth begin to spread throughout her body as he kissed her mouth.

When at last she was able to speak, she said, "You don't need to worry. I'm not changing my mind. I looked at the calendar again this morning. Let's see if we can leave on Friday evening at the beginning of the break. If we're back by Monday night, I'd still have a few days to help Dad get organized before the troops arrive."

Mark hugged her tightly. "I'll be like a kid crossing off the days before Christmas with a big red magic marker. It's going to be wonderful. Paul's got a fantastic apartment, and he'll leave the key to his scooter, so we'll tour the whole island in style." He pulled Alexa to her feet. "Come on, love. Let's head back and see what the girls are up to. I feel as if I could run all the way."

They met Sarah and Angie coming out of the barn. "Aunt Jo says if we stay we can have roasted hotdogs at the barbecue pit, and she'll make an apple crisp. Is that okay, Dad?" Sarah asked anxiously.

Mark looked at Alexa who nodded. "As long as Angie calls her mother and gets permission. I'm going to find Jo and offer my services as sous chef. She's wonderful, but she doesn't need to work all the time."

"What's a 'chouchef'? I don't know that word," Sarah said and waited for Mark to offer an explanation.

Jo was peeling apples in the kitchen when Alexa poked her head around the door. "Let me do that. You've been so good to us, and I don't want to feel like a guest."

"Sure. Help yourself to a knife from the rack, but it's no trouble. Sarah loves being here, and the animals keep her busy. My two are old enough to take care of themselves and keep an eye on her as well. Mark knows she's welcome anytime."

"If you're free, I want to invite you and Ray and the kids to come for Thanksgiving. Dad and I are planning a dinner for Monday evening, and we'd love to have you."

Joanne beamed. "That would be great, and I'll tell Mark to bring Sarah here on Saturday. You two need some time together without her tagging along."

"I like Sarah." Alexa knew she sounded more than a little defensive.

"I know you do, and it shows, but Sarah's going through a very confusing time. I'm not going to pull a hissy fit and start in on Jane. It's just that Sarah misses her mother, and she clings to Mark." Reading Alexa's expression, she went on, "You've been told this a hundred times, but she is a good kid, and she'll get through this bad patch."

Alexa sighed. "I wish I could get over the feeling that what she'd really like is to stuff a poisoned apple into my mouth."

"I don't think you need to worry. Sarah's pretty transparent. If she truly disliked you, she'd let you know. A friend of Mark's from school used to go to the house sometimes, and Sarah gave her the silent treatment. Mark told me that once Sarah took her pack of cigarettes and threw it into the toilet. The lady wasn't happy."

Alexa grinned, imagining that scene with Julie. "So far so good then. I don't smoke, and usually Sarah will talk to me."

"Then don't get too discouraged. We want to keep you around. Everyone loves you, and you've done so much for Mark."

Alexa could feel her cheeks growing hot. "He's done a lot for me too."

As the others came into the kitchen gathering up hotdogs, buns and mustard to take to the fire pit, Joanne said, "Rachel, be a sweetheart and get the coleslaw out of the fridge, and I think there's a bag of marshmallows in the pantry. The girls might want to roast marshmallows."

"I'll put on a pot of coffee," Mark offered.

"There's cider too, but you'll have to get it from the freezer in the basement. Just pop the jug into the microwave."

"My sister, the organizer," Mark teased, as he smiled at Alexa.

Angie and Sarah chatted all the way home from the farm. "I'm going to live on a farm when I grow up," Sarah told her. "And I'm going to have a lot of animals just like Uncle Ray except I'll have horses instead of cows. You can come and visit. We'll go riding together."

They dropped off Angie, and when she got home Sarah found Stuart and went upstairs for her bath without prompting. After a few minutes she called down, "Which one of you guys is going to read to me tonight?"

"I'm bringing the English teacher," Mark called back. "She can read to both of us."

They went up to the bedroom where Sarah sat cross-legged in her pyjamas on the spindle bed with Stuart beside her. Mark lay down next to them and rested his head on one of the pillows while Sarah and Alexa took turns reading the next chapter of *Emily of New Moon*. By the time they had finished Mark's eyes were closed, and he was breathing heavily.

"Look, Alexa. Dad's asleep," Sarah said in a loud whisper. "Are you going to stay here tonight?"

"Not tonight. I've got to go home to mark some tests for my kids. We have parent-teacher interviews next week at Riverside."

For a moment Sarah looked disappointed. Then she pulled up the quilt and snuggled down beside Mark. "Okay, I can read to Stuart for a while."

Alexa resisted the urge to ask if she could have a good night hug.

As she got up to leave, Sarah said, "Thanks for the Emily books, Alexa. They're super. Way better than Harry Potter."

Alexa smiled to herself as she walked home. She knew Mark would be embarrassed when he woke up and found that she had gone, but she was euphoric. On a night like this she wondered if she really wanted to leave the glass cage.

CHAPTER SEVENTEEN

"*H*ey, Miss Corbett, are you busy?" Alexa looked up from the stack of tests she was grading to see Jim Callaghan and his vice president, Kelsey James, whom Carol Helmer always referred to as 'the wannabe', standing in front of her desk. With a sigh she put down her red pen. "Not at all. Do I look busy?"

As usual Jim had a pencil behind his ear and wore a typically harried expression which indicated that student politics was an unending round of obligations and responsibilities. "The council and the boys' senior basketball team are planning a surprise birthday party for Mr Anderson on Wednesday after school, and you're invited."

A horrible thought struck Alexa. Was she known as the Official Girl Friend? Gulping, she replied aloud, "Are you expecting the whole staff?"

"Pretty much," Kelsey said easily. "We're just trying to get a head count. Mr Anderson's been so great as our advisor that we wanted to surprise him with a cake. But you know these things sort of snowball, and if a lot of people are coming we thought we should have some other munchies."

"If you're looking for contributions, count me in. I'll make something. Maybe stuff some mini pitas."

"Great!" Jim checked off her name on his clip board and wrote down "pitas" with a flourish. "We're going to sweet-talk Mrs Campbell to see if the food services class can make us some fruit punch."

"Good idea. They catered for us at the last staff meeting, and the food was wonderful."

"What did they make?" Jim asked. "I was wondering if..."

"Come on, Jim," Kelsey interrupted in exasperation. "We're running out of time. I've got to be at volleyball practice in five minutes. Thanks,

Miss Corbett," she added. "Just let me know where you put the food on Wednesday. We're going to set up the stuff in the Health Room at the end of last period and then we'll surprise Mr Anderson when he comes in from bus duty. We'll have a card, and everyone can sign it when they come."

"You sound well organized, but if you want some help, let me know."

After Jim and Kelsey had left, Alexa finished marking the tests. She and Mark planned to celebrate his birthday in style with dinner in the city on Saturday, but it was typical of the Riverside kids that they had discovered the date of Mark's birthday and wanted to do something special. Mark would be embarrassed but pleased by the recognition.

When she and Carol went to the Health Room on Wednesday, Carol's jaw dropped slightly. Kelsey and her committee had transformed the room using decorations with the school colours. There were blue and white helium balloons everywhere and blue and white streamers canopied the ceiling. "At least the cake isn't blue and white," Carol muttered cynically, as Warren approached them with two pieces of chocolate cake wrapped in paper napkins.

"Here. I've been fighting off the hordes to save these," Warren handed them the cake. "Alexa, your pitas looked great, but I could only get my hands on one, and I devoured it. The kids scoffed the rest."

"Unbelievable!" Alexa said, as she took the cake from Warren. "I got Martin to help me last night. When I ran out of filling, he went out for a barbecued chicken, and we stuffed the last bag of pitas with chicken salad. We made so many that I thought the staff would be eating them for days."

"Dreamer, kids are always ravenous after school. When Roger's at work I've given up on dinner, and Kerry and I eat at four thirty as soon as I get home. Thanks for thinking of us, Warren. That was good." Carol had already finished her cake and was wiping icing from her fingers. "Now for something to drink after the sugar fix."

"Okay, my turn," Alexa replied. "I'll try to fight my way over to the punch bowl, but you may have to settle for coffee in the staffroom." Waiting in line for some cups of punch, Alexa turned around to find Julie behind her. "We have to stop meeting like this," she joked, remembering that she and Julie had met in the barbecue line at the Fletchers' party.

Julie gave her a coolly appraising glance. "So what are you planning to do next semester? I just heard today from one of the kids that Murray Dean is back in February. It's amazing how they're always the first to get the scoop."

"Yes, I got that newsflash too." She knew that Warren had finally told Lisa and Mark about his job at St. Mike's, but the news hadn't reached the staff. "I don't have any definite plans yet. I took a leave from my job in the city, so I could always go back there."

"Well good luck," Julie's tone suggested that Alexa would need all the luck going around.

"Thanks, Julie," but Alexa was thinking, "I bet you'd throw a party as soon as I left Riverside, and Mark would be number one on your guest list." She managed to balance three cups of punch and got back to Carol and Warren. "Too crazy," she said. "The kids should have had this shindig in the gym. At least we could've moved around."

Just then Jim Callaghan stood up on a chair and blew a whistle for silence. When he had the crowd's attention, he ignored a few catcalls such as "No speeches" and launched into one. "Mr Anderson, we couldn't let your birthday go by without telling you how much we appreciate what you do around the school. Thanks for the early morning practices and the late night meetings and for giving up so many of your weekends."

"And thanks for all those detentions, sir," someone at the back yelled.

Jim ignored the comment. "We kept trying to find out if this is the big Four-Oh, but no one would tell us. Please accept a small token of our appreciation for all your hard work." He intoned the cliche as if he had invented it.

"F for lack of originality, " Carol whispered to Alexa, but she was smiling.

Jim hopped off the chair, and Kerry came forward to present Mark with an elaborately wrapped box.. Mark opened it and then held up a navy blue school sweatshirt with "I'd rather be playing basketball" stitched in white letters across the back.

"Try it on," someone yelled, and Mark obliged.

"Thanks, everyone," he said grinning. "I wish I'd come earlier and had some food, although I hear there's a piece of cake with my name on it. No, it's not the big Four-Oh – not yet, but some mornings when

I get up for our seven o'clock practices, it feels like the big Five-Oh." The kids laughed. "Seriously, times like this make it all worthwhile. By the way, there's no truth to the rumour that we cancelled tomorrow's practice. Guys, I'll see you at seven on the court."

The kids clapped and whistled as he began to move around the room, talking to teachers and students until at last he made his way over to Carol and Alexa. "I don't know how the kids pull these things off. I saw Jim and Kelsey in the halls last period before the bell and made a mental note to give them the word about missing too many classes. I'll have to postpone that lecture for another day."

"Take off the vice-principal hat for a moment. Relax and enjoy," Carol told him. "By the way, where's Lisa? She was invited and she always loves these things."

"She's at a meeting with the superintendent, fighting for more staff for second semester. Some of the science classes are really big, and we should split them."

"What's your prediction?" Carol asked.

"About staffing? Who knows? Our enrolment is up, but finances are tight." He smiled at Alexa. "We always have staffing changes half way through the year. I know Lisa's going to advertise some positions after Thanksgiving."

Driving into the city on Saturday Alexa and Mark talked about the surprise party. "The kids at Riverside are really something else. They appreciate you and they took the time to show you."

"I think there's a lesson here somewhere." He took her hand in his and intertwined their fingers. "Have I told you yet today that you're special?"

"Keep it for later," Alexa teased. "I haven't even given you a birthday present yet."

"I don't want a present. Spending the whole day together is enough."

They drove in comfortable silence for a few minutes. Then Alexa said, "I went home from school on Wednesday and wrote a note to Justin's grandmother and I sent her a copy of Justin's essay on his grandfather. Knowing Justin, I'm sure she never saw it, but maybe it will help her in a small way. Justin really admired his grandpa."

"Good for you. I know it's hard to find the time to do something like that."

"It must be so hard for her to go on without him."

"You think about Justin a lot, don't you?"

"He was special, one of those kids who could have done anything with his life when he got it together. He just didn't have the time. I hate what he did, but I can't hate him. Imagine losing a kid like that. What are his parents going through?"

There was silence. Both of them were thinking about Sarah. Mark could not imagine what it would be like without her. "Okay, no more talk of Riverside or Davenport today," Mark said, squeezing her hand. "Where do you want to go first?"

"Let's do some shopping for Sarah for Christmas. She'll be with us the next time we come into the city to see *The Lion King*. She gave me a list of the books and videos she wants, and if I can find girls' bathing suits at this time of year, I thought she'd like to wear something jazzy when she goes for her swimming lessons."

Alexa flinched as Mark's cell phone rang. The reception was bad, so he pulled off the highway and got out of the car. Alexa could see him nervously pacing back and forth as he talked. She studied his face and hoped that nothing was wrong at Joanne's. Then her thoughts went to Dara. In spite of her promise, she hadn't called Alexa.

Mark got back into the car smiling. "I panic when the phone rings. I always think Sarah's fallen out of an apple tree or been kicked by a cow, but Jo says she insisted on calling me because her loose tooth finally came out. She wanted to know if she could wait until tomorrow night to put it under her pillow."

"Does she think the tooth fairy will miss her at the farm?"

"Who knows what kids think? I told her she could wait until Sunday night, and Jo promised to put the tooth into a glass jar to keep it safe until she comes home. What an anticlimax! I was expecting a real catastrophe." He looked amused but exasperated.

"When you're eight years old, this is a catastrophe!"

They spent an hour at the World's Biggest Bookstore, and by the time they went to The Harbour for dinner, Alexa had found everything she was looking for including a beautiful tole-painted Christmas angel for Sarah's tree. "Remember this is your birthday present. The sky's the limit," she told Mark as they scanned the menu.

"I've always lived in a landlocked part of the country, but in a past life I think I lived on the ocean. I don't know why I'm reading this menu. I know I want Lobster Thermidor if that's not going to push your credit card too much." Alexa chose Norwegian salmon and ordered Coquilles St. Jacques as an appetizer. They lingered over the meal. Mark had bought a tourist guide to Bermuda at the bookstore, and they began to put check marks beside everything they wanted to do in three days.

When they came out of the restaurant, it was beginning to rain heavily. "Remember the night I drove you home from Lisa's party?" Mark asked. "You were so wet you looked as if you had been swimming."

"I remember that when I put a towel over your shoulders and we kissed, you looked as if you were going to run away. Did you think I had designs on you?"

"No way, " Mark sounded like Sarah. "I wasn't that hopeful. When I kissed you, I was afraid you'd think I was hitting on you, and you'd be furious."

"Really?" Alexa spoke incredulously. "It's amazing how men and women can miscommunicate."

When they finally drove into Davenport, Mark gave her a lopsided mock tough-guy grin, "Your place or mine, kid?"

"Mine. That is, if you want another birthday present."

"You said dinner was my present," Mark protested. At Alexa's apartment, Mark poured them drinks while Alexa retrieved a large silver box from her bedroom closet.

"For you," she said, handing it to him. "Happy birthday." He untied the silver bow and took off the lid to reveal a beautiful dressing gown in heavy blue silk.

"Wow!" he said appreciatively. "You didn't buy this in Davenport."

"No, I could only find plaid flannel here. On-line shopping has its advantages. Do you think it's a little over the top?"

"I love it! I've never had anything like this before. I'll feel like a pasha or rajah or Clark Gable in *Gone with the Wind* when I wear it."

"I don't remember Clark Gable lounging around in a dressing gown in that film although you might look a little like him if you grew a moustache. Put it on."

Mark obliged. He kissed her and then took it off, carefully placing it over one of the diningroom chairs. He handed her a glass of Merlot. "To us, and thank you. Let's make the most of tonight. At last we're together without a thousand kids watching. I want to dance with you. You choose a CD."

Alexa went over to the corner cabinet and looked through her collection. "What are you in the mood for? How about Diana Krall?"

"Perfect." When the strains of "I Remember You" came from the speakers, Mark put his arms around her. "Let's slow dance," he said. "We couldn't do this in the Riverside gym."

In his arms Alexa felt utterly content. "I can't believe we're doing this."

"Why not? It's our time."

"I Remember You" blended into "Cry Me a River." At last he led her to the couch, and they sat quietly almost afraid to break the spell. "You're not as wet as the first night I was here," he whispered, "but your hair is a little damp from the rain." He brushed it back from her face and slowly unbuttoned her silk shirt, his lips warm on her face and neck.

After a long time they moved as one into the bedroom. The room was dark except for the glow of a streetlight, and the music came dreamily from the living room. Alexa felt Mark's lips on her shoulders and then on her breasts. As he undressed her, his lips covered each part that he revealed. His hands explored her body, and he softly kissed her belly and legs. "You're so beautiful," he whispered. When at last he moved inside her, she felt the miracle of completeness as they fit effortlessly together. They began to move at first slowly and softly. They rocked together, and Alexa felt her whole body trembling. When at last they reached their crescendo, Mark leaned on his elbows looking down at her. Then he whispered into her neck, "I love you. Don't go away."

"And I love you," Alexa murmured. The last thing she remembered was lying beside Mark with his arms around her. She thought that he leaned over and kissed her as he shut off the light.

Even before Alexa was fully awake the next morning she unconsciously found herself turning to Mark trying to snuggle into his warmth. With a start she opened her eyes to find only an empty space beside her. The smell of coffee was an incentive to throw on a robe and go out to the kitchen.

Mark turned from the stove where he was stirring eggs to enfold her in a warm hug. He opened his arms, and Alexa went into them. "Good morning. Are you okay? No regrets about last night?"

With her head buried against his chest, Alexa shook her head and whispered, "It was wonderful." Then she pulled back to look at him dressed in Dockers and a shirt with rolled up sleeves. "Where's your dressing gown? I want you to wear it."

"I can cook, but no one ever said I was neat. I didn't want eggs all over it. I'll model it later." He bent to kiss her again. "I've been awake for hours watching you sleep."

"With my mouth open, I suppose," Alexa teased.

Mark kissed her harder this time. "You're beautiful, asleep or awake. I'm a morning person. Usually I'm out of bed at the crack of dawn or before, trying to get some work done before Sarah wakes up. But this morning I didn't want to disturb you. Finally I decided if I brought you breakfast in bed, you might want to wake up."

"What time is it anyway?" Alexa asked with a huge yawn.

"Late, almost seven o'clock. Come on, I don't want to waste the day. This is almost ready."

"Seven o'clock on Sunday?" Alexa asked in disbelief. "Don't I at least get breakfast in bed?"

"Breakfast first, then perhaps bed," Mark answered smiling.

Alexa found that she was very hungry. The scrambled eggs and English muffins disappeared, and they were drinking a second cup of coffee when Mark got up from the table. "I'll be right back, " he said. Moments later he reappeared wearing the blue robe and entering the kitchen as if gliding down a runway.

Alexa clapped enthusiastically. "You look great. Nice change from basketball sweats and a whistle." As he reached for his coffee she asked, "What time do you have to pick up Sarah?"

"I told her I'd be there shortly after ten. She wants to go to Sunday school. Will you come to church with us?"

"Sure, if we can pick Dad up en route. I promised I'd go with him today. I think he's feeling a bit down, and we planned to make pumpkin pies this afternoon."

"Where's Heather?"

"She's spending the weekend with Jan, her married daughter, and her family. She and Dad are good friends, but I don't think they're ready to blend families just yet."

"Perhaps that will change."

"Perhaps," Alexa said without conviction.

Mark reached for her hand across the table. "Alexa, we'll spend the rest of the weekend with your dad, but right now let's talk about us. I know it sounds crazy, but I feel as if I had never been with anyone else, and I'll never want anyone else again." His voice thickened. "Right now, I just want to take you back to bed and love you."

He came around the table, and they kissed. As he slid his hands inside her robe, Alexa felt herself responding. "This is definitely the best offer I've had this morning," she whispered.

In the bedroom Mark loosened her robe and knelt beside her kissing her breasts and teasing her nipples. Alexa lay back, holding his head and stroking the taut muscles in his back. "I've wanted to do this for so long," he murmured. When he moved inside her, she was wet and almost trembling with eagerness. They made love slowly. It was not a game for either of them. The passion was real.

At last they lay in each other's arms on the bed. "I wish we could stay here," Alexa whispered as he stroked her hair, brushing it back from her face. "I hate the thought of going back to the real world of Mr Anderson and Miss Corbett."

Mark raised his head to look around Alexa's pale blue bedroom. "It's a pretty room, but we might want to go out for food occasionally. The real world isn't so bad, Alexa. I promise we're going to have a life together away from school, and Christmas and Bermuda will come soon." He paused. "You need to think about second semester. Lisa's going to post the staff vacancies next week, but is Riverside what you really want? If you decide to go back to the city, I could apply for math jobs there. It would be a change from being a vice-principal. I'm not always sure I want that track."

Alexa shook her head emphatically. "Mark, you're a wonderful administrator. Don't even think about that." Looking over at the bedside clock she added, "We've got to shower and dress. Sarah won't be happy if you're late."

But after they arrived at the farm, Sarah was nowhere to be seen. When she finally came downstairs, she ran to Mark exclaiming, "Dad, Stuart has a girlfriend!"

Joanne laughed. "This is the most important thing that happened all weekend. It even eclipsed the tooth."

"Are you serious? I was hoping this was a joke."

"A friend of Ray's who was visiting on Saturday offered us a purebred Angora rabbit. Ray took it, and now Stuart and his friend are inseparable. Of course Sarah wants to take it home."

"But is it housetrained?" Mark was clearly looking for a way out.

"It seems to be. It used the litter box all weekend."

"I named her Esmeralda," Sarah explained to Alexa excitedly. "She's so beautiful. I'll bring her downstairs now, and you can see her."

"Listen, Sarah," Mark began, "if Aunt Jo agrees, you can keep Esmeralda, but you have to understand that we live in a small house. If Stuart and Esmeralda begin producing bunnies every few months, the babies have to go. Otherwise we'd be overrun with rabbits in no time and we'd have to move out."

Sarah looked as if she were going to pout, but she finally said "Okay" with resignation. Then she brightened. "Maybe we could sell rabbits and make a lot of money. I know Angie wants one. We could start a business and pay for our trip to Disneyland."

Mark was beginning to look a little desperate. "Let's not plan too far ahead, Sarah. We'll see how Esmeralda likes her new home before we plan on a rabbit dynasty. We have to leave now if you want to go to Sunday school. Are you packed?"

When Sarah went upstairs to get her backpack, he said, "Jo, do you know anything about the sex of rabbits? Is Esmeralda a female?"

"Sorry, Mark, I have no idea, but you'll probably find out quite soon." Mark groaned, picturing endless litters of rabbits, but his sister laughed as she asked Alexa, "What time would you like us for dinner tomorrow?"

"Come whenever you like, but we'll plan to eat around six. And, Joanne, thanks so much for taking Sarah. We had a wonderful weekend." Sarah wanted to decorate for Thanksgiving, and they loaded the car with pumpkins, corn stalks, ears of Indian corn and squash. With Alexa holding the jar containing Sarah's tooth, and Mark organizing the rabbits, they managed to drive back to Davenport, stop at Mark's house to unload and meet Dan Corbett on the church steps just as the bell was ringing for morning service.

After lunch, Alexa and her father began preparations for Thanksgiving dinner. Alexa noticed that her dad was moving around the kitchen with a pronounced limp. She stopped rolling out the pastry for pumpkin pies and looked at him carefully as he pulled a chair over to the table and sat down to chop onions for the stuffing.

"Dad, I've been watching you. Are you in pain?"

"A little," he admitted. "We've had nothing but rain for the last few days, and this weather doesn't help my arthritis. I can always tell when it's going to rain by consulting my right hip." He smiled at her, "Don't look so serious, Alexa. I'll live. It comes and goes. It'll get better."

"Are you taking anything for it?" He gave her a quizzical smile. "I know. You'd rather be a martyr than admit you need something. You used to drive Mom crazy because you never wanted to see Dr Blair."

"You miss her, don't you." It was a statement, not a question.

"Of course, we both do. Desperately at times. But I like Heather. She's not a substitute for Mom, but she's a neat lady. I wish she could have been here this weekend with us. I guarantee her pies would be better than mine," she added, trying to make him smile. "Martin's going to bring some butter tarts, so we can always eat those if the pumpkin pies are a disaster – which they may be."

Dan smiled absently. "Heather's got her own family, and that makes it hard at holiday time."

"Maybe we should have a big Open House on Boxing Day and invite Heather and her family to come. Kate's dying to meet her."

"That's a good idea. What are Mark and Sarah doing for Christmas?"

Alexa paused and chose her words carefully. "Dad, Mark and I are planning to go to Bermuda the weekend that school gets out. He has a friend from college who'll lend us his apartment. We'll be back on Monday night, so we'll still have lots of time to organize Christmas before Kate and her family come. I'd like to invite Mark and Sarah for Christmas here and Martin if he's not travelling. We can include Joanne and Ray and their kids in the Open House. What do you think?"

"That sounds good. Mark's very special. I'm happy for you. I wondered if the capricious Sarah would turn you off."

Alexa couldn't help smiling. Her father didn't miss a thing. "That was a distinct possibility. She's a good kid, but it's hard to be around someone who acts as if she hates you. Mark and Sarah are definitely a package deal, and I think she's starting to come around." She stood on tiptoe to look out the window. "The decorating must be done because right now she's trying to interest Robbie in retrieving a ball."

"She'll need lots of patience for that. You should explain to her that he's a terrier. Show him a groundhog hole, and he acts like a pup again, but playing ball, as Sarah would say 'No way José!' He loses interest after two minutes. Your mother used to swear that Robbie hid the ball when he was tired of playing."

Alexa wiped her flour-covered hands on a towel and went over to give her father a bear hug. "You need to get away this winter. Why don't you and Heather pick a sunny island and take a holiday? You and Mom used to love to do that."

"I thought you were going to be my travelling companion," he teased.

"I'd love to, but there's going to be an opening at Riverside for an English teacher in semester two. I'm going to apply for it, so I may be busy."

"It would be great having you around on a permanent basis, and if you're not available Heather and I need to talk. Perhaps we can juggle our work schedules and take some time off together."

Alexa wisely said no more. She had planted some seeds and hoped for the best. "I'd better get my act together. At the rate we're going we'll be eating Thanksgiving dinner next weekend."

When she got back to her apartment that evening, the familiar red light was flashing on her telephone. There was no message, only a hang up. She wondered if David or Tony had called and reflected that she could write a book about how not to break up with a man. She was collecting a wealth of experience. Then her thoughts began to circle around Dara. She told herself that she was going to call her and schedule some tutoring time. That would be a convenient pretext to ease her concern. Snuggled in bed, she longed to have Mark beside her.

In spite of all her misgivings the Thanksgiving dinner was a success. She felt comfortable with Mark's family, and her father could talk to anyone on any subject. Sarah was delighted to be the centre of attention with everyone complimenting her on the holiday decorations. Even Robbie was happy, mesmerized by one of the corn stalks in which some field creature had found a home. When Rachel arrived, she announced to everyone that she had become a vegetarian, but she happily filled her plate with salad, wild rice, and yams and ate two helpings of dessert.

In the kitchen Joanne lamented to Alexa, "This is a new phase, but I'm not saying a word. When you live on a farm, there's always lots of veggies around, and I'll make sure she gets some nuts or legumes every day. All her friends are into body piercing, and I'd rather live with a vegetarian than a daughter with a pierced tongue."

"Ouch!" Alexa grimaced in pain at the thought. "I haven't seen too much of that at Riverside, but tattoos are definitely in. All the senior girls seem to be getting them on their ankle or shoulder."

"She'd never admit it, but Rachel's actually pretty conservative. She loves her patched jeans, but she doesn't go for either the rapper or the hooker look, and I can handle tofu better than tattoos. This is a good reason to buy a new vegetarian cookbook. I've been eyeing Moosewood Kitchen."

Mike, Rachel's brother, still seemed shy, but he talked up a storm with Mark and her dad about basketball and thanked Alexa shyly for dinner. Alexa wondered what it would be like for Sarah to have a little brother, and with this thought she felt a warm languorous sensation spread throughout her body as she remembered the way she and Mark had made love. On Monday night she finally fell asleep imagining that his arms were around her, and his body warm against hers.

Although Alexa was at school very early on Tuesday after the holiday weekend, when she went to open her classroom Dara was sitting outside her door, her back against a bank of lockers. "Dara, this is great! I was going to call you today, but what are you doing here?"

"I tried to call you on the weekend, Miss Corbett. I just got your answering machine, so I didn't leave a message. You'll never guess what happened! One of my entries was awarded first prize for senior poetry in the writing contest."

Alexa was ecstatic. "That's wonderful news! Congratulations! I'm going to take you out to celebrate."

Dara was flushed with pleasure and looked prettier than Alexa had ever seen her. "I couldn't believe it! I got the award for 'Cat Walk'. That was my weakest entry! I thought they would choose 'December Night.'"

"Listen to yourself, girl! You've come a long way in just a few weeks. You've become your own best critic. You'd never have had the self-confidence to say that when I first met you."

"I guess you're right. Talking with my counsellor every week helps a lot, especially when my mother comes too. Things are better at home than before."

Alexa gave her a thumbs up. "If you're free on Friday night and like Italian food, I know a neat place where we can go. I'm going to speak to Mrs Helmer. She'll want to come with us."

On Friday night Dara was beaming. Carol had been able to get her an old word processor which the computer department was planning to cannibalize for parts. "You're really a writer now," Alexa teased her, "with your own computer."

Alexa had made a reservation for the three of them at Fasooli's. Mark was working late dealing with a robbery at school. When they entered the restaurant, Alexa had a fleeting thought of the evening with Tony. It seemed long ago and was quickly forgotten when they began talking about Dara's applications for university.

"I have a business proposition for you," Carol told Dara. "My husband's a police officer who works a lot of weekend and evening shifts. A few weeks ago we decided we needed a real holiday and started to plan a trip to England and Scotland next July. I want to go down to southern England to Devon and Cornwall where my grandmother lived. Then our daughter Kerry found out that there's a good chance she can have a volunteer job as a park recreation leader. At fourteen, that's more important to her than a family holiday. Could I book you as a housekeeper for July? Kerry would be very insulted if I said 'sitter', but we need someone to keep an eye on her, the dog, and the house. Of course we'd pay you for taking on the job, and it would give us both some peace of mind."

Dara was almost speechless. "Do you mean it, Mrs Helmer? I'd do it for nothing if you think that Kerry and I would get along."

"As if! Don't sell yourself short, girl. We'll pay you, and I'm sure you and Kerry would hit it off. She acts like an airhead at times, but she's a huge reader and she's writing some short stories. You two have something in common."

"I'd love to. I can get some part-time work in my father's office, but I'll need all the money I can earn for university. I'm going to see Mrs Fitzgerald again next week. I'm still registered for semester two, and I think I might go back to Riverside. I don't get as much out of the correspondence courses as classes."

"She misses us," Carol told Alexa, and then she said to Dara, "We're thrilled, but I should warn you the cafeteria food is as bad as before. The kids are about to stage a protest."

Dara smiled. "I can handle that."

Alexa felt happy as she drove drive home after dropping Dara off. She wasn't out of the woods yet, but she had come a long way in becoming her own person. Sarah was having her first sleepover at her friend Angie's house, and she would have a chance to be alone with

Mark. When she turned onto Martin's street, Mark's car was already parked in the driveway. She opened the door to her apartment to see him stretched out on the couch and couldn't resist calling out, "Honey, I'm home!"

Mark woke with a start. When she bent to kiss him, he said, "You're really here, love. That means we actually survived the week!"

"You look whipped. Did the police have any leads on the robbery?" Alexa asked, hanging up her jacket.

Early that morning Mark had called Alexa from school. "Lisa and I have been here for about an hour, " he told her. "Someone broke the window in my office last night or early this morning. A police officer driving by noticed the broken glass and contacted Neil Chisholm, who called Lisa. Whoever broke in took my computer and overturned the filing cabinets. The place looks like a disaster area. There are books and papers everywhere. It won't be a great day. I'll be camping out in the nurse's office until I can get it back together."

Now Mark looked tired. "No incriminating evidence so far. Apparently you can't lift fingerprints from paper. I'm cynical enough to wonder what Ben Copeland was doing last night. He's not exactly president of my fan club. And I keep asking myself what idiot would install a security system in a school and not wire the vice-principal's office. Whoever came in the window seemed to know that they could create havoc in the office as long as they didn't step out into the hall. Luckily the filing cabinet was locked, and the office is so small that they couldn't actually do much damage except throw things around. I think my ego can stand having obscenities about me written on the walls. Apparently I'm attracted to young girls and animals."

"That's an interesting combination. Will the school insurance pay for the computer?"

"Not a chance. I think the deductible is ten thousand dollars. Lisa will have to replace it from the school budget." He brightened for the first time. "Roger Helmer dropped by the school this afternoon, and I gave him the gears about the lack of police protection these days. Actually the boys and girls in blue do drive by several times in every shift. That's how the robbery was discovered in the first place, but whoever was responsible either knew their patterns or was just plain lucky." He looked at her intently. "You're glowing tonight. You must have had fun at dinner."

"We did." Alexa sat down beside him. "Things are going so much better for Dara now, and Carol offered her a summer job. I've never seen her act like a kid before. When I think of what she was like in September.... What a change." Her voice trailed off, as Mark put his arms around her and pulled her close. She felt an instant response as he began to massage her back.

"You see. You've made a huge difference in her life. That's what makes our jobs worthwhile in spite of the Ben Copelands of the world."

"Do you really suspect him?"

"Yes, but I may just be a little paranoid. It goes with the job." He smiled and then went on, "Ben's got a reason to dislike me, and he's a sneak. The police are going to talk to him and to some of his friends, but they probably won't get anywhere." He shrugged. "I've got to forget about it. Now that the police have taken the pictures they need, Neil is getting a crew together to paint the office walls this weekend. It'll be business as usual by Monday."

Alexa looked sympathetic. "Did you get something to eat tonight?"

"I ordered a pizza and shared it with the custodians."

"Do you want something to drink?"

"Sure. A beer if you have one." He followed Alexa into the kitchen, putting his arms around her from behind and lightly resting his chin on the top of her head. "I found a little love note in my mailbox last night."

Alexa froze. "Was it as bad as the first?"

"Pretty much the same."

"Can I see it?"

"You can if you're sure you want to. I have an idea that I wanted to talk over with you. If you agree, I think we should go to see Roger Helmer and show him both letters. He comes across all kinds of bizarre things in his line of work and can give us an idea of what, if anything, we can do about this." He pulled the envelope out of his pocket and handed it to Alexa.

She held it in her hand wondering if it would be better not to read it, but her curiosity was too strong. "I feel comfortable with Roger," she said finally, "and I know he'd be completely professional." Then she opened the envelope, noting again the pale typing with the illegible "o's." She read:

Mr Anderson, I am disappointed to see that you did not heed my first letter. I understand that you and Alexandra Corbett went away together this past weekend. It is my Christian duty to remind you again that if you continue this relationship you are not setting a good example for your child. Nothing good can come from it. You have a wife although you do not live with her. I pray that you will search your heart and ask God to help you make the right choice.

This time Alexa was surprised by how calm she felt. She read the letter again and turned to Mark. "This is too much. It just can't go on. I'll wonder every day when you'll get the next one. Let's make an appointment to see Roger whenever he's on duty."

"Are you sure that's what you want?" Mark asked with concern in his eyes.

"Definitely! Obviously I'm not happy about this, but I don't feel as threatened as I did before. I'm no expert on anonymous letters, but I don't feel in any danger. I just want this madness to stop."

Mark reached for the phone. "So do I." He dialled the police station and got through to Roger, who was on duty for the entire weekend. They agreed to meet early on Saturday morning at the station.

That night after they made love Alexa lay in Mark's arms. She felt warm and safe. Even if someone was watching her every move, this was where she belonged. She felt defiant. She had found happiness at last, and no one was going to snatch it away.

CHAPTER EIGHTEEN

❦

*T*he next morning when Roger showed them into his office he took a few moments to reassure Alexa. "Mark said that you two have a problem you want to discuss with me. I think you know that anything you say here is entirely confidential. I never talk about work at home or outside the station."

Alexa nodded, "I understand that." Together she and Mark described receiving the two anonymous letters, and Alexa added, "Before you read them, I want to tell you about something that happened to me in high school." As she had told Mark, she felt comfortable talking to Roger about her pregnancy and miscarriage. He listened attentively and took some notes. Then he studied the letters.

After a few moments, he looked up. "Who would have known about your pregnancy?"

"No one except my family. I never told Tony Benoit what happened. He left to play hockey that summer, and we didn't see each other again until this fall when I came home."

"Are you sure you didn't talk about it to anyone outside your family?" Roger asked.

"Positive."

"Okay, let's think carefully. Do you have any ideas about other people who somehow might have known? Perhaps a friend or a neighbour?"

Alexa thought carefully before saying, "The first letter was such a shock. I couldn't get it off my mind, and I began to wonder if Verna Murphy, my father's neighbour, knew. There's something about the language in the letter. It's so stilted that it reminds me of the way she always speaks. She's very formal and never misses a chance to refer to an all-powerful deity."

Mark looked at her in surprise. "You never said that before."

"Because I have no proof. It's just a gut feeling."

"What can you tell me about Verna?" Roger asked.

"She's lived across the street from Dad as long as I can remember. She's basically a good person, but when you're a kid she's the kind of neighbour you love to hate. My older sisters were very polite to her. I was the rebel of the family. She always seemed to be preaching at us, and it used to make me crazy because she watched everything my sisters and I did and then she'd talk to my mother about things she'd seen. When I began to date Tony, we joked that she stood behind her living room curtains and watched every time he picked me up or took me home. We used to stage scenes for her benefit. And almost every day she'd drop by to see my mother. I'm sure she would have known when I left home at the end of the summer before my senior year even if my mother didn't talk to her about it. She may have put two and two together and got five. I was gone and then suddenly I was home and back at school."

Alexa thought for a moment, and then went on. "She retired from the bank a few years ago, and for the last year she's been trying to take care of Dad. My sisters and I tease him about her. I know she wasn't happy when Dad's friend, Heather Robinson, started spending some time at the house."

Mark had been listening carefully. "I remember when she brought Sarah back and told us she'd almost been hit by a car. I thought at the time it was odd that she made a point of mentioning that she'd met Jane, Sarah's mother."

Roger asked a few more questions and then he said, "These letters are annoying and constitute a type of harassment, but unfortunately there's really no solid evidence pointing to Verna Murphy. Based on our conversation, I can't get a search warrant issued and go to her house."

"Of course not," Alexa agreed. "I didn't expect you'd do that."

"The language in the letters certainly suggests they're written by an older person and one with a religious bent. Does that describe Verna?"

Alexa nodded.

Roger continued, "It's unusual today to see letters which are typed instead of printed on a computer. That makes me think it's not a student's idea of a joke. Not that a student would know anything like this about you, Alexa. I'd like to keep the letters if it's all right with you."

"Sure," Alexa and Mark said almost together.

"Let's play a waiting game. The chances are good that you'll get another letter."

Mark and Alexa's eyes met. Mark had been wondering how Alexa would handle the interview at the police station, and he was relieved that she seemed so calm. "Thanks, Roger," he said. "It's actually a relief to talk to someone about this."

"No problem. I'm glad you came. And, Alexa, try not to worry. We'll get to the bottom of this eventually. Contact me if you can think of anything else that might throw some light on this." He paused, "Mark, I called Lisa Fletcher just before you arrived. I have something interesting to tell you about the robbery at school. Could I speak to you for a moment?"

Alexa waited for Mark in the car. She too felt relieved that they had brought the problem to someone who was used to dealing with bizarre incidents.

When Mark opened the car door, he looked at her appraisingly and then leaned over to kiss her. "You look calm and cool."

"For once, that's the way I feel."

"Then I have a piece of news for you to keep under your hat. Roger told me that he had a phone call from someone he knows who was a little concerned because his son had been offered a chance to buy a used computer at a very good price. When the kid came home with it, his dad wrote down the serial number and called Roger. It's the one taken from the office."

"And the vendor was ...."

"Ben Copeland," they said together.

"Do you believe it?" Mark asked. "He's not even a smart thief. I wonder if the Copelands and the Sawyers are still defending the indefensible?"

"Do you think Stacey's involved with the robbery too?"

"Probably not. Roger said that there were a couple of other kids he had to talk to. Probably Ben's buddies, playing lookout. I have to keep telling myself that for every Ben there are twenty good kids like my basketball players. I'd be completely jaded without them and you."

He kissed her again with such intensity that for just a moment, she wished there was no Sarah, and they could go home and spend the afternoon making love.

As if reading her thoughts, Mark said, "I'm sorry, but I have to pick up Sarah at the sitter's. Let's take her out for lunch. If you can stand the golden arches, Sarah will be in a good mood for the rest of the day."

"Let's do it. I can always order a salad. Anything but turkey!"

That evening they sat in front of the fire at Mark's house. The logs crackled, sending showers of sparks up the chimney, and Alexa felt herself relax. The changing colours of the flames were hypnotic. They sat in a comfortable silence for a few moments, and then Mark said, "Lisa's going to advertise a full-time English position for semester two. Are you going to apply?"

"I told you I was. I've already written the letter. Why would you ask me that again?"

"I want to be sure that's what you want. I keep telling you that I'm not chained to Riverside. We could both apply somewhere else."

Alexa put her arms around him and leaned her head on his chest, "We could," she said, "and maybe someday we will. Somewhere warm would be nice. But right now I need some roots. I think I've done enough travelling for a while."

This time they didn't jump apart when Sarah came into the room. She was holding Esmeralda carefully in her arms. "Dad, can you feel her tummy? She's getting fat. Do you think she's going to have bunnies?"

Mark took Esmeralda from Sarah and felt the rabbit's stomach. "I'm not a vet, but I'd say she's fatter."

"That's good, because Angie still wants a rabbit." She turned to Alexa, "Did you know that Angie's going to have a baby sister?"

"That's exciting! How do they know it will be a girl?"

"They have pictures of it, " Sarah explained in a tone that said, *Don't you know anything?* "Do you think you'll have a baby some day?"

Alexa gulped. Sarah never ceased to surprise her. While she debated how to answer this question, Mark interjected, "Anything's possible, but right now we can hardly handle baby bunnies."

"I think a real baby would be more fun."

Later that evening when Sarah had gone to bed with Stuart and Esmeralda, Mark asked, "When we go to see *The Lion King*, I'd like to visit my parents. Will you come with us?"

"Of course I will." Alexa was puzzled. She realized that Mark and Joanne who were constantly in touch with their aunt and uncle almost never mentioned their mother or father.

"I'm not close to them," Mark said with his uncanny ability to read her thoughts. "I told you that every summer they shipped Jo and me to Aunt Dorothy and Uncle Jim, and they were wonderful. Somehow they became our surrogate family."

Alexa had heard that note of bitterness in Mark's voice before when he spoke of Jane. "You mentioned your older brother once," she said tentatively. "His death must have been traumatic for all of you."

"It was," he said shortly, "but even before that we weren't exactly playing *Leave It to Beaver*." After a minute he added half seriously, "Maybe I need counselling as well as Sarah."

Alexa sat quietly. She hoped that Mark would be willing to open up, but she knew she would have no luck in forcing the issue.

At last he exhaled sharply. "Do you really want to hear about this?"

She nodded.

"My father's an engineer, and when we were growing up he always seemed to be away on major ventilation projects. He travelled a lot throughout North America and Europe. I remember once when Timothy was still alive Dad spent several weeks in Oman, and then my mother joined him for a holiday in England. Timothy was in charge. He was five years older than me and sort of a natural leader. We had a housekeeper, but both Jo and I listened to what he said."

He hesitated. "It sounds as though I'm romanticizing, but he really was one of those golden kids who do everything well. He got straight As and was thinking of studying medicine, but he also played sports especially basketball. And he loved theatre. My mother said that when he was really young he wanted to be an actor. She took us to see him play Snoopy in Charlie Brown. And he played saxophone in the school band."

"That must have been a hard act to follow."

"I suppose it was, but I never thought of it that way. He was just Timothy. The world really was his oyster and of course that made his death even more terrible."

"What happened?"

"I remember it was just after my birthday. Dad was away in Nova Scotia. His firm was doing the ventilation work on the old fort at

Louisbourg. My mother picked up Jo and me after school because we had dentist appointments. We got home around five o'clock. Timothy had a basketball practice after school, and we didn't expect him to be there yet. I was the first one into the house, and as soon as I opened the door I knew something was wrong. There was a strange smell like smoke and also like a barnyard. A really strong smell. I took off my jacket, but I had a horrible feeling that something wasn't right. I looked in Timothy's room. The door was partly closed, but there was no one inside. Finally I went down to the rec room. I could hear my mother and Jo moving around upstairs and taking off their coats. The smell was even stronger downstairs. Then I opened the door to my father's study, and I saw him."

He took another deep breath. "He was lying on the floor and most of his face was blown away. The smell was blood. He had shot himself using a revolver that my father kept locked in one of the desk drawers."

Alexa cradled Mark in her arms. She was horrified. She began to rock him as she would Sarah or one of her nephews who had hurt himself. She could not find any words that could touch this pain.

"It's okay," Mark said at last. "I've been through this so many times out loud and in my head that I'm almost completely drained of emotion." After a moment, he went on, "I think the worst part was that there was no note, no explanation. I guess every suicide defies all reason, but that's how I think of this one."

"And you never knew why?"

Mark shook his head. "My parents spoke to everyone at school. Timothy was a star academically, acing all his courses. He had picked up his university applications from his guidance counsellor. Basketball was going well."

Alexa unconsciously rubbed the side of her face. "Did you have any idea what drove him to that?"

"Jo and I still talk about it. When we were at college, we sat up late one night and went through it all again. Timothy never really had a girlfriend. Jo thinks he might have been worried about being gay. Most of his buddies were dating, but then lots of guys don't get into that until later. I wondered if he had experimented with drugs. They were always around at school, but he didn't seem like the kind of guy who needed them or would be part of that scene. My parents blamed each other. I told you that my father was often away, and my mother was there but quite aloof. Her parents had money, and she was brought up in a sort of sterile environment, and she brought that into their marriage."

Alexa was listening intently.

"The worst part was that Jo and I were just two average kids. I think we both had survivor guilt. You know, why Timothy and not us? We tried to play happy family with my parents, but it was tough going. Once, a few years after Timothy died, I wanted to have some kids over for my birthday. Nothing major, just pizza and videos and cake. My mother absolutely refused. It was the worst time of year for her. I lost it and yelled at her, 'He's dead. We can all be miserable, but he's not coming back.' Do you know what she said?"

Alexa looked at him mutely and shook her head.

"'The difference between Timothy and me is that he died quickly. I've been dying slowly since it happened.'"

Alexa took his hand. "Mark, that is truly awful. I don't know how you managed to live with her."

"I spent almost no time at home. I went over to friends' houses, and I played sports. And there was always Jo to talk with. When I got to college, I lived in residence or with a friend." He smiled ironically. "Do you still want to meet them? Don't worry. We'll all be very civilized."

In response, Alexa put her arms around him and drew his face down to hers. For a few minutes they simply held each other. Then they kissed long and hard. Mark softly circled her tongue with his. When at last they broke apart, Alexa said softly, "Mark, I wish I could change the past, but I can't. Just remember that we're together now, and you and I and Sarah are a family." They kissed again, and gradually she felt Mark relax against her. Alexa remembered how passionate Mark had been about getting professional help for Dara. He cared about all the students, but now she understood why he had been so concerned about her and why he continually asked how she was coping.

Despite Mark's warning, her first meeting with his parents felt like a performance of theatre of the absurd. Mr and Mrs Anderson lived in a high-rise condominium, an imposing concrete and glass structure standing across from a city park. After they were buzzed inside, the lobby was large and bright, all green trees and tastefully arranged rattan furniture covered with floral prints. Mark politely greeted an elderly gentleman with thinning hair who stood waiting for a taxi or perhaps a relative inside the front door. His liver-spotted head and hands were visibly trembling.

Sarah instinctively moved closer to Mark and took his hand. When the elevator doors closed behind them, she asked in a loud whisper, "Why was that man scared, Dad?"

"What makes you think he was afraid, pet?"

"He was shaking."

Mark exchanged glances with Alexa. "I don't think he was afraid. I think he has a disease called Parkinson's which makes people lose control of their muscles. They can't stop shaking, but it doesn't mean they're afraid of anything."

There was no time for more conversation before the elevator doors opened, and they were greeted by Mark's mother standing at the door of the apartment. Sarah was carrying an autumn bouquet of asters and chrysanthemums which she thrust into her grandmother's arms as Mrs Anderson bent to kiss her cheek.

"Why, thank you, Sarah. We must find a place for these," Mrs Anderson murmured vaguely. She was a tiny woman, elegantly dressed in a pale mauve skirt and matching sweater set, a single strand of pearls around her neck, pearl studs in her ears, and her silver hair perfectly coiffed in an upswept style. Alexa had no doubt the pearls were real.

Mark valiantly performed introductions. "Mother, I'd like you to meet a friend of ours, Alexandra Corbett, who teaches at Riverside."

When Mrs Anderson extended her hand, Alexa suppressed a very uncharacteristic desire to laugh. She wondered if Mark's mother would have called her "Jane" if Mark had not intervened. Would she have noticed that the tall red-haired woman whom Alexa knew only from pictures in Sarah's bedroom had been replaced by a petite brunette?

Inside the apartment Alexa took in the room at a single glance. It was completely white, a white leather love seat opposite the window which provided a sweeping panorama of the city, two matching armchairs nearby, a standing lamp, and a low coffee table with a pottery bowl. There were no books or magazines, no family photographs. She could not help wondering what people did in such a room.

"So good of you to visit, dear," Mrs Anderson was saying to Mark. "Your father is changing. He was a little late getting back from his gym this afternoon."

"I'm sorry we can stay only a few minutes, Mother," Mark said, not looking the least sorry. "I told you that we have tickets to see *The Lion King* this evening." He did not say that they had already been in the city for several hours, shopping and taking Sarah to her favourite theme restaurant.

Mrs Anderson was still standing with the bouquet in her arms. At last she said, "Your father bought a cake. I hope you can stay long enough for that."

Mark's father entered the room, a tall man carrying himself with an almost military bearing. Again there were introductions and a dutiful kiss from Sarah.

"I'll just find a container for these," Mrs Anderson said, "and we'll have cake and tea."

"Could I help?" Alexa offered.

Taking silence for consent, she trailed behind Mrs Anderson into a gleaming galley type kitchen where a convenient ceramic vase accepted the flowers. Opening the door of a stainless steel refrigerator, Mrs Anderson took out a gold cake box embossed with the name of a patisserie. While she filled the kettle, Alexa carried a tray loaded with plates, silver pastry forks and linen napkins into the living room to find Mark and his father discussing golf. Sarah sat on the love seat beside Mark, her head swivelling back and forth between her father and grandfather like a spectator at a tennis match.

"Let me help you." Mr Anderson rose to his feet to take the tray from Alexa. He set it down on the coffee table and went to the dining area to bring back an additional chair upholstered in pale grey leather.

When Mrs Anderson joined them, she brought the cake on a silver stand. "We missed your birthday, dear, " she said to Mark as she began to serve the torte. "We thought Sarah might enjoy this."

Sarah was on her best behaviour. "Just a small piece, Grandma, please."

Mark and Alexa smiled at each other, knowing that Sarah had recently eaten a huge lunch followed by an ice-cream sundae. Alexa sat down in one of the white chairs as Mr Anderson remarked to Mark, "My game really improved once I was able to play three or four times a week, so there's hope for you yet." Alexa reflected that it would be many years, if ever, before Mark had enough time to play more than twice a month and she wondered if golf would eventually hold the fascination for him that it clearly did for his father.

"Are you a teacher, Alexandra?" Mrs Anderson asked.

Understanding that Mark's mother had missed the reference to Riverside, Alexa began, "Yes, I teach English in Davenport. Actually I work at the same school as Mark."

"And perhaps if you took some lessons it would help correct your slice," Mr Anderson was suggesting.

Sarah had finished her slice of torte and was now licking her pastry fork thoughtfully. "What's a slice, Dad?" she asked at last.

Mr Anderson launched into a long and technical description of a slice and its perils in the game of golf. By now Sarah was looking distinctly bored, and unconsciously she began to kick her feet against the front of the love seat. Mark automatically put his hand on her legs to stop her.

"I found that a lesson or two really corrected my habit of hesitating too long at the top of my swing," Mr Anderson went on.

"I'm sure you find the children at school delightful," Mrs Anderson was saying to Alexa. "They must be so creative at that age." Alexa reflected that if Mrs Anderson could spend five minutes with the Pathways kids, if she did not die from shock, she would find them somewhat less than creative. Realism was more their strong suit. She still thought often of Justin and could imagine what his comments would have been after visiting an apartment like this.

"Dad," Sarah began, "What time...."

With an effort, Mr Anderson broke off the golf monologue and for the first time looked directly at his wife, "Elizabeth, don't we have some gifts ready?"

"Of course, dear." Mrs Anderson rose dutifully and left the room.

Alexa thought irrationally that if they gave Mark a golf club, she would lose control and disgrace herself in front of Mark's parents by breaking into wild guffaws.

Mrs Anderson returned with a small gold package and several holiday gift bags. She presented the first to Mark, "Happy birthday, dear. Although a little late. And the bags are Christmas gifts for you and Sarah since we'll be in Palm Springs then."

"Open your birthday present, Dad," Sarah piped up, looking interested for the first time.

Mark complied, carefully removing the gold wrapping to reveal a Palm Pilot. Sarah crowed with delight. She loved technical gizmos and would have spent hours on the computer if Mark had not restricted her time which was carefully scheduled on their family calendar. Mark looked decidedly uncomfortable. "Thank you so much. It's a great gift. We'll program it tonight. Now I'll have no excuse to miss school council meetings," and he smiled at Alexa.

"Glad you like it," Mr Anderson said expansively. "All the younger engineers in the office claim they couldn't survive without one. Don't like to get too far behind them, so I bought one for myself as well."

Mrs Anderson smiled faintly as Mark bent to kiss her. "Thanks for the Christmas gifts, mother. We'll get together when you're back. Sarah bought a present for you today, but we're not organized enough to have it wrapped and ready to give you."

Sarah was entranced by the magic of *The Lion King*, and on the way home she quickly fell asleep, wrapped in a car rug on the back seat. Mark drove slowly, holding Alexa's hand. "I'm sorry. I should have prepared you a little better for meeting my parents. I knew it would be quite an ordeal."

"Don't apologize." Alexa hesitated and decided to go on. "Mark, is your mother okay?"

"She had a slight stroke last year. But the doctor said that she made a good recovery. I just find she seems more detached than ever."

"Maybe that's it. When she opened the refrigerator door to take out the box with the cake, I noticed that there was almost no food, but there was a shelf of cleaning supplies. I just thought that was a little odd."

"Like what?"

"Oh, just the usual. I remember a bottle of Windex, and I think there was a bottle of Sunlight and some Javex. Mark, please don't say anything about that. I'd feel as if I were a nosey guest snooping in the fridge when her back was turned."

"Don't worry. I won't mention it, but I'll call my father at his office before they go south and just say that I was a little worried about Mother." He exhaled sharply. "At least I had Sarah primed to behave well."

Alexa wondered what impact the visit had upon Sarah. She reflected that even as an adult she might well be paying a therapist to help her resolve her childhood traumas, but she replied, "She's really wonderful.

Most kids couldn't sit there without entertainment."

"I know. It's expecting a lot. Usually when we meet my parents, we go out for dinner and that keeps her amused. She'd better make lots of money when she grows up or marry someone who does because she's developing expensive tastes. The last time we ate with them she ordered Surf and Turf and finished it all." He interlaced his fingers with hers. "Alexa, I love you. Thanks for being patient."

"Patience isn't my strong suit, but your family is part of you, Mark, and you're part of me."

"You really mean that, don't you?"

"You know I wouldn't say it otherwise. We all have our idiosyncrasies and eccentric relatives. Wait until you meet my sister, Tanya. She's a neat freak. Her house looks like an operating theatre, which is appropriate because she's a surgical nurse."

"I wish I could stop the car and just hold you."

"Let's do that later."

CHAPTER NINETEEN

*T*he next Friday morning Davenport awoke to the first snowfall of the season. The world was made new as soft, furry flakes coated tree branches and transformed gardens into quiet pools of whiteness. To Alexa there was always something incredibly innocent about the first snow. She remembered a glass paperweight which had always stood on her mother's desk. Inside the globe a tiny man and woman stood in skating costumes, locked inside a perfect world. The arrival of winter made her feel that she and Mark were safe in their own protective bubble of love.

Winter exhilarated the Pathways students. Ignoring the school rules, they threw snowballs at each other, and the hall floors were slippery with the packed snow which they stamped from their feet as they came into the building. Alexa felt almost as much excitement as the kids. She had signed a contract for semester two and invited Patti and Chris for dinner at Mark's to celebrate.

After school she wished Carol and Warren a happy weekend and went out to brush the snow from her car. She and Sarah could make a snow man to greet their guests. When Mark arrived, he smiled at the snow figures lined up in front of the house. Sarah had found an old apron and a straw hat for Mrs Snowman, while the baby clutched the rope of an old sleigh in his red mittens.

"What about Mr Snowman? Doesn't he get any clothes?" Mark asked. "Give me a minute. I'll find something for the fellow." He disappeared into the house and came back with a battered fedora and a long, plaid scarf . While Sarah was dressing her creation, he kissed Alexa and asked, "What can I do?"

"You can make the salad if you like. I've got everything else under control. I bought some shrimp on my way over here. We can have them before dinner."

When the Barrys arrived, Sarah took Cheyenne and Nick up to her room to see Stuart and Esmeralda, who was now noticeably pregnant. Patti and Chris sat on stools at the kitchen island while Alexa made hollandaise sauce, and Mark grilled the salmon fillets. Patti had brought a bottle of champagne. "I know it's not New Year's yet," she said, "but when Alexa called and told me that she got the job for semester two I was dancing. I was so afraid that she'd be bored after one semester in Davenport and head back to the city."

Mark finished tossing the salad and replied with mock seriousness, "I'm here to make sure that doesn't happen. It's my job and I'm going to do it well."

"Stop talking about me as if I'm not here, you two," Alexa protested. "I had some part in this too. It's actually got nothing to do with Mark. I looked at my *cv* and decided that no one would ever hire me again unless I stayed longer than one semester in each school. I'm about to prove that I don't need to move every year."

Alexa had set up a small table for the children at one side of the dining room. When it was time for dinner Sarah automatically took charge, cutting up Nick's fish and giving nonstop instructions to him and Cheyenne. "You can have some more rice as soon as you finish what's on your plate," she told them.

"I love Sarah," Chris said to Mark. "Do you think we could bring her home as a nanny? I can't imagine what it would be like to eat a meal without getting up ten times or refereeing an argument."

Alexa looked around the room as they talked. The children were eating with their fingers or scooping up the rice in their spoons when prompted by Sarah. Mark and Chris were teasing Patti, who had agreed to host their hockey team for a Christmas potluck on the condition that the men did the cooking. "We'll have pots of spaghetti and chili, " Chris was predicting. "It's the only thing most guys can cook."

"Don't move, Alexa," Patti instructed her as they finished their meal. "I brought a tub of praline ice cream and I'll serve it." Alexa exhaled happily, contrasting the comfort of the evening with the ritualized dessert they had shared with Mark's parents. She felt completely happy as Mark's eyes met hers and locked.

It was late that night when they were finally alone. Alexa was curled up on the couch with Mark's arms around her. "Christmas is going to be wonderful this year. I'm so happy that you'll have a chance to meet

Katie and Bill. It's hard to believe that it will be almost six months since I saw my nephews and nieces. I think Sarah will love Bailey."

"What about Tanya? Is there any chance that she'll come with her husband? I'd like to meet her after your description."

"Probably not. She and Terry like to visit Dad in the summer when they have more time. They live close to Terry's parents and usually go there for the holidays. I'm going to invite Martin for Christmas dinner unless he's travelling."

"We talked about inviting everyone for Boxing Day. Why don't we do that here? We could have a sort of open house and invite everyone from both our families to come any time in the afternoon or evening. That way we'd have more chance to visit with them."

"Knowing my family, they'll come at the beginning and stay all day. You're going to love Katie. She's a lot like Jo. I think she wanted six kids, but Bill's from a small family, and he's a little overwhelmed right now with four."

Mark laughed. "This is going to be fun. We'll keep it simple. We'll have finger food and order pizzas if people stay for supper."

"Or we can make turkey sandwiches."

Mark groaned. Then he reached for her. His kiss was long and lingering, his tongue probing. At last he broke away and murmured softly. "Planning together like this is wonderful. I love you so much."

"And I love you."

They kissed again with deeper intensity. Alexa felt herself yearning for his touch.

"But you still worry?"

"That's just the way I'm wired. At times I feel really close to Sarah, and there are other times when I'm sure she wishes I'd disappear from the planet."

"I think she's a typical kid. Sarah talks about you a lot. I know she likes you, but even with me she's becoming her own person. At times she blows me away with her opinions. She may be totally out of control as a teenager."

"I keep wondering if at some point Jane will see what she's missing and try to reclaim her."

"I think that's one thing you *don't* have to worry about. Jane's got her own life now."

The hours went by as they talked about Bermuda and Christmas.

"I bought Dara the perfect present," Alexa said. "It's the *Oxford Book of Canadian Verse*. She's going to stay with Kerry next Saturday night while Carol and Roger have a weekend in the city. I think it's a trial run for the summer."

Mark smiled. "Kerry will keep Dara busy. I predict that in a year or two we'll see Kerry running for a position on our student council executive. She's already a good home room rep."

When the fire began to die down and the house grew cooler, Alexa stood up and went over to the window. "It's snowing again," she said looking out at the street lights which cast shadows on an untrammelled expanse of whiteness.

Mark came up behind her and put his arms around her. "That settles it," he whispered. "You can't possibly go home. Please stay tonight."

They went upstairs with their arms around each other. Sarah was sleeping soundly with both Stuart and Esmeralda on the foot of her bed. It was the first time Alexa had stayed overnight at Mark's house, and at first she felt unexpectedly shy. His bedroom was so stark, just a framed photograph of a much younger Sarah, a computer and piles of books on every available surface, but the look of love in his eyes made her ache for his touch and to feel him next to her. When she slipped into the bed beside him, he put his arms around her. They lay quietly together for a long time as she listened to the beating of his heart.

At last Mark said, "We're home. I've waited so long for this, just to have you here warm beside me on a winter's night." As his lips began to move over her body, she shivered with excitement. Their lovemaking was quiet but intense, clinging to each other while they moved on a mounting wave of passion.

In the morning Mark got up early and built another fire. By the time Sarah came downstairs, the house was warm, and they had made a stack of pancakes. "Hi, sleepyhead," Mark teased her, brushing the tangled hair back from her face. "I thought you were going to stay in bed until noon, or until we'd eaten everything."

Sarah looked at Alexa. "Did you sleep here last night?"

"Yes, I did."

Sarah seemed to consider this. "You two have a lot of dates," she said at last. "Does this mean you're going to get married?"

"What makes you ask that?" Mark hedged.

"That's what the big kids say at school. You get a boyfriend and go on dates, and then you get married."

"That's often the way it goes." Mark was smiling. "Do you want some breakfast now?"

Sarah squealed when she saw the pancakes on the stove. She sat down at the kitchen table and reached for the jug of maple syrup. "You should be here every morning," she told Alexa. "This is my best breakfast. Dad always makes French toast."

As Sarah concentrated on her stack of pancakes, Alexa smiled at Mark. "We've got a surprise for you," she said to Sarah.

"I knew it! I dreamed about it last night. We're going skiing this morning, aren't we? Do you have any skis, Alex?"

"If I can find my old skis in Dad's basement, we thought we'd go cross-country skiing at the golf course."

When Sarah left to look for her ski pants, Mark turned to Alexa. "Kids! They take everything in stride. Sarah just accepted that you'd be here at breakfast. Going skiing is the most important thing on her mind."

"I'm being lulled into a false sense of security. If this goes on, I'll begin to think that she accepts me." Mark shot her a half amused, half exasperated glance.

When Alexa and Sarah walked through the garden and knocked on Dan's door, they were surprised to find the house empty except for Robbie, although her father's jeep was in the driveway. "It's such a beautiful morning. He must be out somewhere," she told Sarah.

Sarah was thrilled when Alexa found a pair of ski boots and skis which had belonged to her sister Tanya. "Do they fit?" she kept asking.

"They'll be okay for this morning."

At the golf course the snow had formed a soft powder, and they were able to ski from the club house with Sarah following Mark's trail. There were enough hills and valleys to give them all a good workout. Sarah became a daredevil, shrieking with delight, whizzing down the steepest hills and picking herself up when she tumbled.

"Maybe we should go to Blue Mountain at New Year's," Alexa suggested when they stopped to watch her. "She's really fearless. I think she's ready for some downhill ski lessons on a bunny hill."

"I'm surprised she's so brave. She just has to learn to snowplow, and she'll be a pro in no time."

Under a cloudless blue sky in the quiet of the woods they seemed very far from town. Mark couldn't help smiling as he watched Sarah skiing doggedly in front of them. At last she began to complain that she was hungry, and they skied back to the car.

"That was the best morning! Now can we have grilled cheese sandwiches and hot chocolate? And after lunch I want to call Angie and see if I can go over to play at her house. Her grandmother's here, and she always lets us make cookies. And she's going to teach us how to knit."

They were changing their wet pants and sweaters when the doorbell rang. Mark went to answer it to find Dan standing on the top step. "I was hoping to find Alexa here," he said.

"Good morning, we're just going to have some lunch. Come and join us," Mark invited. "Alexa will be right down. We took Sarah skiing this morning, and they're getting into some dry clothes before we eat."

As Mark hung up his jacket, Dan took a deep breath and brushed the hair back from his forehead. "Dad, are you feeling okay?" Alexa asked coming down the stairs and slipping her arm through his. "You look tired."

"I'm all right, just a little overwhelmed. This has been a strange morning."

"Come and sit down in the kitchen," Mark invited. "I'll put some coffee on and make hot chocolate for Sarah. What have you been up to? Alexa said you weren't home when she and Sarah went over to your place this morning."

Dan pulled out a chair and sat down at the kitchen table. "I had a telephone call from Evelyn, Verna's sister, around eight o'clock this morning. Verna was supposed to go to her place for the weekend, and when Evelyn called her, there was no answer. She was worried, so she called me. I hadn't seen Verna for several days, and I said I would go over and check on her, but the house was locked."

He broke off as Sarah came into the kitchen with her eyes bright and her cheeks flushed. "Hi, Mr Corbett," she said. "We went skiing this morning."

"Hi, Sarah. You look as if you had a good time."

"It was awesome. There was one really long hill, and I skied all the way down and didn't fall until I reached the bottom."

"That's good. I know that hill. I used to fall halfway down."

"Sarah, why don't you take your hot chocolate and go upstairs to call Angie now?" Mark suggested. "We'll eat in just a few minutes, and I'll call you as soon as the sandwiches are ready."

When Sarah left the kitchen, Dan continued, "I called Evelyn back, and she was so worried that she decided to come into town. She has a key to Verna's house, but she didn't want to go in alone, so I went with her." He paused and cleared his throat. "At first we thought the house was empty, but we found Verna on the floor in the living room. I called 911, and the paramedics arrived right away. She was unconscious. They think she had a heart attack last night or early this morning."

"Oh, Dad!" Alexa put her arms around him. "I'm sorry! I wish you'd called us before you went to Verna's."

"It was much worse for Evelyn than for me. As you can imagine, she's really in shock. She's still at the hospital. The doctor on duty gave her a sedative, and she's sleeping. She's going to stay at Verna's house. That way it will be easier for her to get to the hospital."

"What can we do to help?" Mark asked.

Dan drank his coffee eagerly. "There's nothing we can do right now. Maybe in a few days Verna can have some visitors." He paused to gulp the rest of the coffee. "After the paramedics left, the police arrived, and I was with them most of the morning while they went through the house."

"Why were the police there?" Alexa asked.

"I called them," Dan admitted. He looked embarrassed. "Probably it was unnecessary, but when we found Verna she was lying on the floor in the living room beside her writing desk. There were several drawers open and papers scattered about. I just wanted to be sure that she didn't surprise a burglar. The police checked the house, but there was nothing else out of the ordinary like a forced entrance." He paused and then went on with difficulty, "Mark, there is something strange. After the paramedics lifted Verna onto a stretcher, they found an envelope addressed to you. Verna may have had it in her hand. The police have it now, but I'm sure they'll contact you at some point."

Alexa and Mark exchanged glances before Alexa said, "Dad, we really have a lot to tell you. I hardly know where to begin."

At lunch they talked about Christmas plans and later in the afternoon when Sarah had gone to Angie's, promising to make her dad a scarf when she learned to knit, they told Dan the whole story beginning with the first anonymous letter and ending with their visit with Roger Helmer at the police station. He shook his head in disbelief.

"It's hard to understand. What makes a person do something like that?"

"I wish I knew," Alexa replied. "At first I was in total shock and then unbelievably angry and upset. But the more I thought about it, especially when I began to wonder if Verna wrote the letters, it just seemed sad. All those years she lived beside us always watching us and coming over to talk with Mom. She must have felt so alone. I didn't think of her that way before, but now it just seems such a wasted life."

Mark leaned over to take her hand as her eyes filled with tears. "I feel so lucky, " she went on. "Our family was always together when I was growing up, and now I have you and Sarah. She had no one except her sister."

"Alexa, remember what you said about not taking on the problems of the world."

"I know, but kids are selfish. To me, she was a nuisance and a busybody, always spying on us and lecturing me. I never thought that she was just lonely."

"Alexa," Dan interjected, "you told me once that we never really know other people, and that's true, but in our little circle of influence we can reach out to others." He smiled sadly. "Arlene and I tried to do that, but it wasn't enough."

Now it was Alexa's turn to reassure him. "Dad, this may not sound cool, but you're my hero. You were always there for me and Tanya and Katie, and you and Mom were super neighbours. I'm not going to sit here and let myself get morbid." She hesitated a moment and then went on. "I'm sure Verna will recover. She's one tough lady. Someday I'm going to confront her about the letters. I'm going to tell her what really happened that summer."

Dan raised his eyebrows but wisely said nothing. After a moment he remarked, "Evelyn wants me to go to church with her tomorrow. She called Reverend Wiseman to ask him to include Verna in the prayers for those who need healing." He smiled quizzically. "If you want to do something, Alexa, come with me. I could use your support."

It was typical of Davenport that the church was filled almost to capacity for the Sunday morning service. Dan sat with Evelyn in the front row with Alexa, Sarah and Mark behind him.

"I like this church," Sarah whispered to Alexa. When Alexa nodded, she whispered again, "The coloured glass in the windows is neat, and look at all the pots of flowers. It's cool." She looked around, and her gaze became fixed on a stained glass portrayal of a group of children. Then she whispered, "I bet lots of people get married here." Alexa nodded again. She wondered if this was the same child who had screamed that she hated her for trying to act like a mother.

Alexa watched her father as he bent protectively over Evelyn. She looked down at Sarah who sat immobile, transfixed by the sunlight streaming through the stained glass windows. Her eyes met Mark's. Sometimes you have to walk in darkness to see the light. She took a deep breath. She felt as if she were home.

CHAPTER NINETEEN

*

*I*n the following weeks, there was no time for Alexa to follow through on her resolve to confront Verna Murphy. Dan reported that Verna had been transferred to a Rehab centre in the city, but Evelyn was hoping that her sister could come home for Christmas with the help of a walker and visits from the public health nurse.

In the days leading up to Christmas break, the school became frenetic. The Pathways students, always the most sensitive to changes in the atmosphere, were frequently out of control, and their classes threatened to degenerate into chaos. Shawn Bethune and Pat Fortier were suspended until after the holiday for fighting in Alexa's room. Normally they were buddies, but Shawn took offence at a casual remark, and soon the two had overturned their desks and were wrestling in the aisle while the rest of the class cheered them on, eager for any diversion from the routine of the classroom.

Samantha McGill, who remained one of the Pathway girls with attitude, directed some obscenities at Alexa during a routine homework check and was also suspended. Alexa shrugged off these incidents with cynical humour. "She suggested that I was a female dog with unnatural tendencies. It goes with the territory," she told Carol. But she was aghast the weekend before they left for Bermuda when Sarah staged a full-fledged temper tantrum.

Sarah had been on a high on Saturday morning, chattering happily about her school play the night before and the accolades she had received as fairy godmother. They were eating lunch with Sarah's favourite bow tie pasta when Mark said casually, "This afternoon we should go through our boxes of Christmas decorations and see if all the indoor lights are working. Next Sunday Uncle Ray's going to take you and Rachel and Mike to cut down two Christmas trees from his bush. Then when Alexa and I get home on Monday night, we can put up our tree and decorate it."

Sarah stopped eating. Her lower lip quivered. "But I want to go to Bermuda with you."

Mark took a deep breath. "Sarah, we've talked about this. We're going to Disneyland in March break, and when Alexa and I are in Bermuda you're staying with Aunt Jo and Uncle Ray. Rachel's got the whole weekend planned. She'll take you skiing, and there's a concert at the church on Saturday night."

He got no further. Sarah pushed back her chair with such force that it toppled backwards with a horrible crash. "I don't want to go skiing!" she screamed. "I want to go with you. It's not fair! You're always going somewhere with *her*! What about me? Why can't I go too? If I can't go, I'm going to run away. I won't be here when you come back."

Unlike Alexa when Sarah had made this threat earlier, Mark did not hesitate to call her on it. "Just where are you planning to go?" he demanded.

"I'll go live with Mom."

"And with Peter?"

"I don't care about him. And it's better than living with *her*." Sarah threw a disdainful glance in Alexa's direction. "I hate her," she pronounced coolly. "I don't want her at our house." She ran upstairs to her room and lay on her bed face down, kicking her feet and sobbing. Even Stuart deserted her, hopping quickly under the bed.

Alexa felt the blood drain from her face. When Mark returned after checking on Sarah, she was blunt. "I honestly don't know if I can stand this. She really does hate me. She'll never accept having me around. Maybe we should forget the whole idea of a holiday. Bermuda will always be there. It's too soon to leave her for an entire weekend and go so far away."

Mark was grim-faced but determined. "She has an appointment with Dr Ahmid on Monday. I'll talk to Laura about this, but as far as I'm concerned we're going. She knows we're not deserting her. She's just being melodramatic." He broke off and then went on, "I could understand her acting this way if she were stuck with some sitter she didn't know, or someone she hated, but she loves the farm. It's like a second home."

Seeing the expression on Alexa's face, he took her hand. "I'm sorry you have to put up with this. I don't know what gets into her sometimes."

"I'll survive," Alexa said laconically, but she felt miserable. Why was she cast into the role of Wicked Girl Friend?

Mark was upset and angry. He wondered how long Alexa would be around if Sarah continued to orchestrate scenes like this one, but to his relief the rest of the weekend passed in relative peace although Sarah refused to speak directly to Alexa, and no one mentioned Christmas holidays or Bermuda.

On Monday morning he called Dr Ahmid, and she assured him that such outbursts were not unusual. "It's perfectly normal for Sarah to test the waters, Mark. Who wouldn't want to go to Bermuda for a long weekend if they could? Sarah likes Alexa, but she keeps checking to make sure that she's still an important part of your life."

"But she is! She must know that."

"She does know that, but keep reminding yourself that she's handled a lot of changes this year. I think she's doing very well, but she's only eight years old. She's going to assert herself sometimes."

"So you don't think we should cancel our trip?"

"No, I don't. What kind of message would you be sending to Sarah then?" Dr Ahmid paused and answered her own question. "You'd be creating a very powerful child if you did that. Keep talking with her about what she'll do at the farm when you're away, and what you'll do together when you come back."

Mark unconsciously let out his breath. "Thanks for the advice. I needed to hear that." After he hung up, he sat for a few moments at his desk. He knew that much of his own repressed anger was still directed against Jane. If only she could be depended on to share the parenting, this would be so much easier for everyone, but there was no point in going down that road yet again.

After school he went up to Alexa's classroom where she was working with the yearbook club. When she had a free moment, they walked out to the deserted hall, and he told her what Dr Ahmid had said. She looked tired as she said with uncharacteristic skepticism, "That's the textbook answer, but I keep wondering what Sarah's really feeling about her mother and about me. Three days in Bermuda isn't going to change anything."

On the Friday evening flight, Mark and Alexa made a pact as they sipped their drinks. "Let's make this a real escape," Mark said. "I'll check in with Jo and Sarah, but besides that let's promise each other no Sarah talk, no shop talk and no talk of Davenport. I almost checked your suitcase to make sure you didn't bring a stack of marking."

"You don't have to convince me. The past few days are only a distant memory. I'll pretend that I'm on a plane with a mysterious stranger, and we're going to an exotic destination."

Mark nuzzled her cheek and whispered, "Do you often come here, my love?"

"Not often, I usually fly to Monte Carlo in the spring and Mustique in the autumn, but I made an exception when I met you."

"You won't regret it, my dear," Mark promised. "My father, the Duke of Cornwall, lies on his death bed, and I'm the heir to his estate and all his Arabian horses."

Alexa dissolved in giggles. "What a pity that I'm allergic to horses."

"In that case, I'll sell them all, and we'll travel around the world on my private yacht – unless of course you're subject to seasickness."

"I'm always nauseous at sea! I want to escape to a simple life, perhaps an island with only a servant or two and a chance to walk barefoot on the beach at sunset."

"We can arrange that, my little bohemian! In fact I guarantee it. I'll give the butler a few days' leave. I'll cook for you myself. We'll drink champagne and dine on caviar and truffles while I have my wicked way with you!"

Alexa was consumed by a huge yawn. She managed to say, "It sounds absolutely decadent," before her head began to nod, and she fell asleep against Mark's shoulder. She woke up only when they were landing at Hamilton.

As they stepped off the plane, Mark took a deep breath of the tropical evening air. "It feels as if we fell into spring. Let's stay forever. I'll send Lisa a telegram saying 'Sorry, impossible to return.'"

"Remember, we said no shop talk," Alexa replied with mock seriousness.

In a few minutes they were waiting outside the terminal for the driver of a taxi van to load their luggage. "First visit to Bermuda, folks?" he asked and provided a running commentary on the drive into

Hamilton. "We've got a little bit of Britain dropped right down here in the Atlantic. My people have always lived here, and I never wanted to leave. In the old days Bermuda was built on slave labour, but now the different races live together without all the fuss you have Stateside. Seems like we got the perfect climate and the world's most beautiful beaches. My only problem's the cost of living. Things are mighty expensive here, so if you folks plan to go to the shops you're gonna need plenty of money and lots of credit cards."

The driver easily found Rose Lawn, an old Bermudian pink stucco home set high in the hills overlooking the city. While Mark got the key from the landlord, Alexa stood on the patio still dazed from her sleep, leaning on the wrought iron balustrade, admiring the pool and gardens and the lights of Hamilton stretched out below.

Paul had thought of everything. The refrigerator was stocked with fresh fruit, juice and a bottle of chilled chablis. "We owe him big thanks for this, " Alexa said. "It's perfect. We may never want to go out at all."

Mark had found several pages of notes which Paul had left. He laughed as he showed Alexa a list of recommended restaurants and attractions. "Does he think we're staying for a month?"

They took their wine out to the balcony and stood with their arms around each other gazing at the city below. "Maybe if we don't sleep, we can stretch out these three days," Alexa suggested. "I'm not tired at all now."

"Of course not. You slept through the whole flight, " Mark teased her, kissing the side of her neck and feeling Alexa press against him. "Sleeping seems like a waste of time, but we want to be up for exploring tomorrow."

As they showered together, Mark's hands massaged the nape of her neck gently. Then he began to run the soap over Alexa's body, soaping her shoulders and back, then her breasts and belly and legs. They kissed deeply, the hot water steaming against their faces. Mark dried her with a huge white towel. "Do you know how beautiful you are?" he asked. Pushing aside the snowy duvet, they made love on the wide bed, moving together until a wave of passion swept over them. As Alexa fell asleep in Mark's arms, she thought that no matter what happened she would never forget the feeling of love she had experienced that night. Her senses were filled with Mark, his smooth skin, his scent, the taut hardness of his body.

Early the next morning they were awake and eager to go out to see the city. "Let's walk down to the Hamilton Princess for breakfast," Mark suggested. "Paul's note says their dining room overlooks the harbour."

"Then we can do some shopping and find a beach when it's warmest. I can't wait to be in the sun after the last few months at home."

Their landlord, Neville Fraser, was already at work in his rose garden as they left the house. He called out a cheerful good morning to them. "You're more than welcome to use the pool. It's heated. You'll find the ocean's too cold for swimming at this time of year. And if you're back in time we always have tea on the patio at five. My wife would be happy if you'd join us and meet the other guests."

Mark and Alexa looked at each other. "Thanks for the invitation," Mark replied, "but could we have a rain check? We've only got three days here, and we plan to head for a beach this afternoon. Do you have any recommendations?"

"Our sons love Horseshoe Beach, but you could stay a month and go to a different one every day. Before you leave, you must see Pink Beach. It's close to town, and it's the one they show in all the tourist photographs."

Mark and Alexa held hands as they walked down the steep hills past the old mansions and luxuriant gardens. "There must be schools here that hire offshore teachers." Alexa was serious. "I could get used to this very quickly. No snow to shovel and swimming all year round. You'd have lots of chance to golf."

At the Princess, they watched the water traffic going back and forth past the windows while they ate. Finally Mark leaned back. "I really pigged out," he said ruefully.

"In December it's hard to resist all this tropical fruit." Alexa was still eating a slice of mango.

When the waiter came with another carafe of coffee, they asked him about the local buses and water taxis. "If you want to go over to the beach at The Southampton, our sister hotel, you can take the water taxi here at the hotel dock. One leaves on the half hour, or you can go over on the bus and come back by water taxi or ferry. It's going to be warm later. Good weather for the beach today, folks. But if you come tomorrow for breakfast, you stay around the hotel for a while, and you'll see the Gumbey dancers. They're a Bermuda tradition at Christmas time."

When he left, Mark reminded Alexa, "We've got Paul's scooter. Maybe by tomorrow I'll have my island legs, and we can try it out. Today I think we should stick to the bus."

"And we can take the ferry. Can you believe this place? It's really a paradise. No wonder our taxi driver didn't want to leave. How could you face snow and ice and grey skies after this?"

Alexa felt as if every dream she had ever dreamed had come true. She wondered if it meant as much to Mark. It was therapeutic just to concentrate on the holiday instead of discussing the events of the last few weeks.

After breakfast as they walked along the Hamilton waterfront on Front Street toward the large department stores, the street was crowded. It was Saturday morning, and people of every race and colour were out shopping. Everyone seemed well dressed and in a holiday mood. "I love it," Mark said happily. "When I went to Cancun or Freeport, everything seemed to exist just for the tourist trade. But this is real. It's not an elaborate stage set they built to capture tourist dollars."

"It's true. In lots of places where North Americans go for a holiday the local poverty arouses my social conscience, and I end up feeling guilty that we have so much. I was just thinking that most visitors couldn't afford to live here unless they had company housing. Look at that, " she nudged Mark, feeling very much the tourist. An elderly gentleman was strolling towards them wearing an impeccable navy blue blazer, shirt and tie, pink Bermuda shorts, and knee socks. "This is perfect. It's exactly what I imagined it would be."

They stopped to admire the Christmas decorations in the windows at Trimingham's and decided to separate to shop. Alexa found the gift department where she quickly made her selections: a banana leaf doll for Sarah, a watercolour of a Bermuda cottage for Patti and Chris, pottery coffee mugs for Joy, and the inevitable golf shirt for Mark. Then she wandered through the ladies' department. She was tempted by a beautiful hand-embroidered blue and gold sweater and matching skirt, and another set in black and white, and went in search of the change rooms.

Later she found Mark at the counter in the duty-free perfume department. He held up an elegant blue bottle. "For Jo," he said. "Luuluu is her favourite, and she deserves to be spoiled. She's helped so much with Sarah. Thanks to her we have a few moments of sanity."

He took some of the packages and then reached for her hand. "Do you think it's time for the beach? Let's go back to Rose Lawn to change." He looked at her longingly, "I think I've just found another reason to love you."

At her quizzical look he added, "You're an amazing shopper. Most women would spend all day in the stores, but it only takes you an hour to buy out the entire gift department."

At the risk of scandalizing the prim salesclerk in her black dress, Alexa reached up to kiss him. "There's so much I want to do here, and anyway some of this is for you and Sarah, so don't you dare complain about my credit card habit."

Following Neville Fraser's suggestion, they decided to go to Horseshoe Bay. While they were waiting for the bus, Mark dashed into a corner store and raced back with cold drinks in a straw bag. "Do you remember what our driver said last night? How do people live here? I was going to buy us some grapes, but they're eight dollars a pound, and I could buy a six-pack at home for a single beer here."

Alexa was mesmerized by the scenery. She snapped pictures as the bus swung past the picturesque pink and green cottages, white sand beaches, and glimpses of ocean. On the South Shore, they passed a seemingly endless fringe of sand and surf bordered by steep cliffs. They got out at the Horseshoe Bay stop and clambered down a steep path to the beach far below.

"This is a fantasy," Alexa breathed. In the distance they could see two horses and riders, but the beach was almost deserted. She put her arms around Mark. "Remember the first time we escaped to the beach at Picton? It seems like a world away."

"How could I forget? That was the day I fell in love with you." They kissed, his tongue teasing hers, his eyes memorizing each one of her features. They put down their bags near a clump of trees and took off their shorts and golf shirts. Mark gave a low whistle at the sight of Alexa's black bikini. "Turn around," he begged. "Did you buy that this morning?"

"No, it's from Costa Brava. I bought it on our girls' getaway weekend."

"Wow! It's too bad you ever have to get dressed. I love it."

They had found a sheltered cove where the water was surprisingly warm. They swam out beyond the surf and then headed back to the beach while the horses trotted nearer. When they were close enough, one of the riders called out, "You're Americans, right?"

"What makes you think that?" Mark called back.

"It's too cold for us to swim, and we're always shocked by the visitors who ignore the temperatures with their polar bear swims."

"A polar bear swim is through ice!" Alexa exclaimed. "The water's actually not that bad."

All afternoon they lay on towels in their private cove or walked hand in hand on the white sands of Horseshoe Beach. "You've changed in the last few weeks," Mark said thoughtfully.

"Is that good or bad?"

"Good, I guess. You seem..." Mark searched for words. "I don't know, less tentative. I've noticed how confident you are at school and somehow happier."

"I am. For lots of reasons."

Mark leaned over and kissed her shoulder, warm and slightly salty after their swim. "Hmm, you're good enough to eat."

"I thought a lot about what Joy said to me. We do the best we can, and we have to forgive ourselves when we make mistakes."

Mark looked at her, waiting for her to explain.

"When I came back to Davenport, I found myself reliving my high school years. I wasn't always a good kid, but I thought of myself as a free spirit when actually like most teens I just went along with the crowd. I still felt guilty for being irresponsible enough to get pregnant. And then I didn't even tell Tony. It was his responsibility too. He should have been part of the decision making, but I just dumped the problem on Mom and Dad. The worst part I told you about. I felt as if I lost the baby because I had unconsciously let her know that I wasn't ready to be a mother. Crazy isn't it?"

"Not really. You were so young, and it was a traumatic experience, especially being so far from home."

"Yes, but I have to let it go. I remember Joy said the most important thing is that we learn to forgive ourselves. I was beating myself up over not doing enough for Justin and Dara, and I needed to hear someone say that. We're only human. We're going to make mistakes, but the important thing is to learn from them and go on, hopefully wiser and less judgmental of others and ourselves."

Mark was listening carefully. Both had forgotten their pact not to talk about school, and for the first time Alexa told him about the opening day of school when she had smelled marijuana on Justin and given him a ride home that evening. "When he was arrested, I kept thinking that I was wrong to try to handle the problem myself. Maybe if I hadn't been so keen on my own 'Save the Kids' campaign, we could have done something to help him get on track."

"Maybe and maybe not. Justin had set his own course by then. A lecture from me or even a suspension wasn't going to change anything. We tried that the year before."

"I hope that's true. We'll never know. I thought I was doing the right thing by letting him know that I was onto him. Mark, thanks, this has helped me a lot."

"How? Sometimes I feel that I've just complicated your life."

"No, you've helped. You've got a reason to be bitter, but instead you try your best in a difficult job, and you bring out the best in the people around you."

Mark looked embarrassed. "I'm glad you think so, but I'm no saint. And I've had someone who helped me too." He pulled her into his arms and began to kiss her neck and shoulders, his mouth cool against her hot skin. They kissed for a long time.

This time it was Alexa who broke away. "The sun's going to start setting soon. Let's climb back up the cliff and watch the sunset from there before we head back." They sat side by side on a pink granite boulder as the Bermuda sunset painted the sky with a brush of reds and oranges. Seagulls uttered their harsh, lonely cry, swooping and darting over the ocean.

Mark turned to Alexa and pulled her close to him. "Promise me you'll never leave. I want you today and for all of our tomorrows."

In the circle of his arms she whispered, "I love you. How could I leave?" She wondered if they could capture this feeling permanently and bring it home with them. Could life really be this magical, or was this only an interlude before the rude awakening of their return to reality?

When the horizon looked like a golden cup ready to catch the sun, they took the ferry back to Hamilton. They stood close together on the deck watching the lights of the city draw nearer. All around were small boats and larger yachts and the sounds of music and laughter. Alexa smiled at Mark. "Do you think if we saved our pennies, we could come back and bring Sarah? We could rent a guest cottage."

" I was wondering about the same thing. Bermuda's magic. Sarah would love it here."

From their balcony they watched the last golden streaks of the sun fade completely until the sky was almost dark except for the beacon of a distant lighthouse. Mark ran his hands lightly over Alexa's bikini. "I love you, " he whispered. "Let me show you how much."

Alexa laughed softly, feeling herself respond even as his lips lightly brushed the skin of her neck.

"By the way, have I mentioned within the last hour that I'm crazy about the nightgown you wore last night?"

"Not within the last hour."

"Then I have to say it again. It's incredibly sensual. Please put it on, and I'll show you how much I appreciate it."

Alexa thought only of Mark as they kissed and fondled each other with the sheer material of the gown between them. His hands moved in gentle circles over her breasts, her stomach, and her legs. She sat astride him, fitting his body into hers, and they moved together for a long time first in this position, then lying side by side. They fell asleep with her arms about his neck and her cheek against his chest.

Several hours later when she felt Mark stirring against her, Alexa rolled over onto her back. "I can't believe we slept. Now I'm starving. Breakfast was a long time ago, and I'm ready for dinner. Where should we go?"

"I wanted to surprise you. While you were changing before we went to the beach, I made a reservation at a place Paul highly recommended, the Waterloo Inn. It's not far from here, and we can eat right by the water." He yawned and pulled her to him for a long kiss. "I'll call home and then I'm all yours."

At the restaurant a waiter showed them to a table on the terrace overlooking the lights of the harbour. Alexa looked around her, taking in the charm of the nineteenth century mansion. "It's a fantasy come true. I want to meet Paul. His taste has improved since the days of Spam."

The service was attentive but unobtrusive. When the waiter poured the last of the wine and offered a tray of sweets to accompany their coffee, the terrace was almost deserted.

Mark reached across the table and took Alexa's hand, "I didn't know two people could be this happy. I want to give you something so we'll always remember tonight."

Before Alexa could answer, he reached into his jacket pocket and brought out a small black jewel box. He handed it to her. She drew in her breath sharply. Inside was a gold ring with a single square cut sapphire surrounded by diamonds.

Mark leaned across the table to kiss her. "Merry Christmas!"

Alexa was totally overwhelmed. She felt her eyes brimming with unshed tears and finally asked, "How did you know that I love sapphires?"

"I asked your dad sort of casually."

Alexa smiled. She could imagine the exchange. Her father was extremely aware of nuances.

"Try it on." He took the ring from the box and slipped it on her finger.

"It's perfect! I can't believe you did this!"

"The sapphire's the gemstone for September, the month we met. It was a rebirth for me," he said softly, his eyes meeting hers.

"And for me."

"I know Sarah can be a terror at times, but once you said that I was part of you. Do you still feel that way?"

"Of course I do."

Mark hesitated. He seemed to be about to say something else. Instead he raised his wineglass, "To us and to our tomorrows."

They sat smiling at each other, their happiness almost tangible, but Alexa could not help thinking that Mark had not mentioned marriage. Was he as unsure of them as she was at times? It was a perfect moment marred only by the thought of what might or might not lie ahead for them. She knew now she wanted this to be forever.

At last she said aloud, "This whole trip has been so splendid. Can you believe that at home people are trudging through snow and scraping ice from car windows while we've found our moment in paradise? And then tonight..."

"I know. I feel as if we came to a new world created just for us."

Alexa couldn't resist admiring her ring, turning her hand so that the facets of the sapphire would reflect the candle light. "I love it, and I love Bermuda, and I love you! The only thought in my head is how happy we are tonight."

Mark brought her hand to his lips and kissed the palm, his eyes sending an unspoken declaration of love.

Later he fell asleep almost as soon as they were in bed, but Alexa lay awake for a long time. It had been a perfect day, but she thought of Sarah. She had fallen under her spell, not only because she was Mark's daughter, but because, like Mark, she was both funny and vulnerable, yet she knew that Sarah had not accepted her and she had certainly never pictured herself as a stepmother. In spite of Mark's words, she still wondered about Jane and the role she might one day want to play in her daughter's life. Mark had called the ring a Christmas present. Was he having doubts about their relationship? What else had he wanted to say at dinner?

Then she smiled in the darkness. On Thursday just before classes ended for Christmas break she had received a large package addressed to her in David's distinctive handwriting. Inside was a stack of books, his presents to her which she had deliberately left at their apartment. There was no note. In his own way, David had succeeded in having the final word. Another chapter in her life had ended.

At last she slept, and even Mark did not wake up until the sound of pealing church bells aroused them the next morning. For once it was Alexa who got up first and padded out to the balcony on bare feet, the tiles cool in the morning air. Memories of their evening at the Waterloo Inn came flooding back as she stood looking at Hamilton golden in the early light.

When she came back into the bedroom, she said, "Mark, I made some coffee. Let's have breakfast and go to a church service. Mom and Dad came here when my sisters and I were very small. I remember they told us about the beautiful singing in the cathedral."

Mark pulled her down beside him for a kiss. His hands were warm on her breasts. "I had other plans, but your wish is my command. I think Paul left us some eggs. I'll turn on the grill if you'll make us some toast."

Inside the majesty of the old Anglican Cathedral they listened to the crystal purity of the boy soprano voices. Alexa felt her eyes well with tears. She thought of her mother and father sitting in the same place where she and Mark now sat. Mark glanced at her and took her hand. It was easy to imagine the long line of men and women who had found solace and refuge here.

At the end of the service, an elderly gentleman sitting in front of them turned around to shake hands. "Come downstairs for coffee or tea," he invited. "We're always pleased when visitors join us. My late wife and I spent a year studying in Ottawa and travelling in Canada. North Americans made us feel so welcome that I like to return the hospitality." Mark and Alexa exchanged smiles while they drank tea and chatted with the parishioners who assumed they were a young couple on their honeymoon and recommended an impossibly long list of things to see and do.

In the afternoon, before trying out Paul's red scooter, they saw a performance of the Gumbey dancers in their colourful costumes. Then, through the light Sunday afternoon traffic, with Alexa sitting behind, her arms around Mark's waist, they found the fabled Pink Beach easily.

"We belong here now," Mark called back to her, his words almost carried away by the wind. "We're travelling like the locals."

They had promised to join Neville Fraser and his wife for tea that afternoon. Alexa had been surprised by the quiet and order of the big house and wanted to meet their sons. "They're at school in England," Mrs Fraser explained while she poured tea from a large urn and offered them finger sandwiches and slices of fruit cake. "There are some excellent schools here in Hamilton, but both Neville and I attended boarding schools, and we feel it gives children an advantage. They're arriving for Christmas holidays tomorrow. They always spend Christmas and the long summer break with us, and for the shorter holidays they go to my sister."

"How old are they?"

"Matthew's eleven and Simon eight."

"You must miss them!" Alexa tried to imagine Mark sending Sarah away to boarding school.

"Of course," Mrs Fraser agreed, a little puzzled. "But we're very busy here with our guests. I've taken up painting and volunteer with the Junior League, and Neville gardens and golfs at his club several times a week."

Alexa managed to nod politely as they joined the other guests and the conversation about island living, but as they walked back to Paul's apartment to pick up sweaters for the evening she couldn't hide her feelings. "Mark, can you imagine sending children as young as eight away to boarding school? Would we send Sarah away? Sometimes at school we joke about shipping the kids off to a boarding school to protect them from their parents, but I'd feel as if someone else were raising my child. We feel at home here because everyone speaks English, but ..."

"Alexa," Mark unlocked the door and pulled her into his arms. "Stop and listen to yourself. 'Would *we* send Sarah away?' 'I'd feel as if someone else were raising *my* child.'"

"Yes?"

"Is that a slip of the tongue, or do you really mean it?"

Alexa could feel her cheeks burning. "I know Sarah isn't mine, but I *do* think that way. I can't help it."

She broke off as Mark let out a delighted whoop and began waltzing her about the room. Suddenly he stopped, drew her to him and looked at her intently. "Alexa, I want to ask you something, but it's a surprise. Would you go out on the balcony for just a moment?"

Alexa hesitated for a fraction of a second. "All right." She stood at the iron railing wondering what Mark was doing. She could hear his footsteps in the living room, but she forced herself to concentrate on the beauty of the night already falling over Hamilton. She tried to memorize the scene, hoping it would be a talisman against the winter chill to come. The sky was not yet completely dark, but the glow of street lamps lit the town and the harbour beyond. From a nearby house she could hear the sound of a piano.

"Alexa," she turned to see Mark standing in the doorway. He held out his hand, and she followed him back inside. Mark had turned off the lamps, and the long high-ceilinged room was lit only by the glow of several white candles. She caught her breath. It was beautiful.

Mark was smiling. "I wanted to create a romantic atmosphere. This was the best I could do on short notice." They sat side by side on one of Paul's love seats. "We've only known each other a few months, but I love you more than I thought was possible. When I gave you the sapphire last night, I wanted to ask you to marry me, but I lost my nerve."

"Why?"

"Sarah created such a horrendous scene before we left that I thought it was terrible timing. But mostly I was afraid you'd say 'no', and then everything would be horribly wrong. I don't think I could survive if we screwed up our relationship again."

Alexa grimaced at the word "again." She remembered the scene in Mark's living room and walking out of the house, refusing even to discuss their problem. "We won't do that. It's too important to both of us. I was the one who was wrong. I should never have left the way I did."

Mark gently cupped her face in his hands. "I love you now and always. Will you marry me?" There was a long silence.

When Alexa spoke her voice was low but sure. "I know now it doesn't matter where we live as long as the three of us are together. Life with Sarah won't be easy, but I'm going to win her over yet, and you're both a part of me." When he wrapped his arms around her, she whispered, "This is home. I'm never going to leave."

EPILOGUE

*A*lmost eighteen months later on a hot August afternoon Alexa and Dan Corbett stood in the narthex of the old church where Alexa and her sisters had been baptized. Dan stepped back to admire his daughter in her simple white gown. Then he leaned over to touch the diamond pendant she wore around her neck on a thin gold chain. It had belonged to her mother. "Be happy," he whispered.

"I will," she replied. "I made this decision with my heart and my head." She touched the sapphire ring, Mark's first gift to her. "The sapphire isn't my birth stone. It's the gemstone for September, the month Mark and I met. It was a rebirth for both of us."

She turned to smile at Patti who was bending over, straightening the skirt of Sarah's long dress. So many people she loved had come to celebrate this special day. Even Mr and Mrs Anderson had accepted the invitation. Joy had absolutely refused to be part of the wedding party, but Alexa knew she was sitting near the front of the church with her new partner, Michel, and Heather. She hoped that Warren and Marielle had arrived in time for the ceremony. She had sent a letter to Dara, and received a note of congratulations in return. Dara was an exchange student now at St Andrew's University in Scotland and hadn't come home that summer. It had seemed fitting that Mark asked Paul to be his best man, and meeting him had been like meeting an old friend.

Sarah looked nervous. Ever since the wedding rehearsal she had been taking her responsibilities very seriously. Clutching her basket of yellow roses, she looked up at them. "I'll remember to walk very slowly. I promise. Dad said he'll give me a signal if I start to go too fast."

Alexa and Patti smiled at her as Alexa reached down for a hug. "You'll do a great job, Sarah. I know you will. And you look so beautiful."

They took their places at the door of the church. Alexa held her father's arm and reached up to kiss his cheek. "Thanks, Dad, for always being there. I wouldn't have made it without you. If only Mom were here, the day would be perfect."

His eyes met hers. "In some way, she is here. I'm glad you came home, Alexa."

The typeface used in this book is Minion,
with Minion Ornaments and Swash Italic initials.
This book was designed and produced by
Laurie Lewis
in
Kingston, Ontario
2004